Don't miss these other Code Name novels from

CHRISTINA SKYE

Code Name: Blondie
Code Name: Baby
Code Name: Princess
Code Name: Nanny

CHRISTINA SKYE

CODE NAME: BIKINI

ISBN-13: 978-0-7394-8420-3

CODE NAME: BIKINI

This edition published by arrangement with Harlequin Books S.A.

Printed in U.S.A.

CHAPTER ONE

Northern Afghanistan
Winter

DARKNESS.

Wind and death.

Trace O'Halloran didn't move. Cold dug under his Kevlar vest as he watched the rugged road below him.

Something moved over the snow-dusted ground near his feet. Another rat.

Red eyes glowed in the faint green light of his night-vision goggles. Only rats could survive in this godforsaken mountain pass in winter.

It was Christmas Eve. Back in the States, families sang hymns and parents assembled dollhouses to surprise wide-eyed children while snow fell in the soft hush.

But here on a rugged plateau in Afghanistan, the cold was merciless and wind cut with icy fingers. Frostbite was unavoidable if he didn't find shelter soon. But the mission came first.

Trace leveled his gaze on the road three hundred feet below his hiding spot. He didn't think about the fresh wounds across his left wrist or the blood that darkened his forearm, courtesy of a difficult high altitude, low opening—HALO—jump.

Abruptly he felt movements in the night. Leaning forward, he read a change in energy patterns. A three-truck convoy crawled through the darkness. Their Korean-made trucks were guarded by soldiers wielding Soviet RPG-7 shoulder-launched missiles.

An equal-opportunity war, he thought grimly.

And this was his target. The convoy carried covert German communication technology extorted from a weapons designer based in Singapore. Not surprisingly, the man had disappeared before he could reveal his blackmailer. In the hands of a trained technician, the new device could track a massive quantity of U.S. communications. Through the application of mathematical predictive models, government assets could be located and areas of vulnerability tapped within minutes. In enemy hands the system could inflict catastrophic damage, and Trace's job was to see that the hardware never reached its destination.

Truck lights carved the darkness. The convoy stopped with a screech of brakes. Agitated voices cut through the cold, still air.

The men in the Korean trucks were ruthless and well trained. They would shoot anything suspicious on their trek to an isolated mountain stronghold sixty miles to the north. But Trace didn't intend to be noticed until he was ready. As he glanced at his watch, his skin burned. Frostbite was setting in.

Ignoring his pain, the SEAL fingered a button on the device in his left pocket.

Something moved down on the road. The first truck pulled sideways and two soldiers jumped out. Arguing loudly, they pointed to a paper flapping in the bone-chilling wind.

Right on schedule, Trace thought. Nice to see technology working right for once. His maneuver had lured them exactly where he wanted them.

Dark fur brushed his arm. Ears raised alertly, a black Labrador retriever held his down position behind a rock, awaiting Trace's next order. The big dog had trained with Trace for months to prepare for this mission, and Trace sensed the dog's eagerness to go to work.

Not yet, Duke.

His hand settled on the dog's head. The Lab watched every movement, waiting for the next touch command.

As the wind keened over the rocky slope, Santa Fe and Christmas cheer were a universe away. Trace couldn't even remember his last Christmas at home. His last two leaves had been cut short because of security alerts. As part of a top-secret government team, code-named Foxfire, Trace trained hard and kept personal attachments next to nil. That was the price of admission for special operations work, but the conditions had never bothered Trace, not when the stakes were so high.

Other people might call him a patriot. But for Trace the job boiled down to very personal terms—protecting family, friends and a way of life from enemies without honor or scruples. If doing his job meant taking a bullet, he was more than ready to pay that price with his own blood.

A silent alarm vibrated at his wrist.

Showtime.

Silently, he pulled a small box from his Kevlar vest. The dog sniffed, then gripped the box's metal handle between his teeth. When Trace touched the Lab's collar in a pre-arranged command, weeks of training kicked in. Duke skirted the rocks, turned and then headed for the road below.

Be safe, Trace thought. *Stay low and move fast.* He

didn't have to project the commands. Duke would do exactly as trained.

Trace leveled his scoped assault rifle and measured his target. A third hostile soldier jumped down, shouting at his teammates. Trace took out the nearest truck's tires and front windshield with a four-second burst.

The insurgents scattered. Gunfire hammered the air above Trace's head. His next volley drilled the middle truck's gas tank. Under the explosive flare of an orange-red fireball, he jumped a boulder and dropped into a narrow wash that snaked toward the road.

Hidden by walls of sand, he followed the curve of the wash, a shadow swallowed by the greater darkness of the night. One short tap on a small transmitter alerted his backup team that the encounter had begun. Now he had only minutes to complete his objective and head for the ex-traction point.

He sprinted to the bottom of the wash and found the big package exactly where he'd left it a day earlier, buried beneath a foot of sand. In seconds Trace had opened the canvas to reveal a blood-spattered body dead for barely ten hours. He rechecked the uniform pockets, then hefted the dead weight over his shoulders.

Hidden by the mayhem of the explosion, he carried the body closer to the road, placed it in the sand and then raced along a second trail barely visible in the light from the burning truck.

It was time to draw fire and alert the convoy to the body. If all went as planned, the insurgents would find the com-munications gear and codes planted on the body and begin using them. Everything they picked up from U.S. sources would be carefully constructed disinformation.

Trace wasn't crazy about using human remains for a mission, but their local allies had provided unidentifiable bodies of insurgents killed in a violent skirmish earlier that day. Now they were dressed and outfitted as American soldiers.

Automatic weapons fire punched the air to his left, and a tracer round whined over his head. For every round he could see, Trace knew there were three others invisible in the darkness. The SEAL followed the rocky slope away from his service dog, who bounded toward a nearby overhang. Once Trace was certain the body had been discovered, he turned into the open and made a clumsy run toward the highest ridge, his movements calculated to draw maximum fire.

The maneuver worked. Down the hill, dark shapes raced toward him, rifles level.

Kevlar was good, but it wouldn't stand up to repeated bursts from an AK-47. That's where the ceramic plates in his vest took over. But a glancing blow hit him with deadly force and knocked him off his feet.

Calculating the speed of his pursuers, he primed a grenade and lobbed it over his shoulder. Rocks shot up, clawing at his back and neck while gunfire burned near his face and tore through his glove. His excited pursuers clustered at the top of the slope below, shouting in delight when they saw Trace fall.

A second burst of fire drilled up his arm, but he didn't move, feigning a fatal wound.

His heart pounded.

Sweat streaked his face.

Footsteps raced behind him. He calculated strike force, distance and probable accuracy as the wind howled over the rocks, and then his fingers closed around another grenade. He yanked the pin and lobbed the deadly metal sphere hard, generating a wall of noise that masked more enemy fire.

The blast was deafening. Sand flew into his eyes and mouth. Another round tore through his right deltoid.

Trace's vision blurred. More shrapnel from enemy fire tore into his chest and neck. He stumbled and then plunged forward, the wind in his face as he hit the cold sand. A chopper crested the mountain, the whine from its engines blessedly familiar.

Another explosion ripped through the night, and the lead truck vanished in a red fireball.

The big Lab had accomplished his mission, planting his C-4 charge under the last truck while the insurgents were distracted by Trace's clumsy run.

Nice job, Duke.

Pain raked Trace's chest. He stumbled as blood gushed thickly over his Kevlar vest, every muscle stiff, every movement strained. Over his head the mountains seemed to darken, blurred between cold wind and night sky.

And then he died.

CHAPTER TWO

SOMETHING WAS wrong.

The air was too clean, too calm. There was no acrid smell of cordite and no rumble of distant artillery.

White curtains danced slowly in a warm wind. The smells of bleach and floor wax filled his damaged lungs.

Wounded. Hospital?

"Nice to see you're finally awake." The voice was vaguely familiar. "You look pretty good for a dead guy."

Trace cracked open one eye. Even that small movement hurt.

Hell, *everything* hurt, but he couldn't remember why.

"Very funny." Trace managed to lift his head. "You look like shit, Houston." He smiled slightly. "Maybe life with my sister doesn't agree with you."

"Kit, hell. I wish I'd been home with her. Instead I flew overnight from Singapore to get here."

Trace tried to sit up and grimaced. "Where's *here?*"

His superior officer, Wolfe Houston, stared at him thoughtfully. "Military hospital. Germany. You're in ICU, pal. Ryker has been spitting bullets waiting for you to come around."

Ryker. The head of his top-secret government operations team. That much Trace remembered.

He didn't move. His throat felt raw, as if he'd swallowed a convoy's worth of gasoline fumes, which he probably had. Slowly the fragments began to return. He'd used all his grenades, and then he'd stumbled across the ridge in clear sight, drawing fire to the location of a second, cached body left where they were meant to be found. More false codes were planted on that second body.

As AK-47 bursts followed a blast from a shoulder-launched missile, Trace had gone down, knocked out cold. Duke had to have jumped the rocks, dragging him to safety while the helicopter drew fire. A second chopper would have shot in low to pick up Trace and Duke.

Otherwise the SEAL wouldn't be here in one piece.

As the rest of his memories returned, his head began to pound. When he sat up, his left arm felt too heavy. "How's Duke?"

"Your dog is A-Okay. He just ate two steaks and ran a mile before breakfast. I wish I could say the same for you." Houston's expression sobered. "You were in cardiac arrest, completely flatlined when our people got you aboard. It took almost two minutes to revive you. Duke didn't leave your side once."

Trace managed a lopsided grin. "Duke did good. He saved my butt after that last volley. I remember he dragged me to the extraction point, not much after that. But…something's different."

"You were dead, O'Halloran. Of course you don't remember much."

No, something else was wrong. Trace shook his head. "My reflexes are off. I can't pick up any energy trails. Everything is quiet."

"Your chips are all disabled. Precautionary measure,

according to Ryker. He told the medical team to close down all your Foxfire technology until you're fully recovered."

Trace stared at the ceiling, trying to get used to the deafening silence inside his head. "I like knowing who's behind me without having to look around. When will I be reactivated for duty?"

"Get well first."

In war, soldiers fought with all kinds of ammunition. Recently the array of weapons had changed drastically. As part of the Foxfire team, the two men used focused energy as a tactical weapon. Thanks to mental training, physical conditioning and selective chips developed in a secret facility in New Mexico, their seven-member team had changed the definition of military combat.

Only a few people knew that the success rate of the covert Foxfire team was unmatched anywhere in special operations. Trace excelled at psi sweeps, spreading energy nets and reading changes made by anything alive in the area. The more difficult the terrain, the better.

Usually, he could have communicated telepathically with his commanding officer. Now there was only silence. Trace was stunned by the difference. With his extra senses closed down, he was locked within the narrow space of his body. The experience made him realize how much he had taken his Foxfire gifts for granted. Now he was flying blind, moving through a world that felt like perpetual twilight.

But chips took a toll on the nervous system, and even good implants could malfunction. Better that his hardware be disabled until his body recovered from the beating it had taken in Afghanistan.

As a test, Trace tried to set an energy net around the small room. Usually he would have succeeded in seconds.

But now nothing happened.

Wolfe Houston watched him intently. "Tried an energy net, didn't you?"

Trace shrugged.

"You okay with this?"

No way. Trace felt out of balance and irritated, and he chose his words carefully. "I'm used to my skill set. Being without any energy sensation is damned unnerving. How do people live like this?"

"I'm told they manage pretty well," Wolfe said dryly.

Trace shifted restlessly. "How bad was I hit?"

"Let's just say you won't make Wimbledon this year."

"Hate tennis. Stupid ball. Stupid shorts." Trace hid a grimace as pain knifed down into his shoulder. "Now how about you cut the crap? How *bad,* Houston? When do I get back on my feet, and when will my chips be reactivated?"

Silence.

He stared at Wolfe Houston's impassive face. No point in trying to read any answers there.

"You're here for a patch job, which you've received. Air evac will transport you to a specialized hospital stateside within the hour. If you do everything right, you'll be back in action inside six weeks."

Trace made a silent vow to halve that prediction. "What about the bodies? Did they take the bait?"

"Swallowed it whole. They're already using the communications unit you secured inside the uniform. That hardware will generate permanent system deviation in the parent programs. Hello, major static."

Trace smiled slowly. "Goodbye, security problems."

"Ryker is thrilled. You've earned yourself some solid R&R. So what will it be, Vegas or San Diego?"

"Forget the R&R. Get a rehab doc in here. I need to start building up my arm." Trace tried to sit up, but instantly something tore deep in his shoulder. He closed his eyes, nearly blacking out from the pain.

A shrill whine filled the room—or was it just in his head?

"Idiot. What happened?"

"I'm just—just a little dizzy, sir." Trace blinked hard at the ceiling. Pale green swirled into bright orange. Did they paint hospital ceilings orange?

"…you hear me?"

The orange darkened, forming bars of crimson.

"Trace…hear me now?"

The room was spinning. Trace had felt the same sensation back in Afghanistan before Duke had roused him, licking his face furiously.

His vision blurred. He tried to stand up, biting back a curse as the whine grew. *Chip malfunction? Can't be. They're all disabled.*

Have to stand up. Have to find out what's wrong.

The room spun faster. Trace didn't see a medical team crowd around the bed, equipment in hand.

He was back in Afghanistan, fighting brutal cold and a hail of tracer rounds.

"Does he know?"

"Not yet."

Two men stood at the end of the deserted hospital corridor, their faces grim. In front of them a fresh X-ray was clipped to a light box.

Trace's surgeon frowned. "He's still groggy from the last surgery." The tall Johns Hopkins grad tapped the black-and-white image. "Torn ligaments. Bone fragments—here,

here, here. We cleaned up everything we found. After rehab he should recover full use of his elbow and wrist, which is a near miracle. You saw him on arrival. I've seen a lot of trauma cases, but nothing like that. What did you people do, shoot him out of a tank?" He didn't wait for an answer, rubbing his neck worriedly. "If he'd lost much more blood, he wouldn't have made it out of surgery."

The other man took a slow breath. His dark, sculpted features bore a resemblance to Denzel Washington's, except his eyes were colder, making him look older than his age. "Tell me about his shoulder, Doctor. I don't like the bone damage here…." Ishmael Teague traced the gray lines radiating across the X-ray. "Will he regain full mobility in his right shoulder?"

"We don't read crystal balls, Teague. With your medical training, you know how risky predictions can be. All I can say is that this man was in excellent shape before this happened, and we'll give him the best support for his recovery. The rest is up to him—and to far higher powers than mine."

Izzy Teague didn't move, studying the network of lines spidering through the X-ray. "I want hourly updates on his condition and round-the-clock monitoring by your best people. Notify me at any sign of change."

"All things considered, he's recovering well. Give me a week, and he'll be starting phase one rehab."

Something crossed Izzy's face. "You've got twenty-four hours, Doctor."

"That's *impossible*. This man needs rest, close observation and at least two more surgeries. Maybe after that…"

"You have twenty-four hours." Izzy's voice was cold with command. "I have a plane inbound. We'll prep him for travel."

"You won't find a better medical facility anywhere in the country." The surgeon scowled. "Don't play politics with me, Teague. He could end up with a ruined joint if you move him now."

"Not now. Twenty-four hours, Doctor." Izzy pulled the X-ray down from the light box. "Orders are orders." His voice was flat.

"You know this is wrong. Fight it. Pull rank."

Izzy looked at the closed door down the hall. "My clout doesn't stretch as far as you think. There are other…factors."

The surgeon glanced at the unnumbered door, which was guarded by uniformed soldiers. The rest of the hospital floor had been emptied. Only this one room was occupied. "I knew something was up when you moved all my patients, but I won't play along. By all rights this man should be dead, considering how much blood he lost. In spite of that he's recuperating in minutes, rather than hours. I don't suppose you're going to explain how that's possible."

Both men knew it was a rhetorical question.

The surgeon made a sharp, irritated gesture. "You won't let me in on your secrets, and you want me to risk a patient because of a whim."

Teague's handsome features were unreadable. "Orders, Doctor. Not whims. We'll be sure he's stable before he's moved. At that point he'll be out of your hands." He rolled up the film and slid it carefully inside his briefcase. "And for the record, John Smith was never here. You never saw him, Doctor. You didn't see me, either."

"Is that an order?"

"Damned right it is."

The grizzled military surgeon pulled a cigar from the

pocket of his white coat and sniffed it lovingly. "Had to give the damned things up last year. I've got a desk full of these beauties, and this is the closest I can get. Life's a real bitch sometimes." He stroked the fine Cuban cigar between his fingers and then tucked it carefully back into his pocket. "Do what you have to do. I never saw either of you." His voice fell. "And just for the record, Vladivostok is the capital of Michigan."

"You never know. World politics are turning damned unpredictable these days." Izzy looked down as his pager vibrated. "Hold on." He pushed a button and scrolled through a data file, his eyes growing colder by the second.

"Is there a problem with John Smith?" the doctor asked.

Izzy slid the pager back into its clip. "Do you remember Marshall Wyckoff?"

"Senator Wyckoff's daughter? Sure, we saw her—what, two years ago? I heard that she'd recovered from her kidnapping. She was an honor student, head of her debate team."

"*Was,* Doctor. They just found her body floating under the third arch of Arlington Memorial Bridge. Three witnesses say she jumped."

"Suicide?" The surgeon looked back to the guarded room down the hall. "Trace was the one who brought her out. What are you going to tell him?"

"The truth. It's what we do."

"Tough bunch, aren't you? Never take the easy way."

Izzy squared his shoulders. "Easy doesn't get the job done."

Neither man noticed the glimmer of light in the quiet corridor outside Trace O'Halloran's door. When the scent of lavender touched the air, they were halfway down the hall, arguing about bone reinforcement techniques.

Neither guard looked up as a faint, spectral shimmer gathered near the door and then faded into the still air.

TRACE DRIFTED SOMEPLACE cold, halfway between sleep and waking, his pain kept at bay by a careful mix of medicines too new to appear in any medical reference books or on pharmacy shelves.

But his mind kept wandering, and none of his thoughts held. He was back in the frigid night again, waiting for an armed convoy to draw close. Distant gunfire cut through the air, and he felt the energy change even before he saw the first glow of illumination rounds.

Three trucks. Ten men. They had no clue anyone was watching them.

Trace strengthened the net, feeling the sounds and invisible movements in the night, his specially adapted senses humming on full alert.

Time to come out of the shadows.

Move fast. Head low, course uneven.

Present no stable target.

In sleep his body was tense, his breath labored. Eyes closed, he ran up an exposed ridge, drawing enemy fire beneath an orange-red fireball. His legs moved, carrying him into a world drawn straight out of nightmares.

CHAPTER THREE

THEY WERE coming.

Gina Ryan heard tense voices echo in the hall. She scanned the big wall clock above her commercial double oven. Twenty minutes early?

Unbelievable.

She took a deep breath and rubbed the ache at her forehead, checking her last row of desserts. What was the point of having a schedule if you ignored it? Didn't people realize that a wedding reception with formal seating required split-second timing and no distractions?

Silver trays laid with white linen napkins?

Done.

Spun-sugar flowers arranged at each seat?

Done.

Mini rum cheesecakes plated?

Ditto.

Three-tier chocolate ganache wedding cake decorated with edible flowers?

Perfect.

Gina straightened the marzipan figures of two Olympic speed skaters, which the bride and groom happened to be. Through a porthole she saw clouds skirt a gleaming row of waves. Another glorious day at sea on a top-rated cruise ship, but she'd be too busy to enjoy it.

Laughter spilled into the room. A door opened and the bride appeared, radiant in a chiffon halter gown with vintage lace that clung at her hips and neck. At her side, the groom stood tall in an elegant black tuxedo. A smile stretched over his happy, sunburned face.

This was it, Gina thought. This was love, exactly the way it should be.

Exuberant and gracious. Taking risks. Staying vulnerable. Not jealous and demanding, calculating selfish returns. And didn't Gina know all there was to know about *that* kind of love?

She pushed the thought deep, buried with all her other sad memories. A wedding was no time to dredge up the past. Besides, the champagne was chilled, waiting to be poured into Waterford crystal beneath a display of Orange Beauty tulips.

Her staff was flawlessly efficient, the menu a perfect mix of classic and trendy for the young, excited bride and groom.

She felt a knot form at her forehead. This was her second wedding that day. On a big cruise ship, weddings were the top guest request, and Gina was known for creating the best wedding cakes on any cruise line.

The bride and groom held hands, flushing as eighty-five guests offered cheers and catcalls. At her nod, Gina's skilled staff poured the first chilled champagne and circulated with tempting desserts.

Music filled the room. Slow and soft, the notes tugged at Gina's heart as she watched the bride and groom exchange lingering kisses.

The dancing began and the regular waitstaff took over. Her team was done.

As she straightened a silver urn of flowers, Gina had a quick impression of wary eyes, short cinnamon hair and a stubborn chin.

Her eyes, her chin. A face too angular for beauty, and eyes whose strength made most men uneasy. Right now pain circled behind her forehead, vicious and swift.

She was getting worse.

The thought filled her with panic. She needed more time.

"Hey, Chief, you okay?" One of her staff, a slender ex-kindergarten teacher from San Diego, studied her anxiously. "You've got that look again. It's like last week when someone smashed your thumb with their heaviest marble rolling pin."

Gina forced a smile. "Hey, it's called resting, enjoying the sight of a job well done." She hid her embarrassment with casual dismissal. "Anything wrong with my taking a rest?"

"Not a thing. But you *never* rest. And for someone trying to enjoy her success, you looked too worried."

Gina made a noncommittal sound and cleared the last serving tray. What was the point of dwelling on what you couldn't change?

Her vision was going. End of story.

It wouldn't happen in a day or a week. Maybe not even in a year. But the deterioration was noticeably increasing. Despite the newest medicines, her vascular problems were eating away at her vision neuron by neuron, robbing her of the career and future she'd planned with such care.

Put it away.

Shrugging, she headed to the kitchen door. "I'm not distracted now, so let's move. We've got another event in four hours."

She took one last look at the bride and groom, who had

joined hands to cut the first wedge of her exquisitely iced white chocolate cake with trailing sugar roses. The pair didn't look back, oblivious to the world as they fell into another slow kiss.

Gina wasn't really jealous. In a world of bad luck somebody deserved to be happy.

She'd believed in love, dreamed of it, felt certain the right man would appear. When he did, she'd know him instantly.

Nice dream. Stupid dream.

When the man had appeared, she'd chosen wrong. He'd robbed her of many things, the most important among them her innocence and trust. He'd taken her job and her reputation. Now she had no dreams left.

One more line item to cross off your day planner, she thought wryly. No Rose Garden wedding with a formal arch of swords. For some reason she'd seen that vision ever since she was twelve.

She blew out an irritated breath and gathered her equipment. At least she'd made a lot of people happy. With every new event she worked harder, pushing her skills. On the days when her headaches and dizziness were too intense, she'd pull out the bottle of pills hidden inside an empty package of Kona coffee and swallow two.

The pills were working for the moment. But they weren't a cure. Worse yet, they created side effects.

Without a word her brawny Brazilian sous chef slid the tray from her hands. No one said a word, but Gina felt the eyes of her staff. *They knew.* They had noticed her unguarded moments of pain.

Funny, she'd been so sure she had fooled them. Maybe you didn't fool anyone but yourself.

As she felt their silent concern, tears burned at her eyes.

Tall, studious Andreas from Brazil touched her arm. Then the others closed ranks around her, two in front and three walking behind.

Emotion engulfed Gina at the unspoken signs of trust and protection. She'd lost her father years before; she hadn't seen her mother in months. This was her *real* family, the people she had cursed and laughed, sweated and trained with.

The only real advice her mother had ever given her was that falling in love was a curse. Nice advice for a teenager. But over time Gina had come to believe it. Lucky for her, she was too busy for relationships to have a place in her life.

She squared her shoulders. "Andreas, Reggie, did you finish tempering that white chocolate for the tea cakes?"

"All done, boss. But I need some help with the spun sugar." Andreas rubbed his jaw. "It keeps cracking at the edge of the petals."

"Did you double-check the temperature and humidity?"

Gently the conversation turned to safer waters. In the sharp argument over the merits of Colombian vs. Mexican chocolate, Gina forgot about her fear and the bouts of occasional pain. She forgot the headaches and the sudden dizziness.

Who needed love or sex when you could make a killer crème brûlée?

CHAPTER FOUR

Foxfire training facility
Northern New Mexico
One month later

TWENTY.
   Twenty-one.
   Twenty-two.
   Sweat beaded his shoulders and chest, and exhaustion hammered at his concentration. Trace ignored everything until only the heat and pull of his muscles remained, strength returning in slow, almost cruel increments. As the weights rose, he focused on his arm, battling against his own weakness. He had work to do, missions to run. Foxfire men were constantly prepped and ready to deploy at the ring of a pager. Each man had unique skills, and Trace knew his absence made everyone's work harder.
   Thirty-three.
   Thirty-four.
   More sweat.
   More pain. Muscles screamed, their boundaries reached and then crossed until Trace was lost in a haze of pure muscle memory and hints of his old, preambush strength.
   His commanding officer appeared in the doorway. "Nice

to see you have a good work ethic. Just the same, you should take it easy."

Trace grinned. "I'll take it easy the same day you do, sir."

Wolfe Houston smiled faintly. "Point taken."

All of the team had been by to see Trace in the past few weeks, offering dry humor and information about current personnel deployment or upcoming missions. Trace had reveled in the details of the job that was his life, the focus of his whole passion for nearly eight years.

It was a job he could discuss with few others, not even his brave, tough sister, Kit, who managed an isolated ranch northwest of Santa Fe, where she trained the finest military service dogs Trace had ever seen.

It was his sister Trace worried about now. But he kept his tone casual as he finished his last set of curls. "Have you seen Kit and the dogs? Is everything okay at the ranch? No sign of any more cougars, I hope."

His commanding officer eased his long legs down, settling into a nearby chair. "Kit's fine. So are the dogs. Damned if those four don't get smarter every day. Last week we were running a bomb-detection scenario and the team figured out where I'd hidden the dummy device even *before* I'd let them off their training leashes. It's a sad day in Red Rock when four puppies make a trained professional look bad." But there was pride in the officer's voice.

Wolfe Houston had good reason to know the state of the ranch. He had just returned from two weeks of canine assessment exercises—and a passionate homecoming with his soon-to-be wife. Although Kit never asked for details about where the dogs had come from, she had enough experience to know that they were special.

Of course Wolfe could never reveal the nature of the secret program that had produced such unusual animals.

Trace was relieved that things were fine at his family's ranch. The unmistakable happiness in Wolfe's face meant that things were fine with Kit, too. It was strange to think of his stubbornly independent sister getting married. But if she had to pick anyone, this man was the right one.

Trace put down his weights and dried his face with a towel. "So they're as good as everyone hoped?"

Wolfe stretched his arms behind his head and chuckled. "Is the Pope Catholic? I've put in a recommendation to Ryker that the four dogs never be split up once they're sent on military assignment." A shadow crossed his face. "Kit is worrying about them already."

"She'll tough it out. By the way, has Ryker finally okayed your request to set a formal date? I'd like to be there to give away my sister, you know."

Lloyd Ryker was a long-time government power broker at the highest levels; he kept his cards close to his chest and ruled the Foxfire facility like a medieval potentate. Because he got results, his foibles were overlooked.

Wolfe frowned. "One day it's yes, the next day it's maybe. When I pressed Ryker, he told me I'd have an answer this week. It might even be true," the SEAL said dryly. "He's not going to be happy when he finds out that I got the marriage license anyway, and our blood tests are already submitted." His eyes narrowed. "Or what will pass for a specimen of my blood." Rules were rules. Any scientific details relating to Foxfire were top secret and that included all team members' medical reports.

"Give him hell," Trace said wryly. "My sister deserves

to be happy, and for some crazy reason she's set her sights on you." His shoulder had begun to ache with a low, dull throb.

Ordinarily he'd agree that marriages involving Foxfire team members wouldn't work, but Kit knew the score. His sister could handle whatever fate—and the U.S. government—threw at her.

So Trace hoped.

It was Wolfe's career choice that gave Trace some bad nights. Who knew better than a fellow SEAL how often work would intrude? Trace knew just how much uncertainty his sister would have to live with. He hoped she could learn to accept the unknown, because virtually every aspect of the Foxfire program required absolute secrecy.

He and Wolfe and the rest of the team had volunteered, and they knew the rules. But could Kit or any other woman—no matter how remarkable—live with the tight constraints that program security imposed?

Trace didn't have an answer for that.

Ryker, the civilian head of Foxfire, had a rule against personal involvement, and for good reason, in Trace's opinion. But Wolfe and a second Foxfire member had gotten involved up to their eyeballs. Now they were part of deep, stable relationships that had to be faced, not swept under the carpet. If Ryker couldn't accept that fact, he would lose two of his best men, including Wolfe, their team leader.

Trace realized that Wolfe was staring at him. "Something wrong?"

"If you keep overdoing your workouts, I'll put someone here to watch you." Wolfe met Trace's glare. "Take this one by the book, hotshot. Your body has been through hell and back. Give it time to recover." He studied Trace through narrowed eyes. "Are you going to do another set to keep your mind off it?" he said quietly.

Trace didn't move.

"We both know Marshall's death is bothering you."

Trace started to answer, then looked down at his hands. He didn't want to talk about Marshall. Hell, he didn't want to *think* about the death of the teenager he'd rescued from particularly nasty South American kidnappers two years earlier. Her death was ruled a suicide, but Trace was having a hard time believing it. Marshall was a fighter and a survivor. Lost and confused, she still had shown the courage of a soldier during her captivity.

It didn't make sense that she'd overcome so much just to give up in the home stretch.

He was fighting to accept her death, fighting to acknowledge his grief. If he'd kept in better touch with her afterward, things might have gone differently. If there were problems, she might have confided in him.

But beating himself up now wouldn't help anyone. It was too damn late to do what friends do—supporting each other, watching each other's back.

And he wasn't going to spill his guts to Wolfe. This was his own problem to work through. "The rehab is taking too long. My shoulder's much stronger now. I keep thinking if I can work a little harder or a little longer—"

"All you'll do is blow out your shoulder." Wolfe faced him squarely. "Do me a favor and get well before you report for duty. Otherwise, you endanger all of us in the field."

Trace knew Wolfe was dead right. Every man relied on his team for life or death backup during a mission. If Trace screwed up on an assignment, he could get other people killed. "Roger that, sir. I'll gut it out."

Even though I'm going to shoot someone if I don't get out of rehab and back to work soon. He wanted his chips functional, too.

He was getting to like the Superman experience.

"Glad you're being reasonable. And in the spirit of being reasonable, Ryker told me to give you this." Wolfe's lips twisted as he slapped a thick envelope on the table beside Trace. "You're shipping out in forty-eight hours."

"Mission orders?" Trace grabbed the envelope and tore open the seal eagerly. "Urban or jungle target?"

"Neither." Wolfe crossed his arms. "You'll be at sea." He cleared his throat. "On a cruise ship to Mexico."

Because he was concentrating on reading the papers, Trace almost didn't hear the assignment. "Puerto Vallarta and Mazatlán? I don't understand. This says—" His head snapped up. "This is a *pleasure* vessel? A cruise ship?" he said, ice in his voice. "I'll be damned if Ryker is going to send me off for ten days on a ship full of *Desperate Housewives* at sea."

"He's dead serious about this. This mission is important."

"On a cruise ship?" The words dripped with distaste. "Why not a Navy support vessel? Hell, even a tramp steamer would be preferable."

Wolfe's eyes narrowed. "I don't have all the details, only that you're to guard a package being conveyed outside normal channels. This is highly sensitive material and you'll be working with a civilian."

A civilian? Trace hated the assignment already. "Anything else I need to know?"

"A Navy SEAL will be aboard with his family. Izzy knows them well. Use him if things get sticky."

"Identity?" Trace asked. He wondered if Ryker had

bothered to cue the guy about the chance that he would be tapped for duty during a family vacation.

Doubtful, he decided. Ryker didn't bother with niceties. If a SEAL was stupid enough to get married and have a family, Ryker would figure the man deserved to live with interrupted vacations.

"His name is Ford McKay. The man is tough and smart. His wife, Carly, has been involved in producing several Navy training films. You may have seen her pictures in *Time* and *Newsweek*."

Trace gave a low whistle. "I'm impressed."

"You should be. She's way above *your* pay grade, pal."

"Exactly what is the nature of the package and the possible threat?" Something cold stirred in Trace's mind. "Not Cruz?" That had to be impossible. Their old enemy and rogue operative was dead, according to all intelligence.

Trace had seen him die.

"No, not Cruz. He went down in the chopper crash in the Pacific." Once the leader of the Foxfire team, Enrique Cruz had been a superb officer and fearless operative, but he had snapped a year earlier, betraying his team and his country with a vengeance. Everyone in the secret project had breathed a sigh of relief when the man had finally been cornered and killed on a deserted island in the Pacific.

"No one could have escaped from that burning chopper." Trace frowned. "Right?"

"Nothing suggests that Cruz escaped. Ryker has a full-time team monitoring the crash region, and they've found zilch."

Some of Trace's uneasiness faded. "What's the threat?"

"Izzy will give you more details before you embark." Wolfe shook his head. "You know how Ryker loves drama."

Irritated, Trace riffled through the papers, pulling out a set of travel documents. "Vacations make me crazy."

"I seem to recall hearing something about that from your sister. Kit says your record visit at the ranch is three days and four hours—and that was only because you were testing some new ammunition for Ryker."

Trace gave a sheepish laugh. "At least Kit understands how I feel." His smile wavered. "She wasn't upset that I haven't visited for a while, right? She loves the ranch and she's great at raising her service dogs, but—"

"Stop worrying. Kit knows the ranch isn't your thing. She's fine with that. On the other hand she told me to make sure that you don't get cut to ribbons someplace with an unpronounceable name. I promised to try my best."

The words were casual, but the strength behind them was unyielding as forged steel. Foxfire men were tighter than family. Guarding each other's back was both a practiced skill and a task of bone-deep loyalty.

"Always glad to have you watching my six." Trace held up an arm brace made of moldable high-tech foam. "This new contraption is pretty amazing, but I'd like to know when I'll be done with the training wheels."

"Ask Teague. He's the go-to guy for tech and rehab."

The door swung open. "Someone call my name?" Izzy appeared with a sleek laptop under one arm.

"Speak of the devil," Trace muttered.

"I'm a hell of a lot more handsome. Better with computers, too. So what's your problem, O'Halloran?"

Trace dangled the tube of molded foam. "I'm ready to roll. And *not* on some half-baked duty aboard a cruise ship. I want my chips operational."

"Not possible until the medical team finishes a complete

assessment. Some anomalies have turned up following your hospitalization."

Trace made an impatient sound. "I'm fit, Teague."

"You're strong and your reflexes max the chart. That's why you were chosen for Foxfire in the first place. The chips enhance, but they don't define your abilities, O'Halloran. They just make you a little stronger and faster than you already are. And throwing energy nets can wait until the assessment is done."

Trace wasn't close to being convinced. He hadn't endured his grueling Foxfire training to be stuck on a half-baked assignment that a civilian could handle blindfolded. "This is kindergarten. Tell Ryker I'm ready for real action."

"Tell him yourself. He's out in the hall finishing a call to the head of the NSA."

The men in the room stiffened. Lloyd Ryker's presence usually had that effect on people.

"I went over your rehab reports," Izzy continued. "I'd say you're good to go. I've already conveyed that information to Ryker."

"Appreciated." Trace drummed his fingers on the pile of travel documents. "But I want a real assignment."

"Better than pacing the floors of the medical wing and scaring all the nurses."

"What nurses? Ryker pulled everyone but Foxfire staff as soon as my last surgery was done."

"He's just being cautious." Wolfe looked around as the door opened again. Lloyd Ryker was shoving an encrypted cell phone into the pocket of his understated Italian suit while an aide zipped papers into an alligator portfolio.

He studied the SEALs. All were standing now, eyes forward. Ryker noted the disciplined response and nodded slightly at Wolfe. "You still say O'Halloran is ready to leave rehab?"

"Yes, sir. Ishmael Teague concurs."

"I saw the reports. I want a guarantee your assessment is correct."

"You have it." Izzy crossed his arms, meeting Ryker's sharp gaze. "The surgery went even better than planned."

"Good. I'll be holding you two responsible for any problems." The civilian head of the Foxfire Unit made several quick marks on a form held out by his aide, then turned to study Trace. "Nice work in Afghanistan, O'Halloran. They found our hardware and were testing it within hours, congratulating themselves on a major success. For two weeks now we've been feeding them 'secret' updates. After our planted information is complete, their stolen equipment will start malfunctioning. The operation is a success."

"Glad to hear it, sir." Trace remained at stiff attention, certain that Ryker had more to say.

Ryker glanced around the room, then frowned. "I'm not convinced you're ready for duty. I can't have anyone on the team operating below full capacity, O'Halloran. You flatlined after that last round hit you and when you died—even briefly—your chips went haywire." Ryker's eyes narrowed. "You're carrying expensive technology. As far as I can see, my only option is to shut everything down until you're completely recovered and I have all the tests to prove it."

Trace shoved his anger deep. Ryker was baiting him, probing for signs of weakness or anger, but Trace wouldn't give any excuse to sideline him.

"Permission to speak, sir?" Trace kept his eyes forward.

"I'm listening."

"I don't like going out unarmed. I am trained and fully field capable, sir."

"Speculation. While the medical team is still running tests, I can't risk a foul-up. The chips are turned off." Ryker's eyes narrowed. "Anything to add, O'Halloran?"

"No, sir." Nothing that wouldn't get him into deep trouble.

Ryker glanced at his watch and then motioned his aide out of the room. "You'll be working this mission with the help of the ship's security director, who has been briefed on your arrival. In the event of problems, he will take orders from you."

Trace kept his eyes forward. The day he'd joined the Navy, he had accepted the fact that working for the government meant twenty-four-hour days and no privacy. It also meant taking orders from SOBs like Lloyd Ryker, who made mental manipulation an art form.

No whining. Do the job or pack your bags.

"Are you clear on your orders?"

"Yes, sir…except for the exact nature of the threat and the contents of the items in transit." In other words, everything important, Trace thought wryly.

His comment caught Ryker midstride.

As the head of Foxfire turned slowly, his cell phone beeped. He glanced at Trace and grimaced. "I'm expected in D.C. in four hours, so I'll make this short. Foxfire has an off-site scientist down in Mexico working on a highly specialized project. I have a man on board the cruise ship who carries sensitive material back and forth for me when necessary. The procedure has always worked well in the past. Who in the hell would expect someone on a cruise ship to be a government courier?"

Ryker shoved his cell phone in his pocket. "But last week someone tried to penetrate security at the Mexican compound. Then we detected an attempt to bypass our scientist's computer security." Ryker picked up Trace's discarded foam cast and stared at it for long moments.

When he looked up, his eyes were very cold. "I'm taking no chances with this transfer. If it was simply a question of data, we could send everything digitally, but there are tissue specimens involved, and their temperature stability is crucial. Your job will be to oversee security and provide backup."

"May I have the name of my shipboard contact?" Trace asked. Leave it to Ryker to milk the intrigue for all it was worth.

"Izzy will pass that info in a briefing packet at the appropriate time." Ryker crossed the room and opened the door. "Before you sail, you have one more assignment. Tomorrow a senator from California is hosting a cocktail party in your honor—4:00 p.m. at the Carlton Hotel. That means spit-shined and polished, Lieutenant. Wear *all* your medals."

Trace hated social events where he was the cocktail centerpiece. Ryker used the events for friendly politicians seeking reelection. A crisp uniform and a chest full of medals never failed to impress prospective campaign contributors.

"I'll be there, sir." *Hating every freaking second, but I'll be there.* Trace kept the irritation from his face. If the senator kept money flowing for Foxfire's expensive research, who was Trace to complain?

I hope some lobbyist's bored wife doesn't fondle my ass, like that last gig in Georgetown.

The woman had suggested Trace join her in the garden for some down-and-dirty sex between cocktails.

She'd been plenty miffed when Wolfe had shown up and spoiled her plans.

"A problem, Lieutenant?" Ryker turned, eyes narrowed. "You dislike attending the social events I arrange?"

"No, sir." *Hell, yes.* Every one of Ryker's team shunned social displays like the plague. But now was not the time for honesty.

"Let me remind you these parties provide the funds to keep our facilities viable. You may forget how expensive this project is, but I am reminded of that fact daily. I don't want to hear a hint of a complaint." Ryker shot a cold look at Wolfe. "Is that understood?"

"Absolutely, sir. May I offer to join Trace, sir? Sometimes two uniforms are better than one."

Ryker's eyes narrowed. "Excellent suggestion. You'll have travel documents ready in an hour. Be sure to give the senator and his wife my regards."

He gestured at his aide and strode out. The door slid shut behind him.

Silence filled the room. Then Wolfe Houston rubbed his neck and sighed. "Me and my big mouth. I swear, if another woman tries to grope my ass—"

"You'll grin and bear it, sir. You are always the height of courtesy." Trace grinned, glad that another one of the team was in the same boat. "That's one reason you're so popular with all the Beltway wives."

Wolfe muttered a graphic phrase. "Don't tell your sister that." The SEAL's expression turned serious. "Kit's the one. As far as I'm concerned, no other woman exists. I hope she knows that."

"You can do no wrong in my sister's eyes." The emotional force that bound the two was overpowering. For some reason Trace felt a little jealous when he saw how happy his sister and his friend looked when they were together.

A flicker of movement made him turn, staring at the door behind Izzy Teague. More like a shimmer than anything concrete, the phenomenon was damned strange. He caught a sweet scent…something almost familiar.

Trace moved swiftly, snapping open the door to the hall. He still couldn't peg the elusive scent.

An alert security officer stared back at him. "Problem, sir?"

"No. None." *Except that I'm hearing, seeing and smelling things that aren't there.* Had the change in his chip status triggered a wave of sensory distortions?

Who the hell knew?

Trace closed the door carefully. Through the window he watched a black helicopter cut through the azure New Mexico sky.

Nothing moved in the quiet room.

"We'll have to double-time it if we're going to catch that chopper." Wolfe picked up his equipment bag.

Trace grabbed his towel and sweatshirt. "I'm ready." He ignored a dull pain at his shoulder. Rehab was over. That was all that mattered.

CHAPTER FIVE

HE HADN'T BEEN to San Francisco in six years, and he loved the chaos as much as ever. A bike messenger was blasting rap music. Two truckers argued over one parking space. A woman with purple hair blew him a kiss.

Trace had forgotten how the colors mixed, how the noise roared and ebbed. Standing on Kearny Street, he caught the drifting scent of Middle Eastern spices mixed with Chinese sesame cakes and fried ginger. His stomach growled. Too bad he didn't have time to stop at the little Hunan restaurant with the blister-your-tongue chile.

But Trace was due to press the flesh at the senator's affair in less than twenty-four minutes, and he still had six blocks to walk. His CO had stayed behind in the hotel to make a last-minute phone call to the Foxfire facility.

His uniform drew a few curious stares, but Trace ignored them, walking briskly. He enjoyed the sea-tinged air, the fog and the pleasant twinge in his legs from climbing steep streets.

At the busy corner of Sutter Street, he swung his shoulder carefully, testing for range of motion, pain and strength. The rehab process was a success. He wasn't quite back to one hundred percent strength, but he was damned close. After ten days on the cruise ship, with as many gym sessions as he could schedule, Trace expected to be at full operational ability.

Behind him a taxi horn screeched.

A bus lumbered past, belching exhaust fumes. Trace sprinted across the street during a lull in traffic and re-checked the address Ryker had given him.

Three more blocks.

With a little luck he'd be there ahead of schedule.

Something shimmered at the edge of his vision. Through the noise, the bus fumes and the cooking smells he caught the bright tang of lavender, the third time that day.

He scowled at a passing Porsche.

The Phenomenon again. That was his word for the random sensations.

As he walked, the lavender scent thickened.

Trace ignored it.

No doubt it was connected to his chips being disabled. He'd write a complete report for Ryker once he was able to detect a pattern, but not a second sooner. He didn't want to be ordered to visit Foxfire's resident shrink, forced to dredge up his past for possible signs of emotional vulnerability.

He knew he was fit for action. His memories of Afghanistan were fading along with his scars, and no shrink would dredge up anything important. The lavender smell had to be a sensory reflex.

His heart pounded. He had a sudden urge to cross the street, coupled with a sense that something important was about to happen.

Neither made any sense. Pedestrians rushed past all around him, but they were all strangers.

There was no reason for him to cut back across Kearny.

He muttered in irritation, staring at a bakery truck double-parked near a fire hydrant. Probably he was dehydrated. Maybe it was the time change and the late-night flight from New Mexico. But he wasn't a man who was unsettled often, so he watched the street, watched the passing cars, watched the way clouds brushed Nob Hill beyond the tall buildings.

And then Trace saw her—tall and slim, wreathed in a bar of sunlight. Light played through her short, spiky hair, cut in layers that framed huge eyes.

A stranger.

No need to stare. No need to feel as if someone had jerked the cement out from under him and kicked him in the stomach.

Something seemed to wrap around his chest, driving the air from his lungs. It made no sense. She was just another woman racing through the afternoon sunlight. Probably going to meet a husband—or a lover, judging by the eagerness in her expression. She wasn't even beautiful, he thought wryly. Most people wouldn't have called her remarkable in any way, yet her long, quick stride and the swing of her hair were doing strange things to his pulse.

Somewhere a clock chimed, but he couldn't move.

He had less than twenty minutes to reach the penthouse somewhere above him. He would have preferred to spend the time pressed against that long, slim body, memorizing the secrets of her warm skin.

Crazy.

Through long months of training Ryker's first rule had been burned into the minds of every man on the Foxfire team. No personal life or distractions were permitted. Even sexual contacts were arranged by Ryker's staff, and the contact was carefully controlled. There was no gentle laughter and slow kisses on a moonlit night. It was physical release and nothing more.

Trace tried to remember the last time he'd laughed with a woman or simply held her hand. Nothing came to mind. The thought left him empty.

Suck it up, sailor. You knew what you were signing on for when you accepted your transfer to Foxfire. You knew all you were giving up.

And you couldn't wait to be part of the team.

As Wolfe Houston always said, there were only three things you could trust in life—yourself, your team and the probability of getting fungus where you least wanted it.

Then Wolfe had defied the rules by falling in love and asking approval to marry Trace's sister.

Despite that, all of them were Foxfire property, pure and simple. They *were* the job, 24/7. Trace had liked that just fine.

Until he'd stood in the afternoon sunlight watching keen eyes and vibrant cinnamon hair.

Around him the noise of the city faded. Even the sunlight seemed strange, wrapping itself around the woman across the street, playing in her hair and brushing the clean lines of her face.

No, she wasn't a beauty, Trace thought. So why was it impossible for him to look away as she cut through the crowd?

A fire truck screamed past. Shouts mingled with car horns and motorcycles. Then in one of the weather changes San Francisco was famous for, a bank of marine clouds poured in over the hills. In seconds the street blurred beneath a shifting veil of fog.

Traffic snarled. Horns screamed. Up the street Trace saw a construction truck back up, its ladder poised above the rear bed.

The woman had stopped. She bent low as she took something from a young man climbing out of a taxi. Both of them cradled big, white boxes, laughing.

Her laugh made the hairs rise along Trace's neck. The sound was full and rich and subtly sensual.

She was a stranger, but he knew just how her voice would sound up close, warm and husky.

A wave of sexual attraction hit him, as thick and sudden as the fog.

Hell. Maybe Ryker was right. Maybe this was about stress, not sex, and he hadn't put Afghanistan behind him.

As the woman headed down the street, she didn't look in his direction once. Trace took a deep breath. It was time to go. He glanced toward his destination, checking the address through pale, trailing fingers of fog.

Down the street he saw the truck turn, ladder creaking. One of the metal restraints twisted and broke free, the metal frame shuddering violently.

The woman and her friend hadn't noticed.

He moved by pure instinct, his heart pounding as he sprinted through a gap in traffic. Neither the woman nor her companion heard his shout as they turned toward the nearby hotel, their boxes held tightly at their chests.

Trace jumped the curb, shoved the woman sideways against a wall, and pushed her companion after her just before the ladder swung horizontal across the sidewalk. Its broken edge was a death blade cutting directly over the place the two had stood laughing a second before.

"Hey, *watch* it." The woman slammed him hard with her

shoulder, muttering angrily. Then she slipped, hit her companion and both of them lost their balance.

Trace saw the two white boxes fly into the air. He stepped back, twisted neatly and caught one in each hand.

A bicycle messenger shot past, making a string of obscene gestures, and the woman with the cinnamon hair shoved at his chest.

"Drop those and you're dead. Big, clumsy ox." She tried to grab one of the boxes. "Give me that now or I'm calling the cops."

Trace frowned at her. Why didn't people say thanks when you'd just saved them from death by sudden impalement?

He turned, pushing her back against the building and out of the way of the still-swaying ladder, while the truck bounced back down the curb. A man in a gray uniform jumped out and tugged at the broken hinges, trying to pull the metal sections back into place.

The woman turned, looking over Trace's shoulder. Her face paled, her body going still. "Shit." She swayed a little, not struggling against him now.

Her eyes locked on the truck bed. "Holy, holy hell," she whispered. "The ladder would have hit us. I didn't see." She took a deep breath, one hand shaking against the wall. She brushed a layer of cinnamon hair from her face while her hands shook harder than ever. "You aren't crazy." Her voice hitched. "You saved our lives."

"Are you okay?" He balanced the boxes, feeling her thighs press against him. The subtle friction made his mouth go dry.

"I'm fine." She took a deep breath. "I'm sorry I was rude. I didn't realize what was happening." She studied his face. "We see a lot of Navy guys in San Francisco. I thought you were just being a jerk."

Her voice was breathy, smokey like a good chipotle sauce.

Trace felt her hand on his sleeve. He didn't know her, would never know her, but the husky catch in her voice was as tempting as the slim, strong legs he felt brushing his.

Strangers or not, he wanted her bad.

Angry, he bit back a curse and moved away, banking the heat. *Trying* to bank the heat.

She looked at her friend. "Andreas, why don't you go check out the room? No surprises, please."

"Sure thing, boss. I'll take this with me." The man deftly removed one of the packages from Trace's hands and left.

"I'll take the other box now."

Trace looked down, feeling stupid as he gripped the white cardboard. "Must be something pretty important in here."

Her smile felt like pure, distilled summer pouring over his skin. The force of it made him forget the cars racing past and the appointment creeping closer.

"You bet it is. You're holding a little piece of my heart in that box."

"Maybe I should keep it then." His voice was gravelly. Hell, what had made him say something lame like *that?*

"News flash—men want sex, not women's hearts." She straightened her big, colorful sweater and shoved more cinnamon hair out of her eyes, then stared across the street. "Oops. My defensive, bitchy side is showing."

Trace heard old wounds and bad memories rather than bitchiness. "What's so important in here?" He raised the box, rattled it slightly.

She lunged, panic sweeping her face. "*No.* If you drop that, I'm dead."

Trace simply smiled. He handled high explosives and

deadly biotoxins regularly with complete confidence. Steady hands and split-second reaction times were part of his skill set. "Relax, your box isn't going anywhere. You still haven't told me why it's so important."

"I need to go. I can't be late."

Before she could answer, his cell phone vibrated against his belt with unavoidable force, yanking Trace back to earth. He muffled a curse as he realized the pocket was out of reach.

He started to hand over the box, but she leaned down and slid a hand into his pocket. His gaze never left her face as she pulled out the phone.

"Least I can do," she murmured, opening the phone. Frowning, she stared at the complex screen of Trace's new government prototype. "How do you—"

"Top left. I'll take it."

Instead of giving him the phone, she pressed the button he'd indicated and held the phone up to this ear.

Trace had seen the caller's number. Wolfe was probably upstairs waiting for him. Still, he didn't like anyone listening in to the call. "Look, I need to—"

"Take the call. I can see that your shoulder hurts, so as soon as you're done, I'll get going."

Shoulder?

How the hell had she known that?

Another twinge of suspicion made him study her warily.

But the phone was already at his ear, and he heard Wolfe's voice.

"O'Halloran, are you at the hotel?"

"Right outside, sir."

"I got held up on a conference call. I'm at least ten minutes away. Go in and press some flesh until I get there."

"Will do."

The line went dead and she closed the phone, returning it to his pocket.

Their skin brushed. He smelled her perfume, a faint mix of oranges and lilac. As gentle as a memory, it slid over his senses, leaving him restless for things he didn't have a name for.

She turned and lifted the white box. "It's a cake, by the way. I'm giving a class upstairs in thirty minutes."

"A cake?"

"Don't look so surprised. I worked five hours on that thing."

"On a cake?" Trace repeated.

"It's special. Ganache icing, spun-sugar flowers." She glanced at his dress uniform and the row of medals. "Impressive jewelry you've got there."

Trace was still trying to get his mind around the idea of a cake that took five hours to finish. In his world you ate whatever appeared on your plate, as long as it didn't move, and even that rule got broken sometimes.

He shrugged off her compliment. "No big deal. Just doing the job."

"That kind of hardware doesn't come easy. Something tells me there's a story behind each one." She tensed and nearly dropped her box as another skateboarder shot past close enough to bump her leg. "Damn."

Trace caught her with one arm and steadied the cake with his other hand. "It's okay. I've got you."

A delicate wash of color filled her face. She didn't pull away, only tilted her head, looking up at him over the box. "You're fast with your hands."

"Fast enough. What did you mean about my shoulder?"

He kept the question casual, watching her face for any sign of calculation.

She shrugged. "You favor your right side. When our boxes went flying, you caught them on the left. So what happened? Gunshot wound? Training accident?"

The explanation was plausible. "Nothing very interesting." He'd died, that's all. He sure as hell wasn't going to discuss that with her.

He crossed his arms. "Are you doing anything later?" At least they could have a drink before he left. Trace didn't have to be at the cruise dock until the following morning.

She cradled her cake, and then her fingers tightened. "No." There was an edge in her voice that hadn't been there before. "I'm sorry, but there's really no point." She gave a shaky laugh. "Believe me."

Trace watched her shift her box, then move off into the flow of messengers, workers and tourists.

Great legs. Strange encounter. She'd probably forgotten him already.

He shrugged off a sense of regret. He had a cocktail party to attend and lobbyists to charm.

DAMN.

Abso-freaking—damn.

Was she crazy?

Gina Ryan gripped her cake, scowling at her own stupidity. She'd been breathless, panting over a complete stranger, a man with trouble stamped all over him. It just wasn't her style.

Oh, she'd been tempted to say yes to that drink. It was the hard set to his jaw, coupled with the hint of danger in his eyes.

Yeah, she was a sucker for a man who knew his own mind.

Trouble, she thought grimly. And she hadn't been lying when she told him not to waste his time on her.

Meanwhile, she had two kinds of crème brûlée and a white chocolate wedding cake to worry about, not the hot challenge in a stranger's eyes.

She waved as Andreas trotted back, carrying a big set of keys. "Room's all set, Gina. You've got a big crowd upstairs." He waved the keys. "These are for the kitchen next to your lecture area. Your big Hobart industrial mixer wasn't set up, so I sent someone to track it down."

Gina resisted an urge to pull out her hair. Without her mixer for the demonstration, this master pastry class was going nowhere fast. "Did they have a record of our request?"

Andreas followed her up a sidewalk bordered by forgotten newspapers and scattered leaves. "They knew about it. They just haven't found the mixer yet."

"I may have to kill someone," Gina muttered. "Maybe myself."

"It won't be so bad. They'll find you something close. You're always quick on your feet at demonstrations." Andreas glanced at his watch. "Twenty minutes to go. Good thing that guy in the uniform caught our stuff." Gina's sous chef stared back down the street. "The man was smoking. Those were a lot of medals, too."

"Really?" Gina cleared her throat. "I didn't notice."

"Like hell you didn't. You two vanished into some kind of alternate reality. Hell, the guy had his arms around you right in the middle of the sidewalk."

"Because he knocked me over and I almost fell," Gina muttered. "Plus, I was trying to hold my cake steady." She nudged the big, white box. "The last thing I need is for this thing to get crushed."

Andreas glanced back, grinning smugly. "Don't look now, but he's following us. Probably wants to ask you out."

"He already did."

"And you said *no?* Come on, Gina, I felt the tension snap between you two. You haven't looked twice at a man in months."

"And I'm not looking twice at a man now." But she had to fight an urge to look back. She wondered if she'd have the willpower to turn down that drink if he asked her again.

"Too bad. He went in a different door."

Gina tried not to care. "Forget about the hunk, *will* you? We've got to find a mixer and test the sound system. Was the chocolate there?" She took a deep breath. "If anything happened to my tempered chocolate…"

Pain stabbed at her forehead.

"You okay, Chief?"

No, not even close to it.

"I'm fine." Ignoring the little blur in her vision, she walked past the uniformed doorman, away from the lobby filled with fresh roses and real Chinese antiques.

"Let's move." She checked her watch uneasily. As she strode past the gleaming marble lobby, Gina was proud of herself for not glancing back in search of a white uniform.

It took all of her willpower.

CHAPTER SIX

THE LOCATION COULD HAVE been worse.

At least there was running water, a decent gas oven and space to lay out her cakes as part of her master class on pastry. But the clock was ticking, and there was icing to finish. When transporting off-site, you never added final embellishment until you were almost ready to serve. Gina had learned that the hard way. Now she had two cakes that needed icing for final display.

Outside the participants were arriving. Stress beat a path down her forehead. "Reggie, where are the edible flowers?"

"Right here, Chief. Your buttercream is on the other side of the table. All three colors, present and accounted for."

"Yet again you save my butt." Without a pause, Gina opened the frosting made in the ship's kitchen that morning and assembled her tools. "Andreas, are you okay with the crème brûlée?"

"Good to go here. The demerara sugar's in place. They'll be ready to torch for your first presentation."

Gina knew that all of her staff were well trained. But the cruise management had insisted that she do the honors. Something about her recognition factor, Gina thought sourly. In an age of media-hungry celebrity chefs, finding time for actual cooking had become harder and harder.

"Andreas, where's my Hobart mixer?" Gina squeezed icing through a small bag and produced the first of two dozen rose petals to cover a white chocolate fondant–covered display cake.

"Supposed to be in the elevator any second. I called the hotel beverage services ten minutes ago and they said it was down at the loading dock."

"Call them again." Gina straightened, frowning. "No. I'm almost done here so I'll go. I need that mixer for the whole second segment."

"You sure?"

As she went back to work, icing swirled beneath her skilled fingers and crimson petals bloomed over a white ground. Carefully she dusted edible flowers over the sides of the cake and the iced cake board.

"Whoa, great roses." Andreas glanced over her shoulder.

Gina didn't look up, securing a ribbon of lifelike petals across the top of the cake. When you dealt with buttercream, there were always worries, always mistakes. The trick was being fast enough and experienced enough to know how to cover them up. "Almost done here. Have Reggie bring the cake stands."

She eased the second display cake from its box. The rich lemon batter had been enhanced by a liberal amount of rum, and the cake happened to be the captain's favorite. Using her turntable, she whisked swirls of white all around the base and then anchored pink hearts cut from marzipan, each one dotted with an edible silver bead.

The result was pretty damned good. She stood back, warmed by a zing of pride.

No matter how many pastries she made, she always felt a glow of pleasure at creating a thing of beauty. She'd never planned to cook for a living. Growing up in a quiet suburb of Sacramento, she'd wavered between being the world surfing champion or a neurosurgeon. Her policeman father had encouraged her in both—right up until the day he'd taken a bullet in the heart during an armored car robbery. After that, life had taken Gina down a very different route.

She centered the cakes on a rolling cart. Behind her she heard Andreas fire up his crème brûlée torch.

Now she had to find that damned mixer.

SHOWTIME, Trace thought.

Staring at the receiving line, he picked out a senator, two congressmen and a whole lot of major-league diamonds. San Francisco society was out in force, it seemed. Ryker's connections appeared to be solid gold.

There was too much loud laughter and too much jockeying for position next to the most powerful people. Trace glanced longingly at the bar displaying cans of ice-cold beer.

Wolfe appeared beside him, carrying two glasses of cola. *"Skoal."*

"Hell, sir, you expect me to drink *that?*"

But Trace only pretended to complain. He rarely drank to excess, and in a crowd like this it would be stupid to drink at all. You never knew who you were rubbing shoulders with. Any casual remark could find its way to the E-ring of the Pentagon within hours, killing a good career overnight.

He glanced at the door, wishing he had an excuse to leave. *Any excuse.*

Trace realized that Wolfe was talking to him. "Sorry, sir. What did you say?"

"The senator's wife just told me that a case of vintage

champagne is held up somewhere down in the hotel's receiving department." Wolfe motioned toward the door. "You are hereby ordered to go find it. It's that or keep explaining to people why you look like you hate these events, so get moving. And I want you back before this thing is finished, clear?"

"Understood, sir. Thank you, sir." Trace scratched his cheek. "But it might take me longer than I think to find that missing champagne. Probably a real mess down there."

"Don't sound so enthusiastic," Wolfe muttered.

Trace grinned. With luck, he'd be back just in time to say his goodbyes.

THE HOTEL LOADING BAY was deserted, half in shadow.

The mixer was still in its box, wedged in a corner next to a row of folding chairs.

Gina tried to lift the box and staggered back, gasping. She'd forgotten how heavy a commercial mixer could be. And there was no one around to help her move the stupid thing.

On the other hand, there happened to be a forklift parked by the wall, and it was screaming her name.

Gina had spent two summers working in a warehouse, so she knew her way around forklift trucks. She hopped aboard, scanned the controls and gunned the motor. It took her less than a minute to maneuver across the small loading area and center the metal arms. She nudged the mixer into position, raised it four inches, locked the long arms in place and then swung wide.

"You mind watching where you aim that thing? I kind of like having my chest in one piece."

And it was such a gorgeous chest, Gina thought, staring at her rescuer from earlier that afternoon.

The broad wall of muscle showed off his white uniform and rows of medals to perfection.

"Mind if I borrow your forklift for a few minutes?"

"Yes," she snapped. What was *he* doing here? She didn't have time to be distracted, not with two hundred people upstairs expecting a killer pastry presentation to begin any second. "Sorry, but I'm late. You'll have to find your own ride. It's every man for himself right now," she said grimly.

Wheeling, she balanced the mixer and turned with small, precise movements.

"You're pretty good at that."

"Summer job," she called over her shoulder.

Learning to drive a forklift had been easy. Getting along with the macho male warehouse staff had been the hard part. But she'd held her own and made good money those summers, enough for all her tuition and more. When summer ended, her male coworkers had been sorry to see her go.

She had almost finished her turn when a man's voice echoed from someplace inside. Abruptly the heavy metal door of the loading bay started to slide shut.

"Hey, *stop!*" Gina shouted, trying to maneuver back out of reach.

But the door kept right on moving.

In her concentration, she barely saw the Navy officer jump up onto the area under the closing door. "Hold on," he called over the din of creaking metal. "There has to be a manual override here somewhere."

He wouldn't find it in time, Gina thought desperately. She maneuvered sideways, her gaze locked on the moving door. Suddenly she felt a hand at her elbow. She was yanked off the truck and pulled against a rock-hard chest.

"*No.* My beautiful Hobart mixer—"

"Can be replaced. You can't," the man said roughly. "That door probably weighs eight hundred pounds. You'd be hamburger, trust me."

"Do something," Gina whispered. Her presentation was going up in smoke before her eyes.

Caught against his chest, she watched in horror as metal ground down against metal. The forklift shuddered, crumpling slowly, with her mixer caught firmly beneath.

The man blew out a breath. "Something tells me I'm going to regret this." He set Gina back on her feet, scanned the out-of-season tools and supplies lining the walls and grabbed a thick rope.

He circled the mixer and pulled hard, bending to the task, his face taut and arms rigid. As the door came lower, the space was plunged into shadow.

Gina heard the scrape of metal as she searched vainly for any kind of wall control panel or power button, but finally she had to give up. "Forget it," she called. "I don't want you to get hurt."

He didn't seem to hear, so she gripped his shoulder and yelled over the growl and grind of metal. "Let it go. It's not your problem."

As her eyes grew accustomed to the shadowed light, she saw that he had worked the big steel mixer several inches closer, but it wasn't far enough. She flinched as the crucial piece of equipment was mangled by the door.

Finally the metal stopped moving. She took a shaky breath and sank against the wall, frantically trying to plan around the loss of the mixer.

"Are you okay?" The man's voice was cool, precise. He'd recovered incredibly fast, Gina noticed. He wasn't even breathing hard now. She, on the other hand, was a total wreck.

"Okay as in not hurt or maimed? I think so. Okay as in anticipating a happy life and a prosperous future? Definitely not. I've got two hundred people upstairs waiting for me and that mixer, and I am *so* screwed." She looked up, stabbing a hand through her hair. "Thanks for trying, Mr.—"

"Trace."

"Gina," she said without really thinking. She stuck out one hand and felt a tug at her sleeve. Furious, she tried again.

No luck.

"What's wrong?"

"I can't *move,* that's what's wrong."

CHAPTER SEVEN

SHE LEANED RIGHT and left. This time there was a definite snag on her right side.

Trace moved closer. "Stay still."

"But I—"

His hard body nudged hers. "Stop twisting around." He ran a hand along the wall and then across her shoulders.

"What's wrong? What did you find?"

"Give me a minute here. The light's not great," he said shortly. "I'll get my cell phone."

"Check the left pocket of my skirt," Gina shot back. "Outside corner right under the snap."

She felt his hand slide along her arm and into her pocket, searching to the bottom.

"How deep are these pockets?" He searched some more. "This feels like plastic. Do you always carry thermometers in your cargo pockets?"

"Knitting needles. Hand them over." Gina turned a knob on the bottom of the long piece of plastic and instantly her hand was bathed in a blue-white glow. "They're for knitting in the dark. I never leave home without them." She held up the bright needle, trying to look over her shoulder, but Trace moved her back against the wall and angled the needle downward.

"I think I see the problem. A big piece of your sweater is caught in the joints of the loading-bay door. It must have happened when you were trying to find the control."

She would never, ever knit bell sleeves again, Gina swore. She gave an experimental tug with her arm.

The man was right. Her sleeve was caught in the cross joint.

"You want me to cut it?"

Her heart fluttered. "Hand dyed cashmere yarn? I don't think so. Do you have any *idea* what cashmere costs?"

His lips curved slightly. "In that case, I guess we're stuck here until someone comes."

We. Not *you.*

That was nice.

Gina's eyes narrowed. Only maybe the man wasn't heroic. Maybe he was a psychotic stalker who waited for opportunities to get women in deserted places and this was definitely deserted. After that he'd—

She remembered how he'd caught her cake boxes and balanced both of them carefully.

Nah. He was hero material, all right.

"Actually, there is another way to handle this," he said thoughtfully.

"Anything. I've got a master class to give upstairs." Desperation made her voice shrill.

He crossed his arms. She felt his gaze brush her face, her chest.

"Then take off the sweater."

She stared at him. This was heading right into psycho territory after all. He even had a faint smile playing around his lips. Better nip this line of thought in the bud.

"Forget it. I can't take the sweater off."

"Why? I'll help you. The sleeve doesn't look that tight."

"It's not the sleeve." Gina took an angry breath. "There's not— I'm not—" She frowned at the wall. "I'm not wearing anything underneath the sweater. Is that clear enough for you?"

His mouth twitched. "I can see how that would be a little problem."

If the man laughed, she was going to hit him in the face.

But he tilted up her knitting needle, studied the sweater and rubbed his jaw. "When did you say your class was supposed to start?"

"Five minutes ago." Damn, damn, damn. She had to *think*. "My cell phone is in my purse. Call security and get them down here."

He fumbled for her phone. "I don't think they'll get here fast enough to be much help."

Gina blew a strand of hair off her forehead. "I can't walk into my class *naked*. Well, half naked."

"Wear my jacket. You can find a cook's uniform somewhere in the kitchen, can't you? That should tide you over."

Why hadn't she thought of that? It just might work.

"That's good. But my sweater will still be hanging here." No way was she losing all that excellent cashmere. The yarn had been worth a week's wages.

"I'll come back for it. I've got to track down a case of vintage champagne. After that I'll drop off your sweater wherever your class is meeting."

She stared at him suspiciously. "Hold on. Why are you being so nice?"

"Do I have to have a reason?"

"Absolutely." She shoved a strand of hair out of her

eyes. "If I know anything, I know this. Nobody does nice for nothing."

"You're wrong."

Gina felt the skim of his hand at her neck, the heat of his body against her thighs. She swallowed. "No way."

"I do," he whispered.

An odd little flutter dipped into her chest. Gina felt something earthier and more reckless than simple gratitude.

She closed her eyes, hit with sudden images.

Her.

Him. Together in a hotel bed, doing things Gina hadn't ever tried, putting herself into the hands of a stranger. Breaking all the rules.

She closed her eyes, forcing away dark images that left her skin hot and aching.

It had been too long, she thought. This was just reflex and cranky female hormones talking, nothing more.

She cleared her throat. "It's a deal. Turn off the light while I get out of this sweater."

The light vanished.

Just like that? No protests or trickery?

She wasn't sure if she should be thrilled or insulted. Most men she knew would have tried to sneak at least one look. She shimmied out of her sweater, clutching the soft cashmere to her chest. "So—are you about ready? I just have to work free of this sleeve."

The sweater came off. Cool air skimmed her naked breasts. She sensed Trace's presence nearby.

Warm cloth settled around her shoulders.

"How's that?" His voice was low and rough.

"F-fine." No, it wasn't fine. It was a very bad idea. Gina realized the uniform jacket was warm with the heat of his body, as intimate as the touch of his hands on her sensitive skin. The fabric also carried his scent, a mix of crisp outdoor air, citrus soap and sweat.

Kill me now, she thought dimly, intensely aware of how close he was standing.

Her nipples hardened as the cloth touched and skimmed, driving her crazy with the thought of his callused hands curved over all the same places.

Hel-lo.

The man is a stranger. Did you lose all functioning cells of your brain when the light went out?

There was only one answer.

Yes.

She felt reckless and hot, her fingers digging into the long sleeves of his uniform jacket. Whatever she wanted, he would do it. Here and now. They were alone and she'd never see him again, so what would it matter to let go, just this once?

"Are you ready to go? Your people will be waiting. Maybe you should call them."

Earth to Mars. The man was dead right. When had her brain blown every fuse? "I'm ready. You can turn on that light again. Then I'll make my call."

She heard the rustle of cloth and saw his chest, rows of hard muscles outlined beneath a white T-shirt, caught in the glow of her knitting needle.

The sight made her knees go soft. Okay, the man had a chest out of her deepest fantasies. So what? You didn't go to bed with a man just because he had a fantastic chest and abs to die for.

At least you shouldn't, she thought wildly.

"My first topic is bed." Gina felt her face go hot. "I

mean, *bread.* Then I'm doing puff pastry and custard-style desserts. Andreas will be able to get things started."

"Bread. I've always loved a hot loaf fresh from the oven. You must be a great teacher. And don't worry about your sweater. I'll bring it to you." He took her arm, guiding her up a set of narrow metal steps.

Sweater? What sweater?

She was worrying about a lot more than some cashmere yarn. Right now her sanity seemed to be at risk.

"I appreciate your help." She tried to ignore the way his muscles bunched and flexed as he moved in front of her to open an interior door.

But she couldn't ignore the way her nipples felt, tight and hot, driving against the soft lining of his uniform. The friction was making her lose all focus as her body came alive.

"By the way, was that Mongolian cashmere? Four-ply?"

She simply stared at him.

All this, and the man knew about yarn, too? *Be still my beating heart,* she thought dizzily.

She managed to make her voice cool and casual. "You noticed that?"

"My friend is a knitter. A fanatic, actually. When she finally scored a whole bag of cashmere on eBay, she went nuts. I heard about it for months."

"Your friend is a she?" Somehow the question just tumbled out. "Not that it's any of my business," she said stiffly.

His fingers cradled her wrists. For a moment he held her lightly, their bodies touching, while the sense of contact between them grew, nearly electric. Gina's throat went dry.

"Miki," he said quietly. "A *she.* Just a friend, in case it's important."

It shouldn't have been.

She barely knew the man, so his friends and background were of no possible significance.

Like hell, they weren't.

"You're not—married or anything? Seeing anyone, I mean." *Great job, Ryan. Spell it out, why don't you? Let him know you're a complete tongue-tied idiot in a major state of lust.*

"No one." He slid one hand slowly over her hair. Just that and no more, letting the warm strands play through his fingers as if they were infinitely interesting. "What about you?"

Gina took a deep breath. "No one for me, either. No time for any of that stuff."

"Good." The word was rough.

He moved before she knew it, and his mouth brushed hers, careful and slow. Gina made a lost sound. Somehow her fingers were locked around his strong shoulders and there was no space between them. With her thigh to his, she felt the sudden tension of his body.

"Hell," he whispered.

"What?"

"This. You. It shouldn't be happening." His tongue slid against hers, hot and searching, and Gina's fingers tightened. He kissed her hard as if he couldn't stop himself, but had to try. His arousal was unmistakable.

The suggestive pressure at the base of her stomach made her greedy for more.

The sharp vibration of her cell phone jolted her back to reality. She shouldn't be doing this. She had never been interested in casual sex. She hadn't been too good with long-term relationships, either. But the slick, damp feeling between her legs told Gina that her body was making up for lost time.

The vibration continued, and she dug in her purse, found her cell phone and answered breathlessly. "Yeah."

"Chief, where are you?" Andreas sounded worried. "I've got Reggie at bat, but the natives are restless. You've got four food critics and six reporters up here, and they want *you*, not us."

"I'm on the way. Ask Reggie to grab an extra white jacket in my size and leave it out, okay?"

"Why—"

"Don't ask. Just stall. I'll be there in five."

"You got it. There's a television crew here, too. Someone from the home office set it up and forgot to let us know."

Gina coughed back a sound of dismay. No need to worry Andreas more than he already was. "Not a problem. We'll start with the bed recipe—I mean, *bread*," she said quickly.

Great.

Silence. "Gina, are you okay? You sound…strange."

She struggled through a haze of major lust and stared up at Trace. He was focused on her entirely, his hands open on her shoulders. His attention—and his control—were nearly tangible.

Another major turn on, she thought. How long since a man had listened to her, watched with that kind of total focus and concern?

Never, a small voice whispered.

"I'm fine, Andreas. See you in five." She powered off her cell phone and shoved it into her pocket. There was so much more to say, so much more that could have happened then.

But her time was up.

"I have to go." Her voice was strained. "I can't let them deal with this without me."

He nodded as if he understood. "The elevator is

beyond those stairs. Make a left and then a quick right. You can't miss it."

"How do you know where the elevator is?"

"I memorized the hotel floor plan. It's a habit of mine."

She frowned, suddenly aware how different his life was from hers and how unlikely it was that they'd ever met.

That knowledge made her push to her toes and rest her palm against his cheek, savoring the heat of his body. "Thank you."

She felt his jaw flex. "I did nothing special."

"Wrong. I'd forgotten there could be giving with no strings. I'd forgotten—a lot of things. You just reminded me."

She brushed her mouth across his, feeling the instant rise of heat.

Him. Her.

They both felt it. His body left no mistake about that.

Wrong place, wrong time.

Gina forced herself to climb the stairs. No point in dragging things out. "After I change, I'll leave your jacket upstairs in the kitchen. It's just off the ballroom. Good luck with the champagne." She smiled briefly. "I'll…see you around."

But she wouldn't. They both knew that.

CHAPTER EIGHT

HE WATCHED HER GO, her hair swinging, her steps fast. Great legs, he thought. A woman with places to go and people to see.

He wanted her to stay.

She was mouthy and stubborn, but he liked her energy. He also liked her sense of loyalty to her kitchen team. Trace knew all about the importance of team loyalty.

But five hours to make one cake?

He felt a dull ache at his shoulder and grimaced. He was regretting his wrestling match with the big mixer, but he hadn't done any real damage. Any pain had been more than offset by her smile of thanks and gentle kiss.

Great mouth, too.

Then he shrugged off the memory. She wasn't his type. He'd always favored leggy blondes or sultry brunettes, women who liked to feel a man's body fast and hard, without much discussion.

He rubbed his neck and wondered why the other women he could remember suddenly seemed pale and uninteresting.

He glanced at his watch.

Vintage champagne, he thought wryly. But first he was going to chew someone's butt for closing the loading door without maintaining direct visual contact with the area.

There was probably an override switch somewhere, but it was nowhere in sight, and someone could have been killed beneath the heavy door. The hotel was damned lucky that their only casualties were a forklift truck and a Hobart mixer.

After he retrieved his uniform jacket from the kitchen, he'd report that problem to security.

"LOOKING FOR SOMEONE?" Wolfe stole through the crowd, his smile forced.

"Just an escape route. I found the missing champagne. The senator's wife seemed very happy." Trace set his untouched glass of punch on a nearby table. "Is it just me or do these things keep getting worse?"

"Yes," Wolfe said cryptically. "Don't look now but the senator is gesturing. We should go make nice-nice."

Trace uttered a sound of pain and eyed the open bar wistfully. "I didn't sign up to play nice. I signed up for det cords and delayed rocket rounds."

"Welcome to the New Navy," Wolfe muttered.

TEN MINUTES LATER Trace stood at the back of the crowded room finishing a shrimp canapé that tasted like cardboard. To his left a journalist was trying to draw Wolfe into an argument about the necessity of collateral damage during wartime operations. Not that he'd succeed.

Finally Wolfe broke away, looking harassed as a woman slid a business card with her phone number into his pocket. "If I'm not brain dead, I will be in another five minutes." Wolfe glanced at his watch, then examined the thinning crowd. "We're done here. Let's roll."

"Hallelujah." Trace headed to the door without a backward glance. He and Wolfe said polite goodbyes to the senator and his wife, then breathed a sigh of relief when they reached the elevators.

Trace consulted his memory of the hotel floor plan and hit the elevator button down.

"Fourth floor?" Wolfe raised an eyebrow as Trace pulled a bright pink sweater out of a brown paper bag. "I don't think pink is your best color, O'Halloran."

"I have to drop this off at a lecture downstairs. I won't be long."

The elevator doors opened at four.

"There's a story here somewhere." Wolfe stared at Trace, then shrugged. "None of my business, though. Downstairs. Five minutes. There's a beer back at our hotel with my name on it."

"Roger that."

ALMOST DONE, Gina thought.

The crème brûlée demonstration had received wild applause, with her cake decorating tutorial a close second. She was pretty sure she had flecks of buttercream frosting in her hair, but she was too tired to care. All she wanted was to get back to the ship, kick off her shoes and unwind.

Then she saw the white uniform at the back of the room and all thoughts of relaxing vanished. He'd actually tracked her down. She'd expected him to be distracted and forget all about her.

She tried to focus on the food critic in the front row. The man tugged at his small goatee, launching into his third convoluted question.

Meanwhile, Trace was handing her sweater to Reggie. The two spoke quietly and Reggie nodded.

Please get his phone number, Gina prayed.

She cleared her throat. "I think this will be our last question." She smiled but made a point of glancing at her watch.

"Ms. Ryan, the *New York Times* recently quoted a food writer who said that imported chocolate is the new sex. Any comment?"

Gina waited a beat and smiled. "Was something wrong with the old sex?"

When the laughter stopped, she cut to a brief review of quality, artisanal imported chocolates, outlining her personal favorites. Then she wrapped up the session.

When she glanced at the back of the room, Trace was staring at her, smiling.

He raised his hand.

"Yes? The man in the uniform," Gina said a little breathlessly.

"Don't get me wrong, ma'am. I like good chocolate as much as the next guy. But the way I see it, sex is always going to have it over chocolate."

Laughter broke in another wave.

He gave her a calm two-finger salute that sent the dark flutter nose-diving through her chest. Before Gina could answer, a man with a camera cut in front of her and she was caught in a TV interview.

When she looked up, Trace was gone.

CHAPTER NINE

One day later

THE SHIP'S LOWER DECKS were packed. While passengers lined up for entrance upstairs, uniformed workers raced past the lower loading areas with cans, food boxes and equipment.

Gina leaned against a rail, watching huge drums of cooking oil being rolled toward the ship's stores. The head of beverage services stood in the middle of the chaos, looking perfectly made up and very smug. Gina wasn't up with all the fashion trends, but she suspected that Blaine Richardson's cropped red sweater was a Prada original. How you could afford designer clothes on a head of beverage service's salary was a mystery to Gina. Then again most things about Blaine were a mystery to Gina.

As a seabird circled overhead, she rubbed her neck, smoothing knots of tension. All she wanted to do was sit down and close her eyes for a few minutes before the dinner madness began, but that clearly wasn't going to happen.

Blaine was gesturing to her from the deck, and talking to Blaine was never a good thing.

Gina crossed the deck warily. "You wanted something?"

"No, but you will."

The mysterious act again. "I don't see any problems,

Blaine. I logged all my stores in the ship's computer three days ago. I'm good to go."

Blaine studied a crimson nail and yawned. "Really?"

Whenever Blaine struck a casual pose like this, disaster always waited right around the corner.

"There's no problem for me. But you've definitely got one. You should have been here earlier when the men began to load. There were space issues inside one of the refrigerated units. You remember when the thermostat started acting up, don't you?" Her voice was sweet.

About as sweet as poisoned fruit, Gina thought. "That thermostat was supposed to be replaced here in California."

"Afraid they couldn't find the right parts." Blaine studied another crimson nail. "That means no repair and no guarantees on anything stored in that unit." She yawned dramatically. "Lucky for me that I'm an early riser. I made sure that all my stores were put in the functioning units. Since you weren't here..."

The workers had diverted her food to a malfunctioning unit?

Gina stiffened, hit by a wave of anger. The day before she had been busy doing a favor for the cruise line bigwigs. Earlier in the morning she had had to catch up with her work on board. Meanwhile, the Wicked Witch of the West had been *here* sabotaging her pastry stores. Any pastry chef knew that chocolate was very temperature-sensitive, with an ideal storage temperature between fifteen and eighteen degrees centigrade. Fluctuations in temperature could result in melting and subsequent recrystalization of the cocoa butter fat. The surface powder or "bloom" was death to good pastry, requiring a new round of tempering.

Now Gina would have to beg, wheedle and trade favors

to find adequate space for her sensitive chocolates and edible flowers in the ship's already tight refrigerated areas. There was no way she'd ask Blaine to share her space.

Not that asking would help.

Never pleasant, Blaine had lapsed into full bitch mode after she learned that Gina was being considered for a food series on national TV. Since that day three months ago, it had become Blaine's sole goal in life to beat out Gina with her own wine series, and her sabotage efforts were becoming more difficult to avoid. Gina had spoken to the head of food services twice, but he had been no help.

No surprise there. Blaine was boffing the man every chance she got. There was little that didn't get noticed aboard a crowded ship, and crew gossip had pinpointed the spots and times, right down to the noise level and positions involved.

Ugh. Some details you just didn't want to know.

"Thanks for all your help, Blaine." Gina's voice was icy. "You're a real team player."

Blaine buffed another nail. "Nobody said it was a team sport, honey. Just remember. If I don't get a TV series, then *nobody* on board does."

"Wow. Now there's a healthy adult attitude."

Much as she would have liked to, Gina didn't stay around to trade insults.

She had a pallet of varietal semisweet chocolate to rescue before it started to sweat.

WHEN GINA TURNED into the corridor to the rear storage area, she nearly ran into her Brazilian sous chef. Andreas looked exhausted and worried. "He wants you and it's not pretty."

"Who wants me?" Gina ran through any recent problems with personnel, management or the captain and was relieved when she found none.

"Tobias Hale from security. He was down at the kitchen ten minutes ago. *And* ten minutes before that. He said you were to go straight to his office as soon as you came aboard."

"Can't. Gotta go save a ton of expensive chocolate from imminent peril. The Wicked Witch sent them over to the malfunctioning cooler."

Andreas muttered a string of harsh words in Portuguese street slang. "You want me to help you with this transfer?"

"I can manage. But come back when you've finished checking on the tarts for dinner. We may have to work fast."

"Nothing to sweat for, boss." Andreas's English was very good, but he occasionally mixed an idiom. "I will come soon. But Tobias—"

"Can wait." The ship's security chief was six feet five inches tall, built like an oak tree and had the smooth, dark features of a slightly younger James Earl Jones. He stopped fights with one glance and shot fear into the hearts of boisterous travelers and drunken crew alike. Because of him the ship never had security problems. The crew scuttlebutt said that he was a former CIA operative; others said he was ex-Delta Force. Maybe both were right.

His orders were never ignored.

But Gina did that now. She had her food to protect.

She was racing along the corridor to the galley so fast that she didn't see a hand truck half hidden by a box of cleaning supplies. Her ankle hit metal and she went flying headfirst, skinning her palms, elbows and one cheek.

Closing her eyes to the sudden burst of pain, she sat up slowly.

A worried face loomed over her. The cleaning man

shoved his hand truck back against the wall. "You okay? I had to use the bathroom. Sorry about that. Hey, you're the one who made the rum cake for my birthday last month. Man, it was great." He offered her his hand and tugged her to her feet.

Gina blinked, feeling a little dizzy. "Glad to hear you liked it."

"Ma'am, you don't look so good. You want me to get someone—like a doctor or something?"

"I'll be fine. Just be sure you store that hand truck so no one else trips over it."

"Sure. Real sorry about that. By the way, Tobias Hale is looking for you."

Great.

Gina dug a tissue from her pocket and limped off. Most of the blood was gone by the time she located her chocolate pallet, just in time to keep it from being loaded into the cooler with the unreliable thermostat. After fifteen minutes of mixed pleas, promises and threats, she found an alternate berth in a different unit, but it meant volunteering to prepare special desserts for staff dinners the following month.

Next time she'd definitely beat Blaine to the dock. And until then she'd remember to watch her back.

When Gina finally reached the kitchen, she sank wearily into a chair, kicked off her shoes and pressed a bag of ice against her bruised cheek.

"Want to tell me what you are doing?"

"Resting?" She didn't look up. She knew that deep voice, and there was no ignoring its edge of anger. "I had to rescue some chocolate." She sighed. "And after that I was trying to avoid running into you."

"In my office." There was steel in Tobias Hale's order. "Five minutes, Gina. Otherwise I'll put you on report."

If she hadn't been so tired, she would have jumped up and saluted. "Aye-aye, sir."

"Don't bother sounding nice and obedient. We both know you'd like to insert one of your favorite knitting needles up my…nose. So stop smiling and get over to my office."

One more fire to put out, Gina thought wearily. What had she done to piss off Tobias so royally?

She rubbed a fresh trickle of blood off her cheek and wiggled back into her shoes. Whoever thought cooking was glamorous needed to have a serious mental evaluation.

CHAPTER TEN

"You should have told me."

"Told you what?" Gina paced Tobias's small office, watching seabirds rocket past the porthole. The ship was two hours out of San Francisco, following the curve of California south to Mexico. Given the hum of the big engines, she put their speed around fifteen knots.

Funny how she'd picked up the maritime life. Now it seemed like second nature. She was going to miss all of this when she left.

When she had to leave.

She prayed it wouldn't be soon.

"Stop pacing like a scrawny, caged cat."

"Who's scrawny?" Gina muttered.

Tobias sat down at his desk and glared at her. "You know damned well what I mean. You're not eating enough. You're not sleeping enough. Scrawny," the big security officer repeated flatly. "Bad-tempered and wound up tight."

Gina started to rub her forehead, then caught herself. Tobias missed nothing. She couldn't give any sign of the headache that was digging in behind her eyes. "You have a cigarette?"

"Why? You gave them up four years ago."

"Right. Then how about some of those lemon drops you think you've kept hidden in the top left drawer of your desk?"

Tobias flipped open a drawer and tossed her a bag of candy. "Don't change the subject. I know what's going on."

What was he talking about? Had she forgotten to return those last two videos of *24* from the ship's video library? Did she owe money for uniform laundry?

No to both. But something had Tobias riled up big-time.

She savored the bite of a sour lemon ball, frowning. "Gee, Tobias, I don't know what—"

"Of course you do. You were pale and shaky out at that damned pastry class you refused to say no to. You were dizzy by the end."

"Oh, that." She should have known Tobias would get reports on staff activities ashore. The man was spooky in his ability to gather information. She shrugged. "Didn't sleep very well last night. Must be too much partying."

"Partying, my ass. You don't party. You don't take time off. You work twenty hours out of every twenty-four and your staff is worried about you."

Gina stopped pacing. "They told you that?"

"I had two worried calls today. Everyone says you looked pale yesterday."

"Things were hectic."

The security chief snorted. "Try again."

So much for fooling her staff. "Look, I—I'm fine, Tobias. I was tired and too rushed to eat. Everything piled up."

His eyes narrowed. "You're still pale. Something else is going on." The head of security steepled his fingers and stared at her. "Level with me, or I'll get really nasty."

Gina cast about desperately for another excuse. "A truck ladder broke and almost hit us. Things were looking nasty."

"I know all about the lieutenant with the medals who saved the day."

"Is there *anything* you miss?"

"Not if I can help it. So did you get the man's name?"

"No. Should I have? We weren't contemplating marriage," she said dryly.

"I'm just curious. And I'll take the rest of those lemon sours, if you're done shredding the bag."

Gina took a breath and handed the bag back to Tobias. "Do you have boxes of these stashed somewhere? They're imported from France, so you can't just pick them up at the local Wal-Mart."

"I could tell you, but then I'd have to kill you." His lips curved faintly. "So they say."

"When are you going to tell me the truth, Tobias? Were you Delta Force or a Green Beret?"

The security chief moved his fingers over the single photo on his desk. It was a shot of a woman at a distance, her face blurred by the sunlight pouring over the mountain at her back. The thick trees could have been in Mississippi or Connecticut or Guatemala. Gina had often wanted to ask about the woman, but Tobias wasn't the sort of man you crowded with personal questions.

"What I was doesn't matter. It's over. That me is dead." He sat up stiffly as if the words had surprised him. "Stop changing the subject."

"Fine. I'll eat. I'll sleep. I'll be more careful in the future." *And I'll learn to lie a whole lot better, too.*

Keen eyes swept her face. "Pressure is part of the job. You've dealt with it before without any problem. Something's different now."

No kidding.

Now my eyes ache and I keep failing my peripheral vision tests. Occasionally colors blur and lines of print wobble. "Nothing important, I promise you."

The dramatically handsome security officer leaned back in his chair. He straightened a pen and pencil near his phone, then looked up. "That's bullshit and we both know it."

No fooling Tobias, Gina thought glumly. But she said nothing. If he reported her as unable to work, she'd have to appear for a medical evaluation, and any serious exam would reveal anomalies in her last set of vision tests. It would only be a matter of time before her condition went on record for personnel and everyone else to see.

No way. This chef was going to die in the saddle. What else could she do but cook? Once upon a time she'd had a different job back in Seattle. She'd been damned good at the job, too.

Ancient history.

Gina knew she'd go crazy if she had to stare at her hands and do nothing while she waited for the color loss and double vision that signaled final optic nerve deterioration.

So she had to lie through her teeth and convince Tobias she was in perfect shape to work. Not that it was a lie; the day she couldn't do her job was the day she'd turn in her resignation.

Of course it was never a good idea to have a blind person working near an open fire.

Tobias leaned back in his chair. "Stop that."

"What?"

"Trying to cook up a lie. It won't work. You know, I thought we were friends. Friends don't lie to friends."

Yeah, they were friends. They'd shared some bad jokes during awful storms at sea. They had worked together for five years on more cruises than Gina could count, and they spent Thursday nights playing poker in a secret, rotating location with only select crew in attendance. She counted Tobias as a true friend.

But some things you didn't share.

After her dad's death, Gina's mother had flaked out completely. Unable to function, she'd lived on medications that left her half asleep most of the day. She hadn't accepted what was going on around her. Instead, she'd built a wall of denial and vanished behind it.

That wasn't happening to Gina.

Tobias had a right to expect the truth from her, but friendship had its limits. How did you tell a friend that you were going blind? That the meds were working, but only to a point and one morning you'd wake up to see shadows and squiggles. About that time Gina's color vision would become unreliable. Outlines would blur and the headaches would ratchet up.

She closed her eyes. Dear God, she needed more time. How could she break the news to someone else when she still hadn't come to grips with it?

"No more evasions." His voice was rough with concern. "Damn it, Gina, I want to help but I don't know how."

It was his baffled anger that finally cut through her defenses. Pity or concern she would have dismissed easily, but anger was something she understood too well. Anger had become her closest companion in the past few months. Little things, nothing things, left her shaken and furious.

Meanwhile, Tobias wouldn't let go until he had answers.

"It's personal, Tobias. I have to deal with this myself."

His eyes narrowed. "Personal how? Blaine trouble?"

Blaine. He thought that was her big problem. If only he were right.

Gina cleared her throat. "I'd rather not discuss it."

He didn't move, didn't speak.

She didn't try to make up a story. The man would spot it in a second. "If things get desperate, I'll come to you— I promise." That was true. Tobias was the only one she could trust. Her staff was too emotional. They would worry and intervene and hover. They'd want medical details and the name of her doctor. They'd need to try to change what couldn't be changed.

Only Tobias would be cool and practical. Gina needed that if she was going to face the truth, not live on wishes and impossible hopes for a cure.

Her throat was raw. She locked her hands, trying to stay calm.

"Here." He held out a white handkerchief. "Your cheek is bleeding again."

She took the soft cloth, feeling her cheek burn as the soft cotton pressed against her skin. "If things change, you'll be the first to know. Isn't that enough?"

"I guess it will have to be. I know you keep your promises. But we can't avoid this conversation forever."

Gina took a long, rasping breath, feeling lost and afraid of the future. It was past time she faced that future.

All at once, she blurted out the words that couldn't be trapped inside any longer. They fought her, demanding to be heard, demanding an honesty that felt like sandpaper on an open wound.

"I'm…going blind, Tobias. That's pretty much it, soup to nuts. It's a nerve degeneration problem and I've got meds to slow it down, but there's no cavalry over the hill and no cure in sight." She sat stiffly. "I didn't want to tell you. Now if you don't mind—I think I'm going to throw up."

"Head between your knees." Gentle hands pushed her forward, rubbed her neck while she gulped in air and tears seared her eyelids.

He didn't speak. When her shaking had stopped, he sat forward. "What's the specific diagnosis?"

Gina said the long, barely pronounceable Greek name. She'd avoided the word for so long that it was a relief to say it out loud.

"Which means?"

"Optic nerve damage of unknown origins. My doctor in Palo Alto says it will probably be months. Maybe I'll get two good years before…" Her fingers twisted, locked. "I need to work until then, Tobias. If I lose that, I've lost everything. Working is what I know best. I've got no family to speak of, and my friends are all here. This will never impact the ship or my staff, I promise."

He didn't speak. He crossed his arms at his chest and stared out the window. Two seagulls dove into churning waves, then reappeared carrying small fish that wiggled vainly.

Gina knew exactly how those small fish felt.

"So you want me to keep your secret, even if it means breaking a dozen company regulations?"

"What are rules if you don't break them once in a while?" She squared her shoulders. She wouldn't grovel. She'd quit first.

Tobias studied the neat piles of paperwork on his desk. "I never break the rules." He leaned toward the picture, then stopped abruptly. "Only once. That was enough." He swiveled in his chair, his face a mask. "Here's the way it will go. This stays between us for now. You report to me every week and I see your medical files. If your symptoms change, you tell me immediately. Understood?"

It was better than she could have hoped. Worse, too, since she hated the thought of giving up her privacy, even to this friend.

Too bad her choices were a little limited at the moment.

"I accept. Thank you, Tobias."

"Don't thank me yet," he said tightly. "It's my job to push." He made a dismissive sound, then looked out the window. After a long time he picked up a set of keys from his desk. "Take care of yourself. And stay away from Blaine. She's gunning for you bad now."

"I got that message, believe me."

"So watch your back. And get Andreas to take over the heavy lifting. He's good, so let him do more."

"Aye-aye, sir."

Tobias frowned. "I mean it. Start delegating or I'll report you." His eyes were steely. "Don't mess with me, Ryan."

"I won't." This time her voice was soft, hesitant. "Delegate." She snapped a small salute. "Even if it kills me."

"It's a hard thing to learn, but your people have to advance sometime." He stood up, shaking his head. "I thought it was money problems, or Blaine. Maybe something with an old boyfriend. Nothing like this."

Gina gripped his arm for a moment. She didn't cry this time. The tears were gone. Saying the words had driven them away.

She stood up, smoothed her hair. "Hell, isn't it? So what happens now?"

"Work. The usual grind. And we live for Thursday

nights." He smiled slightly. "You got all that stuff we ordered in San Francisco?"

"Safe and sound in my cabin. Andreas brought the second box himself. Brown paper wrappers, just the way you asked."

"One more thing." His forehead furrowed. "A friend of yours contacted corporate to set up some time with you. The cruise brass okayed it." Tobias glanced at his computer screen. "Carly McKay, wife of Ford McKay. Three children traveling with them."

"Carly's here? But she isn't supposed to be taking the cruise until next month."

"They boarded three hours ago. Her husband looks like an interesting guy." Tobias scrolled through the passenger information, his eyes intent. "Navy, I see." He kept on scrolling. "A man who's been a lot of places."

"Something wrong with that?"

"Not that I can tell. Your friend has your ship e-mail address and she wanted to get together later today if you have time."

Gina hid a grimace. The first few days at sea were always hectic. Tonight would be worse than usual due to the malfunctioning refrigeration unit. But she and Carly had been college roommates. It had been far too long since they'd been able to meet. How could she refuse?

"Okay, I'll e-mail her back. I'll check with the captain about—"

Tobias waved one hand. "Already done. Strings have been pulled. As long as your work is complete, you can see your friend whenever you like."

"I appreciate it, Tobias."

"Thank corporate. All I did was field the calls." He cleared his computer screen and stood up abruptly.

"Tobias? Is something wrong? You look like you've seen a ghost."

The tall man let out a slow breath. "Turns out that McKay and I have…friends in common. Not that it matters." He pulled a set of keys from his top desk drawer. "The doctor tells me a nasty strain of flu has hit coastal Mexico. He wants everyone down for flu shots in the next twenty-four."

Blaine. Medical files to Tobias. Flu.

What else could go wrong?

"I'll get my staff lined up. Nothing for me, though." Gina worked at a knot in her neck. "I'm under strict orders not to combine anything with my experimental meds." She laughed dryly. "But the good news is, I won't be losing my sight because of any flu."

Tobias stared at her, his gaze cold and angry. "That isn't funny, damn it."

"I guess not." Gina let out a slow breath. "Sorry. My humor's been a little…warped lately. I'll try to keep it to myself."

"If it bothers me, I'll let you know." He glanced at his watch and held open the door to the outer office. "Remember Blaine's out there somewhere, and she's one very hungry shark."

"Warning noted."

As she walked back across the hall toward the kitchen, Gina ran through the night's pastry platings and calculated her staff assignments. Suddenly she felt a sharp prickling at her shoulders.

She stopped across the hall from Tobias's office, looking in both directions. One of the purser's staff walked by with a paperback and a bottle of water. One of Tobias's security team moved down the hall, his walkie-talkie squawking.

No one else was in sight.

Stress. Lack of sleep. She had enough problems without conjuring any new ones from her imagination.

Gina leaned against the wall and rubbed her eyes gently, using the exercises the doctor in Palo Alto had shown her. Though they wouldn't reverse her problem, they reduced some of her pain.

But even after she walked into the pastry kitchen, the probing sensation between her shoulders remained.

TOBIAS HALE CLOSED his door and stared at the paperwork forgotten on his desk. He was reeling with the news Gina had just given him.

Blind.

And he thought *his* problems were bad.

Rules or not, he'd find a way to protect her as long as he could. He only hoped it was the right thing to do.

How did you ever know until years later?

Meanwhile there was Ryker to consider. Damn Ryker for hanging on to him when he had worked so hard, paid so dearly to sever all ties and put the past where it belonged. But old debts never got repaid, and the past didn't stay forgotten for long.

He'd done what he thought was best all those years ago.

Now he owed Ryker. One favor to make his family safe forever. That one favor became ten and then twenty.

Tobias studied the two photos on his desk. His callused fingers traced the worn wooden frames the way he had daily for seventeen years.

It had all seemed best at the time.

It had seemed the safest for those who counted most.

But people had a way of growing up and making their

own choices, even if they didn't understand the truth. Tobias had no doubt that Ryker had manipulated everyone to suit his own purposes. No one did manipulation like Lloyd Ryker.

Now Tobias was trapped. It was too late to go back, too late for explanations or amends.

Too late for everything that mattered.

He stared at the photos on his desk for a very long time. Then his head fell, braced on his hands in the empty room that was the only home he had allowed himself since he'd left the government.

CHAPTER ELEVEN

TRACE WASN'T SURE what a cruise ship security office was supposed to look like. He didn't have a clue what to expect of his contact on board, either.

The man was probably overweight, fiftyish and an ex-Marine with delusions of operational grandeur. Probably read *Soldier of Fortune* religiously.

A balding, middle-aged man in a brown uniform walked out of the Security office.

Figured.

Trace frowned at him. "Are you the security chief?"

"No, I'm Riley from engineering. You want Tobias. He's inside his office. And you'd better have a good reason for bothering him, because the man's in one cranky-ass mood today."

The engineer vanished around the corner, shaking his head, a clipboard under one arm.

Inside the office a tall black man with broad shoulders walked toward a coffee machine, cup in hand. He was neither overweight nor fiftyish, but he did have the tight stance of an ex-Marine.

Trace walked inside, and the man looked him over in silence, then nodded slightly. "You're taller than your picture."

"And you're older." May as well get all the attitude out on the table.

"Not so old that I can't get the job done." The man sipped his coffee, studying Trace intently. "I hear you had an accident. Got torn up bad."

"Nothing important." So Ryker was calling the ambush in Afghanistan an accident, was he? Trace made a mental note to keep his story consistent with Ryker's.

He glanced around the outer office, looking for concealed electric lines and slight differences in paint color, which would signify security equipment upgrades. He pointed to the ceiling. "Two fish-eye lenses in the overhead light canisters. Primary and redundant wiring in the side wall. Motion sensors behind the potted plants."

"You missed the pressure-sensitive plates outside the door." Tobias relaxed slightly and held out a beefy hand. "Hale. And you're O'Halloran. Have a cup of coffee. It isn't Starbucks' finest, but the way I make it will keep you awake a whole lot longer."

Trace poured himself a cup of coffee, took a sip and nodded. "Pretty bad. Then again, I've always liked it strong enough to melt a spoon."

"You came to the right place." Tobias opened the door to the interior office. "Have a look around."

Trace glanced around Tobias's private office. He hadn't expected anything so subtle and well appointed. Asian prints lined two walls and a raw silk couch in sage green faced the desk. The effect was soothing as well as efficient. "Is the safe in here?" Trace asked quietly.

Tobias closed the office door and nodded. "Behind the second print. "Number coded, with security connection to my pager, which I keep on me at all times."

"Power backup on the monitoring equipment?"

"Two separate units. One here. Another hidden overhead in the ceiling."

Trace nodded. "Sounds like good coverage."

"I'm always open to suggestions." Tobias leaned back in his chair. "Not that I'm expecting any problems this run."

The words hung in the air between them. Trace realized the man was fishing for information.

"That would seem to be the case. Ryker didn't brief me about detailed problems."

Hale blew his coffee. "That makes two of us." He sat back, eyes narrowed. "I'll give you the formal tour in a few minutes. First we need to discuss your cover. You're on record as a tourist, Ryker says. I've told my people that your father was an old USMC friend of mine, and that you and I are planning to shoot the bull during the cruise. That should give you credible cover for any meetings we have."

"Noted."

"If anything develops, I'll connect via your cell phone. Ryker gave me all the details. Encryption up to date?"

"Of course." Trace nodded, finishing his coffee. He didn't mention just how high the encryption levels went or the new technology Izzy had devised to beef up the phone for difficult conditions at sea. "You arranged my cabin location? I see that it's just two decks up from your office, with direct corridor access to the staff stairs."

Hale gave a Cheshire cat smile. "It was the least I could do. By the way, you're not going to ask what I'm transporting in my safe?"

"No."

"You're not even curious?"

"No. If something goes wrong, I'll recognize the package. Ryker's man filled me in with a description."

Tobias stood up. "I guess that brings you current, O'Halloran. If you come this way, I'll brief you on the new infrared sensors and their scan patterns. Then I'll call some of my security people and introduce you. May as well get your cover initiated immediately."

The security chief bent down and straightened the picture at the corner of his desk. There was a precision in the movement that told Trace this man would be nobody's pushover.

Maybe this mission wasn't heading south as fast as he'd thought.

THE FORWARD DECK WAS hot and sunny, and women were everywhere. Some wore sarongs and some were in halter tops. Most were wearing scraps of fabric that skirted legal limits.

Trace frowned.

Red, purple and black. Striped and plain, with serious skin on display. He should have enjoyed the sea of microbikinis, but there was way too much grabbing going on. He'd just had his butt fondled twice in the buffet line and once in the elevator.

Now a woman in a skimpy string thong number was staring at his thighs while she licked salt from the rim of her margarita glass. Every stroke of her tongue was slow and blatantly suggestive.

It should have left him feeling something—simple lust at least, but it didn't.

He had a sudden memory of the pastry chef at the hotel, wheeling across the loading bay in a forklift truck. The memory stirred emotions more complicated than lust, and for the life of him he couldn't figure out why.

Before he'd left the hotel, her assistant had given him her last name and e-mail address. No phone number. Probably she was careful about giving it out to strange men.

He wondered where she was now, what she was doing. Probably baking another cake and setting up for a big event. Judging by the enthusiastic clapping, her pastry class had been a big success. Trace was no cooking expert, but he guessed her decorated cakes wouldn't come cheap. All of which meant she was a busy lady. Most likely she'd forgotten him already.

He frowned, reaching up to rub the small scar near his collarbone. Before his return from the mission in Afghanistan, a chip embedded beneath the skin had enhanced his control over his heart rate and brain waves. Another chip provided continuous GPS data to Foxfire monitors. A third chip had allowed him to carry out controlled energy sweeps and monitor all nearby movement, visible or invisible.

Trace had added his innate abilities of strength and speed, which allowed him to push his skills to the max.

Now the chips were all inactive, and he felt naked without them. But until he was back to full physical and mental strength, Ryker had ordered that the chips had to go dormant.

So he would deal with it. As a SEAL he was confident in his ability to adapt and improvise, using whatever tools were at hand. Instead of getting irritated, he shut off his mind and tried to relax.

It wasn't as if he was likely to see action on this trip. According to his last briefing with Izzy, the mission security was fully intact.

Ryker was probably being too touchy. With a new experiment in the works, his scientist required a transfer of sensitive material or equipment. It figured that Ryker would want a second layer of protection, using a civilian outsider as a courier. Tobias Hale fit the bill.

Trace wondered what Ryker had on the civilian to ensure his compliance. Probably he was calling in a favor. Trace doubted the job was based on simple friendship. Ryker had no friends.

Somewhere nearby water splashed, and a woman laughed loudly to Trace's left. Suddenly cold water drenched his chest.

Two people in the nearby pool appeared to be involved in a no-holds-barred splashing contest. Did people generally turn insane when a cruise ship left sight of land, or was it something in the drinking water?

A woman in a black microbikini walked in front of his chair. Silhouetted against the sun, she stood with one hip thrust out as she held out a bottle of sunscreen. "Would you be a love? I never can reach all the way to my back." She puffed out glossy lips as she eyed him closely. "Something tells me you're good with your hands."

Trace gave a mental sigh. He was out of touch. He knew more about fighting than socializing.

He was trying to relax and blend in with the other passengers, but going with the flow had never been part of his repertoire. He'd always considered *relax* a four-letter word.

He poured sunscreen in one hand and worked it in, trying to ignore the breathy little sighs of pleasure the woman made as she wriggled under his touch. If she was trying to simulate sex, she was doing a good job.

"So are you from California? I mean, you're very tan.

It looks like you work outside or climb mountains or something. Are you some kind of athlete?"

"No, ma'am." Let her decide which part he was referring to. *Go with the flow,* he thought grimly.

Finished at last, he leaned back in his chair and closed his eyes. With the sun warm on his face and shoulders, he began to relax.

Abruptly the woman leaned closer. "Honey, you look lonely, and I can do something about that. What do you say?"

Trace cracked open one eye. "About what?"

"About us. Your cabin or mine?"

Trace opened his other eye. Ms. Microbikini's improbably large breasts were threatening to pop free. Mascara smudged the edges of her eyes. Something told him the woman had a scorecard she was determined to fill before the ship reached its final port.

Because he felt a little sorry for her, Trace kept his voice casual. "Sorry, I'm meeting someone here." He made a point of checking his watch. "Man, is she running late."

"Well, you could have told me sooner that you were attached." Towel twitching, the redhead shot to her feet and stalked off in search of more productive company.

Trace eyed her bikini appreciatively, but it was only a reflex. He wasn't really interested.

He drummed his fingers on the table and stood up.

If he had to be aboard the damned ship, at least he'd be productive and work on some strength training moves.

HE WAS ON HIS THIRD SET of overhead presses when the buzz started behind his left ear. At first Trace thought it was just the exercise buzz hitting, along with the good pump of blood. But something shimmered at the corner of his eye.

Then he smelled the faint scent of lavender.

He shrugged it off.

There had been a few weird sensory moments since his hospitalization.

Trace shrugged off the events as the Phenomenon. Nothing to get bent about. After all, Izzy had told him to expect some distortions following his chip shutdown.

Except that the lavender smell was getting stronger.

Marshall had loved lavender. Trace remembered the night he'd found the senator's daughter curled up in a ball, covered with dirt and cuts. When he'd slipped inside the mercenary camp to the tent where she was held captive, he'd gagged her to prevent an outcry that could have gotten them both killed.

She'd fought him at first. Then Trace had given her a picture of her family dog, whispered a warning, and pulled out a small cloth to clean her face and hands. She had whimpered, tears coursing over her cheeks.

By the time he'd wiped away a month of grime, she had trusted him.

Strange how the memory came back now.

Trace took a deep breath, pushing away the dark images of Marshall's captivity. He still couldn't believe she'd taken her own life.

He pumped two more sets and leaned back against the weight machine, sweat covering his face. He closed his eyes, breathing hard.

Cool fingers touched his forehead.

He shot up, dropping his water bottle.

A faint outline shimmered in front of him. Her hair was pulled away from her face, and her eyes were guileless, just as he remembered them.

Except now Trace could see the wall behind her.
Through her.

This wasn't happening. It was just another chip malfunction. He closed his eyes, counted to five. When he looked up, she was still there, only now she shimmered above the weight rack.

Six feet above the floor, in thin air.

A hallucination of some sort. Trace wondered if he should report the malfunction to Izzy.

She seemed to frown and the air felt colder.

Trace stared at the swirling light above the two rows of weights. Marshall Wyckoff was dead. Drowned.

This was some kind of projection, born out of his guilt.

He smelled the drifting perfume again, stronger now, carrying hints of cinnamon and lavender. Something cool moved over his neck. The light gathered as she stared straight into his eyes, almost as if she was waiting for something.

Trace picked up his towel and water bottle and walked away.

Marshall followed—or the shimmering and insubstantial illusion followed him, her eyes unreadable.

Trace closed his mind and looked away, walking out onto the promenade deck, where he faced the cutting wind, letting his mind go blank.

The shimmering figure appeared on the ship's rail. She frowned at him, her mouth moving. "Can't go away." The words formed into a whisper. "Something's wrong. Have to stay until…"

She looked into his eyes, as if willing him to understand.

But Trace didn't.

He ran through all the scenarios. Most likely, she was one of Ryker's off-the-wall psych tests, some kind of chip-based projection to determine if Trace was focused and ready for action.

One thing that a life lived in dangerous places had taught him was that you didn't sweep your problems under the rug. Problems got faced until you found solutions, and then you moved on. Denial was ineffective and downright stupid.

And this...*thing*...looked like a ghost. Like a teenage ghost, her face too pale and her eyes too dark.

She appeared and disappeared like a ghost.

Except ghosts didn't exist. This had to be the result of a chip error of some sort.

As a member of Foxfire, he knew that under the right conditions images could be shaped and directed. The process was part of his specific Foxfire training—or it had been until he'd nearly died and Ryker had disabled all his implants.

But Ryker lied when it suited him. Maybe he'd left one device in place, its function hidden from Trace.

He was hit with a sudden urge to know what had happened under the bridge in D.C. If he could understand how Marshall had died, he could put this aberration behind him. But there was no point trying to interrogate a hallucination.

He forced himself to walk away. He wouldn't buy into this fantasy.

Don't shut me out.

He froze, willing the words away.

Something's wrong.

The scent of lavender grew, wrapping around him.

Find her.

"Find who, damn it?" Trace spun around, the words coming in an angry rush.

Find her.

The silent command came again.

He took a deep breath and shoved his hands in his pockets. When he looked across the deck, the image was gone.

There was no more shimmering. No voice in his head. *Find her.* What the hell was that supposed to mean? There were women all over the ship.

The vibration of his cell phone cut through his irritation. He glanced at the LED and answered.

"Yeah."

"Everything squared away?" Izzy's voice sounded as if he were right across the deck.

"More or less." Trace chose his words carefully. "I checked in with security and verified the arrangements. They look A-Okay."

"Something else bothering you?"

Trace stared at the line of clouds dotting the horizon. "I'm having some sensory…disturbances. Auditory and visual."

"Type and frequency. Location pattern, too." Keys clicked at a computer.

Trace gave every detail of what he'd seen and heard. If there was any possibility of serious sensory breakdown, Izzy needed to know.

When Trace was done, he shoved one hand through his hair and stared at the faint line of the horizon, blurred by mounded clouds. "So what do you think? She—I mean, *it*—looks like Marshall, but we both know that's impossible."

The computer keys stopped clicking.

"Teague?"

"Right here. And if you're asking me do I believe in ghosts, the answer is no."

"Glad to hear it." Trace watched a seagull cut cleanly

across the deck and plunge toward the water. "Then it's a chip error. One of them wasn't shut down properly."

Silence.

"This isn't some half-assed psych maneuver by Ryker, is it? A test to evaluate my response to Marshall's death? He's done things like that before, but if he's toying with my mind through Marshall, I swear I'll—"

"Ryker didn't do this." Izzy's tone was cold. "I have a complete medical file on you, and that includes a chip evaluation." Papers rustled. "According to my records, everything but a GPS locator was turned off in your last surgery."

Trace's hands tightened on the cool teak railing. "Then what in hell is happening to me?"

CHAPTER TWELVE

BIRDS SCREECHED.

Waves churned, sullen foam spilling into restless gray water.

Trace stared without seeing any of it. "If you tell me I'm going crazy, I'll be seriously pissed off, Teague."

A chair creaked. Paper rustled. "Your last psychological evaluation gave you the highest marks ever noted for stability and adaptability. You're not crazy." Izzy took a slow breath. "But I can't explain what's happening until I do some tests at this end. You've got third-generation chips, and I'll start by running a search for any reported anomalies in the series. That would give us someplace to start."

Trace had hoped for more. "How long?"

"Twenty-four hours. We rule out production and design error first. After all, your chips were shut down, not removed completely. Then we look at the human factor. Is this interfering with your mission capability?"

"No." *Not yet.*

"If that changes, I expect to be notified immediately. Is that understood?"

"Loud and clear."

"Note any patterns. Keep a log. Anything you can give me will help."

"I'll get right on it."

"I'll be in touch as soon as I have something concrete."

Izzy rang off.

No wasted words. No morale-building talk, which was fine with Trace. He was a big boy.

He scanned the deck, relieved that the shimmer was gone. No voices or lavender scent, either. By reflex, he rubbed his shoulder, feeling a slight twinge from his earlier workout. He thought about going back to the fitness center and finishing his last sets. He had nothing important to do until 1800 hours, when Tobias was going to introduce him to several of the security crew.

More women passed.

More bikinis.

A blonde in a thong leaned against the rail and gave him a slow, thorough inspection. When she was done, Trace knew what it felt like to be beef on the hook, weighed, measured and stamped Grade-A across the center of his forehead.

He had to get away before he shot someone, so the gym it was. The blonde gave him a sour look as he crossed the deck, picked up his fallen paperback book, then stopped to watch a whale breach far out at sea.

Amazed, he leaned his elbows on the aft railing, feeling the wind in his face.

A shadow moved past his legs.

A four-foot shadow with pigtails.

"She wasn't your type. She smelled a little funky, too."

Trace glanced down at the vision in pink flip-flops and an oversize Scooby Doo T-shirt. "Who?"

"The lady with the teeny suit and the big…um, bosoms. My mom says that's what we should call them, but Stephie at school calls them—"

She was neatly pushed sideways by a second vision in flip-flops. Clearly, this was her identical twin. "Forget what Stephie calls them. It's rude, Daddy said. And we're not supposed to talk to strangers, remember?" Twin number two stuck out a hand laced with purple friendship bands that matched her purple swimsuit and sandals. "I'm Olivia. My sister is Sunny. What's your name?"

"Trace. Glad to meet you two ladies."

"Listen, Sunny. He thinks we're *ladies*." Twin two snorted a little and then recovered her dignity. "How do you like that book?" She leaned her head sideways, reading the title. "Our dad says it's unrealistic trash without any military verisimilitude." She pronounced the last word calmly, as if she'd used it often. "Our dad says the author should be dropped from a chopper without a parachute."

Trace hid a smile. "Can't say. I haven't gotten very far yet." He recalled the media blitz about this particular book. "Your dad could be right."

"He's usually right. Our dad is *really* smart. Our mom is totally smart, too. She does effing stops."

Trace gave a startled cough. "She does what?"

"Not effing stops, stupid." Twin one rolled her eyes. "F-stops. That means camera apertures. One of her photos was picked for the cover of *Time* last year," she announced.

Trace nodded gravely. "Your mom must be really good."

"You bet your butt she's good." Miss Purple—Sunny— giggled a little. "Stephie says that a lot."

Trace grinned. It was impossible to be serious around these charmers. But surely their parents would be looking for them.

He saw at least fifty adults and scattered children, but no one seemed to be searching for the two girls in flip-flops. "Your parents swimming in the pool over there?"

"Nope."

"Are they in one of those deck chairs in the shade?"

The little girls turned, scanned the shaded chairs and shook their heads. "Nope."

Trace was starting to feel a little uneasy. "If you're lost or something—"

"Oh, we're not lost. We're on the aft Lido Deck, and we don't have to be ready until the first dinner seating. Everything's right on schedule." Sunny opened a little mesh beach bag and pulled out a purple diary. "But there's some weird stuff going on here. The lady across the hall cries a lot. The man next door to us hasn't come out of his room once and he's really noisy. He groans like he's climbing a hill or something." She wrinkled her perfect nose. "It makes Dad get all red in the face. He says we're going to have to move to another cabin." She traced the wooden deck with her flip-flop. "I wonder why we have to move. It's just a little noise."

Trace cleared his throat. He had a pretty clear idea what the huffing and puffing was all about. "Maybe you should find your mom and dad. They could be worried about you."

"They certainly were."

A tall woman in a white gauze shirt looped her arms across the girls' shoulders, frowning. "You were *supposed* to stay with Daddy and guard our chairs while I went to the bathroom."

"We did, Mom. Then we asked Daddy to get us some ice cream and we followed him a little way. But Olivia lost her notebook, and then we found it. We only went a few rows away, just around the corner from Daddy at that ice-cream counter."

"It's not the distance, honey. When he turned around, you were gone. He's very upset about losing sight of you. It's also the fact that you made a promise. You should always keep your promises."

The girls looked down, crestfallen. "Sorry," Sunny muttered.

The woman ruffled their hair, then gave Trace a thorough scrutiny. "I hope they weren't bothering you, Mr...."

"O'Halloran." Suddenly Trace stiffened. Looking into calm, intelligent eyes, he realized exactly who the woman was. "No bother, ma'am. Your girls are way too charming for that. They told me you had a photograph on the cover of *Time*. That's pretty impressive."

She smoothed Olivia's hair. "No photos this trip. We're all on vacation." She smiled, waving at a tall man in a black T-shirt as he rounded a line of deck chairs. Three ice-cream cones were melting in his hands.

His eyes were dark with worry. "You two are in serious trouble for leaving without telling me."

The two girls looked glum. "Sorry, Daddy."

"Sorry doesn't always help."

"They won't do it again." A third little girl in lime-green flip-flops took her sisters' arms.

Triplets, Trace thought. His briefing file had mentioned that, but seeing three identical faces was still a shock.

So this was Ford McKay and his family. A Navy SEAL with all McKay's decorations and experience would be a definite asset in a pinch. So would his wife, judging by what Trace had read in Ryker's files.

"I was just telling Mr. Trace about Mom's effing-stops." Sunny gave a bright smile. Something told Trace that in about nine years that smile was going to drive men straight to their knees.

"F-stops, darling. Not effing stops," her mother said calmly.

Ford sat down and sorted out the melting cones. "After that little stunt you two pulled, I should toss your cones overboard."

Sunny and Olivia looked guilty until McKay relented. "But you get one more chance. Here you go. Vanilla and vanilla."

Sunny giggled. "Oh, Daddy. You know we hate vanilla. These are what we wanted." A natural-born leader if Trace ever saw one, Sunny gave her father's cheek a little pinch. "You always get it right. Pistachio. Butter pecan. Chocolate chip cookie goo."

"Dough," their mother corrected, smiling.

"Yeah, that one." Sunny tucked into her wafer cone. "We don't like vanilla because vanilla is for geeks." She smiled at Trace. "Even if we like most geeks. When Stephie Andrews called Olivia and me geeks, I called her a big, nasty womb."

Ford McKay choked on his frozen latte. "You said *what?*"

"I read it somewhere. In the *Wall Street Journal,* I think. They said that wombs were—"

"Okay, okay." Ford looked harassed, while his wife seemed to be enjoying his discomfort.

Was that an I-told-you-so look on her face? Trace wondered. He felt a nearly tangible bond of emotion between the two, even when no words were shared.

Maybe that was what it meant to be in love.

Nah.

Trace knew better. Most of what people called love was the result of hormones, boredom and abstinence.

The Navy SEAL held out his hand. "I'm McKay."

"Trace O'Halloran."

"Were they bothering you?"

"No way. We had a nice talk before your wife tracked them down."

The little girl in lime green held out her hand. "We haven't met yet. I'm Cleo." Her calm formality was blinding. If there was such a thing as American royalty, Trace figured it would look like this.

"I'm Trace."

"It's a pleasure to meet you, Mr. Trace. You have nice eyes."

Trace scratched his cheek. *Nice eyes?*

Ford swung an arm around Cleo and Sunny. "Okay, troops. Time to hit the cabin for unit evaluation before dinner."

"Yeah."

"Yes, Daddy."

"Cool."

The words spilled out as the three girls immediately lined up, their faces bright with excitement.

"I finished my security sweep of the ship," Olivia said proudly. "I found no security breaches in the passenger-side Internet outlets."

"And I checked out our key card. It only accesses our cabin, and no one else can use their cards in our door. Our cabin steward showed me how to use his." Sunny looked thoughtful. "His key works for any room on his floor, so if we ever get locked out, he can let us in."

Cleo cut in. "I spoke with the captain. He was very

polite when I asked to see his digital compass. He invited us all to dinner at his table tomorrow night."

Ford frowned. "Sit at the captain's table? I don't know—"

"Darling, the girls would love it. Why don't we discuss it downstairs?" His wife took his arm. "And I love how handsome you look in your tux."

The man was definitely outgunned.

For some reason, the thought made Trace slightly envious.

"I feel hot," Sunny announced loudly. "And the ice cream…uh, I don't feel good."

With the instant resourcefulness of mothers everywhere, Carly gathered Sunny close and felt her forehead. "You do feel a little warm."

"Sunny's got a touchy stomach. It's her only Achilles' heel, believe me." Ford McKay gave him a long, focused look. "Spent some time in the service, have you?"

Trace knew he'd have to step carefully, since his current military deployment was a highly guarded secret. "Here and there."

Ford started to ask more, but his wife touched his arm.

"If you two start talking shop, the girls and I may do something dangerous. I'm thinking spa outing for four. Full pedicures, no expense limit."

"Can we, Mommy? Pretty please." Sunny wiggled her toes. "I want *pleasure-me-purple* polish." She frowned. "What does pleasure-me purple mean, anyway?"

Ford crossed his arms, waiting for his wife's answer.

"It's just a name, darling. And we'll all choose nice polish that Daddy will like, won't we?"

"I don't wear nail polish." Olivia frowned. "The toxin load isn't healthy."

"I'm sure they have healthy kinds." Carly McKay smiled at Trace. "It was nice to meet you, Mr. O'Halloran. I'd better get my unit back to base before they exhaust us." She took Sunny's hand. "Let's go take your temperature." She waved at her husband and Trace. "You two have fun."

Ford McKay stared after them for a moment and then his sharp gaze settled on Trace. "Delta?"

"Different deployment." Trace gave no additional information. Any spec op soldier would know what that kind of silence meant.

Under the radar. Highly classified. No questions.

McKay nodded. "I figured as much."

Trace decided to change the subject. "Great family you have. Those girls of yours must keep you in good shape."

In a few years Ryker would probably be trying to recruit the triplets.

Ford watched his wife and children cross the crowded deck. "Sometimes I feel outclassed. Cleo is a walking, talking diplomat already, and Olivia is nine going on forty-nine. She knows organic chemistry that I haven't even heard of. Sunny could command a tank battalion." He shook his head. "The thought of high school scares the beejesus out of me. Dating. Drinking." His voice fell. "*Sex*. Hell."

"You ought to be very proud of them. I'm sure they have great judgment." Trace slung his towel over his arm. "Guess I'll hit the gym."

Ford gave him another measuring look. "We'd be happy for you to join us at dinner, if you don't have other plans. The fact is, with another man around, I might not feel so outnumbered."

Trace needed to finish his ship orientation tonight and

walk every deck. He was also slated to meet Tobias Hale's security team.

He thought fast. "Sorry, I can't. Maybe tomorrow, assuming you don't have dinner with the captain?"

"You're on." Ford picked up his khaki tote. Trace saw two books on encryption technology inside it.

He gestured with one hand. "A little light reading?"

"Pays to stay ahead of the wave. Because there's always a wave out there somewhere, and it's usually gaining on you." McKay slung the tote over his shoulder. "Something tells me I'll be seeing you around, O'Halloran."

SUNLIGHT SHIMMERED.

Seabirds dipped low, circling in the wind.

As Trace turned, Marshall's dim outline walked out of the shadows behind one of the bulkheads. She wore a black leather motorcycle jacket and ripped vintage jeans.

Her eyes were filled with sadness.

Trace felt a humming noise near his neck. He turned away, dizzy and angry. He didn't have time for hallucinations or guilt.

She drifted, then reformed at his side, her face strained. Her mouth moved in silence as if she was struggling to form words.

She closed her eyes and shook her head in frustration, then tried again, and this time the humming turned into a whisper. "Are you finally ready to listen?"

CHAPTER THIRTEEN

TRACE GLARED at the drifting figure. *Go away,* he thought angrily. *I don't need you, want you or believe in you.*

"I can't go away." The words sounded hollow, somewhere near his ear. "Not until this is done."

Maybe it was his new meds. There were always side effects, and Ryker's tech team had told Trace these were a new, powerful mix.

"I'm not coming from your medicine, Trace. Don't try to make this complicated."

Trace started to say life was always complicated and hers was such a mess that she had ended it, but he didn't really believe that was true. Meanwhile, saying the words aloud meant that he believed she was real, which he damn well didn't.

So he said nothing.

Across the deck, near the interior doors, the girl in purple flip-flops looked back at him and waved. Trace waved back.

"For the record, Sunny has a crush on you."

Trace blew out a breath. "Can it, Marshall," he muttered.

A woman nearby turned and stared at him oddly. He realized he was talking to himself.

Great, O'Halloran. Talking with a ghost makes a hell of a lot of sense.

"Ford McKay doesn't trust you. Right now he's placing a call for a background check on you."

He was making all of this up, Trace thought. It was a simple projection of exterior possibilities within the dramatic structure of a two-way conversation.

But it was all within himself. No ghosts or apparitions were involved. End of story.

The thought made him feel better. Gripping his towel, he strode down the deck toward his cabin. As he stepped into the elevator, the scent of lavender followed him.

Trace made absolutely certain he didn't look back.

"They're in danger," Marshall said quietly, drifting near his right shoulder. "All of you are. You'd better start paying attention before it's too late."

This brought Trace up short. This warning stuff was getting harder to ignore. "What kind of danger?" he snapped.

There was no answer.

When he turned around, the corridor was empty.

THE TWO NEW LINE COOKS from Guatemala were arguing. Andreas was muttering as he plated a crème brûlée for the captain.

Someone had used all of Gina's confectionery sugar, and the backup dishwasher was acting up again.

All of it felt good. A typical day at sea, Gina thought.

She pulled a tray of cheesecakes out of the oven and slid them into the flash freezer. As she stared at the ice-covered walls, she thought of the pristine white uniform of the man who'd saved her and her cake back in San Francisco. He'd looked damned good in that dress uniform.

Great shoulders, she thought. Good hands and reflexes. The man would make a fantastic line cook.

Yeah, right.

He had the focused, intent look of someone used to dealing with danger. He was probably long gone on some covert mission. Clearly, he was no desk jockey. The deep calluses on his hands proved that.

Goodbye, Navy. It was fun while it lasted, forklift and all.

Behind her, Andreas set out the first platings of fresh apple pie, which were picked up by servers and raced up to the dining room, still hot. Now Gina and her team had twelve dozen cheesecakes to finish in four hours.

They had done twice that many in a pinch. Her team was sharp and experienced. They could hold their own any- where, anytime. Despite Tobias's warning, she wouldn't be cowed by Blaine's off-the-wall threats.

Sometimes she wished that this TV opportunity had never happened. It had complicated her life and added more pressure to her already insane schedule. But a series would mean great promo for the cruise line and all her pastry staff. With TV experience on their résumés, they would all have broader choices if they decided to move on.

On a personal level, she hoped the contacts would lead to voice-over jobs when her vision loss meant kitchen work was no longer an option. If she was smart, she'd start to tackle Braille now.

But she wasn't ready to be that smart. It would feel like giving up on all hope of a cure.

So her life became more and more insane. She agreed to every new set of interviews and demo videos. She enter- tained visiting media planners from L.A. and New York and even created signature pastries for the pilot, sending samples via courier to L.A. as a special enticement to the TV management.

Now the network bigwigs were checking their demo-graphics and trying to make up their minds about possible ratings, which could take five years, she thought wryly.

The sounds of laughter and the friendly boasting calmed her down, reassuring in their familiarity. In a real sense these people were her closest family, and she wouldn't let Blaine ruin her confidence or destroy the mood of her staff. They'd trained together too long to be psyched out by a…

Well, by a psycho.

There were plenty of stories circulating about Blaine's prior employment stints. Someone in the purser's office claimed to have a detailed list of everyone Blaine had slept with to get to be head of beverage services. There were sup-posedly twenty-six men on the list. The woman worked fanatically, obsessed with making it to the very top, over-seeing all beverage services for the entire cruise line. She had also announced a plan to marry one of the owners and then retire before she was thirty.

Directed therapy would help her more than getting married, Gina thought, dropping the last strawberry into place on a chocolate-strawberry mousse.

Not that she cared what Blaine did with her life, as long as the witch stayed far away from Gina's kitchen.

High heels tapped hollowly behind Gina's prep station, an unusual sound in the kitchen. Gina and her staff always wore athletic shoes. It was safer given the constant motion of physical work aboard a moving vessel.

"I need to talk to you."

"Sorry, I'm busy." Gina kept sliding cheesecakes out of the oven and into the flash refrigerator. She savored a brief but satisfying vision of shoving Blaine into the flash refrigerator right along with them. "Can't talk right now. Try me in an hour."

"*Now.* Someone has moved my best Merlot."

Gina juggled another tray. "Which concerns me how?"

"Because it was one of your staff. Henry, my beverage assistant, saw their uniform."

"Blaine, *all* of my staff have been here in this room helping me prepare for dinner for the last hour. Now if you'll excuse me—"

"You're trying to cover up for them." Blaine pointed a red-tipped nail at Gina. "News flash to all of you. It won't work, because I have documentation and a witness. Whoever did it will be tossed off at the next port. If you try to cover up for them, you'll go with them."

"I have no idea what you're talking about." Gina stepped around Blaine to reach another tray and felt an elbow dig into her ribs.

Blaine gave her a hard shove. "*Listen* to me when I'm talking."

As her rib throbbed, Gina froze. Something unraveled inside her. She'd taken too much from the schemer. She wouldn't take any more. Being a victim wasn't in her life plan. She shoved back, sending Blaine against the polished steel wall of the refrigerator. "Do *not* bring your skinny size-two butt into my kitchen again without a written invitation. And do *not* give me orders. Understand?"

"You hit me." There were two spots of color in Blaine's cheeks, and something like triumph in her eyes. "You twisted my arm."

Gina looked down. As if from a distance, she saw her fingers gripping tanned skin. She took a hard breath and then stepped back. "Leave."

"I'll have bruises on my arm." Blaine smiled thinly. "You are as good as fired already. You know there's a zero-tolerance policy for fighting."

Gina's eyes narrowed. "It's always lovely to chat with you, Blaine, but some of us have actual work to do." She nodded to her assistant, who was already headed their way. "Andreas, why don't you show Blaine and her skinny butt out of my kitchen?"

"You can't just—"

Gina's Brazilian assistant moved in front of Blaine, looking stiff and protective and very angry. When Blaine tried to step around him, her heel slipped and she caught herself on one of the counters.

"Touch me and I'll scream," she said shrilly.

"Andreas didn't touch you. I didn't touch you until you attacked me. We've got cameras here that will back me up," Gina said coldly. "Remember that when you plan to lie about what happened. Also it's a stupid idea to wear high heels when you're in a kitchen."

"*Some* of us prefer to look like women. I guess you wouldn't understand that." Blaine's voice rose, carrying through the whole room. "Who exactly did you sleep with to get those TV scouts here? We both know it can't be because of your cooking or your looks. Maybe you're just good with your mouth."

Andreas moved directly in front of Blaine and closed his hands to fists. "You're leaving." Two of Gina's other staff moved in to flank him. All three watched Blaine with palpable hostility.

"We'll see who's going to leave. And I mean permanently." Blaine stalked out, her high heels echoing like gunfire.

"Well, the Blaine show is over." Gina took a deep breath

and tried to shrug off the tension in the air. Blaine had nothing to base a complaint on. It was an empty threat.

Andreas crossed his arms, standing protectively near the door. "That woman is definitely going postal. A set of thermometers was missing from my station yesterday. Last week one of the mixers was broken," he said quietly.

"You didn't tell me that."

"I thought it was a coincidence. Now I'm starting to think it was the Wicked Witch."

Gina set down a tray of cheesecakes. "You think Blaine got in here without any of us seeing?"

"Either that or she had one of her staff slip in." Andreas shook his head. "Did you see the *look* on her face? She would gladly have stuck a knife in your neck if she'd had one handy."

"As long as she keeps her distance, we'll be fine." But Gina had an uncomfortable picture of Blaine sneaking around the pastry galley, snooping at her desk and accessing her computer files. She could have sabotaged Gina's recipes and staff e-mails while she was at it.

As a matter of fact, several of Gina's e-mails had gone missing the previous week. Nothing major, but odd just the same. Now it was starting to make sense.

Andreas's eyes narrowed. "What did she do now?"

"I lost some e-mails. Tobias has been telling me to beef up the password security here in the galley, but I didn't think it was important before…"

"Before the witch went postal. Tobias is right." Andreas paced the narrow work area. "I've gotten some strange spam and newsletters from sites I've never visited." His lips curled. "Very bad sites."

Pornography? Gina knew all of her staff well. They were normal, healthy and curious, but she just didn't see

Andreas or any others involved in that behavior. Besides, the man was gorgeous. With his high-voltage smile and liquid Brazilian accent, he could have his pick of women on the ship's staff.

"So Blaine is trying to set us up through the computers." Things were more serious than she'd imagined. "Do you think she has that kind of digital skill?"

Andreas jammed a hand through his spiky dark hair. "That I cannot say. I'm no tech expert. But I think we need Tobias to put up those hot walls right away."

"Firewalls," Gina's pastry assistant from St. Croix cut in. Imogen was almost six feet tall and as regal as any runway model. She could also belt out a mean reggae tune with complete moves to match. "I know a little about computer security. We had a course at my local college."

"Great, Imogen. You be our tech liaison with Tobias. And until our security is beefed up, all of us use our own passcodes. No more generic codes, understood? I want to know exactly who is on the system, when and why."

Andreas gave a rueful laugh. "Busted. I always forget my code."

"Write it inside your underwear or on your foot, but don't forget." Gina bent over her computer terminal, accessing the pastry portal. "I'm deleting the general access code right now. Imogen, you and Tobias set up a serious defensive wall in here. If Blaine's trying to cause problems in our department network, I want her stopped. I'd also like proof of this in case I need to document the tampering."

"Count on it, Chief." The tall woman flipped her apron in the general direction that Blaine had left. "Bad smell. That woman, she gives me one huge pain in my butt."

"No kidding." Gina studied each of her staff one by

one. "From now on we all have to be careful. Report anything odd to me or to Tobias. Keep an eye on all your e-mails and be sure to log out when you leave the area. It would also be a good idea to passcode-protect any important or personal files." She turned away, sneezing. "Fine, my allergies are back. Count on Blaine to stir them up." She scanned her desk and shifted some new paperwork. "Where did I put my time-release antihistamines?"

"No worries. You can use mine." Imogen pulled a foil package from her apron. "These work for twelve hours and they don't even make you sleepy. My brother is a pharmacist in St. Croix, and he tells me exactly which ones to buy."

"Thanks, but I'm supposed to take a specific brand. All the others put me right to sleep. It's a genetic thing." Gina dug through her desk, muttering. "I know they were here. I saw them yesterday."

"These?" Andreas crouched and pulled a small plastic bottle from beneath Gina's desk. "You must have dropped this earlier."

Gina didn't move, staring at the floor. Was she seeing a new pattern here? Had Blaine been tampering with her medicine and going through her desk, as well as hacking her computer?

Or was that total paranoia?

Gina stared at the bottle.

"What's the matter?" Imogen leaned over her shoulder. "You think something's wrong with these?" She poured out two gel tabs onto her palm. "They look like the ones you always take. And they have the green letters C-R on one side. If they're counterfeit, then someone went to a whole lot of trouble to make them look good." Imogen frowned. "You don't think that Blaine—"

"Trust me, she's not smart enough or quick enough," Gina said flatly, even though she wasn't convinced. Meanwhile her staff moved uneasily, circling the bottle. If something didn't restore morale fast, they'd be spooked and work would suffer. When you were moving fast in tight quarters with hot dishes, the last thing you needed was distractions like this.

"We need to be careful, but not let Blaine make us crazy. She's not Superwoman, after all." Gina checked the pills, saw the C-R imprint and grabbed a bottle of water from her desk. "I'm sure these are fine." She downed one as proof.

Then she fell against the wall, grabbing her neck with a gurgling sound.

"Help her!" Andreas and Imogen were at her side in a second. "Go get the doctor."

"Gotcha!" Gina stood up, grinning. "Sorry, but I couldn't resist. All of you looked like we were dead already. Don't let Blaine spook you like that."

Andreas blew out a little breath. "This is good idea. We'll watch the kitchen and our computers. She won't have the way to touch us now."

As Gina finished cooling the last cheesecakes, she prayed that her assistant was right. But she remembered too clearly the hate on Blaine's face.

Watch your back, Tobias had warned her.

Apparently, she was going to have a war on her hands. As insurance, she decided to send Tobias a written report of all the incidents noted by her staff.

The timer pinged on her desk.

"Hey, Chief, aren't you supposed to meet your friend? It's almost five-fifteen."

Gina spun around and chewed on her lip. Where had the

afternoon gone? She still had the day's food usage to tally and a new set of pastry tools to order through the executive head of catering.

"I'll finish the decorating tool order," Andreas said quietly.

"And I've got the food usage tally started anyway," Imogen announced. "Go meet your friend."

"I can't let you—"

"Why? Last week you worked my station twice while I had the flu," Imogen said. "Are *you* Superwoman now? Take the night off for once."

"As your next in command, I agree." Andreas pointed to the door. "Get going, Chief."

"Ganging up isn't fair." Gina rubbed floury hands on her jacket. "There's still time for me to do the food tally."

"That's why you have smart, efficient, brilliant and gorgeous staff like us." Imogen waved a notebook in the air. "See? Nearly done. You go have a nice time with your friend. Everything will be fine here. Blaine's probably forgotten all about us by now."

THE CABIN WAS DARK. Low, sultry jazz drifted from a small but very expensive stereo unit.

Blaine crossed her legs, letting her skirt ride higher up her tanned thighs. "I've only got fifteen minutes."

The man opposite her watched every move, his eyes unreadable. "This shouldn't take long. I brought what you wanted."

"You brought the first item on my list. What about the other things?" Blaine tried not to stare at the long, fairly recent scar below his right eye.

The man shook his head. "These files go back ten years. Digging any further will take some time."

Blaine stretched, slipping her skirt higher, pulling her silk camisole tight across her breasts. Her nipples were already hard. She liked how they felt against the sheer silk. "They told me digging was your specialty, that no one was better." She stood up and crossed her arms. "I guess they were wrong. That means this meeting is over."

The man sitting across from her reached into a leather portfolio. "I'll get the earlier information you want. Meanwhile, these aren't what you expected." He held up a manila envelope tied with string. "They're very detailed. And they're going to cost you more."

Blaine leaned over and ran her fingers along his arm. "What did you find?"

"Old e-mails. Newspaper files. She got a lot of media attention back in Seattle, only she had a different name then."

Blaine's eyes glittered with excitement. "What kind of media attention? Something I can use against her?"

He laughed shortly. "You're a real bitch, aren't you?"

"It never seemed to bother you before."

"It doesn't bother me now. I'm just surprised at how much you hate her. Is it because she's more talented, or is it just that other people like her and hate you?"

Blaine cursed, shoving his hand off her leg, but he moved faster than she'd expected, twisting her arm and yanking her against his chest. "That just made my price double. If you want this file, it's going to cost you twenty thousand."

She stopped fighting and relaxed, tracing his mouth with a long red fingernail. "Maybe I can throw in something besides money," she whispered.

He seemed to hesitate. When her hand slid slowly down his chest, he shook his head. "You really are one hell of a bitch, aren't you?"

She smiled coldly. "And you love it. Let's see how much." She found his zipper and jerked it down.

The man with the scar held the file out of reach, watching her fight to reach it. "I hear you're good at what you do."

"Oh, I'm very good." Blaine unbuttoned her blouse slowly. "Believe it." She stared hungrily at the thick file as her fingers moved, searching past his zipper, finding hot skin.

Her sheets hit the floor. In seconds the last of her clothes followed. She gasped as their bodies strained, then slammed together.

Soon his panting was drowned out by the slap of their sweating bodies. When the precious file toppled from the bed, she caught it with her free hand.

Her smile was icy and very satisfied.

CHAPTER FOURTEEN

GINA KICKED OFF her comfortable cooking clogs and tossed her chef's jacket over a chair. Her bedside clock read 5:22. She was barely going to make dinner on time.

Skimming off clothes right and left, she ran a brush through her hair and tugged on black pants and a white cotton top. She prayed that Carly was just the same, still unconcerned with fashion and everything except f-stops and light angles. Now that her college friend had three little girls, the photography would have serious competition.

They'd been roommates all through college, had laughed over freshman orientation rituals and bonded over basic physics. Both had hated it, but they'd struggled through economics, grilling each other before tests. They'd passed physics with solid marks and gone out to celebrate in the dead of a Chicago winter.

Singly they were strong. Together they had been invincible.

After that they'd seen each other when they could, sharing job woes, boyfriend complaints. Then had come Carly's marriage and the birth of her triplets.

After leaving Seattle, Gina had fallen out of touch with her friend. Before she knew it, years had raced past. Carly's babies were almost ten now.

Maybe they had both changed beyond recognition.

Staring into the mirror, Gina pulled on the shrug she'd knitted. The design was simple, but the knitted lace panels hugged her shoulders, and the misty blue flattered her complexion. She frowned into the mirror above her simple oak dresser. Why was she so freaked out about meeting an old friend? Was it because Carly had always seen through her excuses and read her mind? Would Carly see the anxiety she needed to hide now?

Not likely. She hadn't seen her friend in years. They wouldn't have the wordless communication they'd shared in college.

Times changed. People changed.

On her desk was a photo of a tall man, a radiant woman and three grinning little girls running over a beach in the Caribbean. Carly had taken the shot using a timer. Only someone with her skill could have caught the palpable sense of love and energy in the scene.

Gina had knitted careful gifts for all of them. She had used lavender cotton in a sweater for Olivia. For Sunny she had knitted a shimmery poncho in recycled Indian silk, bright with crimson and pink and lime green. Cleo, the third girl, was more formal, according to Carly, so Gina had made her a small tank top with lace at the hem. For Carly she had made a lace shawl in alpaca fine enough to pull through a key ring. Ford had been the most difficult of all. Gina had decided on socks of brown and tan and forest green in camo colors.

She studied the wrapped gifts nervously. Maybe she should have scrapped the whole idea and bought gifts from one of the shops in Mazatlán or Cabo.

She straightened her white camisole, grabbed her purse

and staff ID, mentally plotting the fastest route to the Lido Deck. On her way, she detoured through a staff laundry area, gaining four minutes. For a moment Gina stopped, hit by the cold awareness that someone was hidden in the silent room stacked high with laundry.

Stress, she thought.

In the days of ultra-high security post-9/11, there was simply no way for a passenger to stow away and remain undetected.

She crossed the laundry room quickly and breathed in relief when she finally reached the staff elevator, where her odd uneasiness vanished almost immediately. In minutes she stood outside the crowded restaurant, feeling self-concious as she gave her name to a waiter.

Staff did not eat in passenger areas except on unusual occasions, but Tobias had helped cut the red tape. Another thing she owed him for.

Bass music drummed from the disco one deck below. Couples and families passed, but none of them stopped. When she didn't see Carly, she used a wall phone to call her cabin.

No one answered.

She glanced at the clock on the wall. More families passed. More honeymooning couples.

No Carly.

At twenty minutes after six, she figured her friend wasn't coming. According to Tobias, they were already aboard, so what had gone wrong?

She tried to check the wall clock again, but there were too many people and she couldn't get a clear view. Down the corridor, she saw empty seats at the ship's latte counter. Feeling uncomfortable, but still not ready to leave, she wove through the crowd and ordered an espresso.

The young Swedish woman behind the counter made a high five. "Hey, I love those chocolate cheesecakes you made for crew night. What are you doing up here?"

"Checking on the pastry. What's selling best so far this trip?"

"Chocolate espresso cheesecake. Can't get enough of it."

Gina sipped her coffee and filed the information, watching more passengers head for the dining room. She now had the unexpected gift of a free evening before her and no idea how to spend it.

Back at work there was nothing her staff couldn't handle. She could curl up on a deck chair in the staff rec-reation area while she watched the ship's wake froth red in the setting sun.

Her fingers curved around imaginary rosewood needles. If any of her old coworkers from Seattle had seen her with yarn and sticks, they would have been incredulous. Knitting didn't exactly fit the kind of dangerous occupa-tion she used to have.

She pushed away thoughts of the past and focused on the night to come. Twilight on deck. Alpaca and silk slipping through her fingers. Talk about paradise. After five years on a cruise ship she had seen flings, passion and high drama. She had even had her own short relationship with a purser from Denmark. It had been fun while it lasted, but nothing ever lasted at sea.

"Were you waiting for someone in the dining room?" The attendant pointed to her phone on the counter. "Because someone's on the phone, asking for you."

Gina lifted the receiver and immediately recognized the quick, breathy voice. "Carly, is everything okay?"

"Cleo threw up when I was about to leave. Now she and

Sunny both have fevers. We had to take them down to the doctor, and everything took longer than we expected. I'm so sorry I didn't reach you sooner."

"Don't worry about me." Someone walking past sloshed wine over Gina's arm and she squeezed closer to the wall. "Are the girls okay now?"

"They're sleeping. The doctor says they should be fine by tomorrow. Ford will keep an eye on them in the morning if you can get away for breakfast. I can't wait to see you." Carly hesitated. "Or will you be too busy?"

"I'll manage." Gina tried to focus despite the noise around her. "How about we meet in the lounge outside the purser's office?"

"At eight?"

"I'll be there. Give them all a kiss for me."

As Gina hung up, a man crossed the corridor. She couldn't see his face, but he had great shoulders. A great butt, too, as a matter of fact. Looking down, she saw the backs of worn brown cowboy boots.

A great butt *and* broken-in cowboy boots? Now that was unfair. What woman could resist a one-two punch like that?

He turned around, staring down the hall behind him, his eyes cool and alert.

Gina nearly choked on her espresso.

No way.

Trace was here on the ship? The knowledge unnerved her. She liked control in her life, everything in its place and everything with a clear purpose. Something told her this man had the potential to destroy her control completely.

Not again. Not ever.

She shoved a hand through her hair. If she kept her back turned, he'd never see her. That was the smart way.

The safe way.

It seemed very important to play this the safe way.

She didn't turn around, her shoulders stiff. Laughter echoed nearby. A woman asked him a question, and there was more drifting female laughter.

She pushed away her unfinished cheesecake, drummed her fingers on the spotless counter and motioned to the waitress. "I'd like a glass of wine."

"Now you're talking. Merlot or Zin?"

"Merlot." One drink, no more. A few sips to smooth out her tension. Once she was sure that Trace was gone, she'd head back to her cabin.

The attendant poured her a glass of Merlot, staring over Gina's shoulder. "Talk about amazing shoulders. That man could shift my transmission anytime he wanted."

Gina didn't turn. She didn't need to look. The man's body was burned into her memory. She pushed away her wine, listening to music spill out of a nearby disco.

The ship's engines changed rhythm slightly, and she estimated they were picking up speed. It would have been nice to spend the evening on a quiet deck, watching sunlight gild the distant clouds.

It would have been nice to explore the man beneath the tough, cool facade.

Right. When pigs could fly.

CHAPTER FIFTEEN

TRACE HEARD HER VOICE through the chatter of two hundred others. A small laugh, a few smooth vowels, and the recognition snapped home.

The chef.

He turned, scanned the room and saw her at the latte counter, exactly the way he remembered. Her hair gleamed in the sunlight coming through the window, and her eyes moved intently in a way that would have made some men uncomfortable.

He wasn't. He enjoyed the warmth of her smile. He liked her low laugh. Her energy felt tangible, feeding an empty place that he hadn't realized was inside him.

She wasn't wearing her white coat now. No white box in her arms, either.

She was talking with the woman behind the latte counter, nursing a nearly full glass of wine. When a man sat down beside her, she shook her head and the man stood up stiffly. As he passed, muttering something that sounded like *loser,* Trace had a serious urge to rearrange his face.

Probably that would be a bad idea.

He stood in the middle of the crowded deck and checked his watch: 6:28.

He had a report to prepare for Izzy and a new paper to

read about quantum entanglement and GPS applications. After that he'd hit the gym, order a steak from room service and make an early night of it.

Good plans, but suddenly his body wasn't listening.

Instead he walked toward the latte counter, feeling an odd little catch at his chest. She didn't look up when he sat down in the empty chair beside her.

Trace nodded to the waitress. "I'll have the same dessert she's having. Black coffee, too."

Gina swung around, surprised. "You? Uh, you're here." She sounded breathless. "I mean—of course you are." She ran a hand through her hair. "How was your bash?"

"As good as can be expected." He took a sip of coffee. "At least it's over."

"And now you've got a vacation. That's wonderful."

"Wonderful," Trace repeated dryly. "Nothing to do but soak up the sun, dance the night away, stare at four walls."

She chewed at her lip. "Is something wrong with your cabin?"

"Nothing like that." He took a bite of cheesecake. "This stuff is pretty good."

Gina stared critically at her own pastry. "It could use a little more butter. It should be served at a slightly higher temperature, too."

"I forgot. You probably notice every detail. I guess that takes the fun out of eating out."

"I can turn it off when I have to." She studied him in silence, cradling her chin in her hand. "Something tells me you don't like vacations. You're a born leader charging through life." She blew out a little breath. "I used to know someone like that."

"You make it sound like a disease." Trace blew at his

coffee. "I call it keeping busy." He watched her cut another bite of cheesecake and inspect it closely. "Are you doing a celebrity cooking demonstration here?"

She shifted on her chair. "Definitely not."

"So it's strictly fun and sun." Trace looked at her glass and nodded at the waitress. "How about a refill?"

Gina cleared her throat. "No more for me. I have to leave soon."

"Heavy yoga session?" he said dryly.

She shook her head. "No, I have to be up early tomorrow."

"Doing research for a shopping day in Puerto Vallarta or Mazatlán?"

She started to say something, then stopped. Instead she cradled her wineglass. "Oh, I'm huge on shopping. Can't miss a sale anywhere. Point me and I'm there."

Trace nearly choked on his coffee. The woman was a terrible liar.

He rubbed his neck. Did she want to get rid of him so much that she'd make up such a bad excuse?

He stiffened at a sudden thought. "Are you…with someone?"

"Me?" Color touched her cheeks. "No. I'm alone."

"Glad to hear it." He pushed away his coffee and stood up. "Right now I'm bored out of my head. You'd be committing a humanitarian act if you'd join me for a walk on deck."

"I don't think…"

A door opened down the corridor, nearly invisible because it was painted the same color as the wall. A man in a waiter's uniform emerged and he stared at Gina, looking surprised.

"You're worried about something."

She took a deep breath. "It's nothing personal."

He leaned forward. "Funny, it definitely feels personal from where I'm sitting. So exactly what's holding you back? Humor me, but a man likes to know these things."

She pushed away her empty wineglass. "I just…can't." She chewed her lip. "You're nice. I appreciate your help back in San Francisco, but I have to work."

Work?

Trace frowned. "Are you a food critic or something? Maybe you're writing a book?"

She looked down at her red handbag, which began to shake and hum. "No to both." She pulled out a sleek black pager and scanned the message. "I have to go."

"Why?" Trace watched anger mix with worry in her eyes.

She stood up quickly. "I have to go because right now someone is trying to break into my office computer. If I hurry, I may catch him. Then I may murder him. Or her." She looked at Trace squarely. "I'm not a passenger. I'm part of the crew."

Trace followed her as she cut across the lobby toward a short corridor. "Maybe I can help."

"It's crew only in the pastry galley, and I don't have time to argue with you right now."

She made a turn and Trace dropped a few feet back, facing a bare white wall. Then he realized she was opening another door painted to blend in with the wall. When she walked through, he followed her.

Inside the door white walls met utilitarian black carpet. Voices drifted toward him, and he heard Gina's sharp questions around the corner. He tracked the sound into what had to be the pastry galley. Stainless steel work tables ran along every wall, topped by metal cabinets. Tobias Hale, the security chief, was standing by a computer console and he didn't look happy.

The kitchen was close to Hale's office, Trace noted. That meant this visit had just become work, not pleasure.

Hale was hunched over the computer screen. "I just missed them." He glanced up at Gina. "Whoever it was stopped keyboarding two minutes ago."

"Did my staff notice anyone come in?"

"No luck. Two of them were in the freezer area on the other side of the room. One had just gone to check the convection ovens."

"Odd that no one was here when it happened. Or maybe it wasn't so odd." Gina didn't move, as if working through the scenario. "They knew that no one would be here. I think they've been watching the kitchen," she whispered.

None of this sounded good, Trace thought.

He made some noise as he came through the door and nodded at Tobias Hale, careful to maintain the cover that had been created by Ryker. "Lieutenant Trace O'Halloran. Nice to see you again, sir."

Hale didn't look happy. "Gina, you know that passengers aren't allowed down here."

"When my pager went off, he followed me. I didn't invite him. I couldn't exactly throw him overboard." Distracted, she shoved a strand of hair off her face. "When did you two meet?"

"I knew Lieutenant O'Halloran's father in the service." Hale stared at Trace. "As a courtesy to your father, I won't toss you out of here, O'Halloran. But you can't wander around unescorted. The ship has a strict security protocol."

"Glad to hear it. So where are the surveillance cameras?" Trace turned, checking the ceiling for the telltale fish-eye lens of a hidden camera. "Look at the footage and see who's been here."

"I just received the alarm," Tobias snapped. "And what makes you think we have cameras in place?"

"Any public vessel of this size has some form of surveillance post-9/11. I'd say you probably have several cameras in every work area. How long will it take to isolate the current feed?"

Tobias rolled his shoulders. "Depends on how many men I can put on it. But these cameras cover only a small area of the galley near the door and refrigerators."

"Is this the only computer that has been compromised?"

Hale's jaw clenched. "So far it is."

Trace nodded at the news. If there had been an attempted break-in on Hale's computer, the mission would have gone to red alert.

"So someone's harassing Gina and all you can do is wait?"

Tobias prowled the small cooking area. "Listen, O'Halloran, your father was a friend, but I don't need an *amateur* telling me how to do my job."

Gina cleared her throat. "He's not exactly an amateur, Tobias. He's in the Navy."

"Hurray for him. If he was any good, he'd be in the Marines." The security officer glared at Trace. "As it happens, I've got my assistant isolating the video footage as we speak. I've also got a computer expert coming aboard to beef up the whole staff network as soon as we reach Puerto Vallarta."

"Good but not good enough."

GINA DIDN'T MOVE. She was acutely aware of Trace standing beside her desk, observing every movement in the room. His expression gave away nothing.

She recognized his thousand-yard stare. Once she had

been good at the same kind of look. It had been part of her job back in Seattle, and nothing had ruffled her then.

Until the day she'd been hounded and torn to ribbons by the press and then fired.

Can't go back. Don't want to go back, either.

This wasn't Seattle, and she wasn't running ever again.

Meanwhile the two men were striking sparks off each other. Typical guy thing, and she had no time for a testosterone contest.

She looked around the galley. All her papers and supplies seemed to be in order on her desk. She shuffled through her recent food requisitions and then scanned them again.

Her last order for bittersweet baking chocolate was missing. For a pastry chef, no single item was more important than baking chocolate. Now the order was gone.

Tobias glanced across the big counter. "Something wrong, Gina?"

"My last food requisition is missing. I left it here this afternoon, after I filed it via computer. At least I hope it was filed." Frowning, she stacked her papers and slid them back into a file on her desk. "Who would take something like that?"

"Same person who tried to break into your online computer file." Tobias gestured at her console. "Check to see that the order was recorded."

Gina logged in and opened the program for her pastry stores. She scanned every requisition, line by line, but her chocolate order didn't appear. There was no sign of any chocolate requisition being made.

"Gone," she said flatly. Something cold crossed her neck. If Tobias's intrusion alert hadn't been triggered, she might not have noticed the problem for another twenty-four hours, too late to arrange a full replacement order when they docked back in California. Talk about a nightmare.

How did you keep two thousand passengers satisfied without chocolate?

She closed her eyes, grimacing. The scheme had Blaine's scent all over it.

"Anything wrong in here?" Tobias moved along the pristine galley, opening doors and checking cabinets. "Is all your food in order?"

Quickly Gina scanned the pastry for the evening seatings. Room-service meals were prepared in a different galley, but that still left twenty-eight hundred dessert platings in one evening. That didn't count almost a thousand more dessert items for the ship's crew and captain.

The captain.

Gina swung open the small refrigerator directly above her desk.

The captain had a standing order for mango-chocolate crème brûlée the first night at sea, and she always kept a platter of ramekins cooled, ready for caramelizing. Now she saw that the platter had been moved. Then she realized that wasn't the only change.

Every ramekin was buried beneath a layer of old potato skins, coffee grounds and what appeared to be debris from the galley disposal unit.

Tobias muttered a harsh phrase beneath his breath. "Food tampering is a serious safety violation." He stared at the debris-covered tray. "She crossed the line this time. This will get her fired." He checked his watch. "Is there enough time to make a new dessert for the captain's table?"

"I have more in another refrigerator. The extras were for you, Tobias." She smiled wryly. "They were meant to be a surprise for your birthday."

The big security officer blinked. "*My* birthday? How in the hell did you know—"

"Andreas is dating the assistant purser. Her cousin is married to the director of personnel back in Miami. No secrets on a cruise ship, remember?" Gina blew a strand of hair from her face, still shaken by the sabotage before her. "Happy early birthday. We were going to surprise you tonight."

Tobias watched her open a second refrigerated unit on the far wall. "Don't worry about me. Keep those for the captain." He shook his head as Andreas began dumping the ruined desserts in the garbage. "Stop. I need some of those for evidence."

"For fingerprints?" Andreas looked confused. "But we all wear plastic gloves."

"Maybe whoever did this wasn't careful. It's worth a shot. I want everything in plastic bags, including that metal tray."

"Good idea. Meanwhile, what about her computer?"

Gina jumped at the sudden intrusion of Trace's voice. He had been so quiet that she'd forgotten he was still there.

"We'll check the crew access number and verify the time of the intrusion. Then I'll start cross-checking location and access against videotapes."

"Only a fool would use his own number." Trace leaned against the big Sub-Zero freezer and crossed his arms. "Obviously, he used someone else's code. And the video-tapes could be useless."

Gina shivered a little. "Can't we do anything to stop this?"

"I'll find something." Tobias studied the debris on a tray. "Maybe we'll get lucky with some prints and—"

"I think I have a better way to get the information you need," Trace said quietly.

CHAPTER SIXTEEN

"I HATE BREAKING RULES." The security officer's mouth flattened. "So how many will I have to break?"

Trace wondered how long Tobias and Ryker had been working together. Working with Ryker for any amount of time would make anyone cynical.

"None. I've got a friend with equipment that can pull a molecule of sweat off a fly's wing." He held Hale's gaze. "Shall I contact him?"

They both knew this was Trace's judgment call. Any anomaly or incident of this sort created security risks.

"No one's that good," the security officer growled.

"My guy is. Trust me on this."

Tobias didn't look ready to trust anyone. He also didn't appear to be happy about the suggestion. "What would your contact need? Assuming that I go along with this idea."

"Clear photos of everything. I'm thinking some infrared shots would be useful. He'd want food samples and your surveillance videos, too, of course."

Tobias shook his head. "Not gonna happen. No outsider would ever be given access to those tapes." He stared down the long row of cabinets, and his hands opened and closed as if he were trying to hold something that couldn't be held. "You'll get the tray and the food samples. I'll get you the infrared photos, too. But you can forget about viewing the surveillance feed."

"Do you want to resolve this or not?" Trace shot back. "If you do, get those tapes."

"Stop growling." Gina strode between the two men, hands on her hips. "Tobias, let's work on those videos."

"I'll do what I can."

Gina spun toward Trace. "And *you* stop giving orders. You're not part of the crew. You shouldn't even be down here," she muttered.

"Maybe I should be. You're obviously understaffed. I could help you out. On an informal basis, of course."

"Out of the question. Passengers aren't even supposed to visit work areas. And no offense, but you're hardly pastry chef material. The job requires patience, focus and excellent reflexes. Some knowledge of chemistry doesn't hurt, either."

"Is that a fact?" Trace kept his expression unreadable. "Do you always rip into people who try to help you?"

"I manage just fine without anyone's help." She glanced at the people gathered uneasily near a big commercial refrigerator. "I need to speak with my staff. Then I want to check those computer access logs, Tobias. I want solid proof of tampering, and I want a name."

She turned her back pointedly on Trace. "Everybody get coffee," she said to the group by the refrigerator. "It's time for us to plan our counterattack."

"SORRY IF I SNAPPED at you." Gina didn't look at Trace as she strode down the hall. "Morale was going south and I had to do something fast. They're worried that their bonuses will be cut or they'll lose their jobs. I can't let that happen. This isn't about rules and security." Her hands bunched against her waist. "It's about people and families."

"You care about them."

"Of course I do." She swung around to face him, stiff with anger. "Andreas sends money home for his sister, who's got leukemia. Imogen's father can't work because he lost his leg in a boating accident two years ago. Reggie's mother…"

Gina stopped, unable to continue. She felt the weight of too many personal stories. Whole families depended on the checks sent back from this ship.

Everyone in the kitchen counted on her. They were family, in the truest sense of the word, and she couldn't let them be hurt because of a crazy woman's vendetta.

"Things are different here. We've all grown very close, and now I've got a responsibility to them." She stuck her hands in her pockets. "I doubt you'd understand that."

"I understand more than you think," he said harshly.

"Maybe, maybe not. Anyway, Blaine has to find out there will be consequences. I'm going to talk to her."

"Bad idea. People who do things like this aren't interested in talking. Let her think she's winning, then ambush her from a rear-guard action. Remember, all warfare is based on deception."

"Is that Navy theory?"

"No, very old military advice from a Chinese genius named Sun Zi."

Gina scowled. "So I can't go kick her butt from here to Sunday?"

"It's not exactly a long-term solution."

"That probably means I can't grip her throat and strangle the last ounce of life out of her, either."

"Nix on the strangulation. Law enforcement tends to frown on stuff like that," he said dryly.

"What kind of date are you? Can't a girl have *any* fun?"

"Is this a date? I thought it was more like a security consultation."

"Somehow it's turning into both, and I'm not sure why. Did I say thank you?"

"Not recently."

"Thank you." Gina stood uncertainly. Something in his eyes made her breath catch.

To hell with being careful. Leaning in close, she kissed him. He didn't move as her mouth brushed his, then settled for a slow, thorough appreciation. Her heart gave a little kick as she felt his hand rise, skimming through her hair.

She meant to pull away but somehow she forgot all about that.

There was more here, she thought dimly. With this man there would be fire and surprise and risk. But the risks would be worth it.

She bit his lip gently and heard his breath catch. When she teased him with her tongue, he responded with the urgent slide of his mouth.

His hand tightened in her hair. Slowly he drew her body against him.

Oh, the man was good. Far too smooth for safety. He knew moves that she'd never heard of.

She felt his hands tense on her cheek, his breath coming fast and shallow.

Nice to know that he was shaken, too. She felt the tension in his shoulders, the weight of his hand cradling her neck. When she closed her eyes, she sighed, adrift in pleasure. Caught in a strange and unexpected surge of…

Belonging.

Impossible, Gina thought dimly. Her heart hammered so hard she rubbed her hand protectively over her chest.

He didn't push her further, and when she pulled away, he watched her in silence. Questions hung between them.

Dangerous. Far safer to act as if she hadn't been knocked dizzy by the force of his touch. But somehow she didn't want *safe.*

"What was that about?" she whispered.

"Hell if I know." He eased a wayward strand of hair from her flushed cheek. "But I'm going to find out." His eyes were very dark.

She blew out a little breath, suddenly aware of people passing and shooting them amused glances. "No fair saying things like that when I'm trying to stay calm and cool. In case you forgot, this is a public place. Gossip on a ship can be brutal."

She stepped back and missed the warmth of his arms immediately. "You don't have to waste your vacation helping me. Blaine is my problem."

"Are you kidding?" He moved easily, matching her pace. "This is the most fun I've had in three days. A few hours ago I was ready to stick a fork in my eye, just for the distraction value."

"You really are having a terrible cruise, aren't you? Usually people love our ship. Gambling, fitness, dancing, we've got it all."

"It's not the activities or the facilities." Trace cleared his throat. "It's the female passengers. There's way too much grabbing."

"Welcome to the brave new world of high seas cruising." Gina glanced down at his hand. "You could try wearing a wedding ring." Then she shrugged. "On second thought, it wouldn't make any difference. Any man who looks like you is fair game."

Trace made a sound of annoyance. "It's not open season," he snapped.

"I'm glad to know someone thinks that. Not that I'm criticizing. If a woman wants mindless sex, that's her privilege. Ditto for the man."

His eyes cut to hers. "Is that a theoretical or a personal opinion?"

"Off topic. This is a security consultation, remember?"

"And a partial date. You need to eat and I'm prepared to feed you." His eyes darkened, bottomless and hungry. "All night long, if you want."

Gina's breath caught in her chest. *Yes,* she wanted. Her body hummed, turning hot at the thought.

But she didn't have sex with strangers, not even strangers who had saved her from professional ignominy twice.

She avoided his eyes. There was no point in drawing things out. "You really don't have to escort me to my cabin. I doubt I'll be attacked while I cross the aft deck."

"I've finally got something to do. You think I'm giving that up now? I was one step removed from body restraints and enforced confinement until this happened."

Body restraints. A hot and very kinky image of Trace naked on her bed left Gina's cheeks hot. Was she losing her *mind?*

She rolled her shoulders. "You really are an alpha-personality gone bad, aren't you?"

"Comes with the territory. Not that your job is exactly calm and quiet."

Gina laughed. "Things can get bonkers when we're

counting down the final minutes before a ship-wide event. But when you work together long enough, you learn to work as a team. The laughter keeps us steady, able to cope."

Trace held open the door as they reached the end of the hall. "Admirable field style. Sure you weren't ever in the military?"

Gina looked away, memories crowding in. Did he see things that others didn't? "I have a feeling your field style is pretty good, too, Lieutenant."

Suddenly she wasn't thinking about Trace's skills at fighting or covert surveillance. She was imagining him in bed, rugged and fierce, making her wild. She imagined finding out how that lean, tough body looked and felt naked under her searching fingers.

Serious meltdown. Time to grow up and stop being a mental case, Ryan.

They took an elevator down two decks, and Gina stopped outside an end cabin, digging in her pocket for her key card. "You really don't have to stay."

"I'm staying," Trace said harshly. "Tobias Hale is nobody's fool, and he seems to think you should take basic precautions, which is right up my alley. Now go find that list of missing e-mails that he wanted. I'll be right outside." His voice turned hard. "Just don't take too long or I may decide to come in and get you."

Gina's throat felt dry. "And that would be bad because…?"

"Because I doubt that we'd get out of your room until morning."

CHAPTER SEVENTEEN

SOMEHOW SHE KEPT her voice steady. "You're pretty cocky, Lieutenant."

"So I've been told."

"You're impossible, too."

"So I've also been told," he said calmly.

Gina tried hard not to stare at his mouth. Why did he make her so distracted? "I appreciate your help, Trace. But if you're expecting this to go anywhere—don't. You'll be disappointed."

"Go?" His face was unreadable. "Not sure I follow."

"Don't play dumb. As in a week of uninhibited cruise ship sex." She shook her head. "It's not happening."

"I'm not angling for…cruise ship sex," he said wryly.

He didn't seem at all ruffled by her warning, which surprised her. So maybe he *was* different from the other men she'd met aboard. After all, a gorgeous man like this could pick and choose, and there was no real reason he'd pick *her.* She'd never rated herself very high in the allure department.

He waited at the door while she searched her desk, found a sheet of notes and flipped off the desk light. When she looked up, he was studying the room. "What?"

"You don't spend much time here, do you? No posters. No photos. No knickknacks. It's strictly a place to sleep."

He was right, and for some reason his dead-accurate assessment made her uncomfortable. "Sleeping is all I have time for besides work."

Trace walked around a big black duffel bag in the corner of her cabin. "Not entirely. I see you've got a fully equipped gym bag in the corner."

"Not for the gym. That's for Thursday-night poker." She smiled a little. "It's become our little institution aboard the ship."

"Glad to hear it, because I love poker. What's your buy-in?"

"Uh—that depends. Tobias usually sets the figure."

Trace looked thoughtful. "How about you wrangle me a seat at the table?"

"No can do, Kemosabe. It's invitation only and strictly for staff. Tobias rules the proceedings with an iron fist."

"Maybe he'd make an exception in my case." Trace toyed with the zipper of her duffel, and Gina bumped away his hand.

"Back off, Ace. Go find your own poker game."

Trace shook his head. "Why do I get the feeling there's something you're not telling me?"

"Because you look for secrets everywhere," Gina muttered. When he didn't answer, she frowned at him. "What now?"

"Things don't match up. You just don't strike me as a cook. You seem comfortable with handling authority, and you know how to read people quickly. Were you always a pastry chef?"

She laughed dryly. "When I was twelve, I woke up and said, 'Gee, why don't I make a mango chocolate cheese-cake today."

Not.

But the truth wasn't any of his business. That meant flippant was best. She changed topics adeptly, waving a stack of papers as she walked back to the door. "Three of my e-mails are missing."

He stood outside the door, legs apart, body relaxed but alert. In full bodyguard mode, she realized.

For some reason the thought was very comforting. But Gina wasn't looking for a protector, and she certainly didn't need to lose her head over a handsome stranger who'd be gone in a week. She would handle Blaine perfectly on her own.

She closed the door to her cabin and took a deep breath. "I'll have to reconstruct all those messages."

"Tobias is right," Trace said quietly. "Stay prepared. Things will get nastier before this is over. So what started your little war?"

She gave a hollow laugh. "Chocolate ganache."

"I don't follow."

"Chocolate and cream, melted together slowly and blended perfectly. It's amazing stuff." She rubbed her eyes gently, the way her doctor had shown her. "I made a ganache cake on a cruise to Honduras last year. Turns out the passenger was a TV bigwig. His wife loved the cake, which I constructed to look just like his favorite car—a silver Porsche GT2. When he saw it, he refused to eat it. It's still wrapped in plastic, frozen in his freezer. Terrible waste of varietal chocolate, if you ask me." Gina cleared her throat, feeling Trace's body too close.

Too strong.

And his scent, a faint mix of citrus and leather, made her want to lean close, pull off that shirt and run her hands over hot, sculpted muscles.

She cleared her throat. "Where was I?"

"Porsche. Waste of good chocolate."

"Right. The next thing I knew, he wanted photos of my other cakes, which are always super-realistic. I did a red Prada cake in the shape of his wife's favorite ostrich handbag, and I made a pair of shoes to match. There were e-mails and a few phone calls, and one morning I found out I was up for a series. *Chocolate Rules* is the working title."

"This chef is gunning for you because of jealousy?"

"Not a chef, the head of beverage services. I should try to keep an open mind, but she's made threats and done some shoving." Gina took a long breath. "When will we know for sure who's behind this?"

"An hour after my guy has the materials. He has skills that haven't even been named yet. He'll pull a print somewhere. Maybe even a fabric sample."

"A print would be enough. All the crew is finger-printed when they're hired." Gina started walking, her expression fierce. "So what do I do next? Because I'm not giving up."

"Simple. You watch your back and trust no one."

Gina shook her head in disgust. "Defensive paranoia. Gee, there's a positive life philosophy." She stopped walking so suddenly that Trace almost ran into her. "We're all up for performance assessment. That's why she's doing this now, so she can hurt me and everyone who works with me." Anger twisted deep in Gina's chest. "Never mind who ends up hurt as long as Blaine gets exactly what she wants. Maybe it's time I kicked her skinny size-two butt."

She took a deep breath and leaned against the wall,

her fingers twisting back and forth. "Okay, so how do I *really* stop her?"

"Increase your surveillance activity. Then update your base of operations and security. Work on field of fire and enemy reconnaissance."

"Field of fire? That may be a little dramatic."

"Symbolic but very real. Protect your back always. Keep records, lock your computers, hide your backup copies and send them to several dummy e-mail accounts for good measure. Watch kitchen access at all times."

That made sense, Gina thought. Why hadn't she started sooner? "Go on. You've got my attention."

"Harassment and interdiction. Use random fire to demoralize the enemy and disrupt their troop movements."

"Okay, this is getting weird." She held up a hand, shaking her head. "I can't live this way, out on the edge suspecting everyone."

"You are out on the edge. Someone's targeting you, remember? Do you roll over and play dead or fight back?"

"You know how this stuff works, don't you?" He was good, Gina realized. Field of fire and base of operations were second nature to him, and he could apply the concepts to vastly different settings.

"It's what I am. What I do," he said flatly. "And since you asked for suggestions, I'll give you the rest." Trace's eyes narrowed. "This is the part you won't want to hear. I'd say someone close to you is passing information to your competition. I doubt this Blaine person is acting alone."

"Impossible," Gina said angrily. She'd worked and sweated and laughed with the dozen people in her kitchen. None of them would betray that trust.

Or would they?

"Better start making a list of who had access and opportunity," Trace said. "Then think about who your real friends are, because someone around you is not who you think they are."

TOBIAS WAS STILL TINKERING with Gina's computer when they returned to the kitchen. He studied her list of missing e-mail messages, noting dates and times. Then he slid the sheet into his pocket. "This should help. Meanwhile, Andreas has everything on track here. There's no reason for you to stay."

"I'm not leaving," Gina said stubbornly. "There's still work—"

"All the early-seating desserts are plated," Andreas cut in. "And we'll be watching tonight." His voice dropped. "There will be two people here at all times. Nobody will get past."

Gina straightened a pile of folded aprons. "I can't leave. Not after what happened."

"Sure you can." Andreas smiled thinly. "It will make Blaine crazy to think she screwed up and you're not concerned."

All warfare is based on deception, Gina remembered. "I really, really hate this."

Tobias finished typing at her computer and then shut down the program. "Hate it or not, Andreas is right. Let Blaine simmer. Go away and forget about this. Have some dinner and let everyone see you calm and happy—*especially* Blaine. We want her angry enough to make a slip." Tobias eyed Trace. "And since you're here, make yourself useful. Keep an eye on her. Just don't keep her out too late. I want you both in my office tomorrow morning so we can work on some new tactics."

SOMETHING WAS WRONG.

Blaine glared at her PDA, networked to the ship's main computer. She repeated the string of letters that had always worked perfectly for codeword entry before.

Nothing happened. For some reason she was locked out of Gina's computer.

"The little bitch."

She tried again, this time aiming to enter the general pastry kitchen computer. None of the old codes worked, which meant that someone had changed them in the past hour. Her covert contact had triggered a response on Gina's computer an hour earlier.

Damn. Blaine stared down at the PDA. Now Gina would know that someone had tried to breach her network.

Weeks of patient work down the drain.

Blaine kicked the side of her bed. She wasn't going to lose. Gina would become a laughingstock and be fired for personal and professional misconduct. When the producers were desperate for a replacement project, Blaine would step in to offer her services. The history and lore of fine wines was a hot subject right now, and the commercial side of wine investment was growing in popularity. With her experience she could handle both superbly.

"Something wrong?" The voice was low and lazy, but Blaine knew the sound was deceptive. This was a very dangerous man. That thought excited her immensely—but not when she had work to do.

"Don't bother me. I'm busy here."

"I told you I'd handle it." Behind her the sheets rustled. A hard arm slid up, covering her breasts. "Come back to bed."

"In a minute." Blaine had to work to bite back a snarl. He was superbly athletic, and his air of barely contained violence made him a perfect lover. But not even world-class sex was going to interfere with all her careful plans.

There was good money to be made on a ship. It flowed effortlessly if you knew the right people and had the right network in place. Wine could go missing or be replaced, if you were skillful enough, and Blaine was definitely skillful. No bitch with a pastry degree was going to jeopardize her careful investment of time and contacts.

The man's arm encircled her waist, pulling her down until she straddled hard thighs. "Relax. I told you I had everything in motion. It's my game now, too."

"I'm almost done here, love." *And if you keep interrupting me, I'll see that you never get between my legs again.*

After a third try with the same code failures, Blaine powered off her Palm device and tossed it across the room.

"The bitch has locked me out of every computer," she snapped.

"Has she now?" The man on her bed held Blaine still, his eyes intent. "Every computer?"

"That's what I just said, isn't it?"

"That would require serious security protection. Not exactly what you'd expect in a pastry kitchen." His fingers tightened on Blaine's waist. "Maybe something else is going on."

"Like *what?*"

His scar looked dangerous in the semidarkness. Blaine felt a little shiver of fear. Who was he really? He had refused to tell her anything personal, while he knew *everything* about her. If the man hadn't been so adept at computer skills and acquiring buried information, she wouldn't have given him the time of day.

Don't forget how amazing he is in bed, a smug voice whispered.

No, she couldn't possibly forget that.

She reached between his legs, finding him hard and ready.

But his face showed absolutely no expression. How did he have such complete control? Sometimes it frightened her.

Here in the darkness it only left her aroused and reckless. But she wasn't going to make this easy for him.

Besides, she had work to do. Her eyes narrowed. "I need you to do something for me tonight." Her voice was smooth, confiding. "It's very important."

The man laughed. "Everything about your job is important to you. For a woman, you've got big balls, honey."

The description made Blaine smile, and she pressed her lips slowly against the erection that was impossible to ignore. "Do you have a problem with my body?" She made a show of pulling away. "In that case maybe I should—"

He yanked her back onto the bed and tossed her onto her back, then studied her naked body. "There's nothing wrong with you, and you damn well know it."

Blaine's lips curved. She traced his thigh, enjoying the play of powerful, conditioned muscles beneath her fingers. "How do you stay in shape? You haven't worked out once."

His eyes darkened. "Must be good genes."

"Did you bring your laptop? I need to—"

"It's in my cabin, ready to network everything, just the way we discussed." He knelt, gripped her shoulders. "Any other questions you're dying to ask?"

There was a warning in the words.

Blaine heard it clearly. The tiny hairs stirred along her neck as she felt the force of his odd, gunmetal cool eyes. Who *was* he?

But his secrets didn't matter to her. All that counted was results. "No questions that can't wait. I'll give you whatever you want."

She was already planning how soon she could get rid of him. It would be tricky because men with the skills she needed weren't easy to find. And this man wouldn't dance to her tune.

Which only made him more fascinating.

His fingers cupped her face. "You know what I want."

Blaine smiled. She certainly did know.

Luckily, she wanted the same thing, with just the same edge of violence. She closed her eyes, her plans forgotten minutes later as her first breathless cry of release echoed in the dark cabin.

CHAPTER EIGHTEEN

THE SUN HUNG BLOODRED to the west, suspended over the restless horizon. Gina felt just as restless, just as volatile. It was a night to throw caution to the wind, to do things she might regret. But somehow she'd never felt more alive.

Torn between work and pleasure, she stood on the promenade deck, surrounded by the salty tang of the sea, while birds wheeled overhead and the deck rocked gently beneath her feet.

She closed her eyes, feeling the wind play through her hair. She'd forgotten how good it felt on her face. How the last bars of sunlight melted liquid against her shoulders.

Now there was a new factor in the equation. A man who stood at her side demanding nothing, yet supporting her even when she told him not to. She didn't want support, didn't need a guardian, but somehow she had one.

Awareness stirred and came alive inside her. A silent promise took shape, hovering between them.

But Gina didn't trust promises and she didn't want romance. Emotion like this fueled impossible dreams and mad indiscretions, making people throw morals and logic out the window.

No way she was falling down *that* rabbit hole.

She took a deep breath. "Humans are a lousy species.

Give us something beautiful and after a week we take it for granted, even something as amazing as this."

"Gotta admit, that's some view you have on your commute home," Trace said wryly. "And your rush-hour traffic is about as beautiful as it gets. Good reason to work on a cruise ship."

Gina leaned over the aft railing. "Some people go their whole lives without seeing this. That makes me sad."

"People always have choices. No need to feel sad for them."

"Stupid, but I've always felt responsible for things."

"Even when they're beyond your control?"

Gina nodded.

"Congratulations. That makes you an excellent leader." Trace leaned against the rail beside her. "And a messed-up human being. For that reason, I agree with Tobias. Take the night off and forget about everything. Your staff is a cohesive unit, so give them their heads and let them perform. It's obvious they're dying to take care of you for a change, and a good field officer knows when to step back, watch and advise without interfering. It boosts morale."

"More military tactics." She turned up her collar against a brisk western wind. "Cooking isn't a war."

"Honey, all business is war. Ask any Fortune 500 CEO."

Gina was almost certain he was right, but she didn't want to think about it. After all, she had become a chef to get away from the harsher realities of her life.

Look how well that turned out, a dry voice whispered.

"You okay?" Trace brushed a strand of hair away from her eyes. His fingers lingered, touching her cheek. "No reason to look so bleak. We'll get your security problem handled."

She looked away, suddenly aware of his warm body

close enough to touch. She fought an urge to lean in closer and find out how that hard mouth tasted all over again.

A shipboard fling?

No way. Gina refused to become a cliché. She didn't fall into bed with strangers, and she wasn't looking for Mr. Right.

Mr. Right had never been born.

But this man was…different. His keen eyes missed nothing. They probed deep, made swift conclusions, assessed risks and then shot ahead to the next challenge.

He had made it clear that he was interested in her, but then said he wouldn't crowd her. So why did she suddenly *want* to be crowded, just a little?

Too many questions.

Confused, she ran her hands through her hair and decided to do exactly what Tobias had suggested.

She would go with the flow.

What was the big deal about taking one evening off?

Tension made her stiffen and she walked into the edge of a deck chair. Pain streaked up her ankle. So much for go with the flow.

Trace took her arm, steadied her, then stepped back. "Okay?"

"Sure."

Not.

She was tied up in knots and that made her angry.

She took a deep breath and forced Blaine out of her mind. As she shoved her hands in her pockets, something rattled and smooth plastic brushed her knuckles. Gina realized it was past time for her medicine. In her surprise over the computer break-in, she'd forgotten.

She gripped the bottle of pills that Andreas had found beneath her desk.

"Headache?"

Nodding, she palmed a pill and swallowed it dry. Only Tobias would know the full extent of her medical problems. She had her pride, after all.

She shivered a little in the wind and felt Trace's linen sport coat slide around her shoulders. Still warm with the heat of his body, the fabric enveloped her, heavy and palpably intimate. She caught the smell of citrus and leather and fresh air.

The faint male scent of *him*. The power of it sent shivers through her body.

Here, Gina thought blindly. Here was the need, the rain, after months of dry days. Here was the hunger, sprouting through urgent, parched earth.

Because she wanted to touch him, she closed her hands and turned away. Forgotten on a deck chair, a paperback book shot across the deck. Carried by the wind, it struck her ankle.

She jumped on one foot, wincing. "That was one plot I didn't see coming."

Trace glanced at the book and shook his head. "Another author writing about war when he's never been farther than the beltway."

"That bothers you?"

Trace tossed the paperback from one hand to the other. "If I had my way, I'd choose fairness. Since fairness usually isn't an option, I'll settle for accuracy."

"Is that a chip I see on your shoulder, Lieutenant O'Halloran?"

"Yes, ma'am. I'm told that I have a definite chip in residence. It's been there so long I wouldn't know what to do without it." He pulled his jacket tighter across her shoulders as the wind picked up. In the process, his hand grazed her breast.

Gina shivered, her throat going dry. Neither moved, struck by an aching awareness that made them feel alone beneath twilight sky and racing clouds. Caught in a sudden shimmer of nerve and need, Gina would have done anything to feel more.

But he had warned her clearly. He was tough and temporary. She'd seen enough to know that he was a professional who got the job done, no matter the risks. That also meant he was the kind of man who would never get too close. He'd walk away without a backward glance.

Did that really matter? She wasn't looking for permanence and white picket fences. All she wanted was to be caught against that rugged body, to lose herself in the power of his touch.

Strangers didn't ask questions. A man like this would have no plan for a future with her. He wouldn't press her or make demands.

She liked that idea. And if he wanted hot, detached sex, what was so wrong with that? They didn't have time or energy to play games, explore mutual interests or learn each other's past. All they had was *now*.

She leaned in closer, surprising herself as much as him when she felt her breast meet his open palm.

His mouth tightened. "What are you doing?" he said roughly.

"Isn't it obvious?"

"Obvious enough. But why?"

"Why *not?* Is something wrong with my touching you?"

He looked down at his hand. His fingers opened slowly,

then went still against her skin. "This isn't you, Gina. You're a long-term, say-the-vows kind of woman."

"Was," she said, feeling dizzy and just a little frightened. "I used to think I needed those things. Not anymore."

A muscle moved at his jaw and his hands rose slowly, settled at her shoulders and tightened. "What happened to make you change?"

She leaned into the wind, feeling it cut across her shoulders. "I...grew up. It happens to everyone, I'm told."

His finger rose to cup her cheeks. "Not if it means settling for less than you want."

She watched him pull his jacket tighter around her, turning his back to block the wind for her. "I'm not asking you for *your* life story. Why all the questions now?"

"Because this feels...wrong. It's too fast, too easy." He frowned. "Because you look tired and a little wobbly, and it would be damned easy to forget that," he said harshly.

Gina definitely felt unsteady. She hadn't been sleeping well, hadn't been able to relax for weeks.

"So carry me back to your cabin." She linked her hands behind his neck and let herself soak up the heat of his taut body. *Time to take a few risks.* "Ply me with drink and talk me into bed. You might get lucky tonight, Navy."

He muttered beneath his breath. "You'd be dead tired and distracted, worrying about your staff. I won't take advantage of you under those conditions."

"If I *want* this, it's not taking advantage." Gina was irritated, confused. What did a woman have to *do* to get seduced?

"Want what? Say the words." His voice fell. "You want hard, impersonal, sweaty sex all night in my bed? Lock the door, anything goes—you're okay with that?"

"Of course I am." She gripped his jacket, feeling her

hands tremble, trying to hide the jolt of nerves at his words. Despite a wave of unsteadiness, she raised her chin, defiant. "I just said that, didn't I?"

"Yeah, you said it, all right, but I'm not buying. Something's wrong. Hell, you're shaking."

"Fine, you're not interested. Goodbye, *sayonara*." She squinted at the dark horizon, feeling disoriented. Why did she feel drunk, too? She'd had barely half a glass of wine. "I think I'll find someone else." She swayed slightly, angry as she pushed away his steadying hand. "Don't need any help. Nice brush-off, Lieutenant."

"This isn't a brush-off, damn it."

The back of Gina's head throbbed. The pain was dull, different from her other headaches, and every movement felt slow and clumsy, like she was swimming through Jell-O.

Something was wrong here.

"Look at me." The voice was too rough, too close. He held her chin, staring down at her in the purple twilight while the first stars shimmered into view over his head.

She tried to shove away his hands. "*You* brushed me off, remember?" Her words slurred just a little. "C-cold, I think. Maybe…flu. Need to go now." She stared around her, blinking.

Twilight had bled into night. The ship's lights were reflected in rushing black water.

None of this was happening the way it was supposed to. Rubbing her forehead, Gina tried to drive away knife points of pain. "Going…now. This has been a r-rotten date."

She faced the wind, holding the rail and feeling dizzy. "Too bad. Nice, sweaty sex would be good." When she rubbed her forehead it felt like slow motion and the deck seemed to shift hard. "Don't feel so good, Navy. In f-fact—"

He caught her as she fell.

CHAPTER NINETEEN

TRACE STILL WASN'T SURE exactly what had happened. One second Gina was arguing with him, the next she simply plummeted. Now she was draped over his arm like a wet towel.

He knew she was tired, cold and stressed out from the sabotage on her computer and kitchen. But more than stress was at work.

As he stared down at her pale features, he remembered she had rubbed her head, then taken one of the pills from a bottle in her pocket.

Headache remedy, hell.

He slid an arm around her waist, steadied her against his chest and managed to take her pulse. Slow but steady. Her color was passable if a little pale, but she'd been pale before. Thigh to thigh, he managed to guide her down the deck. She stirred once, shoving at his arm and muttering something about crème fraîche and a candy thermometer.

Trace almost smiled. She was back in a world he knew nothing about, and she was damned good at handling that world. His world held death and torture and manipulation, while she spun sugar and layered chocolate into unforgettable fantasies.

But he couldn't get the idea of pill tampering out of his mind, and it was making him see red. He considered carrying her down to her cabin, but he didn't want to cause undue attention. Something told him that taking her to the ship's doctor wasn't a good idea for the same reason. Better to go back to his cabin one floor up and let her rest until she came around.

A young couple passed, smiling as they saw Trace's arm around Gina and her head on his shoulder. The very picture of romance.

Except she was completely disoriented, and Trace was sure it was because of tainted medicine.

Keeping one arm around Gina, he worked his secure cell phone from his pocket. Ryker never stinted on backup hardware for a Foxfire mission, and this phone was enabled for use anywhere in the Caribbean as well as Central and North America. As Trace hit speed dial, he smiled calmly at another passing couple.

Izzy Teague picked up immediately. "Joe's Pizza. We've got a special on pepperoni and anchovies tonight."

Trace snapped back the code words. "I never eat pizza on Sunday."

"Glad to hear it, Ace. Is that wind I hear?"

"Aft deck starboard. No change on my surveillance target. But I need a favor."

Instantly Izzy was all business. "Hit me."

"A pastry chef named Gina Ryan just passed out on deck."

"Too much to drink?"

"She barely had half a glass of Merlot."

"Allergic reaction to food? Did she eat shellfish or peanuts? Is she showing signs of breathing problems?" The questions came rapid-fire. "If so, you need to get her medical care immediately. You don't mess around with anaphylactic shock."

"I thought about that, but she hasn't eaten for over an hour. She had coffee, a slice of cheesecake and a little wine, but there was no sign of a problem then. This started minutes after she took a pill she said was for a headache. They might have been doctored."

"Get me a sample when you dock. Do you have the pre-scribing physician's name?"

Trace fished in Gina's pocket until he found the plastic bottle. He read Izzy the pharmacy and physician informa-tion. "Hold on. There's something else here." He read what appeared to be a brand-name.

"That's a new one on me."

Trace heard the quick tap of a keyboard as he kept walking Gina aft, keeping their pace casual. With one hand he cradled her head against his shoulder, adding to the picture of two lovers out for a slow, romantic stroll. He was almost at the main door leading inside when a woman in tight black capri pants and a black lace top crossed the deck, holding a PDA.

She was a looker, Trace thought. She had the kind of sleek, well-maintained body that made a man think about rough, no-holds-barred sex.

And she knew it.

She surveyed his body long and thoroughly, then glanced over at his partner, and Trace saw the exact moment she recognized Gina. He also saw the naked jealousy that crossed her face. This had to be Blaine, the person who'd set up the kitchen raid.

He kept right on moving.

The woman in black slipped her PDA into a leather case and then moved directly in front of him, blocking his way. "It's good to see that someone is enjoying this gorgeous night. Having fun, Gina?"

"Mwwwwg." Gina turned her head away, huffing out a breath.

The woman moved closer, trying to see Gina's face in the darkness. "I didn't hear you."

Gina swung one arm sideways and sighed sleepily. "Nhhwa."

"Honey, are you okay?" The woman sounded deeply concerned. Her act was polished and convincing.

Except Trace saw her gaze flicking up to meet his, and her smile was a little too practiced for his taste.

He turned, holding Gina toward the far side of the deck out of Blaine's line of sight. "We're both a little tired. She's had a busy day and she needs to eat."

"Really? There are no big events planned tonight that I heard about. By the way, I'm Blaine." She stuck out a cool hand, and Trace saw the glint of something that looked like diamonds at her wrist. "I'm executive head of beverage services. I don't think we've met."

"Trace O'Halloran. I'm an old friend of Gina's." He lied calmly, a casual smile in place. "Once we started talking we couldn't seem to stop. You know how it is." Hearing Izzy return to the line, he cradled the phone at his ear. "Hold on a minute."

"So you're one of the passengers?" Another wide smile. "How lovely for Gina. It's such a romantic night, too. I wish I had time off to enjoy it like you two clearly are." She leaned sideways, once again trying to see Gina's face.

"Gina, remind me about that cooler problem in the morning, okay? I promise I'll look for some space for your chocolates."

No answer.

"Gina?"

"Fwwhmmng."

Blaine stiffened. Her eyes narrowed. "She's drunk."

"Just tired. She fell asleep on deck while we were talking."

Blaine stood stiffly. "You think so? I've heard a few rumors about a problem with alcohol, but—" She shook her head. "No, I won't pass on empty gossip. It's just not professional."

"Glad to hear it." Trace smiled comfortably down at Gina. "Tired, aren't you, honey? Say hello to Blaine."

"Whhmmm. Bssssh." Gina stuck out a hand, but Trace curved her fingers against his palm and smiled at Blaine. "I guess we should go. Nice to meet you, ma'am." He kept walking, glad for the darkness that would mask his hand, holding Gina upright.

Now the gossip would begin. He figured Blaine wouldn't waste any time telling everyone that Gina was drunk.

"Have a lovely night, you two. And call me Blaine, please, Trace. I hope we can see a whole lot more of each other," she said in a sultry voice.

Not if I can help it, lady.

As soon as her heels tapped off into the darkness, Trace raised his phone. "Teague, you still there?"

"At your service. Pizza delivery and computer encryption. We're a full-service agency."

"Was there anything in those pills that would cause this kind of side effect? She's out cold."

"Checking." A desk chair creaked. "It's not a medicine I've seen before, but I remember a journal that mentioned—" The chair creaked again, and then silence fell.

"What did you find?"

"I found a reference, but it's pretty vague." There was another silence, followed by the click of a keyboard. "Shit, this thing is still in clinical trials. I may have to call in a few favors."

Gina muttered and snuggled closer, her breath warm across Trace's skin.

Her breast pressed against his arm, soft and full, and she moved suddenly, reaching out as if to pull trays out of an oven. Trace thought he heard her muttering about a crème brûlée torch that needed fuel.

"I need an analysis on some food samples, too. There's been a case of food sabotage on board, and if I can help the chief of security ID the culprit, the man will owe me." Trace frowned. "I'm not thrilled at the thought of getting ground-up kitchen refuse in my chocolate cake."

"Leave it to me. I'll get you something to score some points with the chief of security. Express those food samples and any equipment that might hold prints."

"That should do it. All staff are fingerprinted when they're hired. How long?"

"Three hours tops, once I have those samples in the lab."

Trace notched the cell phone under his chin and pulled out his cabin key card. Gina made a little huffing sound as he propped her upright. With one arm under her shoulder, he swung open his door. After a little maneuvering, he half lifted, half walked her inside.

"Gotta go. Sleeping Beauty is starting to thrash."

"Check her pulse. Be sure she's got an open airway, and keep an eye on her breathing."

Trace wasn't a trained medic, but Foxfire missions required detailed experience for unit members. He could manage a decent evaluation with the items in his locked bag, but instinct told him that she wasn't in immediate danger. "Will do."

"Go by the book on this, O'Halloran. If the chef's been given some kind of toxin, things could go south fast. If her condition changes, get her to the clinic on ship immediately."

"Roger that."

Trace powered off the call, then shoved his door shut with his boot. Sleeping Beauty was mumbling about dough surfaces and chocolate melting points as he walked her toward the bed.

He knew he'd made the right choice to bring her here. Trace knew that most cruise lines had zero tolerance policies for drinking problems among their staff, but without solid evidence or witnesses, Blaine's comments about drunkenness would fall on deaf ears.

The Babe in Black wasn't getting her way tonight.

As he settled Gina on his bed, her arm tightened around his shoulder. She snuggled closer and sniffed his neck. "Cinnamon. Smells good."

Her hand slid along his chest and worked under his shirt, pulling him closer. "Ummmh."

Uh-oh.

Trace tried to ease away. "Time to hit the sack, honey."

"Mwggh." She buried her face in his chest, licking his skin in a way that sent his whole body into overdrive.

"Let's get you tucked in."

When he tried to move away, Gina turned restlessly, one arm stretched across his shoulder. Her other hand tunneled under his shirt. She found his belt.

Trace began to sweat.

Focus, dog-brain.

He worked to maneuver her onto her side, but she stiffened, looking confused. Then, with a little sigh, she collapsed onto his chest.

She whispered his name, the sound wistful and low. Her leg slid along his thigh.

Trace's jaw locked as her fingers worked beneath his belt and burrowed toward the hot, aching skin beneath.

CHAPTER TWENTY

HER FINGERS SEARCHED.

Trace bit back a curse as her hands closed around him.

Talk about trouble. He didn't want complications, yet here was an unforgettable one staring him in the face.

Gently, he pulled Gina's hand out of the red zone and rolled her across the bed. She muttered a protest and tried to roll back, but he ignored her.

His hands shook a little as he took her pulse and verified she was breathing well. Her color was good and her pulse normal.

Meanwhile his own pulse was unsteady.

He'd seen more women naked than he could remember, so there was no logical reason for the sight of a fully dressed woman stretched out groggy on his bed to leave him fully aroused.

But the evidence was unavoidable. The tight stretch of his zipper reminded him how long it had been since he'd had a woman in his bed.

No, not going there.

Grimly, he pulled off her shoes while she twisted, tangled in his sheets, muttering something about rose petals and buttercream. Cooking again.

Right now the only food Trace could think of was Gina.

Naked and hot beneath him. Ready to be devoured by his slow, expert mouth, whispering his name blindly as he took her over the edge.

He took a harsh breath and forced his eyes away from her breasts, outlined perfectly against soft white cotton. But the minute he looked down, she twisted restlessly. Every movement gave him a glimpse of long, trim legs and gorgeous thighs. She had curves in all the right places, and the sight of her on his bed was giving him a serious erection.

He closed down his emotions. This was work, not pleasure. He couldn't deny the personal attraction, and he couldn't pretend that her body didn't drive him right up the wall, but personal interests were irrelevant. When he'd joined the Foxfire team, he'd accepted that rule unconditionally.

Now as Trace stared down at Gina, he found himself wondering what would happen if he forgot just once that duty came first. For one night, what would it be like to hear her laugh and feel her fingers in his hair while he lay down beside her and brought their bodies together?

Muttering, he looked away.

What in hell was happening to him? They were strangers with absolutely nothing in common. This woman's life was wedding ganache and lemon cream; his life was free-fire zones and high-yield det cord.

But she was here now, and he couldn't take his eyes off her. Nerve ends rasped and sweat trickled down his forehead as he fought a dangerous temptation to do more than just look.

She was smart and prickly and sexy and he would have her moaning for him in seconds, making soft, breathless sighs as he wrapped those long legs around him and brought them both to a brain-gelling climax.

He closed his eyes. No, that was one X-rated fantasy he was *not* pursuing. The lady was off-limits, and he had work to do.

First he had to find one of her pills for Izzy. Searching in her pocket, Trace touched the outline of what felt like a bottle.

Instead of medicine, he pulled out some kind of roller for dough.

He remembered taking the bottle from her pocket. He'd read the label to Izzy and then dropped the bottle into his own pocket. Talk about addled brains.

Reaching across her, he lifted her arm and eased his jacket out from beneath her. Her purse was wrapped around the sleeve of his jacket. The fiber was soft, almost like it was knitted, but Trace had never seen knitting so thick and dense. He'd have to ask Miki the next time he saw her.

Which would probably be at her wedding to one of his Foxfire teammates.

He smiled at the thought. To Ryker's fury, his no-relationship rule was being challenged right and left. As much as he continued to fight it, he was in a tough spot. He could either give in and maintain his control, or he could lose some of his best men and start all over again with a new set of recruits.

Personally, Trace considered the rule a sound one. Foxfire team members weren't in one place long enough to handle a lasting relationship. All the technology in the world didn't change that. Even if they were, families or loved ones made for security nightmares.

On the bed, Gina sneezed and pulled his pillow over her head. When she turned, Trace managed to free his jacket and retrieve her pills, pocketing one as a sample for Izzy.

When he slid the bottle into her purse, a paper fell out

onto the mattress. Trace saw a name and cabin number scrawled on the back.

Carly and Ford McKay.

Trace sat down on the end of the bed, frowning. So Gina knew the SEAL and his wife. There was yet another complication.

He hated complications, and this mission was turning out to be full of them.

"Brioche. Cheesecake—not done." Gina twisted restlessly and shoved his quilt aside. Her lacy sweater pulled up, revealing a glorious curve of stomach and the edge of red panties.

He tried hard not to stare at the line of lace.

Work, not pleasure, O'Halloran.

But the increasing strain at his zipper said otherwise.

Grimly, he tugged down Gina's sweater, pulled the quilt squarely back in place and flipped off the light. In a few minutes, he'd call Tobias and let him know where she was—and why. Then Tobias could run interference while she slept off whatever was causing her condition. With a little luck no one else among the crew would ever be the wiser.

Except Trace had learned very young that luck usually took a hike when you needed it most. Any experienced soldier knew that guts, control and cold reasoning power were more powerful than luck anyway.

And right now this woman was ripping his control and reasoning power to pieces. She was too close, too soft. Too damned distracting.

Shaking his head, he stalked to the far side of the cabin.

Even there he caught the faint scent of her perfume, a blend with lilac and apples that made him think of springtime back on his family's ranch north of Santa Fe.

His nerves hammered. Every muscle tightened. It had been years since he had thought about sharing his bed just to see a woman's smile when she woke up beside him in the morning. Right now he couldn't get the sleepy, tousled image of a naked, happy Gina out of his fogged brain.

And that kind of distraction could be very dangerous.

Gina tossed once and then muttered restlessly. The quilt fell onto the floor, exposing the pale line of her legs and a large swath of her stomach.

After one look Trace nearly gave in to the temptation to touch, to take what her soft body promised.

Disgusted with himself, he opened the door quietly and walked onto the small covered balcony. To the west, the moon drifted above the horizon, dusting his tiny balcony with silver light. Leaning against the cold railing, he closed his eyes, feeling the sea wind cut into his face.

He had always loved the water. Even as a boy he'd been mesmerized by books about the sea, but growing up in New Mexico, there'd been little opportunity to see the real thing. In spite of that he'd known that one day his life would center around water.

The desert was rugged with a clean, vast grandeur and the sunsets went on forever. The mountains rose above his ranch like a benediction. But it was the ocean that had always gripped Trace's imagination, and he savored that cool beauty now, watching the lights of distant vessels rock through the ghostly wake that churned away from the big ship.

For the first time in hours he relaxed slightly. He had to check in with Izzy about Gina's condition and medicine, then request any updates on ship security.

After that a quick run up on the jogging deck would help to dissipate some of his restless energy. Hard physical exertion always left him clearheaded and balanced. If he was lucky, the focused exertion would also help pinpoint the source of his sporadic hallucinations about Marshall. Either one of his disabled chips was malfunctioning, or the image was coming from his suppressed guilt.

Trace stared out at the restless water, feeling the bite of the wind. The Foxfire shrinks were bound to have a better and more scientific description of the effect. Probably they'd peg it as acute post-traumatic stress disorder with complications of survivor guilt.

Not that the names would make the experience any easier. Until Trace knew why Marshall had died, he wouldn't be able to let her go. As he stared out into the darkness, he couldn't shake the feeling that if he'd handled things better—if he'd stayed in touch in the last year—Marshall would still be alive.

Maybe. Maybe not.

His callused fingers locked around the cold teak rail. *Since when do you decide who lives and dies, O'Halloran? No one made you God.*

The truth should have been simple. If anyone held blame, it was her kidnappers in Thailand, and he doubted that any of them were losing sleep over what they had done.

But his guilt remained, like a bitter and greasy taste that wouldn't go away.

Wind played over his shoulders. The air seemed to carry the faint scent of lavender, tinged with the smell of the sea. Words formed out of the wind.

Protect her.

The lavender scent grew around him.

It is close. When you're not prepared, it will come.

The words echoed hollowly, rising and fading as if caught in an invisible current.

The hairs prickled along Trace's neck.

But the balcony was empty.

GINA WAS STILL OUT COLD half an hour later. Trace had finished a quick walk on deck, checked in with Izzy and then settled for some chin-ups and running in place in his stateroom rather than leave Gina for any length of time.

He checked her pulse and breathing, then tucked the blanket around her shoulders, careful to avoid any contact of skin to warm skin.

He needed to work on this detachment thing. It was a skill set he'd never had to think twice about before. Meanwhile, it was time to brief Tobias on the situation.

He had already committed the number of Hale's secure cell phone to memory, and the security officer answered on the second ring.

"Security, Hale."

"O'Halloran here. There's a woman stretched out unconscious in my bed."

The security officer snorted. "You asking for advice or a medal?"

"Neither. It's Gina. I think something's wrong with her."

"What do you mean?" Tobias growled. "Is it serious?"

Trace relayed the night's events, adding the details of their encounter with Blaine.

"Figures that the witch would manage to be on the scene."

"My guess is that she tampered with Gina's pills."

"Very serious." Tobias murmured a rough phrase. "Jealousy can be a sickness. If anyone is capable of it, Blaine is. I've heard some rumors that she hounded other workers who got in her way."

"Are we certain it was Blaine?"

"No. As the head of security, I'm supposed to be logical and not jump to conclusions just because someone is a royal pain in the butt and enjoys torturing her fellow staff members. So the answer is, *I don't know, but I'm working on it.* Even if I'd like to haul her ass off into custody this second. But if you forget the rules and start acting like a wild gunman—hell, that's a very slippery slope."

Straight arrow, Trace thought. Just his kind of guy. "There's another angle you need to consider. This thing suggests teamwork. I wouldn't expect a beverage manager to have the advanced computer skills to hack in to your ship's network. There had to be some decent security in place."

"You've got a point. Where is it leading?"

"If Blaine's got outside help, they could be testing other shipboard systems, as well. They may be looking for additional information, or they may be looking for specific items, things of value to them alone." Trace considered his next words carefully. "The possibility leads beyond the safety of the ship, to a threat against the safety of the mission."

Silence.

Tobias muttered a low curse. "Someone could use the situation to creep around in our network and find out everything valuable that's aboard. That's a very bad scenario you're painting, O'Halloran. The good news? They'll find no mention of my safe or my sideline work. Not *anywhere.*"

"That's good news. Meanwhile, I suggest you get tough on the Blaine front. Have her followed, discreetly of course. See who she contacts aboard and monitor her phone usage. I assume you have a way to do that."

"I do," Tobias said tightly. "It's highly unethical, but I see where you're leading. So you think Blaine has a deeper target than Gina?" He sounded skeptical.

Neither man mentioned the item currently hidden in Tobias's office safe, but the message was clear.

"It's possible, and because the risk is there, you need to move fast and track anyone she's dealing with. There could be variables here we haven't even begun to consider."

"I'll put someone on it. He'll be discreet."

"Good. I've already contacted the friend I mentioned. He's waiting for me to express him the samples tomorrow."

"I appreciate the help." Tobias made a low sound of irritation. "Of course this means I owe you, and I hate owing anyone for anything."

Trace smiled slightly. "I'll try not to call in the favor."

"Do that." Static filled the encrypted cell phone line and the older man hesitated. "You're sure Gina's stable? Whatever she took isn't doing more than making her sleep, is it?"

"I'd say it was only meant to be career-threatening, not life-threatening. But I'll keep an eye on her."

"Don't even think about taking advantage of the situation," Tobias growled. "Most men would."

"I'm not most men. What the hell do you think I am?"

"A soldier who's done some rough work recently. An open, giving woman like Gina would be a major temptation to someone in that position."

Fury tightened Trace's voice. "If you think she's in danger, get up here and take her away."

"Cool down, Lieutenant. I didn't say she was in danger. If you were going to try something, you wouldn't have called me first. But that still doesn't mean I like knowing she's vulnerable," Tobias said curtly. "A lot of people here think Gina is special. We're—hell, I don't know. I guess you could call us some kind of family. We watch out for each other. And Gina has other issues on her plate right now. Remember that."

Before Trace could ask what those issues were the line went dead.

He tried to sleep, but he never needed much. He read four pages in a mystery he'd brought with him and then gave it up to pace the silent cabin.

He didn't want a mystery. He didn't want sleep. He wanted Gina.

Scowling, he stretched out on the edge of the bed, careful to keep plenty of space between them. Ignoring the curve of her thigh inches away, he focused on the pitch of the water and the familiar drum of powerful engines as the ship cut through the sea.

Suddenly Gina rolled over. Her hand slammed against his shoulder and Trace froze as her fingers opened. They feathered down his cheek, almost as if she'd recognized him in her sleep.

Hell.

He was determined to do the right thing, but she wasn't making it easy. She sighed, and her breath was gentle against his neck as she curled her body into his. Her head sank onto his shoulder, trusting and calm.

Trust him? A man who had killed ruthlessly and would no doubt kill again? A man who didn't know the meaning of intimacy or permanency?

Right or wrong, Trace couldn't find the strength to push her away. Her body was too soft, her touch too honest. The contact shouldn't have been as precious as it was, but Trace didn't lie to himself.

This moment with her head on his shoulder was more intimate than all the show-stopping sex he'd had in his life. Hell if he'd give it up. This *counted.*

When her leg slid against his thigh, desire shot straight

to his groin, and he turned away, fighting a blind urge to pull her down on top of him.

But he didn't. He would do the right thing, no matter how hard. He didn't move, letting her leg drape over his. Her body shifted and snuggled until she found her peace and drifted back into deep sleep.

Time was a funny thing, the SEAL thought.

There had been missions in the jungle when time had snapped like a rubber band, jolting him through a cold tunnel that separated him from everything normal and warm. There had been other missions when he'd hunched down in cutting winds, running surveillance and waiting for a delayed incursion order. Then time had been a vast thread pulled out and then pulled out again, stretching without end while nothing happened and his nerves screamed.

Time stretched out now, but instead of pain it brought peace. He had never felt so calm, so aware of the seconds, counted out in the skim of her pulse and the soft brush of her breath.

He felt his focus narrow, caught at the inches where their bodies touched. Every movement she made tangled his senses. When her cotton tank top rose, revealing the curve of her full breasts, he shifted, covering her carefully, though covering up that hot, rich beauty was the last thing he wanted to do.

She sprawled against him, completely open in her sleep and secure in her trust for him.

Trust. When had a woman really trusted him? The knowledge softened old scars and opened deep, hidden parts of Trace's battered heart.

As dawn crept into the room, he realized that something had changed. When Gina touched him, she had inexorably drawn him across an invisible boundary. Now he wandered in trackless and unfamiliar territory. Yet a strange, reckless joy beckoned at every turn, if only he had the courage to grasp it.

Trace had forgotten what joy felt like.

He had forgotten the textures of hope.

He didn't know how to approach it, how to control it and what it would cost him to lose it. But risk or not, he couldn't go back. He never wanted to give up feeling so alive.

Seconds passed. For Trace each one was a lifetime of joy and quiet belonging, precious beyond imagining.

With her hands curled against his chest and her hair spilling onto his cheek, he finally drifted down into sleep, fought briefly and let himself follow her.

MACHINES HAMMERED.

A clock ticked.

Inside the basement of a facility marked on no government map, Izzy Teague hunched forward, running detailed searches of every medical database in North America. He knew most of the pharmaceuticals in public distribution and it bothered him that the name Trace had given him rang no bells.

And for Izzy, the bigger the challenge, the harder he dug. Now he scrolled swiftly, frowning at the trade names and chemical terms flashing across his sleek, encrypted laptop.

Suddenly the flashing stopped.

A trademarked compound appeared beside a blinking cursor. Izzy scanned the medical condition it was designed to treat and let out a long breath.

Not good to be taking this medicine. Not good at all.

He scanned six medical abstracts, punched in another clarification and then sat back, steepling his hands.

The woman was in a bad place and it was going to get worse. She didn't deserve this. She's had enough hard knocks in her life, according to what Izzy had found out about her. Though it wouldn't affect the mission, Trace would have to be told about her medical condition.

Izzy wanted all his facts straight before that.

He noted the name of the head of the research institute in charge of the first clinical trials. Silent, he drummed his fingers on the desk and planned his next move. Once his story was complete, he pulled out his private cell phone.

The author of the journal article answered on the second ring. His enthusiasm at hearing from Izzy was real. The two had met over a matter of some stolen documents and a possible IPO nightmare a year earlier. A friend of a friend had suggested Izzy could help out.

Forty-eight hours later the documents were recovered and the disgruntled employee behind the theft was on his way to jail.

It was always nice to have people owe you a favor, Izzy thought. He was going to call the favor in now.

"Delson? It's Teague. Yes, I'm doing fine. No, still burning the candle at both ends. No vacation time in sight, so we'll have to wait on that fishing trip to Montana. I'm calling about one of your new products. I have a few questions." Izzy glanced at the printout he had made earlier and mentioned the name Trace had given him. "I'd like to know the range of conditions it treats and all possible side effects."

As he listened, he made notes on his laptop and planned how he would deliver the news to Trace.

Already he sensed that the SEAL's question had been

personal. Trace had a reputation for avoiding emotional entanglements and skirting any kind of relationship.

Something told Izzy all that was about to change.

CHAPTER TWENTY-ONE

SHE WOKE UP SLOWLY.

The noise—or the lack of it—hit her first. Gina realized she was on a higher deck than her own, one well away from the throb of the engines.

So she wasn't in her own cabin. Not in her own bed.

She opened her eyes and stared into the darkness. Her hand stretched to meet the edge of the bed.

Queen size.

Hers was a twin.

This mattress was firm. Hers was soft.

She blinked at the darkness. She was lying half-asleep on a strange pillow in a strange bed. A stranger had his hard fingers on her waist. She lay tense, feeling his hand rise, tracing her ribs in a way that made her pulse skitter.

Okay, Ryan. Time to think. Time to remember every detail of the night before. She tried to inch across the bed and pain stabbed through her forehead.

She studied the clock nearby: 5:04. A hint of gray peeked around the blue curtains across the room and felt the resistance of rising seas.

She closed her eyes, but the images of the night before remained a blur. There had been a problem with her kitchen computer. Someone had attempted access, triggering a warning, and she remembered Tobias waiting for her in the kitchen while he checked out the system.

Someone else had been there with her.

Cool eyes. Hands with the steady confidence of a man who faced danger often.

Heat washed into her face.

How had she ended up in bed with Trace O'Halloran?

He had followed her after she'd received the page from security. Then he had grilled Tobias like someone with extensive computer experience.

Afterward, Trace had insisted she eat. They'd gone on deck, watched the sunset, argued a little.

After that everything faded. Vainly Gina kept trying to string together the fragments of the evening. Had she fainted?

She remembered taking a gel tab while they were on deck. The foggy feeling had begun shortly after.

Her pills had never affected her this way before.

She remembered that Andreas had found the bottle under her desk.

Contaminated.

Gina couldn't believe any of her staff were responsible. It had to be Blaine.

Blaine.

She closed her eyes, stunned at the hatred that would cause such an attack. For long moments a sense of personal violation left her disoriented.

How far would Blaine go in this vendetta?

But Gina's train of thought vanished as warm, callused fingers slid up her leg. Under her skirt.

Across her thigh.

Her skirt was hiked up slowly, stopping at the top of red lace bikini panties. A rush of heat shot into the pit of her stomach as Trace turned. Muttering, he worked one finger along the elastic just below her waist.

She was still fully dressed. Nothing had happened between them. They hadn't...

Relief struck her. But in its wake, desire stirred and need curled through her chest. Gina held her breath as he buried his face in her hair, his leg pinning her to the bed.

One very muscular and very warm leg.

His chest was inches away from her face, every sculpted line close enough to touch. She swallowed hard, imagining her fingers trailing over those hard lines, bringing him awake with the liquid warmth of her mouth.

She'd never wanted to explore a man's body the way she did now, reckless and urgent. Her body felt heavy with rich anticipation, and she yearned to follow every instinct and press closer.

All the more reason that she had to leave immediately, before she did something that she'd seriously regret.

She inched away, slipping out from under his leg. When he gave no sign of waking, she slid to the edge of the bed and eased one foot onto the floor.

Still clear. She started to stand up and then felt the lace at the bottom of her knitted shrug pull tight. Looking back, she saw that the sleeve was caught on a small chain around Trace's neck.

First the forklift. Now a chain. Maybe knitting was dangerous to her health.

Gina gnawed her lip. She'd have to slip off one sleeve to free herself. Otherwise the lace border would be torn. Considering that it had taken her a month of knitting to finish that particular ruffled lace edging, there was no way she'd ruin all that work.

Carefully, she leaned back over Trace. Trying not to breathe, she inched the sweater lower. Her movement made a small silver medal of St. Christopher slip down his naked chest.

Light glowed over his skin, rising and falling gently in sleep. The two of them were caught closely, the small silver links wrapped around fine yarn, locking her against him in a way that was quickly reducing her brain to mush.

After more twisting, she finally felt one side of her sweater slide free. Now she had to untwist his chain and free it from the knitted lace hem.

Holding her breath, she traced the chain's length, her face inches from Trace's cheek. At any second she expected to see his cool gray eyes snap open.

He didn't move.

Time seemed to slow down as she carefully untwisted the chain. The silver was still warm from the contact with his skin as it slid through her fingers.

She tried to ignore his chest, to ignore his tight jeans. Half-zipped, they gaped slightly over lean hips. Dark hair arrowed across his stomach, disappearing beneath taut denim, and Gina tried not to think about what would happen if she pushed that denim lower. The mental images tormented her.

The chain slipped free. His eyelids flickered, but he didn't move. She wriggled away from him, fighting emotions that seemed to belong to someone else. It wasn't like her to be so reckless.

Gina realized she wanted to stay. She wanted to draw heat from his heat, strength from his strength.

Nothing about her life made sense. She valued control and order, but she didn't feel in control of anything now.

Thanks to Blaine, she was cornered and confused, under attack from all sides.

He stretched.

His jeans pulled open a little farther.

Gina tried to look away. She had never wanted the physical strength of a man's body like this, never been so aware of her own body responding in turn. Need churned through her. She wanted more and she wanted it *now*.

With him and only him.

Which was exactly why she had to leave.

Panic made her hasty, and she half fell off the edge of the bed, trying not to stare at the place where his jeans opened above lean thighs.

Forget it, Ryan. Forget the spectacular thighs, the lean abs and everything else about him.

You thought you were ready for reckless, but you aren't even close.

Even then she couldn't fight a wave of regret. With quick, silent movements she retrieved her purse and shoes. Like it or not, she'd have to leave her sweater. She couldn't keep tugging and risk waking him.

Or, God forbid, risk deciding that she should *stay.*

Dawn light outlined the windows and Gina heard the cry of seabirds as she slid open the door and tiptoed out into the hall. Only then at the door did she look back.

Trace was motionless, one hand open on the blanket. He looked strong and contained, peaceful in sleep, and the sight feathered through her chest. He looked like a man she could trust. Maybe even a man she could spend the next seven or eight decades of her life with.

Alarm bells went off in her head.

Sharing was not in her day planner. Gina knew from

personal experience that sharing was an illusion you had until the day you woke up and found out the other person was just using you until he'd squeezed out all you had. Then he'd ditch you and take all your credit cards with him.

Okay, that definitely sounded cynical.

Too damned bad.

No use pretending there were roses and picket fences ahead. Or wondering why she suddenly wanted them, when she never had before.

Gina took a deep breath. This was too confusing. Why was one man making her throat dry and shaking up her life completely?

She closed his door, shaking her head, relieved to be gone.

There were twenty trays of brioche to inspect in her kitchen. Everything else would have to wait.

TRACE LET HER GO without a word. It hadn't been easy. In fact, it had been downright painful.

He crossed his arms behind his head and watched light shimmer behind the drawn curtains. Maybe it was the vulnerability he'd seen in Gina's eyes. Or maybe he was just turning soft.

He stabbed a hand through his hair and sat up slowly. Her fragrance still drifted on the air. Light and soft, it reminded him of sunlight on wildflowers in one of the high meadows where he'd grown up back in New Mexico.

Sunlight and wildflowers, O'Halloran? You are dead in the water, pal.

He took a hard breath, turned and felt something squish beneath his shoulder. He realized it was the edge of her lilac sweater, one sleeve twisted around the silver chain that his mother had given him the day he'd joined the Navy.

Good luck, she'd called it, adding a small St. Christopher medal that was about two hundred years old.

Trace had taken neither off since. Once down in Colombia a drug lord had tried to cut it off with a machete, but Trace had taught him the error of his ways.

That story belonged to the memories of a younger, more hotheaded SEAL.

He stared up at the ceiling, his body sheened with sweat. He still felt the slide of her hips and the gentle nudge of her fingers as she'd tried to pull the damned sweater free. He hadn't given any sign of noticing.

Talk about torture.

He'd managed not to groan when her leg slid over his. He'd been aroused beyond anything he'd ever known, tormented by her wriggling and small, soft sighs of exertion. He closed his eyes, wondering what it would feel like when they actually made love.

They'd probably melt down the whole damned ship.

Trace knew that it was going to happen. Sometime during the walk to his cabin, with Gina half asleep in his arms, he'd come to the decision.

When the time was right.

As the room filled with light, he listened to the rush of the sea and the sigh of the wind. He'd grab another two hours of sleep before he took a walk to check out Tobias's progress. They would have to pack up the samples of the previous night's mess along with the pill he'd taken from Gina's bottle. A courier was already waiting at the port.

Later.

Trace's eyes closed.

He didn't smell the lavender scent that drifted, filling the air as he slept.

CHAPTER TWENTY-TWO

FRESH PASTRIES WERE COOLING in the refrigerator. The last set of brioche was perfect. One of Tobias's men was finishing off a croissant warm from the oven, smiling at an attractive young pastry intern from Guatemala as Gina surveyed the kitchen anxiously and tried to relax. But every time she tried, Trace's long, lean body jumped into her mind.

What if she hadn't gone foggy all of a sudden? What if they had—

She closed her eyes and blew out a breath. *What if* was pointless and self-destructive. All you could do was hang on tight while change blew through your life like a storm.

The security officer noticed Gina looking at him. "Sorry to barge in, but Tobias told me to drop by and see how things were going. He said to tell you there's a repairman coming by to fix your refrigerator unit sometime this afternoon. He also said to remind you about the thing tonight. He said you'd know what he meant."

Gina knew, all right. She had everything set. "Tell Tobias it's a go."

"I'll tell him, even if I don't understand a word of it. By the way, the captain came in as I was leaving the security office. He told me to check if you had any iced mocha coffee available."

"Coming right up. Give me three minutes and you'll be ready to roll."

"Since I was coming down anyway, Tobias—" The young officer cleared his throat, looking embarrassed. "Tobias wanted to know if you had any beignets. If it's not too much trouble."

"Yes, I do and no, it's not."

"How do you manage that? I mean, if Tobias or the captain wants something, you always have it."

It wasn't a mystery, of course, but Gina knew better than to reveal her secrets. One of the first things she had learned after being hired was that the captain had a major chocolate addiction, so she was careful to keep excellent chocolate ingredients ready at a moment's notice. It gave her pleasure to do little things for people she liked.

She sent Tobias's junior officer off with the chocolate drink, three beignets for Tobias and one additional pastry of his own. His gratitude was touching. Life on a ship was a self-contained world, and Gina enjoyed feeding as much of that world as possible.

The short night was catching up with her, and she had a pounding headache. It felt like a small hangover, though she had barely drunk half a glass of wine.

She suppressed a yawn and studied her crowded desk. In the cold, clear light of day, the idea of her sleeping in Trace's bed was beyond embarrassing. She'd probably snored. What if she'd *drooled?*

With luck, she wouldn't see the man for the rest of the cruise. One night's disgrace was more than enough.

But the question of her pills was sobering. She had found her bottle in the pocket of her skirt when she'd reached her room. The gel tabs had looked completely normal. Even up close she had seen no signs of tampering, but probably a tiny syringe needle would leave no traces.

She wouldn't touch any remaining pills in the bottle. Luckily, she always kept extra medicine in the small safe in her cabin. That supply would get her through the rest of the cruise.

As she sat at her desk, she checked her papers and drawers for any signs of new tampering, but nothing was out of place. There had been no alarms from the computer and no intruders in the kitchen.

She rubbed her head and suppressed another yawn.

"Busy night?" Andreas stared at her closely. "I think those are bags under your eyes, Chief. How late were you out with GI Joe?"

Gina flushed. "Not so late."

Andreas avoided her eyes. "Blaine is telling everyone who will listen that you were staggering drunk."

"I…there was a reaction to my allergy medicine, that's all."

Gina looked around the kitchen, feeling a strange tension crawl along her neck. It was almost as if she were being watched.

She stood up slowly and walked through the kitchen. No one new was working. No one else was doing anything out of place. There was no reason to shiver as if something cold had slipped between her shoulder blades.

She frowned as one of the interns leaned toward the oven. Safety came first in her kitchen.

But Andreas reacted before she did. "Sleeves," he called out sternly. "Roll them up or tie them off. Otherwise you're going to drop a pan and get badly burned."

The young blond intern flushed beet red. "Yes, sir."

Gina realized the intern had a case of hero worship for

Andreas. Judging by her assistant's expression, he didn't have a clue.

She decided to give the two a little nudge. They would be a good match, and she knew Andreas had finally begun to recover from an affair that had gone sour. She made a mental note to give him an extra night off this week, coincidentally the same night that her intern had off.

With kitchen safety restored and a romance nurtured, Gina poured herself another cup of coffee.

Near the porthole Andreas slid a ball of dough deftly onto a marble rolling board. "Another great day out there."

"No kidding." The sun glittered over miles of teal water, while the gray-brown mountains of coastal Mexico rose in the distance. "But one thing bothers me." Gina rubbed her neck, staring out at the ocean. "Maybe we *are* crazy. We go around with sugar in our hair and chocolate under our nails. We get burned, banged and cut and we work like galley slaves. Then whatever we create vanishes in hours. Why do we do this again?"

Andreas and Imogen spoke together. "Because anything else would be stupid and *boring*."

"Right. I keep forgetting that."

As the smell of fresh, buttery croissants filled the air, Gina scanned her e-mail, saw nothing urgent, then logged off her computer.

The minute she finished, Andreas set a brioche in front of her. Imogen added a cup of herbal tea.

Family, Gina thought. Not the kind of family you grew up with from birth, but the sort you grew into over time, which was the best sort anyway. You bickered and nudged, supported and one day you turned around to find out you were family in the truest sense. Pride made her smile.

"What is this?"

"It's called buttering up the boss." Imogen crossed her arms, frowning. "If you keep forgetting to eat, you're going to be sick, girl."

She already was sick, Gina thought. All the food in the world wouldn't help that. She forced the thought out of her mind. "No sign of Cruella De Vil yet?"

"No. She probably didn't get her blood delivery yet."

The running joke about Blaine being a vampire had taken hold after she had summarily fired three employees in an hour without showing a hint of emotion. It was no secret that morale was bad, and jobs in beverage services were nearly impossible to fill now.

A plate slipped somewhere behind Gina, bouncing across the floor and cracking. A tall ex-soccer player from Argentina bent over to reach it and swayed.

"Edouardo, are you okay?"

"Tired. My stomach's been a little off since last night, too."

Andreas jerked a finger toward the door. "Get up to the infirmary. It might be that new flu Tobias mentioned."

"I'll be fine," the ex-athlete said stubbornly.

"*Go.*" Gina gripped his arm as he swayed again. "You should have called us, then gone straight up to be examined. I'll take over your morning station. I'll call Carly and change our breakfast date to lunch."

"No way. It's almost eight now. I'll take over for Edouardo." Imogen swung past, cradling a tray of fresh croissants. "Get moving, Chief."

"I'll fill in from eleven," Andreas called, busy rolling dough for apple pie.

"Are you sure?"

"Not a problem."

Gina stared down at the brioche on her desk as she rubbed her face and wished for a long nap. She had food in plenty; it was energy she needed. The excitement the night before had taken its toll, and she was fading fast.

Not that spending the night in a man's bed was earth-shaking. After all, nothing had happened between them. She'd gone blotto and he'd carried her off. End of story.

At least she didn't *think* anything had happened.

She took a deep breath. No, Trace wasn't the kind of man who would take advantage of weakness. He had a code of ethics a mile wide.

"Why are you still here?" Imogen was making shooing motions. "Go. And where are all those cute presents you made for the girls?"

"Back in my cabin. I forgot in all the...rush."

In all the distraction of escaping from Trace's bed.

"Move it, girl."

"I'm on it." Gina pulled off her apron, tossed it over her chair and swore to forget all about Trace O'Halloran.

"THIS COLOR MAKES ME look washed out." Carly McKay held up an aqua silk blouse. "See? Awful," she stated.

"You look great, honey." Ford McKay wasn't sure whether to curse or smile. His wife had photographed presidents and poets, athletes and generals. As long as he could remember, she'd never broken a sweat at meeting anyone.

Now she looked a little crazed.

"I hate red. Why did you let me buy all these red things?" She tossed a pair of fuchsia capri pants over her shoulder, followed by a crimson jean jacket. Abruptly she made a sound of distress and dropped all the clothes on the floor. "It's me. I'm nuts. Why am I going to pieces here?"

Gently, Ford pulled her into his arms. "You're not nuts, you're perfectly normal. You haven't seen your friend in almost a decade, and you want it to be right because it matters." He brushed a strand of hair off her cheek. "Things *matter* to you. I've always loved you for that."

She huffed out a little breath. "Just because we were best friends once doesn't mean that things won't change. Gina probably doesn't remember anything about college, and I'm fine with that."

Like hell she was, Ford thought, hiding a tender smile.

"Like hell I am," Carly muttered, slipping her hands around his waist.

Quiet footsteps crossed the floor behind them. "They're kissing again," Olivia muttered. "Why do they do that so much?"

"Because they like each other." Sunny frowned. "When grown-ups like each other they do dumb things like holding hands, and doing tongue stuff."

Ford froze.

Doing tongue stuff? Was it time to tackle diagrams of sex and adult relationships with their three live-wire girls?

He felt sweat break out on his brow at the thought.

"Why is Mommy so nervous, Daddy?" As usual, Cleo had a book under one arm. "There's nothing wrong with red. One of the magazines at school had a whole article about sizzling fashion trends." She said the three words with the cool detachment of an anthropologist describing a primitive culture. "They said red is the new gray." She looked confused. "What does that mean, Daddy? How can red be gray?"

Hell if Ford knew.

Carly draped a red pashmina shawl over one shoulder.

"Red is the new gray, Cleo?" She frowned. "I was at a photo shoot with three fashion designers from Paris last week and none of them mentioned that red is the new gray." She tossed the red shawl onto the bed. "I hate it. I hate everything. I'm *not* going." She closed her eyes. "She's going to hate me," she said in a very small voice.

"No way," her three girls said in unison.

"We'll be stiff and formal, and everything will be awful." Carly stared at her reflection in the mirror. Sunny ran to her first. Sunny the born leader. Sunny the brave and absolutely unstoppable. "Don't worry, Mommy. Your friend will remember. Once I didn't see my friend Mei-ling for a whole month, but when she came back we remembered each other."

Smiling, Carly sank down next to her daughter. "Of course, you're right, Pumpkin. Mei-ling remembered. So will my friend Gina."

"You should wear this, Mommy." Cleo held up a purple T-shirt against her chest. "I'd wear this one if I were bigger. I like that it has just one shoulder."

"So do I," Ford said wolfishly. He gave a low whistle that made his daughters giggle.

"Maybe purple is the new gray," Cleo said gravely.

"It looks good with your red hair, Mommy." Olivia checked her watch. "And if you don't go now, you'll be late."

Carly looked at her three daughters. "So wise. Okay, I give up." She threw out her arms. "Make me beautiful."

Immediately she was buried beneath flying scarves and batik sarongs. Laughing, Carly caught the girls and dragged them down onto the bed, tickling each one until they all screamed with laughter.

Watching the familiar scene, Ford remembered the first

day he'd seen Carly, on a cruise ship just like this one. He had saved her life in Barbados and lost his heart completely.

The work he did was dangerous, making him a target for hatred and violence, but that hatred would never be allowed to hurt his family. He had almost lost Carly once when he'd underestimated a twisted enemy. Worse yet, he had underestimated Carly's own bravery, but Ford had never made those mistakes again.

Sunny, meanwhile, had found a black-and-white dress with little red beads around the neck. "Wear this one, Mommy. Olivia, get the red sandals from the closet." Olivia ran to complete the mission, and Cleo held up a pair of red and purple wooden bracelets.

"Have I told you three how smart you are?"

Cleo giggled. "Two minutes ago, Mommy. And last night when we went to bed." Sunny handed her mother a red straw handbag and a bead necklace that the three girls had made together.

"Perfect." Carly toed on her sandals and spun slowly. "How do I look?"

"More gorgeous than any woman has a right to look." Ford picked up the bag by the door. "Don't forget your camera," he said.

But his wife surprised him. "Today is for feeling and remembering. No pictures and no camera."

STANDING WITH HIS THREE daughters at the edge of the deck, Ford watched his wife cross toward her old friend. The reunion was hard for her, something she would do best alone. There would be time to bring the girls to meet Gina later during the cruise.

Meanwhile, the three girls were already tugging at his

hands. No sign of separation anxiety here, the SEAL thought proudly.

"Who's ready for cruise camp?"

"We are."

He took a last look across the deck. His wife had found a table with her friend. Ford thought the pastry chef looked nice. She also looked tired. He figured that running the kitchens of a busy cruise ship had to be a 24/7 job.

His keen eyes swept over his girls. "Everyone have their pagers?"

The girls nodded. The ship's purser provided communication for all families, which was one of the reasons Ford and Carly had chosen this particular cruise line.

"I've got my camera, too." Sunny held up a small digital unit. "I'm shooting the promenade deck at camp later."

"Watch those F-stops," Ford said.

"Look, there's that man who had the book you said was awful, Daddy." Sunny pointed across the deck. Trace O'Halloran looked a little harassed today, Ford thought.

A woman stuck a piece of paper in his back pocket, leaning close and brushing her hip against his thigh. Trace didn't seem happy about it.

"Why does that lady have her hand on his leg, Daddy?"

No way was Ford answering *that* question.

"I'll explain later." In about twelve years, Ford thought.

TRACE WAS TRYING TO GET through the second chapter of a convoluted mystery when the rich scent of coffee wafted past his shoulder.

"I figured you could use this." Tobias Hale held out a cardboard cup. "Free coffee is one of my best crew perks."

He sat down, nodding toward Gina and her friend across the deck. "That seems to be going well."

Laughter drifted closer.

"Yeah, I'd say so."

"I've got some bad news. Blaine—the woman you met on deck—filed an anonymous report that Gina was drinking."

"If it was anonymous, how did you find out?"

"I'm head of security. Nothing that happens on this ship gets by me."

Trace snapped the book shut. "Only a fool would think she was drinking."

"Doesn't matter. The cruise line has a zero tolerance policy for alcohol. Any report of intoxication receives immediate attention."

"So, they'll do a little research and find out it was a problem with her medication. End of story."

Tobias studied the passing guests, his gaze always moving, always assessing. "Probably. But there will be blood tests, medical forms. Probably drug testing, too. She'll be put on probation until everything is settled. She'll hate that." Tobias's eyes hardened. "That means any additional problems in her kitchen will get her fired." He held up his hand as Trace started to argue. "I agree completely, but those are cruise line rules, and they get broken for no one." He leaned back in the chair and rubbed his neck as if it hurt him. "I can't shake the feeling that I'm missing something here." He stared toward the horizon. "You know that feeling you get when you're crouched in a foxhole, waiting for the first artillery round? You're jittery, and your whole body is telling you that something bad, really bad, is coming."

Trace had had that feeling less than two months ago on

a cold Christmas Eve in Afghanistan. "I know," he said quietly. "Anything you can put your finger on?"

Tobias shook his head. "If I had something concrete, I'd order a cabin search for all crew along with a complete inventory of ship's stores. Hell, maybe I'm losing my edge and it's nothing."

"Have you turned up anything on Blaine's contact?"

"I've got discreet surveillance in place. She knows most of my people, so I have to be careful. She's always in motion, checking stores and overseeing the beverage and bar areas, but if there's a pattern, I'll find it."

Trace smiled coldly. "I could always toss her overboard one dark night."

"A lot of people would like to see that, me included. Too bad we're the good guys." Tobias pushed back his chair and stood up. "Stick close to Gina. When she gets the news about her probation, it's going to hurt. Right now this job is her whole life." He stared at Trace for long moments. "I'm counting on the fact that you're good for her, O'Halloran. Don't prove me wrong or you'll regret it."

CHAPTER TWENTY-THREE

CARLY HADN'T MEANT to bring the pictures, but somehow they landed on the table in front of her. "This is Olivia finishing her docent week at the art museum. She was their youngest ever," Carly said proudly.

Gina picked up the next picture. "Cleo, right? She likes books."

Carly smiled. "She's going to be a world-class writer or a terrifyingly good diplomat."

As the two talked in the sunlight, seabirds wheeled overhead and the years fell away.

To Gina, it could have been spring of their senior year again. With money tight, they'd made a breakfast of cheap coffee and doughnuts last until dinner.

"Triplets." Gina sat back and laughed. "I'm still amazed that you can tell the three apart."

"Ford and I were wrecks for months. If Olivia cried too loudly, Ford wanted to call the doctor. If Cleo went through too many diapers, he wanted to call the doctor. We were lucky that one of his friends had medical training. Ford called him on the sly for medical advice." Carly frowned. "Come to think of it, I haven't seen Izzy in ages."

Gina lifted a picture of a determined-looking toddler who was trying to climb onto the back of a docile German shepherd. "Riding lesson?"

"That's our Sunny, racing through life on three wheels, always the first at everything. You have no idea how close she's come to being really hurt." Carly rested the photograph on the table beside the others. "Our girls. That's pretty much what I do these days."

"That and take pictures of the president of France," Gina said dryly. "I may work on a cruise ship, but I read magazines. Everyone wants to be photographed by you. Somehow you make people drop their defenses and reveal who they really are. It's an amazing gift."

Carly flushed, uncomfortable as she always was when people analyzed her work. "I've been blessed with good subjects."

"Didn't you shoot footage for a cruise line? I seem to recall that's where you met Ford, when he was your model."

"It was a little more complicated than that." A frown worked between Carly's eyebrows. "But everything worked out fine in the end." She reached across the table and squeezed Gina's hand. "I have to say, I never would have guessed you'd become a pastry chef. You were always set on law and justice."

Gina shrugged. "Things change."

No details. She still wasn't ready to probe old wounds.

Carly's eyes narrowed. "You've got burn marks on your hands."

"Goes with the territory. Cooking can be dangerous if you do something stupid." She glanced out over the ocean and vowed she wouldn't be stupid again, not in cooking or in life. Trace O'Halloran might be a major turn-on, but trusting him would get her hurt.

"So tell me about this TV series in the works," Carly said. "And when do I get a taste of your signature chocolate espresso cheesecake?"

TRACE WAS ON HIS SECOND cup of coffee, sitting in a small lounge near the children's camp. He had made two rounds of the ship and decided to break for caffeine when he saw Ford McKay's girls shoot giggling into a neighboring bathroom.

Whatever they were doing, it couldn't be good, judging by their guilty looks.

Trace held up his newspaper, making certain they couldn't see his face, and his vigilance was soon rewarded. One of the girls in a blue sweater—Olivia or Sunny?— strolled out of the bathroom with a book under her arm. The one who liked books was Olivia, he remembered. He frowned as she raced back into the children's activity room.

Where was the other one?

Listening closely, he heard Ford's daughter tell a counselor that her sister had an upset stomach, but she would be out in a few minutes. Meanwhile, Sunny crept out of the bathroom, glanced up and down the corridor and shot in the opposite direction.

He scanned the deck for signs of McKay and found none. Apparently he had just volunteered for babysitter detail, Trace thought wryly.

Sunny had a small camera hanging over her shoulder, and she darted off to the left down a corridor as if she had been there before, while Trace followed surreptitiously.

She took some random shots and then checked her watch, pacing restlessly outside one of the unmarked doors to a small utility room. She was obviously waiting for someone.

As Trace ducked behind a fake palm tree, footsteps approached from the opposite corridor. A pair of legs in a blue crew uniform flashed by. The man was short and appeared to be in his midtwenties. He was carrying a wicker box, and he lifted the lid slightly, showing something to Sunny.

The little girl beamed.

Trace's hands clenched into fists. If the man tried to sell Sunny drugs or entice her into leaving with him, Trace would rip him from limb to limb. He was just about to take charge of the situation when he heard a sound come from inside the basket.

The muffled cry of an animal.

He drew back, waiting. The meow of a cat drifted across the corridor.

Barely able to contain her excitement, Sunny reached into the basket and pulled out a white kitten with icy blue eyes. Cradling the wriggling ball of fur, Sunny slipped around the corner where she couldn't be seen and began feeding the kitten scraps of food from her pocket.

Trace revised his plan to break the crewman's neck, but he wasn't about to ignore the fact that Sunny was sneaking around the ship unsupervised. Crossing the deck, he knelt beside her.

Her eyes widened. "Mr. Trace?" Vainly she tried to shove the wiggling cat under her shirt, but the white tail switched back and forth like a windshield wiper.

Gently, Trace extracted the animal from her grasp. "Who's your friend?"

Sunny's shoulders squared and she looked at Trace with an expression of bull-nosed stubbornness. "You *can't* have him. Miguel found him wandering in the engine room and they were going to drown him. I *hate* them." Her eyes filled with tears. "He's not sick or anything. He's healthy and his fur is beautiful and—and probably he got lost and snuck aboard in San Francisco." She reached out for the cat and tucked it protectively against her chest. "I won't let anyone *hurt* him."

The little white ball began to purr loudly. "See? All he wanted was food and water. My sisters and I will take care of him until we reach Puerto Vallarta. Then Miguel will take him to his sister because she's nice and has lots of cats. Trouble will have a good life there."

"Trouble?"

"That's what we call him. It was really hard to keep him hidden." Her eyes shimmered for a minute. "I wish I could take him home with me. He could sleep right on my bed. But there's probably all kinds of stupid adult laws about taking him back to the United States." Her lips began to quiver, and she looked away, rubbing a hand quickly across her eyes. "I'd ask Daddy, but I don't want him to get in trouble."

She fed the hungry kitten another piece of food, sniffing furtively.

Trace tried to harden his heart to the kitten and failed. "What's that you're feeding him?"

"We saved our sushi from dinner because he likes raw fish. Olivia did some research on the Internet, and they said it has to be cut up very fine, so we did that. See?"

The kitten went right for the mush, smearing tuna all over his white face.

"It sounds like you three know what you're doing."

Sunny's gaze shot to his face. "So you won't tell on us? You won't get Miguel in trouble, either? He was just trying to save the cat. Then Trouble got free and we found him wandering around outside the spa yesterday."

Trace tried to ignore the plea in her big green eyes. "I guess a few hours won't hurt." He gave the cat a gentle scratch behind the ears and then stood up. His tone hardened as he looked at the nervous crewman. "You found the cat?"

The man nodded.

"You shouldn't have gotten these girls involved. I'll keep the cat with me until we reach Puerto Vallarta. Then I'll make arrangements to give you the cat to take ashore. There's no need for you to bother the girls again."

"Yes, yes. That is very good. I do not like to involve them, but to kill a cat is a very bad thing."

"You're going to take the cat, Mr. Trace? Can I come see him in your room?" Sunny danced from foot to foot. "Can my sisters come, too?"

"We'll see. Right now you are heading right back to Cruisers' Camp. You can't walk around the ship alone without telling your parents. They'd be sick with worry if anything happened."

Instantly Sunny's smile fled. "I didn't want anyone to worry and this was the simplest way, don't you see? My sisters and I have a feeding schedule and a time that we meet Miguel when his cabin is being cleaned. He needs to hide the cat then, so we take turns." Her little chin rose defiantly. "We had it all figured out. Then you had to come walking by." Her eyes narrowed suddenly. "You were *watching* us." She shoved her hands onto her hips. "You shouldn't watch people. It's not nice."

Maybe not, but watching people happened to be a big part of his job, Trace thought.

The young crewman was listening intently. "He is right, Sunny. You should not leave the campers' class again. Your parents will be very angry. I tell you this already."

"Okay." Sunny moved closer to Trace as he opened his sweatshirt, slid the cat inside, then closed the zipper halfway.

Little claws kneaded his chest.

When he looked down, Sunny was giggling at the little white face burrowing out above his sweatshirt.

"Mr. Trace, he *likes* you. Hear how loud he's purring?"

Trace figured anyone within six feet could hear, which would pretty well shoot any chance of secrecy. "Let's get you back to camp," he said gruffly. "Then I'll take our friend to my cabin and make him a box."

"A box?" Sunny frowned. "Oh, you mean for poop."

Trace nodded to the young crewman, who seemed only too happy to escape.

Trace realized he might have bitten off more than he bargained for. What was he going to use for kitty litter? And how was he going to hide the cat when his cabin steward came in to clean?

Just the same, he couldn't help putting a protective hand around the kitten. Maybe he'd let Gina in on the secret. She would be able to come up with food and—

Trace looked up, sensing a change in the corridor. Energy seemed to snap around him. The cat meowed loudly and climbed up Trace's chest to stare over his shoulder.

Trace gripped Sunny's hand and turned, his uneasiness growing. They were half a mile off the coast, traveling past barren beaches and rugged, unpopulated mountains. Houses dotted an isolated cove, and small trawlers dotted the distant harbor. A short way inland a white truck raced along the road that paralleled the coast.

The energy changed, sharp and focused and churning.

And in that heartbeat, everything fell apart.

CHAPTER TWENTY-FOUR

A SENSE OF DANGER STRUCK Trace with overpowering force, drilling into his neck and chest. Sweat broke out as he watched the truck crawl like a white bug in the distance. But it wasn't the truck he was worried about. It was something much closer.

Something that waited in shadow, hidden and lethal.

Only one stimulus caused this kind of response. Like every man in the Foxfire program, Trace had been equipped to respond to one specific threat.

Enrique Cruz.

But he was dead. Had to be dead.

Once again the oily energy skittered through Trace's senses like a sickness that would not die.

He was certain. Somehow Cruz had escaped from death in the Pacific.

Cruz had once bragged that a military exercise wasn't over until *he* said it was over. He had always been the first on the training field and the last to leave. The fastest and the strongest among the Foxfire operatives, Cruz had abilities that no one could match. If he had cheated death again, what would he be capable of now?

Another disorienting wave of energy cut across the corridor, slamming into Trace. Pain shot behind his eyes, bringing nausea in waves. He pushed a dial on his watch, reviewing precise GPS coordinates. A second button recorded the coordinates for later reference, so that Izzy could order a satellite flyover at the exact location.

"Mr. Trace?" Sunny stared up at him anxiously. "You're sweating and you don't look good."

"I'll be fine, honey." They were almost at the youth camp now, and Trace was itching to be gone. In a matter of seconds his priorities had changed completely. Hunting Cruz took precedence over all other directives, even safeguarding the material in Tobias Hale's safe. "Is your sister Cleo back inside?"

"Oh, that was Olivia. Cleo had her turn being sick yesterday." Sunny gave the cat a quick pat and then ran toward the entrance of the children's camp. "I'll check to be sure."

With growing impatience, Trace stood in the hallway assessing scenarios and probabilities. Sunny appeared, flanked by her two sisters. All three were staring fixedly at his chest.

He gently pressed the cat's white head out of sight while the girls giggled and returned to camp. Meanwhile, the energy was fading. Trace tried to localize the source, but with his chips disabled, it was like looking for a black thread in a dark room blindfolded.

Was Cruz ashore in the white truck he'd seen? Or maybe traveling in one of the fishing trawlers in the cove?

He stared down the companionway, frowning, considering a third scenario. Could Cruz be somewhere aboard the ship right now? If so, had he picked up Trace's presence yet?

Highly unlikely. With his chips inoperative, Trace wouldn't stand out unless the two met face-to-face and

Cruz was too smart to be wandering through any public areas.

He was watching for the elevator when he felt someone behind him. He spun around, silent and fast, his focus centered on maintaining flexibility and lowering his center of gravity.

Gina was staring at him oddly.

He tried to move past her into the elevator, but she blocked his way. "I can't talk now," he said.

"We'll talk right *now* or I'm taking you to Tobias." Her shoulders were stiff. "I just saw Sunny and she told me you were outside the camp. She said you've been watching her. I want to know why, and it had better be convincing."

The elevator doors hissed shut.

"Sunny was mistaken. I was simply taking a walk," Trace said calmly. He reached around and pressed the elevator button. "We can discuss it later, after I make a call." The elevator doors swung open.

Gina's eyes narrowed on his face. "Are they in some kind of danger?"

"I can't discuss it now." His voice was low, but the edge was growing sharper.

Gina stepped back. "I want answers. If Carly or her family is in danger, Ford needs to know that. He's a Navy SEAL and he could help."

Complications.

The last thing Trace needed right now.

"Trace, did you hear me?"

He moved past her into the elevator. While she was still staring at him, Trace unzipped his jacket, pulled out the squirming cat and pressed him into her arms. "Take care of Sunny's cat for me, will you?"

The white kitten burrowed against Gina's chest.

"A *cat?* I can't have a pet aboard ship. Hey, stop licking me—"

The elevator doors closed, cutting off her protest.

INSIDE HIS CABIN, Trace pulled out a small titanium suitcase and shot the bolts. His encrypted satellite phone housed in molded plastic was the latest model, to be used only in critical circumstances.

Anything that involved Enrique Cruz counted as a critical circumstance.

He listened to a brief hiss of static, followed by three short clicks as the call was rerouted to another secure location. More static cut across the line.

"Ace Pizza. What's up?"

"We've got a problem." Trace didn't bother to identify himself. There was no need, since he was the only person who would use this secure phone. "Our man is back."

The sudden silence felt heavy. Neither man mentioned Enrique Cruz by name.

"You saw him?"

"No direct sighting, but a definite sensory response triggered with multiple distortion. It's our man, I'm sure of it."

"The King is in the building," Izzy said coldly. "Location and condition?"

"Condition unknown." Trace punched a button on his watch and passed on the GPS coordinates he had recorded earlier, along with the details of his sensory response.

Izzy's tone was brisk and precise. "Dizziness. Nausea. Visual distortion. How severe?"

This was the voice of a medical authority talking, and Trace considered his answer accordingly. "Twenty-five-percent disruption. Performance ability affected but only temporarily."

"Duration of attack?"

"I didn't clock it. I'd say three minutes."

"Any significant observations ashore?"

Trace heard the fast click of a keyboard. Every detail would be carefully recorded for transmission to Lloyd Ryker, Foxfire's head.

"A small cove with a rocky beach. Probably ten small motorboats and five fishing trawlers visible. Four houses near a little adobe church. I saw a white truck moving south along the beach. The truck felt important, but that is speculation."

"Understood." More typing. "Any localization aboard your ship?"

"Not that I could sense. I'd say it was more of a protective move, not an attack. With my enhancements disabled, I would assume I'm off the radar to the man in question," Trace said carefully.

"That is correct, as far as we know. But I'll be phoning back within the hour, so stay within reach of this phone."

"Will do."

Trace flipped off the satellite phone and looked out at the shimmering line of the ocean. Clouds were piling up in the west. The sun was hot overhead.

And Enrique Cruz had reappeared.

Some part of his mind refused to accept that his old teammate was still alive. He had watched Cruz's chopper explode in a fireball though Cruz's body had never been re-covered afterward. Given the violence of the final explosion, the lack of a body had not seemed significant.

Trace schooled his thoughts to absolute calm. What

happened next would not be his decision. The most important thing he could do now was stay flexible and alert, while preparing for every possible scenario. Given the importance of the material Tobias was chaperoning, an attack there zoomed to the top of Trace's scenario list.

Somehow Cruz could have caught wind of the new technology and decided to go after it. If so, Trace would have to fight without any of the skills that he had come to rely on. In short, he would be a flea squaring off with a tiger.

FUBAR.

CHAPTER TWENTY-FIVE

LLOYD RYKER WASN'T HAPPY to be disturbed. From what Izzy had seen, few things seemed to make Ryker happy.

"O'Halloran was certain about the sensory phenomena? You believe it indicates Cruz is in the vicinity?"

"I'd give it a ninety percent probability, sir."

"How close?"

"Impossible to say yet."

"Any problem with our man? He's still field capable, I take it?"

"That's affirmative, sir."

"Then I want Dakota prepped and sent in as backup. Bring him up to speed and have him ready to fly within the hour."

"Understood, sir."

"We need absolute deniability on this whole situation. Is that clear, Teague?"

A pause. "Understood, sir."

Ryker cleared his throat. "Anything else you need to tell me?"

"No, sir."

It was a lie. Although the source was unclear, for the past month Izzy had been receiving garbled messages on his computer. One week earlier he had received a coded e-mail, short and to the point. The message listed the street address of his mother's home outside Baltimore, along with her precise times of leaving and returning. Whoever had sent the message wanted Izzy to know that his only existing family was under close surveillance. Furious, Izzy had called in a favor from an old friend on the local police force. Although she didn't know it, his mother's house was now under round-the-clock protection.

Despite all his searches, Izzy had no more to go on. He had traced the message to a public Internet café in one of the busiest neighborhoods in Singapore. The computer time had been purchased in cash. The proprietor had noticed nothing strange about the Caucasian man who had rented the Internet time, and no camera surveillance was available.

Dead end.

"Notify me when Dakota is outbound for Mexico. And see what you can pull from satellite coverage of that area. I want to know every speck of dirt on that white truck. Is that clear?"

"Already on it, sir. We should have the first visuals within the next fifteen minutes."

"Excellent. I don't need to remind you that the man is dangerous, Teague. He nearly killed you in New Mexico."

Izzy was highly unlikely to forget that encounter. Cruz had broken several of Izzy's bones and attacked Trace O'Halloran's sister. Izzy wasn't going to let the man escape again.

"Call me as soon as you've gone over the satellite feeds. I'll expect a complete report by 0400 hours." Ryker didn't wait for an answer, and the line went dead.

Instantly, Izzy went to work, scrolling through maps of Mexico to pinpoint the GPS coordinates Trace had given him. He was in the middle of searching police reports from the area when he heard his incoming e-mail program chime softly.

More orders from Ryker already?

But the incoming message wasn't from Ryker or anyone else whose e-mail address Izzy recognized. The content appeared to be gibberish.

He stared at the screen.

Then he typed in a line of code. The letters shifted continuously in seemingly random patterns as a powerful program went to work analyzing the message for all possible word strings. At any other time Izzy would have felt a deep sense of pride that his newest program decrypted the message in less than three minutes.

We'll be sure to say hello to Marietta.

The single line of text blinked ominously, jolting Izzy to his feet. If he didn't act fast, someone very close to him would die.

He stared at his gray metal desk and the secret files stacked in neat, organized rows. He saw the new encryption equipment he was building on a nearby table. He registered the half-eaten tuna sandwich next to a cup of coffee that was rapidly growing cold. And he had the jarring sense that his whole world, the normalcy of his life as he knew it, had just spun on its axis and fled.

Which was exactly what happened whenever Enrique Cruz hit the scene, he thought grimly.

But he swore the people he loved would not get hurt by Cruz's treachery. He reached for the telephone in the corner of his desk, then stopped, his eyes on the blinking red lights that registered calls through the facility's general phone system. Frowning, he pulled his personal cell phone out of his pocket.

He didn't need to look up the number. He had known it by heart for years.

She answered on the second ring, sounding breathless. "Hello?" Izzy's eyes softened at the sound of the voice, low and smooth and cultured. "Teague residence."

He frowned. No matter how many times he told her not to answer with her name, that the world was a dangerous place and you didn't give away information unless you had to, his mother was still southern and a creature of manners.

She didn't argue. She simply did what she wanted.

"Mom, it's Izzy. Everything okay?"

"Well, it certainly is now, honey. I was just thinking about you. Those bulbs we planted together last year have come up and I've never seen a prettier sight." She laughed, a soft ripple of sound. "Of course, the sight of you carrying your suitcase home for a visit would be a prettier sight still, but I won't say that. How are you? I've got a feeling you've made some new electronic discovery or broken a new code since we last spoke. Am I right?"

She was, but Izzy couldn't tell her the details. Now that he was certain she was safe, he cut through the preliminaries. "I'm fine, Mom. But I need you to do something for me. I want you to go up to Maine and visit Uncle Harris. No questions."

His mother's laughter rippled. "Go to Maine now? Why, honey, the gardening season is just starting. I've got the whole backyard to finish—"

"Mom, please." Izzy's voice took on an edge. "I need you to do this for me now."

A silence fell. He heard the sound of ceramic as if she had rested her favorite teacup on a fragile plate. "Now?" she repeated the word, thoughtful this time. Not frightened, but measuring. "So something is wrong," she said quietly.

"Are you hurt again, honey? If something has happened to you, you need to tell me."

"I'm fine. I'd tell you if anything was wrong. I promised you that, remember?"

"But something bad has happened."

"Mom, I've got to concentrate. I'll probably have to travel on a moment's notice, and I need to know that you'll be safe."

Izzy's uncle Harris was an ex-Delta man with highest-level sniper training. Half a dozen of his military friends with similar training were now retired and scattered through the area. Oh, yes, Izzy's precious mother would be safe in Maine.

But first she had to get there.

"Honey, I can't just—"

"We agreed, Mom. I don't ask often. When I do, you need to leave. Go to Uncle Harris."

"It's something very dangerous then." She didn't sound frightened, simply put out by the disruption of her schedule. "Very well. I'll check the airline schedule tonight, then finish my new mulch. I should be packed and ready to go by morning."

"Now." Izzy's voice was firm. He didn't want to betray his fear, but he needed her compliance. "Don't pack, don't plant more flowers, don't put away your tea. Take your purse and go next door. Ask Elias to drive you straight to the airport. You have the credit cards I left you. When you get there, stay in a public area and buy the next flight to Portland."

Silence fell. His mother took a little breath. Now there was a hint of worry in her voice. "It must be something very unusual. Are you safe, honey?"

"Mom, I'm fine. But you need to go *now.*"

"Very well, I'll leave with nothing but the clothes on my back. I can see Elias out in his yard now. That's funny."

Izzy felt a wave of cold skim knifelike across his neck. "What's funny?"

"There's a man with Elias. A man in a courier's uniform. He's holding a box and pointing to my house. But I haven't ordered anything."

Fear raced to the base of Izzy's stomach, so tight he couldn't breathe. "Do not accept any packages. Get your purse and go straight out the back door. Stay behind the rose hedge and walk to Elias's side porch. Are you listening to me, Mom? No matter what happens, do not get near any package of any sort."

"Oh, yes, honey. I've seen the movies. It could be an IED, couldn't it?"

Improvised explosive device.

Somehow on his mother's lips, the definition sounded neat and tidy, like a home bread-making unit. Except that Cruz wasn't into baking.

Only into ripping lives apart.

Izzy held the phone tightly. He had to talk his mother through this. There would be no time to summon help. "Mom, do you have the cell phone I gave you for Christmas?"

"Of course I do, honey. I keep it upstairs in that nice little box you gave me."

Izzy suppressed a curse. He'd given her the highest technology available, and she used it as a doorstop in her sewing room.

He took a deep breath. This is exactly why you didn't deal with family: because family clouded up your vision, tangled your emotions and generally turned all your logic skills to shit.

He looked down at his fingers tensed to a fist. Slowly he forced the muscles to relax. "Okay, I'm going to tell you exactly what to do. Listen to me and walk upstairs while I talk. Can you do that?"

"Of course I can, honey. I'm not senile yet."

"No one said you were, Mom. Now walk upstairs, get the cell phone and turn it on. Then walk back downstairs, take your purse and go next door. Are you walking yet?"

"I'm going." Izzy heard what sounded like a box rattling. "I've got the cell phone, honey. It looks so pretty, too."

Advanced encryption technology, superior clarity and international dialing capability—and she called it pretty. Suppressing a sigh, Izzy glanced at his watch, noting the time. Every second seemed like an eternity now. "Is the battery in? Do you know how to turn it on?"

"Of course I do. Everything's all set. It has the time showing just like you said it would."

"Good, Mom. I'm going to dial you and when I get through I want you to hang up the house phone." As he dialed his backup cell phone, Izzy heard the ring on the other end of the line.

His mother answered crisply. "Yes, I'm here. But I must tell you, all this cloak and dagger business—"

"Is necessary." Izzy's voice was firm, cold. His mother had only a vague idea of the work he did. She knew it was important, secret and all consuming. But Izzy had purposely kept her in the dark as to the dangers he faced. Now he regretted that. "Where are you now?"

"Getting my purse. Now I'm walking outside and locking the door." Izzy heard a door latch. "Everything's fine. You see? You're going overboard with all this spy business. No one is going to jump out from behind a tree and fire a gun at me."

Her voice broke up, caught in static for a moment. "Mom, are you there?"

No answer.

"Mom." Izzy gripped the phone, sweat beading his forehead. He could hear the sound of the wind and a distant call of a bird. Damn it, why didn't she answer?

Static hissed and crackled.

Izzy stared at the telephone, willing his mother to answer him in a calm, normal voice and tell him to stop worrying, that everything was all right.

More static.

And then out of the empty air he heard an explosion roar through the phone, followed by his mother's scream.

CHAPTER TWENTY-SIX

"PROBATION? You can't be serious."

Gina stood at a long steel counter, melted chocolate streaking her cuffs and cheek as she glared at Tobias. "I've never had a complaint, never even been written up before."

The security chief shifted his weight from side to side. "I know that. You're on probation, just the same."

"Why? We tossed out all the food that was tampered with. You saw us do that." She shoved her hands onto her hips, in full battle mode. "Nothing like that would *ever* go out of my kitchen."

"It's not about the food." Tobias stood stiffly. "Blaine reported you for drunkenness and fighting. She said you threatened her and shoved her, too."

"That's rubbish. No one is going to believe that."

"She has a witness to back her up," Tobias said quietly.

"That's impossible. No one else will support her. Besides, I didn't say anything that was a threat."

Tobias held out a sheet of paper. "Not according to Imogen. She corroborated Blaine's story."

Gina put a chocolate-covered hand on the counter, shaken. "Imogen? I don't believe it. She wouldn't back up Blaine." But there was no mistaking the name and signature on the bottom of the official complaint form.

Imogen had worked with Gina for almost four years. Gina had met her family in Mazatlán a year ago. This couldn't be happening.

"Where is she? I need to talk with her."

"She's in the infirmary right now. The last I saw her, she was throwing up, spiking a fever. Intestinal virus or the flu, probably."

"I'm still going to see her."

Tobias shook his head. "You can't discuss this with her, not after a formal complaint has been filed. You know the procedure."

He was right. Gina closed her eyes, wrapping her arms around her chest.

Probation. It felt like a sudden body blow. That Imogen, a friend, had signed Blaine's complaint made the news infinitely more painful.

"I'm supposed to get a chance to dispute this at a public hearing."

Tobias nodded. "When we dock in San Francisco, you'll have your chance. We'll all have our chance to speak," he added grimly. "Meanwhile, watch your step. If Blaine finds one more area of complaint, you will be relieved pending a review."

"Cruella De Vil isn't going to drive me away." Gina glared down at a plate of éclairs cooling from the oven. "This is one battle she won't win."

But Blaine had picked her time well. Andreas had been struck by the same bug, which left Gina seriously short-staffed. It would mean twelve-hour days to keep up. Since she was understaffed, it would also be easier for an outsider to sneak into her kitchen for more sabotage.

So she would sleep here at her desk and never leave the

kitchen, if it came to that. She was drawing a line in the sand. Blaine's sabotage was ending here and now.

Ignoring a pang at the thought of Imogen's betrayal, Gina turned back to stir her chocolate ganache. She cleared her throat. "I may have a little problem. Actually, the problem is a kitten."

"You can't have a pet on board, Gina. You know ship policy."

"I know, I know. But one of the children found a stray cat. She gave it to Trace about an hour ago." Gina was still furious at the way he had brushed her off. What had changed him from calm and controlled to tense and curt in a matter of hours?

"The cat is downstairs in my cabin. The girls told Trace that the engineering crew was going to drown him. He's very cute."

"Who cares if he's cute? Do you know what will happen if you're caught? Especially now?"

"I know. That's why I'm asking you for a favor. No one will be looking in your cabin, so I thought maybe…"

Tobias stared at her, incredulous. "You expect me to break out the Meow Mix?" He shook his head. "I'm regretting this already, but okay, I'll take him until we reach port. Then he goes ashore."

"No problem," Gina said eagerly. "I'll go get him from my cabin now."

"Never mind. I'll send one of my crew. He'll know enough to keep his mouth shut," Tobias said. "Meanwhile, remember that Blaine is on the warpath."

Silence descended, sudden and unmistakable. When Gina turned around, Trace was standing in the doorway.

An effortless sense of command crackled around him.

He was doing the thousand-yard stare like a real pro. "We need to talk."

Gina knew the look well. Soldiers and police officers counted on it for control and intimidation. She had seen her share of it.

Though he didn't move a muscle, didn't say a word, it was clear that he was in full command mode. With one look at his face her kitchen staff had gone silent. Even Tobias seemed to feel the effect.

"We need to talk *now*," he repeated flatly.

Gina had three workers out sick, a temperamental oven to babysit and 780 cheesecakes to oversee for the dinner seating. She shook her head. "I can't go anywhere."

Okay, she was still irritated about the way he had brushed her off in the hallway. So this was payback, but it was also a way to fight her curiosity. "Maybe later." She turned away, reaching for a clean candy thermometer, and gasped when a callused hand gripped her shoulder.

His body was too close, his face too hard as he leaned down. *"Now."*

Gina looked at his eyes, saw the cold focus there. Unnerved, she felt the thermometer slip from her fingers, roll across the counter and drop toward the floor.

He lunged with one hand and caught the metal with reflexes almost too fast to imagine.

She took a step back, stunned by what she had just seen. There was a difference about him now, an alienness that made her skin prickle and the little hairs stand up along her neck.

He saw her look of surprise. "Patience, focus and excellent reflexes," he murmured. His eyes cut across to Tobias. "You're coming, too. Where can we talk privately?"

Whatever he read in Trace's face made Tobias nod slowly. "My office. It's just across the hall."

Trace shook his head, glancing quickly around the kitchen. "Somewhere else."

"Up on deck. I know a place."

Trace seemed to consider the idea, then shook his head. "Not on deck. Somewhere below. Somewhere with noise."

Noisy so they wouldn't be overheard, Gina realized. Noisy so that listening devices would be useless.

Cold air seemed to play across her neck and shoulders, making her shiver. Something had changed.

After leaving detailed instructions with an assistant, she removed her chef's jacket and keyed out of her computer station. "You've got fifteen minutes. That's all I can spare."

Trace glanced at Tobias. "Somewhere close. Maybe a utility area down in engineering."

Tobias was already moving.

"THERE'S NOT MUCH I can tell you." Trace scanned the small room lined with nautical ropes and spare lighting equipment. "It's classified. But I can tell you that we are facing a threat situation."

"So you're not a regular passenger. This is part of your job?" Gina stood stiffly near the wall. "Is the ship in danger?"

"Not that we know of," Trace said.

"Who do you work for?"

"Irrelevant. What matters now is that you do exactly what I say."

"If there's a threat to this ship, I need to report it immediately." Tobias looked angry. "I also need the source of this information."

"You'll be told everything that's permissible. That decision is not mine to make," Trace said.

"Then whose?" Tobias snapped. "I have a duty to my ship, my captain and to one hell of a lot of civilians."

"Someone will be waiting at the dock tomorrow in Puerto Vallarta. He'll fill in the blanks."

Gina threw up her hands. "You're telling us nothing. And why are we standing in this stuffy little room whispering?"

"It's the only place currently secure. We have no reason to think that the ship as a whole is being targeted, but we'll be watching for any signs of that."

"Not good enough." Frowning, Tobias moved past Trace toward the door. "I need to report to the captain. Otherwise—"

The walkie-talkie in his pocket suddenly crackled with static. "Tobias, you are wanted on the bridge. Immediately."

The captain.

Trace crossed his arms. "The captain will be told all that he needs to be told. There will be full approval for whatever orders come down."

"Are we talking about one man or a group of men?" Tobias stood by the door, waiting for answers.

"One man, but he's like no other man you've ever encountered."

Tobias looked back at Trace. "This sabotage in the kitchen—is there any connection?"

"We have no reason to think so."

"But there could be."

"Highly unlikely. But not impossible," Trace added. "Meanwhile I will be in and out of the staff area and kitchen, and I'm going to need an ironclad cover."

"Don't think you can work as part of my staff. We

already discussed that. Besides, you'd practically need a presidential order to get it past corporate."

Trace's mouth quirked slightly. "Let's not bother him if it isn't necessary."

Gina's mouth fell open.

"You could do that, couldn't you?" Tobias said quietly.

"Not me. It's…the job." Trace's voice was cool, precise.

Tobias strode back to the door. "You've bought yourself one hour. Before that time is up, I expect to have e-mail corroboration of everything you've told me. Make sure it's believable and confirmable."

The heavy door hissed shut.

After he had gone, Gina started toward the door, but Trace took a step in front of her. "We're not done here."

"I'd say we are. I don't like secrets and evasions." She blew out an angry breath. "And if something important is happening, why would you want to hang around in my kitchen?"

"Because it gives me acccss to places I need to be. It stops questions when I appear at odd times either day or night. People won't wonder if they think it's personal." Trace put up one arm, leaning against the wall. The same movement brought their bodies closer.

"Personal how?"

"I need you, Gina." His voice was low.

"Need *me?*" Gina stood stiffly. "How?"

"I need *us* together, in and out at all hours, looking happy and distracted and absolutely caught."

"Caught in what?"

His hand curved, slipping along her cheek. *"This."*

CHAPTER TWENTY-SEVEN

HIS LIPS BRUSHED HERS, then locked hard. He pressed her back urgently, her shoulders to the wall and her thighs cradled between his.

Fires raced over Gina's skin. She couldn't seem to breathe, definitely couldn't think straight. "Wait. You—you want me to pretend we're in love, having wild sex on walls and countertops?"

"Bingo."

"But you're not telling me why it's so important?"

Something came and went in Trace's eyes. Impatience changed to wariness. "I can't."

But Gina was tired of secrets and evasions. Caution had its place when you were tempering chocolate or heating sugar for caramel, but not in a relationship.

Or *whatever* this tenuous thing was between them.

"Why don't you find a stranger?"

He gave a tight smile. "I wanted to. A stranger would be smoother, safer." His voice was rough, in stark contrast to his gentle touch. "Because it's been personal since the moment I saw you tottering along Kearny Street, balancing that cake box as if it were a jewelry delivery from Tiffany's. I can't get you out of my mind, and that's a distraction I can't afford."

The words tumbled out, driven by anger.

Gina felt them seep right through her skin into her heart.

"Why didn't you tell me last night?"

"I needed to think things through. This feels like being kicked by a horse." For once he hid none of what he was feeling.

Control would be as important as breathing to a man like this. He didn't look in control now, with hunger etched on his hard features.

"What do you want from me, Trace?"

"You naked in my bed to start."

Heat welled up as his thumb smoothed her mouth slowly.

"Except that's not on the agenda. This is cover, a performance. It's got to look absolutely real, but—" His voice tightened. "But it's going nowhere. Can you live with that?"

She looked at him, her pulse hammering. "Probably not."

He bent his head, his lips feathering across her cheek, along the sensitive ridge of her ear. His tongue followed, making her toes curl with aching pleasure. He was slow and expert, driving her body to respond with a sudden will of its own.

Gina fought an urge to say yes to whatever he wanted.

Her career was in shambles; her health was hanging by a thread. She could be blind tomorrow, trying to feel her way from one side of a room to the other without tripping. She had no business saying yes to anything like this.

She clenched her hands tightly. Otherwise, they were going to slide up and link around his shoulders.

She took a step back.

"Make it clear." She tried to stay stubborn, aloof. "What are you asking me to do?"

His thumb circled the line of her lips. "A performance.

The two of us caught up in a reckless shipboard fling hot enough to convince anyone who's watching."

"This is stupid and pointless. This is—"

"Necessary."

She took a sharp breath, hit by lust. She wanted to feel him against her, inside her. For her, at least, it wouldn't be an act.

Then the deeper meaning of what he'd said hit her. "You think someone is watching us? Here on the ship?"

"I doubt he's here, but he could have people onboard working with him."

She swallowed. She wasn't going to think about sex with that gorgeous body and that dangerously keen mind. "You didn't tell Tobias that."

"I will when he's done with the captain. But first I need your answer. Can you give me a cover that will buy me time? Tobias could be in danger, too, and I need to stay close without triggering any suspicion."

That was hitting below the belt. First he stirred up gut-wrenching lust, and now he made a plea for a friend needing help. How could she possibly say no?

Damn the man. "For how long?" Her body ached with tension. Logic fought with needs she didn't want to face.

"For the rest of the cruise."

"So we do a little bit of *Love Boat,* a little bit of *An Affair to Remember?*" She laughed unsteadily. "Don't ask me to walk in front of a bus."

He looked blank. "What bus?"

"Cary Grant and Deborah Kerr. You never saw it? What kind of life have you led, poor child?"

"Claymores and C-rations. And no, I never saw it."

"It doesn't matter. So you want us to spend the days together. What about the nights?"

His eyes were like brushed steel. "Same thing. Your cabin or mine. Preferably mine, since I've got surveillance equipment there."

"And while we're there…" Gina let the question float unfinished.

She needed to understand the ground rules. She had to know exactly what he expected.

"You sleep, I work. Same room, nothing more."

"I see." She didn't. Not for a second. The lust was mutual. He'd made that clear. So why didn't he want to act on it?

His hand slid up her bare arm. "You need to understand that there's danger involved. There will probably be surveillance that we don't suspect." His hand stopped. "If I had any choice, I wouldn't ask you."

Gina already knew there would be risk. She wasn't stupid. "I can live with that."

Meanwhile, there were other questions to be asked. "Does this involve our country? Is it a question of our security?"

He frowned. "It's important. That's as much as I'm able to tell you."

"And there's one man involved? Only one?"

"In this case, one is more than enough." Trace's voice was grim. "He's as dangerous as they come."

"Why?"

Trace shook his head.

"I don't get a name or description, either?"

"No."

"You don't ask much do you? I pretend to be involved in a gritty affair and risk my neck for a reason I'll never know, to fight a man I'll never see."

"Yes," he said simply.

Gina looked at his calm eyes and her decision came far too fast. "When do we start?"

Trace let out a slow breath. "Be certain. There's no going back once this begins. Any change would be a clear tip-off."

"I'm sure." She put one hand on his arm for emphasis, felt his muscles tense. The movement made her throat turn dry.

She felt the flex and play of his sculpted muscles under her hand and his breath against her cheek. When had every sense become so acute, her body turning traitor to her mind?

"I can handle the risks," she snapped.

"Can you? Can you stay detached, even if I'm touching you? Even if we're kissing slow and wet?" His voice turned harsh. "And looking like we want to have blind, reckless sex on every possible surface every hour."

Oh, the image burned. White-hot, it drove right into her skull. Oh, yeah, she could look like that…without even trying.

She could start right here, in fact. Maybe *he* was the one who'd have trouble staying detached.

"I'm not sure I can trust you."

"I'm not sure you can, either." His voice was harsh. "You twist my guts when you're in the same room. I won't be acting." He made a flat, angry sound. "Around you everything seems too alive, too vivid. But we can't cross the line. Sex—good sex—requires time and a commitment, neither of which I have."

Looking into his eyes, Gina saw his rough honesty and the deep code of ethics that he lived by. A little voice told her to run while she still could.

A braver voice told her to take what time there was and forget about tomorrow.

Even if he left her with nothing but memories and a broken heart.

"Okay," she rasped. "No crossing the line. Are you going to tell me how we do that? Because I sure as heck don't have a clue."

A muscle moved at his jaw. "If it were just us, you'd be upstairs in my bed right now. You'd be sweaty, naked and exhausted." His eyes were hot. "And I would just be getting started."

Desire crackled, filling the small space. Gina's body flushed in hidden places. "You must be pretty good, Lieutenant."

"I'm good." No false modesty. "With you, I'd be...unforgettable." He muttered a curse. "You're entitled to something better than a few nights, Gina. Meanwhile, I have a job to do, and I don't intend to screw up. You understand?"

She blocked a string of hot images and smiled crookedly. "Sure I understand. *Love Boat* in the corridor, *Leave it to Beaver* once the door is closed."

He didn't smile. "That's the playbook. It has to be. Can you stay calm and be convincing, even if things turn messy?"

Oh, she could be convincing. It would be as easy as breathing. Gina decided to prove it. "Like this, you mean?"

She gripped his shoulders and moved in fast, before he could answer. Just one hot kiss, she thought. That would be proof enough.

But when she pulled his head down, her eyes closed and her heart fluttered. She skimmed his mouth and then bit his lower lip, her tongue wrapped around his.

He made a harsh sound.

As his hands tightened on her hair, she smoothed the small bite with her tongue, tasting his mouth while the kiss turned hot, veering to the edge of control.

Dangerous, she thought. And perfect.

Trace didn't move, feeling the top of his head go up in flames. The woman was sleek and stubborn, and one touch had him tied up in knots.

But with Cruz in the equation, there was no room for distraction or mistakes. So he leaned back and kept his expression cool, hiding the fact that this woman might just have torn out his heart.

"Not bad, Ryan."

She pulled away, hands on her hips. Color burned across her cheeks. "Not bad?" Her breath came in short, angry jerks. "Why don't you take your mission plans and shove them up a small, dark place?"

Definitely steamed, Trace thought. "No need to shout. The kiss was perfect," he said roughly. "You know it and I know it." He cupped her hips, pulling her closer until they were thigh to thigh, heat against heat. "I'd like to take you right here, naked against this wall. It would be the best sex you or I ever had, honey, because I'd make damn sure of that. It would be wet and noisy and we'd both come out of here changed people."

He felt her shiver.

"Then why are we wasting time with talk?" The question was low, almost unwilling. She met his gaze with fierce honesty.

No coyness. No evasions.

Trace shook his head tensely. "Shouldn't. Can't. Won't. End of story."

He only wished it were that simple. Wished he could stop smelling her faint perfume and dreaming about her slim, strong legs wrapped around him as she took him deep inside her.

He wanted to hear her first moan as he drove her over

the edge in passion. He wanted to watch her as he sent her up again before the first climax had ended.

No, for him this wouldn't be a performance at all.

Because she seemed too calm, he ran his hands over the rise of her breasts, pleased when he felt the crests tighten instantly. His thumbs moved slowly back and forth until her breath caught.

But he forced himself to stop, to lower his arms as if he had touched a brick wall rather than a living, breathing, infinitely desirable woman. Irritated by his need, he gestured toward the door. "Let's go. I don't want to leave Tobias alone."

Her eyes darkened. She seemed to jolt down to earth the second he said her friend's name. "Tobias," she whispered. "Right. We—we should go."

Trace watched her fumble with her hair, vainly trying to smooth the tangles left from their hot grappling. Her jerky movements amused even as they seduced him. There was no reason for him to be so enchanted. There was no excuse for feeling so dangerously moved.

Except that she filled some hole, some dark space he'd never allowed himself to acknowledge before.

Was that part of the magic?

The SEAL took a slow, hard breath. He was prepared to push his emotions deep, where they wouldn't threaten his mission. But for one moment he didn't move, savoring the sight of her flushed face and clearly aroused nipples beneath her shirt.

Simple, yet stunning. The woman he'd wanted forever, without knowing it. He'd never have enough of seeing her aroused this way, her eyes dark with passion.

He looked away. Cursed mentally. Counted to five.

When he turned back, she was trying to brush her hair

out of her face. Every motion outlined the perfect curve of her breasts, trembling and tight against her white cotton T-shirt.

Kill me now, Trace thought.

But he couldn't drag his gaze away.

Tugging her hands anxiously through her hair, she glared back at him. "What? Why are you staring at me like that? Is there lettuce between my teeth?"

She had a small streak of chocolate beneath her left ear. Trace had wanted to lick it away the moment he'd seen her thirty minutes before. He thought about how he'd make her come just by the touch of his hands and the slide of his tongue.

Hell.

Sheer lust had never left him so out of balance, with his control shredding. Yet as he stared at her, something hot and possessive gripped his chest. He recognized the lust without a problem. He had felt it before, for women he had forgotten an hour later.

He'd never forget this woman.

Now his lust was mixed with other emotions he had never felt before. Deep and confusing, they wrapped him up in a way he had never felt before. He felt a dangerous tenderness, a bone-deep urgency to protect her from harm, and beneath both a primal need to claim and possess. The force of those feelings infuriated him.

He moved away, keeping his face blank. "Tell me about Tobias."

"He never talks about his past or family or any of the things he did before he came here, but we all know it was something important." Her eyes clouded. "If a man as strong as Tobias can be hurt, then God help the rest of us."

Trace thought that she was just as strong and resourceful as Tobias in her own way, but all he did was shake his head. "Everyone has weak spots."

"I doubt that you do."

He never had before he'd met her. She had become his only point of vulnerability. God help them if Cruz discovered that. "In my line of work, weak spots are a definite negative."

"What exactly *is* your line of work?"

"This and that. Here and there."

"So it's classified. I'm glad. If you're that good, you'll keep Tobias safe." Her hands smoothed her T-shirt. "I'll do whatever you need."

Another man might have found an excuse to take advantage of that promise, but the temptation never entered Trace's mind. He tucked a wayward strand of hair behind her ear, skimmed his hand around the neckline of her T-shirt to slip the label back inside. When his hand moved lower, her breath caught in a sigh.

She looked away, bit her lip. "Maybe—you should stop. No one is watching us now."

He wanted to take all day. He wanted to watch more color flare into her cheeks. This was another thing Cruz had taken away from him.

He smoothed the shoulders of her T-shirt and stepped back. "I need food." His voice was harsh. So much for this being a performance. "Why don't you give me some kind of dessert for Tobias? When I deliver it, I can have a closer look at his office and go over preparations for forced access." He wouldn't give her more details than this.

She nodded slowly. "I can do that. His éclairs were still on the counter when we left."

She turned. Her shirt was straightened, her hair now sleek

and tidy. She looked every inch the cool professional. "How do I look?"

"Good enough for me to eat." His voice was hard. "Very slowly."

There was the heat, flaring into her cheeks.

Another time, Trace thought.

With luck when this was over...

He pushed the thought away. There was only *now*. Only the mission. Distractions got you killed.

Enrique Cruz had to be stopped for good. Twice before the man had escaped death against impossible odds, walking out unharmed.

No matter the cost, Cruz couldn't escape again.

CHAPTER TWENTY-EIGHT

TOBIAS HALE FINISHED his paperwork.

On the wall to his right, a false piece of plaster hid a fire-proof safe. He should have been thinking about that safe and the precious technology hidden inside it. The package had to be dropped off in Puerto Vallarta when the ship docked. Until then, he was an uneasy babysitter, and Trace O'Halloran's warning had hit him hard. So much for the easy, uneventful trip that Lloyd Ryker had promised.

He checked his e-mail. Then he crossed his hands tightly. Closing his eyes, he felt the weight of his past press down like a moving tank.

His life had held memories of too many hard decisions. The past came back to mock him now with choices made and roads not taken. At the time his choice to walk away had seemed the only way to protect those he loved.

Tobias had regretted that decision every day of his life for the past seventeen years. Yet he knew he would do it all again.

Two pictures rested against the wall at the corner of his desk. Gently, he lifted the closer one, the same way he had done every day for almost two decades.

A slender, anxious boy stared into the camera. One hand gripped the old-fashioned bicycle he had just purchased with hard-earned savings. That day, rich with the drone of cicadas under a hot, hazy sky, was as clear to Tobias as yesterday. He closed his eyes, ran one hand over his face.

Too many regrets.

There had been another person there that day. Shining black eyes. A strong, slender body and capable hands.

A kiss that could drop a man to his knees.

The boy's mother had opposed the bicycle, determined that every precious penny go toward college. It was the only time Tobias had disagreed with her on anything important. A boy was entitled to a bicycle, he had argued. The happiness flaring across his son's face had convinced him it was the right decision.

Two weeks later, everything had crashed down around him. His career. His wife's respect. His son's love.

All destroyed by unscrupulous men caught in their hunger for money and power.

Old news, Tobias thought wearily. He rested the photograph back on the corner of his desk, staring at the face of his son seventeen long years past.

Too many regrets.

Too many secrets.

He turned slowly in his chair, his eyes bleak. His hand moved toward the telephone, dialing the number that he had long ago committed to memory.

He stopped before he finished the area code. There was no point in doing more because there was no way to go back.

Maybe it was fair that someone was targeting him now. But he didn't want anyone else caught in the crossfire. Not Gina, not her tough naval officer. Not anyone aboard the ship.

He stiffened as the phone on his desk rang shrilly.

He glanced at the number, noted the unfamiliar area code and was tempted to ignore it.

But Tobias had been a professional too many years to ignore his duty now. He took a deep breath, swept up the phone. "Security."

Static crackled.

"Hello?"

He heard a click, as if the phone call had been routed.

And then the voice swirling out of the past. Deeper than he expected. Cool and hard and professional. The sound brought pleasure and unbearable pain—along with a jolt of immense pride.

"I'll be coming aboard tomorrow. I'll be with the first group on deck in Puerto Vallarta. We'll meet in your office at 1100 hours."

"Who is this?" Tobias had to ask. He had to hear the words.

"You know damn well who this is."

His hand closed on one of the cold picture frames. He saw the boy the way he'd once been, full of hope and love, standing with a used bicycle that might have been a rare treasure made of gold. "Say it. Say the words."

"Still giving orders?" The tough voice cut like cold steel. "Too bad for you that I stopped listening years ago. So let's get one thing straight. This is business, pure and simple. I'll do what I have to do, and then I'll leave. Don't read anything into it because I'm *not* your son, and you're definitely not my damned father." The phone slammed down.

Ishmael Teague.

Once Ishmael Hale, before he'd taken his mother's maiden name in a move that had severed the last strand of connection between them.

Tobias didn't move. He felt a sharp, burning pain at his chest. He forced himself to relax, to take steady, controlled breaths. He needed his work more than ever now. Without it he would go right over the edge.

He and Gina were alike that way.

So he sat in his desk chair, working to stay calm. Finally he succeeded.

Years before he had been assigned to work a mob-connected case in Hollywood for the FBI, and his cover had been as a stuntman. He'd been damn good at the job, too, Tobias thought. One day, after a grueling scene in which he'd been dragged by a runaway horse, he caught the attention of the Duke himself. John Wayne had leaned back in his lanky way, stretching long legs in front of him. Tobias could never remember the exact words, but the message had been clear.

If you have a choice, die in the saddle.

It was advice Tobias meant to take seriously. It had prompted him to help Gina and buy her some time.

He glanced down at the pictures on his desk, shoving away all the pain and cold regrets.

He damn well wasn't going to go out any sooner than he had to. Meanwhile, he had the safe to recheck and a call to make to Lloyd Ryker in New Mexico. After that there was a stubborn witness waiting to be interviewed in the infirmary.

IZZY TEAGUE STARED DOWN at the neatly sorted papers, the carefully chosen ammunition next to maps of coastal Mexico, all stacked in water-tight bags on his desk. His eyes were as cold as the memories that flooded over him from a past that had finally stopped waking him up at night.

His first sleep-away camp.

His first bicycle.

His first fishing trip.

His hands clenched as he bit off a curse.

Old news. He wasn't going to waste his time in a tearful trip down memory lane.

He had no regrets. On a bright summer day in August his father had packed his bag and left without an explanation or a backward glance. That same day Izzy had learned the price of letting anyone get too close.

He had never made that mistake again.

His mother hadn't remarried. Stubborn and energetic every day of her life, she had made a lonely, outcast boy feel loved and valued when he was too smart or too fast— or too black—to fit in.

Izzy didn't miss his father. Only a bastard would walk out and leave his family flat, without one letter or phone call in the years that followed. Izzy figured he was better off without that man in his life.

Now fate was tossing them together again.

He pushed back his chair, shouldered his single travel bag and flipped off his office lights. Lloyd Ryker had apologized when he brought up the mission. Agents had no business dealing with family, he had explained. Emotions clouded judgment, brought conflicts of interest and forced painful choices.

Not for him, Izzy had said flatly. The man named Tobias Hale was a stranger in every way that mattered. The blood tie between them was an accident, an irrelevant twist of fate and nothing more. If he had wanted to, he could have found Tobias anytime, using the security and surveillance skills that made him a key asset to the Foxfire program.

But Izzy had never had the slightest interest in looking. His father was dead. He had died the day he walked out on his mother without any sign of regret. The memories of that man were buried in the same trash with all the other broken and ruined things from Izzy's past.

He walked outside and kicked his door shut with one foot. All that mattered now was tracking down Enrique Cruz and taking him off the board for good. The last time they had met, Cruz had nearly killed Izzy.

Oh yeah, this was definitely personal.

Cruz would not be walking away this time. The rogue agent's extraordinary abilities had to be contained before he inflicted more suffering on innocent people. And he'd struck cleverly, hoping to force Izzy's support by threatening the life of his father in half a dozen anonymous e-mails.

Except Cruz hadn't done quite enough research. Because Ishmael Teague didn't care a damn whether his father lived or died.

ENRIQUE CRUZ TOOK his time looking at her.

She was well worth looking at, with skin like silk. Golden hair that tumbled around flushed cheeks. She was hot and reckless and didn't give a damn about ethics or rules.

When he'd heard about the job she wanted done, he had been shocked at his good luck for putting him exactly where he wanted to be. Of course Blaine hadn't guessed that. As far as she knew, he was a freelance computer hacker with a general grudge against authority.

Every employer knew Cruz by a different name. In Asia he had been Rock Malone. Hollywood movie names always impressed them.

In France he was Peter DeNiro. He always let them think he was a distant relation to Robert.

In Colombia he was simply known as Carlo. He had killed the only two men who had asked for his real name.

Now people knew better than to ask.

Here on the cruise ship, he used a completely new identity based on papers set up months before. After completing his work at the security office, he'd vanish into the night, find his waiting car and collect his millions from an eager buyer.

But he had time before the drama began, and he intended to enjoy it.

The cabin was dark. The handcuffs swaying in his fingers clicked softly. He wasn't surprised that Blaine couldn't take her eyes off the cuffs. Her face held revulsion—along with curiosity. They always wondered what it felt like to give up control, he thought grimly. Even the tame, quiet ones.

And Blaine was definitely not tame and quiet.

He gripped her hands, snapped the cuffs in place. He liked the fear that darkened her eyes, paled her cheeks.

"What are you doing? Damn it, I never agreed—"

"Of course you didn't. That's the whole point."

"But—"

"Shut up, Blaine." It took only a flick of his wrist to toss her back onto the bed. In less than twenty-four hours he'd be off the ship with his stolen package. In forty-eight hours he'd be somewhere south of Fiji sipping absinthe on his private beach.

It bothered him a little that the job seemed so easy. The security chief was experienced, but an amateur, and there had been no sign of any Foxfire men aboard. If so, Cruz would have picked up their energy immediately.

Of course, he hadn't gone out for meals or any activities. He wasn't about to push his luck. The stubble he'd grown covered his features nicely, and cosmetic surgery had filled in any gaps. Even if Wolfe Houston or Lloyd Ryker stood next to him, neither one would have recognized him.

A pillow hit the floor.

Blaine's eyes glinted with fury. But she couldn't look away. Cruz knew that his scar fascinated her.

He slid his hand along her chest and over her thighs, watching desire smoke in her eyes. She was a real little bitch, his Blaine. Too bad he couldn't take her with him afterward.

But there could be no loose ends once he left the ship. Ryker would have dogs and men combing every inch of deck and checking every contact.

Cruz's eyes hardened. He'd never go back into Ryker's cage. His millions would buy him a few more years of safety and time to plan his next act of revenge.

Meanwhile, Blaine was cursing, trying to wriggle free.

But her eyes gleamed, hot with fear and excitement. And Cruz had a few hours to kill.

CHAPTER TWENTY-NINE

TRACE DUCKED A PAIR of volleyballs, skirted a limbo contest and strode across the deck. By habit he assessed the passengers around him, alert for any movement that seemed out of the ordinary.

Gina was in her kitchen making *pâte à choux,* whatever the hell that was. Tobias was running his monthly scan of all employee ID cards and checking for current invalid photos, which would keep him safe in his office for another two hours while Trace ran an errand.

He was going to have to brief Ford McKay on the new developments. The man was not going to be happy when he learned there was a threat aboard the ship, and Trace couldn't blame him for that. But he owed it to McKay to warn him. Navy SEALs had a tendency to jump right into a problem, and Trace couldn't chance that.

He checked both fore and aft promenade decks, hoping he could engineer a "casual" encounter, but the McKay family was nowhere to be found. He had made it his business to know that the triplets were at the junior camp, where they were now learning the intricacies of nautical knots. He had spotted Carly McKay hunched over one of the shipboard computers, manipulating an arcane photography program. That left her nice and tidy, too.

So where the hell was the SEAL?

"Hey, honey, are you free for dinner tonight? We could have an amazing dessert. Your cabin or mine?" A slightly drunk female voice drifted across the deck.

Then he heard a familiar voice in response. "Thanks for asking, but I'm having four gorgeous redheads for dinner in my cabin. Prior arrangements." Ford McKay was carrying a water bottle under one arm and a child's lunch box under the other. He smiled politely at a brunette in a bathing suit that could have fit inside a medicine bottle.

The woman blew out an angry little breath. "Some of us have all the luck." She flounced off, showing an extraordinary amount of cleavage.

Trace glanced at Ford McKay. "They hit on you, too? Even with the wedding ring?"

"Morning, noon and night," McKay said. "It drives Carly nuts. My girls think it's pretty funny. Of course we told them that the ladies want to go have ice cream. I figure we can buy two or three more years of innocence before we have to explain the intricacies of serial dating and protected sex." McKay gave a little shudder. "Just thinking about it gives me gray hairs, pal."

Trace chuckled. "And you've got to do it not one time but three times. Good luck."

Ford's eyes narrowed. "No way. That's one conversation that's taking place as a family unit."

This was a different side of fatherhood, something that Trace had never envisioned. It amused him to see the tough Navy SEAL sweating over a family biology session.

It also, in some obscure way, left Trace feeling jealous. "How about a run up on the sports deck? If you can't escape them, at least you can outrun them."

Ford's eyes narrowed. "Works for me. Except something tells me we won't be discussing table settings or party drinks."

The man was sharp, but Trace had expected nothing less. He simply nodded, and neither man spoke as they made their way across the crowded exterior deck, up a flight of stairs and onto the jogging track. They had a 360-degree view of the ocean, shimmering blue and cool as far as the eye could see. Seabirds circled madly.

Off to the west, Trace saw a gray body breach in an explosion of white foam. "Damn, that was a whale."

"I'd say so." Neither man moved, stunned by the majesty of the water's largest mammal engaged in a leap for sheer pleasure.

Trace preferred the bustle of a working military ship any day, but he had to admit that a view like this would be hard to forget. He slipped his water bottle into a pocket and set up an easy pace, matched by Ford.

"Let's have it. My girls told me about the kitten, and I chewed their tails big-time, but you're not frowning at the Pacific because of a stowaway cat."

"I wish I were. I was told to speak to you by someone you know. Izzy Teague," he said quietly.

"I know Teague," Ford said flatly. "If he's involved, things aren't good."

"I gather you two worked together once or twice?"

"Not at liberty to discuss it, O'Halloran." Ford's mouth was set in a flat line as he glared out at the sea. "I sure as hell didn't come on this trip to take care of business. If there's a hint of a risk, I want my family off the ship now."

"We have no reason to think the ship or its passengers are in danger."

"It's Diaz in Colombia, isn't it?" Ford's voice was cold as a North Sea wind.

"Not Diaz. He came up clean."

"Diaz is never clean." Ford stared out at the water, waiting for Trace to fill him in. "You need backup? Is that it?"

"It may become necessary. Mainly I need to know you and the redheads are safe. We can't afford any surprises."

"So you're warning me ahead of time to stay out of it unless you give me the signal?"

"That's about it."

Ford stared out at the water. "You can't tell me anything more?"

"Someone has targeted the Chief of Security aboard the cruise ship. The man may attempt to board sometime during the cruise if he isn't already here."

"You've got my help." The SEAL's voice hardened. "But I want my family put off at Puerto Vallarta."

"We could do that, but it would be a signal to anyone running surveillance that we are aware of the plan and taking precautions."

"I won't put my family in danger," McKay snapped. "When the bullets fly, anyone nearby can get hurt. What about the rest of the passengers? Aren't they entitled to protection?"

"They'll get protection. We have an undercover team coming aboard tomorrow." Trace didn't mention the Foxfire divers who were boarding the ship from the seaward side sometime in the night, ready to be placed in secure cabins. They would remain out of sight as backup in case the threat escalated.

The fewer people who knew that fact, the better. There was little doubt Cruz had eyes and ears on board the ship.

McKay shook his head. "Not good enough. I want my family out of range. Make up some excuse. We'll have Carly pretend that she got an urgent assignment."

"And you would stay behind? Another tip-off, I'm afraid. Anything that calls attention may actually put your family in danger. So I have to ask that you leave them right where they are. We don't want our suspects to panic and run. Or worse, start shooting."

"I knew a backyard vacation was a better idea," McKay said grimly. As the two men jogged along the windblown deck, he scanned the horizon. "When I married Carly, I swore I would never allow my job to put her at risk. I can't go back on that promise now."

"Izzy is bringing someone in especially for them. She comes highly recommended."

"She?"

"You have blinders about women in field positions?"

"They're just as good as the men I've fought with. Some were much better. If Izzy picked her, she will be the best of the best." McKay rubbed his shoulder slowly. "I just don't like the idea. You and I both know there are no guarantees."

"We also know it's a bad idea to rock the boat."

McKay wound down his run and walked to the rail, staring out over the water. "I'm trying to believe that." He leaned one elbow on the rail and turned. "So what's the magic code word, just in case things heat up?"

"Izzy will find you. But don't waste sleep. We've got everything covered."

But with Cruz, nothing was ever completely covered.

THE MAN WAS DEFINITELY good with his hands.

He had grated, sliced, whipped and pureed his way

through almost three hours of nonstop work. Gina frowned, shoving her hair back out of her eyes. Through it all, Trace was precise and uncomplaining. His spatial sense and reflexes were impressive.

And with both sleeves rolled up high, he had fantastic forearms. He could be a line cook for her any day.

She reminded herself he'd be gone as soon as his business was done. Maybe in hours.

Footsteps approached behind her. "Brownies are done." Walking past from the oven, Trace ran a hand along her waist.

Her pulse kicked.

As he turned back from the refrigerator, he leaned down for a swift, hungry kiss that left her cheeks warm with color.

"You can't…"

"Sure I can." He pulled her closer and his tongue brushed hers, hot and unexpected.

She frowned, shoving her hair back out of her eyes, seeing the challenge in his eyes.

An act.

Take this for an act, then.

She turned, wrapped her arms around his neck and forgot that she was in a busy kitchen. Forgot that he was leaving and this was just a performance she had agreed to carry out.

Because it was definitely no act for Gina when she slid her body against his and felt his thighs tighten. His fingers locked on her waist.

She didn't want him to let her go. Not ever. She didn't want to stop feeling this alive and reckless.

This *happy.* Crazy or not, he made her pulse skip and the air dance.

Someone cleared his throat behind her.

Gina looked up to see John Riley, Tobias's youngest security officer, standing beside the stainless steel counter.

"Sorry to bother you." He looked a little embarrassed. "Tobias asked me to come and see if you needed help." He glanced at Trace, then looked away. "I mean, carrying the stuff for the meeting tonight. The poker stuff, I mean."

Gina smoothed down her hair and tried to settle her jangled nerves. "Tonight. Sure. I've got the things ready. If you want—"

"She doesn't need help," Trace cut in calmly. "I'll manage whatever she needs to carry. But thanks for stopping by."

Riley glanced at him again and smiled a little. "Sure. Whatever you say." He gave a little nod at Gina. "I'll tell Tobias that everything's covered."

TRACE WAS AS SUSPICIOUS as hell.

He had the uncomfortable feeling that jealousy might have played a small part in his reaction, but he wasn't letting Gina walk anywhere with anyone he didn't trust.

And that meant just about everybody.

At seven-forty-five on the nose they took the elevator down to the third level crew deck and stopped outside a room like any other. Beyond the door, Trace heard male laughter and the drone of a TV football announcer.

Yeah, he was suspicious, all right. "You sure I can't come in?"

Gina shook her head. "Sorry. It's one of our rules. Pain of death, no outsiders."

Trace frowned. "You must play for high stakes."

Gina made a noncommittal sound. "High enough. But we don't discuss it with anyone. Another one of Tobias's rules."

Trace leaned down, sliding his fingers along her cheek. "I could convince you." He bit her ear gently.

"You think?"

He moved closer until their thighs brushed. He felt her breath catch. "Honey, give me five minutes and I'll kiss you until you forget how to breathe. Then you'd let me in."

The double entendre was deliberate. He wanted her to feel the same heat he was feeling. This had gone beyond being an act.

Truth be told, it had never been an act for him.

Laughter echoed down the hall. Tobias was coming closer, making a joke about his favorite hockey team. Trace leaned down, his mouth brushing Gina's. His hands skimmed her ribs, closing beneath her breasts and tracing slow circles that left her shivering.

Tobias walked by and raised one eyebrow.

Somebody else gave a good-natured whistle.

The cabin door opened to the noise of a football game. The two men vanished inside.

"Distracted yet?" she murmured.

"Which side are you on, honey?" Trace released her and put her canvas bag into her arms. "You know, I really love to play poker. Are you absolutely sure I can't go in?"

"Absolutely sure. Tobias's rules."

What the hell was so secret about a poker game?

The door opened, and Tobias stuck his head out. "You coming in or not, Gina? We're ready to deal."

Trace had a quick view of small tables set up with poker chips and beer. A big TV on the far wall displayed ESPN.

Poker, all right.

"Go on, honey. Knock 'em dead. I'll pick you up later."

CHAPTER THIRTY

INSIDE THE SMALL CABIN, ESPN was blaring and beer was cooling on ice. Chips and pretzels and six kinds of dip were scattered over the various surfaces. Most of the men had their feet up with cigars in hand.

Unlit cigars.

As soon as Gina closed the door, they zipped open their basic black gym bags.

A beer can popped. Someone sat back and sighed. "Hell, have you ever seen mohair like this? Talk about soft."

"It had better be at $32 a ball," Tobias grumbled.

Suddenly there was yarn everywhere. Knitting needles appeared.

Riley opened a can of beer and nodded at Gina. "Did you get the stuff in San Francisco?"

"All here. Merino wool for you. Homespun alpaca from Uruguay for Tobias. Three new sock patterns and a set of cable needles. Six skeins of hand-painted cotton, too." Gina smiled. "In case anyone wants to make a lace tank top."

She ducked as chips and paper cups flew in her direction. "Okay, okay, just joking."

As she opened her bag, she answered questions, took cash and doled out the yarn and knitting supplies she'd been delegated to pick up in San Francisco.

The Thursday-night poker club didn't exactly play poker. But the seven men would have yanked their own teeth before they'd admit their guilty pleasure to the rest of the ship.

Gina dug in her own bag, pulled out a ball of hand-dyed cotton and frowned.

Tobias looked over his shoulder. "What's wrong?"

"I lost two of my new doublepoint needles. They're my good metal ones, too. It will take two weeks to get another pair ordered for pickup when we dock."

Instantly four men offered up replacements.

She finally settled for a set of ebony needles from Tobias. He had broken his guilty secret to Gina several years earlier when he'd noticed her knitting. Several other men had joined over the following months. As the group sailed furiously through raglan sweaters and self-striping socks, they stopped to pound the table when their team made a bad play.

Gina enjoyed every second.

"Hey, Tobias, what do you make of that thing with the yacht today?" Riley passed around a bowl of chips, grinning. "Two women trying to flag down a cruise ship seems a little strange to me."

Tobias shook his head. "They were drunk. Maybe more than drunk. It's lucky they didn't end up pinned to the bow of the ship." He waved his unlit cigar. "Some people shouldn't be given boating licenses, not for any amount of money."

"I didn't hear anything about it." Gina put up her feet and started purling the sleeve of her unfinished shrug. "When did it happen?"

"About 7:20. The ship slowed down slightly, but the passengers wouldn't have noticed. The captain isn't broadcasting the incident."

"Yeah, but you're leaving out the best part." Russ Wilhelm, the head of engineering, dug into a bowl of popcorn. "The women were almost naked. They could barely walk. All they kept saying was that they'd run out of gas and would we give them a tank." He shook his head. "Trying to flag down a cruise ship for gas. Very funny."

"Very dangerous," Tobias snapped. "Hold on, here comes the play. Turn up the sound, Riley. If my guy makes this pass, you all owe me twenty bucks."

Gina had finished half of her sleeve when Riley sat down beside her. "So this guy in the hall. It's getting a little...serious?"

Gina made a noncommittal sound.

"Not that I'm prying." Riley shifted a little, looking embarrassed. "I just don't want you to get hurt. I mean, he's a passenger."

"Actually, he's an old friend of Gina's. I know his father, too." Tobias looked across the top of tortoiseshell reading glasses. "He's got juice, too. Knows one of the cruise line brass. He's got approval to do just about whatever he wants on board." Tobias laughed shortly. "If he wants to waste a perfectly good vacation slaving in the pastry kitchen, who are we to complain?"

"So he's working?" The head of engineering raised an eyebrow. "He must be pretty sold on the head pastry chef. Not that it's any of my business." He looked straight at Gina. "That report Blaine made is crap. Everybody knows it's crap. Don't let it worry you."

The others muttered agreement, and Gina felt a wave of affection for these men offering her their quiet support.

Then Tobias looked around and stabbed his unlit cigar at the air. "Hey, Riley. Stop hogging those chips, will you?"

AT 11:10 TRACE WAS out in the hall pacing.

He checked his watch every two minutes, listening to the dim sounds of the football broadcast in the cabin.

What the hell were they really doing in there? Gina had never mentioned liking poker.

He took a deep breath. He wasn't going to be suspicious. Gina was as straight as they came, and he trusted whatever she did. There had to be a good reason she was invited and no strangers were allowed.

He just couldn't figure out what the hell it was.

He'd passed by Tobias's office twice. All alarms were set and no motion of any sort was indicated. He'd rigged up a remote alarm to his wristwatch, thanks to directions from Izzy.

His cell phone vibrated.

"Yeah."

"Joe's here." Izzy sounded more tense than usual. "Have a report on those meds you mentioned."

Gina's pills.

"Hit me."

Izzy gave him the facts in cold, scientific detail. He didn't omit the optic nerve damage or the negative prognosis. He didn't omit the fact that the medicine was experimental and would only delay progress of the nerve damage, not stop it.

Trace put one hand on the wall. "Shit."

"That's not the technical term, but yeah. I have to agree. There's more, but you don't need it. Basically, she could be blind before the year is out. I'm…sorry."

After he hung up, Trace stood staring down the row of cabin doors, feeling as if he were in a tunnel that was closing in fast.

Gina...blind?

He took one hard breath, feeling sick.

CHAPTER THIRTY-ONE

WHEN THE DOOR OPENED, Tobias was carrying a gym bag over his shoulder. "Some game. You all owe me a twenty, remember that."

Gina was the last to leave, flipping off the lights behind her. She smiled when she saw Trace.

"Are you broke?"

"No, I did pretty well tonight." She shook what sounded like a lot of change in her pocket. "Straight flush. Who knew?"

"Wait. You dropped something." Trace leaned close, pointing to a bright thread on her sleeve.

"Oh, that's just…lint. It must have gotten on there in the laundry."

"Doesn't look like lint. It looks like…fiber or something." He'd find out exactly what, Trace thought as he pocketed the piece of red string. The mystery of the Thursday-night poker session was far from over, as far as he was concerned.

The others were talking about the Cowboys and the Colts and who had screwed up worse than usual. They were all relaxed and grinning. It definitely sounded like a poker game.

Trace decided to forget about it for the moment.

He gestured to Tobias, who dropped back and walked beside him, out of range of the others. "It was all quiet upstairs. I checked three times. But I'd like another look at those surveillance cameras you set up in there."

"Be my guest." They were nearing the kitchen when Tobias called back to Gina. "You have any more of that white chocolate carrot cake?"

"I made one this afternoon."

"Maybe your 'assistant' here could drop some off. I've got a pile of paperwork to finish before I call it a night."

"Sure thing."

Trace took her bag and kept on walking. After a moment, he shook his head. Her bag definitely felt too light to be holding cards or poker chips.

THE SECURITY OFFICE WAS empty when Trace carried a wedge of cake across to Tobias. "Did Izzy contact you?"

"Around seven. We made some modifications to the alarm system by phone." Tobias glanced up at the ceiling. "The cameras have redundancy in case one of them gets smashed."

Trace checked the walls and ceiling, then walked into Tobias's private office. "Behind the plaster?" he asked quietly.

"Upper left. The safe is cut right into the molding."

"Nice camouflage job." Trace put his plate down on the desk. "Gina says to enjoy. And you shouldn't think about the calories."

Tobias groaned. "I didn't until you brought it up."

Trace sat down in a chair opposite the concealed wall safe. "Open it. I want to check the chip we programmed in my watch."

Tobias slid a finger along the molding and a small crack

appeared. He entered a random set of numbers in the recessed keypad.

Three seconds later Trace's watch lit up like Times Square on New Year's Eve. "Everything looks fine here." He watched Tobias reset the safe code and then close the door. "Did Izzy Teague tell you about his mother?"

Tobias turned sharply. "What about his mother?"

"Our man in question has been trying to turn Izzy for six months. His latest trick was to send Izzy's mother an IED via fake express courier."

Tobias's hands closed to fists. "And?" he said very quietly.

"And Marietta Teague is one tough cookie. Knew all about IEDs and didn't go anywhere near the thing. It went off, but all it did was blow up two of her favorite azalea bushes." Trace grinned. "I hear she's mad as hell about that."

Tobias seemed to fall, not sink, into his desk chair. "So all it hurt were her plants?"

"That's what Izzy said. He seemed pretty shaken. You okay, Hale?"

"Fine." Tobias leaned back, his eyes very cold. "Any other developments that might affect my ship and passengers?"

"Nothing yet. But load up on coffee, because the night's still young. And remember," Trace said quietly. "Alarm or not, you check in with me every twenty minutes or I'll be in here breathing down your neck."

WHEN TRACE GOT BACK to the kitchen, Gina was working on a last-minute cake order for a midnight wedding.

He liked watching her work. He liked the way her hands were sure and quick. He liked the way she blew upward when her hair drifted around her forehead and the way she

muttered to herself as she sculpted white petals out of buttercream icing.

He liked just about everything about her.

Usually that thought would have scared the hell out of
him, but not tonight. He didn't fight the feeling. Instead he
analyzed every detail, since analysis was his strong suit.
What he discovered was simple.

He was in deep, caught in emotions he had never felt
before.

Across the room Gina blinked, leaning an arm against
the counter and rubbing her forehead. Trace said nothing
as she dug in the pocket of her chef's jacket and pulled out
a bottle of pills.

A different bottle from the tainted ones. He assumed that
she would have extra medication in a safe place in the
event of loss.

She turned, saw him looking at her and quickly
dropped the bottle back in her pocket. Clearly, this was
nothing she wanted to discuss. Trace followed along, pretending not to notice.

She was entitled to some secrets.

"Anything more you need me to do with these raspberries?"

"We'll flash freeze them, and then I'll make a puree for
the cake topping as soon as I finish this ganache."

She gave her pan a final stir, sprinkled a hint of salt over
the rich mix and took a sample taste. "Umm. After all
these years, good ganache still gives me a jolt."

Trace watched her mouth slide over the small wooden
spoon, drawing out every bit of chocolate with loving attention. The sight stirred rough heat and made him harden at the
thought of his body receiving her slow, thorough attention.

"The raspberries?"

She was staring at him. He realized she'd been talking to him. *Time to focus, meathead.*

"Right here. You want them in the freezer, right?"

Gina looked away, grimacing a little as she nodded. More pain, he thought.

Andreas emerged from a counter work area. "I'm dropping these petits fours upstairs. You two need anything?" He pulled off his work apron and picked up a tray covered with foil, still looking a little pale after his short bout with the flu.

"No, we're good." Gina leaned forward a little, rubbing her neck. "We're almost done here, anyway."

After Andreas left, Gina took a deep breath and rolled her shoulders. "Thanks for being a good sport about the poker meeting."

"I wasn't a good sport. I was damn curious. Still am." He put down his raspberries and leaned around her, reaching for a spatula. His arm nudged her hip and he leaned closer, catching her scent.

Oranges and chocolate. As vibrant and straightforward as she was.

"But I'm smart and I pick my battles. It's one of the first things you learn in basic training." The kitchen was silent, empty. Trace put away his cooking supplies and leaned down to wash his hands. "How are you doing over there?"

"Two more tarts to go. Um, sounds kinky." As she spoke, Gina rubbed a spot on the side of her neck.

Trace moved her hand and took over massaging the tense muscles. "Better?"

She sighed, leaning back against his chest. "I knew you had great hands. I was watching you work. I mean, your hands are *really* good." She made a low sound of pleasure as he followed the curve of her ear. "Oh, yeah. Like that. Just don't stop, whatever you're doing."

Her husky tone made Trace think of other ways he'd like to touch her. Ways that involved her naked beneath him. He couldn't get the images out of his mind.

Time for a distraction.

"You get these headaches often?"

"What headaches?" Her eyes flashed open.

"You're in pain, honey. It doesn't take a genius to see that."

She relaxed a little, her eyes closing again. "They come and go. Everybody has something, right?"

He drew her back, his lips to her neck. "Yeah. Everybody has something." His hands opened over her waist. He inched under the heavy cotton apron tied around her waist. "How about a distraction?"

He could see the door to Tobias's office from where he stood. They were alone, and he wanted her. He also wanted her free of pain. He could give her that much without compromising his mission.

He guided her along the counter until they were away from knives and food—and the kitchen's two surveillance cameras. The knot at her waist slid free and the cotton apron fell. He kissed the curve of her neck while his other hand slid along her waist.

"What—"

"We're alone. Let me touch you."

She started to speak as his callused fingers pushed past lace, edging her heat. She gave a soft gasp. "Trace, I can't—"

"Sure you can. I'm good with my hands. Let me prove it to you."

Her head turned and she found his face, pulled him close to meet her kiss, tongue to tongue.

"Shh." She was damp, shuddering blindly, but Trace took his time touching her, learning her. The moment was rich, filled with his yearning as much as hers. His focus was absolute as he slid deep and felt her open to his slow fingers.

He knew the second her senses clouded and muscles tightened.

Her skin was hot velvet as he slid a finger inside her, stroking in spirals until she whispered his name brokenly.

She bit his mouth, drawing his lip between her teeth. "Don't," she whispered. "Don't stop—"

Watching her, Trace had to have more. With the counter to hide them, with the room silent and empty, he teased through hot, slick folds until she moaned.

Moaned his name, moaned the way he'd imagined she would. Beautiful in her desire, she strained for the thing he had to give. The thing he gave freely.

And then she shuddered and came apart in his hands, her body driving against him while she closed around his fingers that were still moving inside her.

Color flared over her cheeks, and her legs gave way. Silent and protective, Trace caught her with a steadying arm.

"Gina."

The name melted on his lips. Her warmth had touched him, marked him.

He wanted to give her pleasure, make her forget the future. He needed to hear his name on her lips when she crested against him again in blind passion.

She took a shuddering breath. Her eyes fluttered open. She looked dazed. "We can't…"

"We just did," Trace said roughly. He caught her mouth

in a kiss that searched for answers to questions he'd never asked before. The quiver of her lips and the husky catch of her breath made a powerful beginning. Maybe in five years he'd have the measure of her.

Maybe in fifty.

He turned her to face him, watching the color fill her cheeks. *Act* and *performance* were no more than empty words now.

The buzz of his watch alarm made Trace stiffen.

Tobias, checking in.

Twenty minutes gone.

But before he could move, Gina pulled away, smoothing her clothes with shaky fingers. "I have to go."

Trace saw her tension, saw the way she avoided his eyes. "You're done here?"

She nodded, still avoiding his eyes.

"Fine, then you go with me. Your cabin or mine." His voice was cool and impersonal. "You agreed."

"That was before." She leaned back, her knuckles white on the counter. "I can't pretend one minute and forget the next. I'm not like you." She took a long breath. "I'll do what you need and play the game out. But the rest—what just happened..." She shook her head. "No."

Because he wanted to reach out for her, Trace stood motionless.

Because his blood was heavy with need, he kept his face blank.

He shouldn't have touched her, shouldn't want to touch her again, but he did. Instead he drew on training and experience, ruthlessly locking away his feelings.

"Your call." He picked up her white apron from the floor and laid it carefully on the counter. "It won't happen again. Now we'd better go. You need some sleep and I have calls to make."

For a moment there was something haunted in her eyes.

She started to speak, then stopped. "I have to write a note for the morning crew. And I should wait for Andreas. I want to tell him about setup for the midnight wedding event."

"Leave him a note," Trace said flatly. "I'll have Tobias send one of his people over here to keep watch until Andreas gets back."

"But—"

Suddenly Trace gripped her arm, shaking his head. Something rustled out in the corridor, lighter than a footstep, and he pulled her around the corner out of sight behind the big refrigerator and touched her lips, motioning her to silence.

She nodded tensely.

The rustle came again. As Trace moved soundlessly around the counter so that he could see outside, a white form streaked past. Trace caught the cat with one hand and carried him inside.

"The culprit," he muttered. "Sunny's stowaway."

"Tobias was supposed to be watching it." Gina took the wriggling shape and cradled him against her chest. Immediately the cat began to purr, and she smoothed her cheek against the soft white fur. "I see why Sunny lost her head."

The cat burrowed beneath her jacket, meowing.

Trace figured the cat was a lot smarter than he looked.

They were halfway to the elevators when a light flashed on Trace's wristwatch. He took Gina's arm and raced toward the closing doors, pulling her behind him.

"What—"

Trace punched the button for her floor. "Does someone clean your cabin while you're at work?"

"No. Why?"

"Then we've found your thief," Trace said harshly. "Someone just unlocked the door to your room."

CHAPTER THIRTY-TWO

HER LIFE WAS SERIOUSLY screwed up.

Gina didn't know whether she was coming or going, what she wanted or didn't want.

No, she knew that much. She wanted *him.*

But she couldn't want him. Everything was a mess since she'd run into him. She liked things neat and organized, her life like a well-arranged kitchen, but being around Trace O'Halloran was like a crash course in chaos theory.

She closed her eyes, remembering the slow, careful way he'd touched her.

No good thinking about that. She needed time and distance to sort out her tangled emotions.

When she stared across the elevator, he was cool and alert, in full professional mode, reading a text message on the wrist unit that was clearly more than a watch.

As he scrolled through a series of screens, Gina saw him frown. He had to have put some kind of monitor on her door without telling her, taking the whole sabotage issue seriously from the start.

Gina prayed the thief was Blaine. Then she'd have the evidence she needed to clear her name and get on with her life.

The cat meowed against her chest, and she slipped him inside the front of her jacket so he was out of sight.

"Stay at the end of the hall until I see if everything is clear."

Gina didn't want to wait. After all, it was *her* cabin that was being burglarized. She wanted to be beside Trace when he closed in.

But she wasn't stupid, and she didn't insist. "Okay. But make it fast. I want to see Blaine's face when you catch her."

"It may not be Blaine," he said quietly.

Gina didn't have any doubt. Whoever had set up these attacks knew the ship inside and out. It had to be Blaine in search of trouble, pure and simple.

The elevator doors chimed softly. Trace stepped out silently, motioning her behind him. As soon as he saw the corridor was empty, he vanished around the corner.

Gina waited, her heart pounding. She expected to hear Blaine's voice, raised in angry curses that exploded down the hall, but the silence held.

There were no fleeing footsteps, no angry questions. She peeked around the corner and saw that the door to her cabin was open. Trace's back was turned as he crouched on her floor, which was littered with what looked like all her books and most of her yarn and knitting needles.

She shot forward, praying that Trace had caught Blaine at work.

But when she reached her doorway, something red dotted the floor. Over Trace's shoulders, she saw a body sprawled in her desk chair. His face and chest were covered with blood.

Her heart hammered as she stared at the dead man's face. It was John Riley from ship security.

Two metal knitting needles jutted from his neck.

TEN MINUTES LATER Gina was leaning against the wall outside her cabin, trying to ignore the voices and the screech of walkie-talkies. Even though her head was turned, she could still see the dead man's face in her mind.

Eyes glassy and staring.

Hands at his throat.

Half-dried blood everywhere.

Tobias came out to stand beside her. "How are you holding up?"

"I've had better days." She closed her eyes. "So did John Riley," she whispered. "It still seems like a bad dream. Who would do this?"

"I'm going to find out, believe me." Tobias's eyes were cold. "We've got another complication. Remember those needles you lost, the ones you mentioned at the meeting tonight?"

Gina nodded, watching Tobias's team cordon off the area.

"I've checked the ones that were in the body," Tobias said quietly. "I'm afraid that they were yours, Gina. I'm going to have to question you in the murder of John Riley."

All the warmth drained from her face. Tobias thought *she'd* done it? "I'd like you to follow me," Tobias said, his voice carefully neutral.

Trace moved in front of her, one arm steadying her shoulders. "Forget it," he growled. "I was with her all night. I'll swear to that, so you've got no case."

Tobias glanced at two security officers crossing the hall. "I have to take a statement from everyone involved." He nodded at the two men. "Escort her to my office, please."

He didn't meet Gina's eyes.

"This is crap," Trace snapped. "You're wasting everyone's time questioning Gina."

Tobias turned sharply. "A man is dead. Do you expect me to ignore that?"

Gina felt the touch of something cold at her neck. If the attack was meant to confuse and frighten, it was succeeding. If it was meant to destroy her career, it could do that, too.

Down the hall a woman's voice cut through the muted conversations. Blaine pushed past a senior staff member and several security officers. "What's wrong? Why are you—"

She stopped abruptly as the ship's medical staff wheeled a gurney into Gina's cabin. "I don't understand. What happened?"

"You'll be alerted in due course," Tobias said icily. "Please go back to your cabin and clear the hall."

"Not until I know what's going on," Blaine shot back. "I have a right to know if there's a problem—" She looked past Tobias, frowning. "That's Gina's cabin. Isn't that—" The question ended abruptly as she saw the gurney reappear, draped in black plastic. "Someone's dead," she whispered.

If she was involved, she was delivering an Oscar-worthy performance, Gina thought.

Blaine pressed one arm against the wall for support. "Who...who is it?"

Tobias moved in front of her. "All of you, clear the hall. I'll need statements from each of you. I'll let you know when."

Sluggishly, as if in a dream, Blaine turned. When she saw Gina, she stiffened. "What did you *do?*" She charged forward, but Trace cut her off, holding her in place.

"Time out, lady. Now get your ass out of the hall, the way Tobias just told you to do."

Blaine struggled furiously until she was escorted away by two of Tobias's men. Like a woman in a daze, she walked away without looking back.

"THESE QUESTIONS WILL BE recorded. Do I have your consent, Ms. Ryan?"

"Of course." Gina sat stiffly, staring forward. "I have nothing to hide."

"You should have legal counsel present. It's the law." Trace spoke from the back of the small room, his voice curt.

"Lieutenant O'Halloran, if you continue to disrupt this meeting, I'll have you removed." Tobias sat with pen in hand, looking distant. "You are here at my sufferance. This is not a formal police investigation. That will be up to the FBI, assuming they choose to exercise jurisdiction. This meeting is strictly to identify the location and activities of all involved."

"She *wasn't* involved. She was with me the whole night," Trace said flatly.

"You will have your chance to answer questions next. And may I remind you that your interruptions are slowing this process at a time when we all have other important things to do."

"Trace, it's all right." Gina glanced back at him, her eyes cool and glazed.

A glaze he'd seen before in himself as well as others on his team. The glaze acted as a shield, blocking anything personal behind cool professionalism. Where had that skill come from?

She was a pastry chef, not a soldier.

"He has to eliminate possibilities before the truth can be reached," Gina said. "You know that."

Trace crossed his arms. Point taken. He did know that, but how the hell was she managing to keep all her emotions in the background where they belonged, when he couldn't?

And the timing couldn't be worse, creating distraction and confusion when they needed to focus on the security of Tobias's safe. It was just the kind of thing Cruz was capable of doing to suit his own ends.

Ruthlessly, Trace concentrated on the facts and what had to be done next.

Emotions had no place here.

He heard a small squeak from behind the door at his back. They'd had time to hide the cat in Tobias's private bathroom, where he was now well fed and tucked up in a drawer lined with a towel. One problem solved. If only the others were as simple.

He glanced at his watch. Izzy and the Foxfire divers had an ETA of 0300 hours, with a stealth entry via exterior cables. They would immediately scatter in arranged locations throughout the ship.

Trace was fully prepared for more attacks before docking.

"Please state your name and crew ID number." For a moment Tobias's face softened. "Job title also. Please speak directly into the recorder."

Trace stood impatiently and waited for his turn.

Over his head the security monitors winked.

THIRTY-EIGHT MINUTES.

As interrogations went, Tobias had been clean and fast. Gina knew that with the rational part of her mind, but the rest of her was angry and shaken. All she wanted to do now was disappear, away from curious eyes. She sensed Trace beside her and knew without looking that his face would be set in the same mask she'd seen all through the proceedings in Tobias's office.

She looked up as he steered her around the corner. "Where are we going?"

"My cabin. You've got to be exhausted."

"Where will you be?"

"I'll be in and out," Trace said tersely.

Something important was going on, she realized. John Riley's murder had to be part of it. "You're not going to tell me what this means, are you?"

"I don't know what it means." His voice was cold. "Tonight could be a very long night. You'd better rest while you can."

They didn't talk, walking through the quiet corridors with the familiar throb of the engines beneath Gina's feet. But now there was menace in every shadow and danger in every stranger's face.

She shuddered, remembering the blood. Riley's glassy stare of shock and fear. The killer was still here, among them.

A hand gripped her shoulder and she jumped.

"Steady. Just me. We're here."

She was surprised to see they were already at Trace's cabin. The bed was turned down. His clothes were folded neatly on a nearby chair. She fought back a yawn as he put a cell phone on his desk and checked his messages. When he looked up, she was still standing in the doorway, too tired to think.

He pulled her inside, shut the door and slipped off her jacket, tossing it on the foot of the bed. "Get undressed or I'll do it for you," he ordered.

No passion or desire now, Gina thought. Seeing a corpse had that effect on people. First the shock, then the denial. Then this frightening sense of detachment.

She leaned over and tried to untie her shoe, but her hands were shaking and she ended up making a knot. There had been so much blood…and her knitting needles in his neck.

A small sound of horror built in her throat.

She felt Trace's hands on her shoulders. Quick and efficient, he stripped off her cotton shirt and slacks, then pulled her back onto his bed, with his arms around her.

He held her until the shuddering stopped, until her body lost its deathly chill. And she slept.

SHE HEARD FOOTSTEPS and then the sound of the shower.

Gina sat up, wide-awake, and saw that she'd slept for barely an hour. In the second of waking, she'd realized how precious life could be, how easily lost.

And how stupid it was to waste what time you had.

Maybe she was a fool to make the decision she'd just made. Maybe it was simply the result of fcar.

But Gina didn't think so. It would have been far simpler to turn away, close her heart and pretend to be asleep when the shower stopped.

The bathroom door opened.

It took all her courage to stand up and block his way. Her heart pounding, she ran her hands along his damp, naked shoulders and pushed him back against the wall.

"You started something tonight, damn it. Now I'm going to *finish* it."

CHAPTER THIRTY-THREE

HER HANDS WERE shaking.

She'd never been so frightened. If he turned away, brushed her off—

Not tonight. Tonight she wasn't taking no for an answer.

A muscle moved at his jaw as she pulled the towel off his rigid shoulders. It flowed through her fingers, snagged and then dropped to the floor.

After his shower he'd pulled on snug jeans left unbuttoned at the waist, and she took her time looking.

"What are you doing?"

"Making up for lost time. Stop distracting me." She took a deep breath and tugged at the waist of his jeans. The taut denim didn't move.

Was she going to mess this up? Would this be another regret, another chance left untaken in her life?

She gripped his jeans, felt his fingers close over hers.

"This isn't a good idea." His voice was rough.

"Wrong. It's the best idea I've had. Now stop talking and let me—"

"Why should I stop talking?" He pulled her hands from his jeans and pressed them flat against his chest.

His warm, damp chest.

Pleasure cut like a beautifully sharp knife. Her breath backed up as she felt the flex of hard muscles.

"Because you'll ask questions and be logical and try to talk me out of this, but tonight I say to hell with being careful and logical. A man just died in my cabin with my knitting needles through his neck." Her voice broke. "Right now careful and logical doesn't look very good. I want hot and reckless."

"You can't have it."

"Like hell I can't." Her hands headed back down, burrowing under his tight jeans.

"Damn it," he whispered. He slid an arm around her, their bodies fusing as if they'd been made just for this time and this moment. "This is adrenaline and stress. Don't mistake it for anything else, Gina."

Love.

He didn't say the word, but she heard it just the same. "No analyzing. No tomorrow. I want your arms and your body, Trace. Forget all about the mind stuff and the sweet promises. Give me the heat."

That was what she would remember after this night ended and he was gone. The knowledge hurt, but Gina had to be clear that he was leaving, that this was just *now,* just *tonight.*

Temporary would be enough.

She rose to her toes. Slowly, tenderly, she bit his lip and heard his rough curse hiss through the quiet.

A little smile ran through her at the sound. Cursing was good. Cursing meant she was wearing down that iron control.

It meant she was going to get what she wanted.

Feeling a little giddy, she skimmed his chest and then followed those glorious muscles down until she worked her hands into the back of his jeans, finding hot skin. He was commando beneath the denim. Warm muscles flexed under her hands.

Any minute she might just pass out from hypoxia.

Her fingers smoothed and explored, and she felt the press of his erection against her thighs. She realized that Trace was saying something to her, but the sounds seemed to echo through a long tunnel, and all Gina could think of was how they fit together and how warm his body felt and how she wanted to be naked with him inside her.

He said something again, and then his hands tightened on her shoulders. "Slow down, I said. It's not a race."

Wrong. For her everything was a race. Within a matter of months her sight would begin to fade. She wanted a full quota of memories to fill the dark that was coming, and this strong body would be the best of those memories.

"I want to hurry," she said tightly. "I want hot and breathless. Stop arguing with me."

He said something that sounded like *impossible* and shook his head.

"Take your jeans off," she whispered, her voice breaking.

His hands softened. "You're beyond impossible, you know that?" His fingers traced her cheek. Then he lifted and turned her in his arms, pinning her against the wall, and his hand snagged the little red bow at the edge of her red lace bikini briefs.

"Nice." His voice was rough.

The bow popped and the lace slid down her legs onto the floor.

"Very nice," he said hoarsely.

Gina slid her arms around his waist, sighing as rough denim rubbed along her sensitive thighs.

"Help me get rid of your jeans."

His eyes narrowed.

She didn't wait for him to argue. She hooked her fingers through the loops on his waistband and tugged.

The man was built, all right. She realized that the zipper wouldn't move because it was stretched taut. She licked her lips, exquisitely conscious that he was naked under that tight denim.

Her fingers shook. She hesitated, afraid she'd do something wrong and end up hurting him.

His lips brushed her cheek. He seemed to sigh. "Hell, you may as well go on. You won't hurt me."

His erection was clear and obvious. Just as obvious as her desire. Gina was determined to be screwed straight to oblivion and back.

She murmured his name, turning as he kissed the hollow between her shoulders just *right* and she felt heat climb, making her heart pump harder, leaving her shaky and alive and wet for him.

"I don't think a woman's ever tried to strip me before."

But they'd thought about it. Gina had no doubt of that.

Which mattered not at all, because she was the one with her hands on his zipper, and she was the one making his breath come fast and harsh. She reveled in the thought, reveled in the feel of his hands sliding inside her tank top to free her breasts.

The floor seemed to pitch. She gripped his shoulders and sank her nails deep.

Something vibrated between them.

Trace cursed softly. "Give me a second," he muttered. Leaning against the wall, he reached for his cell phone on the desk. "Yeah."

Gina felt his words rumble through his chest as their bodies pressed closer. Dimly she realized he was talking to Tobias.

"Sure. Let me know if that changes. Yeah, twenty minutes will work."

He flipped the phone shut and dropped it on the desk. "We've got twenty minutes. Damned if I'm going to rush through this and walk away."

"Rush," she said between little breathless gasps. "Twenty minutes is a lifetime." Her hands searched and suddenly his jeans were open.

The hot friction of his erection was maddening against her skin.

"*Very* nice," she whispered.

She thought he might have laughed.

Then his fingers tightened in her hair and he brought his mouth down onto hers with an edge of violence. "You're not afraid of fast and rough?"

"Let's see." Driven by a primal need to claim him, she pulled him against her heat.

His jeans rode lower. The denim scraped her thighs with maddening precision.

"How do you do this to me?" His hand slid along her ribs, traced her stomach and nuzzled between wet folds. Slowly he found the tight knot of nerves and stroked her until she shuddered.

With a smooth slide of his hand he sent her up and over, tumbling dizzy and blind while the room spun and she gasped out his name.

He didn't move. Over the pounding of her heart she felt his muscles, rigid and controlled.

Too controlled.

As soon as she could breathe again, she hooked her fingers in his jeans and shoved them blindly to the floor.

Then only need.

Only hot skin against hot skin and the hammering of her pulse.

He kissed her hard and anchored her against the wall. His hand parted her and she felt the sudden fullness as he drove into her. Deep, but not nearly deep enough.

She bit his neck, her body urgent.

He muttered that she was killing him and then their thighs met with hot, tormenting friction. The glint of a smile twistcd his mouth, and she felt his rigid length in long, hard strokes that clouded her vision and echoed in the pounding of her heart.

Sensation claimed her. Their bodies strained, hazed with sweat.

He caught her hips and shifted, then pulled her down slowly while he filled her and Gina moaned with the pleasure of the joining. Inch by inch, ruthlessly controlled, he drove deeper.

His face was taut when she reached down to touch their joined bodies, reveling in the intimate contact. She bit the rugged outline of his shoulder. "I think I'm getting addicted to you."

"Fine with me. I've wanted you this way since I saw you standing on that noisy street corner." He caught her with an arm around her waist and she thought she heard him say her name before he pulled her leg up around his. Hc stopped moving. "Hell. Are you protected?"

Gina stared, desire pounding through her veins. "What?"

"Never mind. I have something in my drawer." He started to turn, but Gina gripped his arm, shaking her head. "There's no need. My medicine has side effects."

He watched her for a moment, his hand moving gently over her face. "We're going to talk about that medicine of yours. That's next on my agenda. But not just yet."

His voice scraped roughly, but his hands were devastatingly gentle as he caught her other leg and wrapped it around him.

"Hold on, because this could get rough."

Rough was fine, Gina thought, feeling the white-hot pleasure start again, her body slick and wet as Trace palmed her, driving her up again. The floor shuddered and the room ran to black.

"More," she rasped, squeezing as she rode down his length.

He groaned her name and she closed her eyes on a sigh as Trace lifted her, then rocked her down, driving her *there* again, their bodies meeting completely.

Now, now, she thought. She couldn't breathe, much less talk, while his hand opened against her. She dug her nails into his shoulder, wanting him to lose that iron control inside her. "I want fast, Trace."

She wanted his control gone.

"Stop protecting me, damn it."

He gave her more, full and hot inside her, and Gina almost passed out with the sudden, thick pleasure. She tensed against him, drawing out his pleasure until his fingers twisted, locked in her hair.

Damp with sweat, he drove her against the wall, drove her hips high as his control finally unraveled and he pounded home inside her. Deep, as far as he could go.

The last thing she remembered was the low, guttural way he rasped her name as he fell with her.

HE COULDN'T BREATHE. Her nails were digging into his shoulders.

Trace couldn't prevent a satisfied smile as he felt her climax. No more questions or suspicion.

Trust.

The knowledge was as potent as any aphrodisiac. In his world, people didn't trust. It was a rule of the game. You watched and waited, and you struck when your enemy was most vulnerable.

If you didn't, you died. Pure and simple.

Trusting felt strange, like trying to walk when your foot was asleep.

Gina's satiated body collapsed against him, and he lifted her up, shifting her in his arms to carry her to bed. She curled toward him immediately, fitting her thighs intimately to his even in sleep.

Hell, the woman was driving him nuts. He'd just had the best sex of his life and he wanted to start in all over again.

As he reached for the towel he'd left on the foot of the bed, he felt a twinge at his collarbone. Another old scar.

Another reminder that trust was a dangerous mistake. For the first time since joining Foxfire, Trace tried to ignore it.

"You were tough with her."

"No tougher than I had to be. I had an investigation to finish. Having a stranger ask the questions would have been far worse for her."

Trace stood on the balcony, where he'd taken Tobias's call. "You could have held off the questions until morning."

"Any unusual routine, remember? That would be a clear sign to this person you say is watching us."

He was right, but Trace didn't have to like it.

"How's she doing?" Tobias asked quietly.

"Sleeping now."

Trace heard the low beep of a cell phone from Tobias's end. "Anything important, let me know."

"Will do."

After the call was finished, Trace paced the balcony, then went back inside. There was nothing else he could do for the moment.

And there was no place he'd rather be than in bed with Gina.

Carefully he stretched out beside her with one arm behind his head, watching her sleep. She did that the way she did everything else, restless and full of energy, scrunching the pillows and shoving her feet out from beneath the blanket. Every few minutes she snuffled and swung around, curling up against his chest, her chin against his neck.

Trusting him absolutely.

Too bad that he was harder than he'd ever been. He was pretty certain he heard her mutter something about a *Bûche de Noël,* whatever the hell that was.

Thanks to his Foxfire genetics, Trace needed no more than four hours of sleep, which had left him time to check in with Izzy, assess the remote camera feeds in the security office and then call Tobias for another update.

Now the rich silence stretched out and every minute felt like a lifetime. He wanted to imagine this moment of contact and trust was real and everything else was the dream. That he'd have long years of watching her sleep and seeing her wake on his pillow.

He pulled out the piece of red yarn he'd found on her sleeve after that poker club meeting. Rolling it between his fingers, he felt a slow grin forming. Like hell she'd been playing poker.

He didn't know how it had happened, but he'd fallen for the woman, from bridge to stern. He ran a hand through his hair and blew out a breath. It was the best thing that had ever happened to him.

It was also coming at the worst possible time.

Trace vowed that he'd find a way to build a future for them. Ryker was going to have to bend his precious rules one more time.

Because Trace had changed somehow over the past few hours. Here in this quiet room, he'd tasted trust.

Now he would never give that up.

CHAPTER THIRTY-FOUR

"YOU KILLED HIM." Blaine stood stiffly in the darkened passenger cabin. "I saw the knitting needles."

"Your friend Imogen did your legwork." Cruz ignored her, keying at his laptop. "You got information, food replaced and a set of Gina Ryan's knitting needles. You'll have to pay her exactly what you promised or she won't keep her mouth shut."

"Forget about Imogen. Why did John Riley have to *die?*" Blaine shuddered.

The man with the scar leaned back, the screen casting restless colors over his face. "He got cold feet. He wanted more cash or he was going to see Tobias. He had to be stopped."

"I never said—we never discussed murder," Blaine hissed. "I never planned anything like that."

"You're in up to your sexy neck, Blaine. Remember that. You planned this with me."

"No." She shook her head slowly. "This has nothing to do with me or Gina. I think you're here for something different. If Tobias knew—"

He knocked her against the wall in one hard blow. "No thinking allowed, *darling.* It could be very damaging to your health. And do me a favor. Don't get cold feet on me."

When Blaine stumbled away, Cruz followed. "If you stick to the rules, you'll come out fine. You may even get your TV series in the end, after the pastry chef is gone." He stroked her tear-streaked face. "But betray me and you're dead, just like our friend Riley. Only in your case, I think a corkscrew might be a much better choice. Or perhaps something less obvious." He stared at her intently, his eyes focused on her throat. Suddenly she went pale and began to struggle blindly for air.

Cruz didn't move, watching her struggles grow.

Then the look in his eyes slowly faded.

Blaine sank against the wall, gasping as she rubbed her throat. "How did—"

"No questions, remember?" He made a dismissive sound. "If you didn't want to play, you shouldn't have come to the party."

She tried to walk away, but he shoved her toward the bathroom. "Go get cleaned up. Your blouse is ripped and you still have work to do for me tonight." He tossed her a piece of black metal the size of a cigarette case. "Don't forget your transmitter."

CHAPTER THIRTY-FIVE

TRACE CURSED SOFTLY as he stared into the darkness. He should have felt wonderful. He'd just had incredible sex with a smart, stubborn woman who fitted against him as if they'd been poured from compatible molds. If Trace had anything to say about it, they were going to have more wild, unforgettable sex soon…and often for a very long time.

The extent of his need scared him. Insatiable, it grew with every glimpse of Gina, every trace of her scent, every sound of her voice.

He stood on the balcony, listening to the scream of the wind. The sound reminded him of old missions and lost friends. As he watched water froth up in the darkness, he realized part of his problem. He was prepared for death. He breathed and lived and slept with it every day. It was life that had him stymied. Life was messy and harsh, with constant change and a demand for painful compromises.

More often than not it was out of control.

Maybe he'd spent too much time in the dark places of the world. For the first time he craved the light Gina promised more than the adventure of his work. Or maybe it was simply the knowledge of Gina in the nearby room, a temptation he should resist and yet couldn't.

It was damn well going to get messy. Trace felt it in his bones.

Restless and edgy, he prowled the length of the balcony, uneasy about something else. Something he couldn't name.

Cruz?

Yet there was no sensation of Cruz's oily energy now. It was something else.

The smell of lavender seemed to spiral up around him, and Trace's mouth tightened. If he was going to have a hallucination, then it damn well ought to be a *whole* hallucination that made some kind of sense.

It's near you both now.

As the words rippled in his mind, he gripped the rail, refusing to turn around.

"Why are you out here when she's inside?"

He knew the voice. He was even perversely relieved that she was back, even though she was a figment of his imagination. Trace didn't believe in ghosts or life after death. Once it was done, it was *done.*

Why didn't this hallucination of his take a flying jump off the balcony?

Dim light swirled across the balcony, and a pale face drifted into view.

"Can't you stop fighting for once?"

Trace grimaced. He wasn't about to answer this gibberish.

A pale body joined the ghostly arm, light rippling out in misty waves. Marshall materialized in front of him, perched on the edge of the railing. Tonight she was wearing black cowboy boots and tight black leggings.

Trace looked out at the sea and tried to ignore her.

"You need to protect her."

He swung around. Since this illusion wasn't going away, Trace decided to face it head-on. "Why are you bothering me?"

"Garbo speaks." Marshall leaned back on the railing, smiling slightly. "You're a tough nut to crack."

"Go away," he muttered.

"I can't. You need help, Lieutenant. You need a *lot* of help. For some reason, I got the job." She frowned, her foot moving restlessly as if she couldn't quite control it. "I'm not very good at this stuff, but let's just say you're my mission. So I have to stay and warn you…until it's too late."

Talk about bullshit, Trace thought. He glared at her shimmering face. "The only help I need is getting rid of you."

"Not gonna happen. Not until all this is done." Her eyes narrowed as she looked over Trace's shoulder. Then she shrugged and turned back toward him. "Stop being afraid. There's nothing scary about you two being together." Nimble, she pushed to her feet and walked precariously along the railing.

Trace fought an urge to leap up and pull her back to safety.

But he was only watching an illusion, and there was no need to save her from anything.

Then Marshall swayed, losing her balance, and he couldn't fight old, protective habits. He lunged forward, reaching for her arm.

His fingers cut through empty space.

She laughed quietly. "That's what being in love is like. You can't touch it and you can't hold it and sometimes it hurts. You want to help someone and protect them from harm and ease their pain, but you can't. That's the way it works. Unless you drive her off. I hope you won't be that stupid."

Trace was about to give her a piece of his mind when she turned sharply. "It's here. I'm not supposed to feel cold, but I do. It's...oily." She shook her head. "I've—got to go." As Marshall stared up at Trace, her features seemed to blur. "It's closing now and it's pushing me away. Can't fight it."

Her outline flickered.

She seemed to be struggling, as if she were walking into a strong wind. "You need to be very careful. Especially now that he is—"

She seemed to shudder, looking back over her shoulder.

Then in the same instant she flickered away, and the balcony around him was empty, filled only with darkness and the rush of the wind.

Trace didn't move, feeling a sliver of uneasiness. He braced his elbows on the rail where he had seen Marshall's image only seconds before. It was too strange to be real— except that she somehow knew things, knew that he was afraid of caring too much and not being able to protect Gina from the dark things in her future.

She'd voiced fears he would barely admit existed in his own mind. Either he was crazy, or this was a clear sign of chip degradation. If it was a chip problem, Izzy would be able to track the source.

The door slid open behind him. Gina appeared, hugging a white bathrobe as she shivered in the wind. "Here you are. When I couldn't find you, I got worried." She glanced around the balcony. "Were you listening to a radio? I thought I heard you talking."

He cleared his throat. "Just humming to myself." *Lame, O'Halloran.* "So why aren't you asleep?"

"Couldn't." She rubbed her neck. "Too keyed up. Which

is pretty funny, considering what we just…" She cleared her throat. "Boy, did we just."

He turned up the collar of her bathrobe and pulled her against him. She was warm and soft, and her hair fell like silk against his cheek.

Maybe Marshall was right. Maybe he had to let go and believe, rather than agonize about details he couldn't control. The problem was, controlling things was what he did for a living. All his life he'd had a playbook in his head.

Places to go. Challenges to tackle. He had always needed to prove something to himself.

Watching her hair slide through his fingers, he spoke without planning or thought, driven to say what he had never said before because now something pushed him to *feel* what he had never felt before.

"I've never thought of a future outside my work, Gina. I've never cared about relationships. Then I saw you on a crowded street corner and I suddenly envisioned a different life from the one I'd lived up until then. Believe me, that scares the living hell out of me."

She tilted her head and ran her finger over his lips, silencing him. "You just said the *F* word, Lieutenant. Future. That's not allowed, remember?"

"The rules just changed," he said harshly. "I want that with you. Damn it, I *need* that with you. One way or another I will make it work."

She took a deep breath. His arms were still around her, yet something separated them.

They both started talking at once.

"Gina, I know about—"

"Trace, I have to tell you—"

They stopped, and she laughed softly. "I go first." She

slid her hands around his waist and took another fast breath. "There's something you should know, since you brought up the subject of a future. I didn't tell you before because—because it didn't matter before. Before there wasn't an *us*." Color flared in her face.

"Now there's definitely going to be an *us*." Trace ignored all the reasons why there shouldn't be. The reasons no longer seemed valid. Now he understood why Wolfe fought fiercely to have a future with the woman he loved.

The rewards overruled any possible risks.

"Okay." She caught her lip between her teeth. "This is harder than I expected." She looked away, her face tense. "I'm losing my…"

Trace waited, realizing the precious gifts she was offering him.

The truth.

Trust.

Things that came very rarely in life.

"I'm going blind," she said in a rush. "Two months or two years. No one seems certain about the timeline."

"That's why you take the medicine?" He wanted to draw her out, to make the details easier for her. If she wanted to talk, he was more than prepared to listen.

He slid his hands inside her robe and massaged her back slowly. Then he kissed the top of her head, and she sighed, curling into his body.

"Pretty much. It all sucks. My plans…all the places I haven't been yet. It's not the same when you can't see."

Something wet brushed his chest. Trace realized it was her tears.

Emotion clogged his throat, tightened his chest. When

was the last time he'd allowed anything or anyone to touch him so deeply?

You can't touch it and you can't hold it.

"So it's definite?"

She nodded, her face against his chest. "Yeah, barring a miracle, and I've never believed in those. I'm trying to do what I can to get prepared." She made a small sound of anger. "No, I'm not. I haven't done *anything* to prepare. I'm still a lot angry and a little frightened. You're the only one I've told, except for Tobias."

"I wish I could change it." His voice was low and fierce.

You want to help someone and protect them from harm and ease their pain, but you can't.

"You're shivering. Let's go in."

"Not yet." She stared up over his shoulder. "It's beautiful out here. I've already made a wish on that big star over there."

Antares, Trace thought. It flashed red above the restless sea, captured in the curve of the Milky Way.

"I wished for us to *be*...somehow. Which is incredibly silly, but—"

"There are always possibilities." Trace needed to believe that. He opened the inside door, swung her into his arms and carried her inside, setting her on the edge of the bed. "We'll handle this together."

But he knew by the calm resignation in her face that she didn't believe it.

"Listen, you have calls to make and work to do. I'll be fine." She gave a crooked grin. "I might even manage to get a little sleep if you're not around flashing that killer body."

Damn it, he wanted to stay. He wanted to make her believe that there were always possibilities.

But his possibilities were currently running a little low.

His gaze swung to the clock. Four minutes until he had to check in with Tobias again. Not nearly enough time to say all the things he wanted.

He pulled her into his arms, feeling her heart beating strong and fast. "I wish this were different."

"You don't have to explain."

"I do," he said harshly.

Her robe gaped open.

The sight of her flat stomach and the dark curve of her nipples made Trace harden instantly. He smoothed the robe shut.

No time.

"I want you to have this." He didn't examine the instinct, because it was too urgent, nearly primitive. He pulled a worn gold chain with a St. Christopher medal from his pocket and slipped it over her head.

"But I—"

His hands closed around hers. "Wear it for me." He thought of Marshall's image out on the railing. "Maybe things exist that we don't understand and can't imagine."

She kissed his knuckles, then opened his palm. "This hurts," she whispered. "Why does love have to hurt?"

"Someone told me that's part of the deal. And if it doesn't make you crazy, you're not doing it right."

"Smart person." Gina took a deep breath and kissed his callused palm. "I'll wear this. Though I'd rather you have it."

"No, I think you were meant to have this one."

His arm tightened around her.

And then, because he wanted to stay and take her again, he moved back.

She smoothed her hands along the glistening chain. "Do you want me to leave? If so, I could—"

"No need. Go shower. This call won't take long."

"Since you probably deserve a smile, ask Tobias about the two women who tried to flag down the cruise ship after they ran out of gas. Talk about crazy."

Trace wasn't really listening as he pulled out his cell phone. "When did this happen?"

"Early evening. I hear they were completely blotto, staggering across the deck of their yacht. It's a miracle they didn't plow into the ship."

Trace turned slowly. "Blotto how?"

"Drunk. Three sheets to the wind."

Something skittered across his neck again. "Tonight, you said? Okay, I'll ask Tobias for the details."

Gina looked at his face carefully and then stood up. "A shower sounds good. Tell Tobias I'm fine. He'll be feeling bad about questioning me." After she left, Trace dialed Tobias, piecing together possibilities and not liking the result.

"Security."

"Checking in. How are we doing?"

"Everything's A-Okay down here. I'm starting to get a little bored."

Trace drummed his fingers lightly on the desk. He checked to be sure the bathroom door was closed. "I understand there was an incident with two women in a boat this evening."

"Drunk as skunks and completely topless. It was lucky we didn't plow them down the way their yacht was circling. The idiots were laughing like it was all a lark, without a clue how close they'd come to dying."

"So they were drunk or maybe on drugs?"

"Hard to say. Whatever it was, they were feeling no pain. It almost caused a stampede when the bridge crew noticed they were topless. I haven't seen binoculars whipped out so fast since review time at Quantico."

"Did anyone check out the boat's registry?"

"The captain reported them to Mexican authorities, but he didn't pursue the matter. Why? You think this is important?"

Trace couldn't shake a cold sense of uneasiness. *Oily,* Marshall had said. Maybe it was time he paid closer attention to that conversation. "I'm not sure. Get me all the information you have on the incident, will you? I need IDs if possible."

"Sure. I'll get right on it. I've got nothing else to do," Hale grumbled.

"You said you were bored," Trace said dryly. "All things come to those who wait."

"Including baldness, senility and death."

"Just don't go to sleep on me. I'll bring you some of Gina's special espresso."

Trace hung up the phone. Was he being paranoid? Maybe this was what happened when you dropped your defenses and let your brain get slammed by lust.

No, not by lust, an inner voice corrected.

By love.

He was about to knock on the shower door when pain shot through his head. Molten steel claws sank into his chest and ripped along his spine. He bent double, feeling the air slowly squeezed from his lungs.

Choking, he dropped his cell phone, dropped the small piece of Gina's yarn he'd left on the corner of the desk. Fighting to stay upright, he gripped the desk while the world faded, running into black.

The pain shifted, then centered on his collarbone.

Desperately, Trace fought to keep from passing out, one hand pressed to his chest even though the pressure didn't help. The pain prowled, then settled down to gnaw.

Only one thing would cause this kind of reaction.

Cruz...

Very close now.

CHAPTER THIRTY-SIX

TRACE STUMBLED toward the bathroom, the phone gripped tightly in his hand. He'd been shot in Colombia and struck by crippling knife wounds in Sri Lanka, but neither came close to inflicting the pain he felt now.

His muscles shifted, trying to expel something beneath the skin. He felt a blinding pain at his collarbone, centered on the one chip that Ryker's medical team had not completely disabled, leaving it intact for passive GPS location. Though it was the slightest of signals, Cruz had to have located Trace through the one active piece of technology that they still shared.

No one had expected Cruz to be alive. Even alive, he shouldn't have been able to locate a chip that was largely passive. His skills had grown off the chart.

A whine filled Trace's head as he opened his cell phone and tried to dial.

"Trace, what's wrong?"

Through a cloud of steam from the open bathroom door, Gina reached out to him. Her hands were cool on his forehead. Like some kind of angel, he thought dimly.

He staggered beneath another assault, and she caught him around the waist, staggering under his weight. "Take it easy. Let's get you to the bed."

"Need to call," Trace rasped. "Get Izzy. He'll know."

"To bed first," she said firmly, grabbing the phone as he dropped it.

Funny, she didn't seem at all frightened.

But of course, she didn't know Cruz.

GINA TRIED TO HIDE her panic. She had come out of the shower to find Trace doubled over, rigid with pain. His face was sheet white, his muscles tight. The last thing she wanted to do was make a phone call, but she took the phone when he insisted.

"Dial two," he said hoarsely. "Izzy—tell him what happened… Tell him—to remember the island…the helicopter had someone else inside."

None of it made sense, but she did exactly what he said, instinctively knowing it was right.

A man answered on the first ring. "Joe's Pizza."

"Oh." She frowned at Trace. "Wrong number."

"*Wait.* Are you Gina?"

"Yes." She didn't offer any other information, unsure who was on the other end of the line.

"Where is Trace?"

"Who are you?"

A chair creaked. "I'm—the man with the pizza. What's wrong with Trace?"

The calm tones of the man's voice reassured her. "Something happened, almost like he was hit. He's gripping his shoulder, and I'm afraid he's going to pass out."

"Stay with me, Gina. I'm going to need your help. Tell me exactly what happened."

"I don't know. I was in the shower, and I heard a noise. When I came out he was bent over in pain."

"No one came inside?"

"No. I would have heard."

"Anything else disturbed? His equipment or suitcase?"

"No. We've been in here for quite a while."

"Okay, good. Can you hold the phone to his ear?"

"He can't talk. He can barely breathe." Panicking, Gina switched the phone to her other ear so she could feel Trace's pulse. "He's bad." She tried to focus. "He said to tell you to remember the island. The helicopter had some-one else inside."

She heard the sound of a keyboard clicking. "Any signs of blood or bruising?"

"None that I can see." And since they had been naked in bed only minutes before, Gina would have seen them.

Trace tried to sit up, but she pushed him back down on the bed. "Steady, tough guy. Give it a minute."

"Izzy?"

"That's right. He said, 'Joe's Pizza.'"

Trace grimaced. "Tell him—he's here…very close."

"Who?" Gina asked.

But Izzy cut back onto the line and she repeated what Trace had said.

"Look at his collarbone." Izzy sounded cold and very professional. "Don't touch him, just look."

Everything was getting very weird. When she looked at Trace's shoulder, Gina saw a dark bruise that she could swear was new. A trail of blood dotted his skin. "He's bleeding."

Izzy didn't sound surprised. "Okay, Gina, you need to do something for me. Touch the bruise. Tell me if you feel anything."

She leaned closer to Trace. "I don't want to hurt you," she whispered.

Trace nodded, lines of pain scoring his face. At the center of the bruise she felt a ridge, as if something hard was wedged just beneath the skin.

"Push it down as far as you can," Izzy said flatly.

"I can't. It hurts him too much."

"You have to, Gina."

Gritting her teeth, she pressed her palm over Trace's collarbone, feeling his muscles tighten against her. The pain had to be vicious, and she was only making it worse.

"Izzy, nothing happened."

More keyboard clicking. Then he spoke quietly, calmly. "Get a knife. You'll find one in the top drawer of his desk. Do you see it?"

"Found it. But I—"

"Listen to me, Gina. Focus. Do what I say. He's going to be fine."

She closed her eyes, trying to believe it. "Okay. Tell me what I have to do."

When Izzy was done, she felt sick at what was to follow. "Trace?"

"I trust you." His callused fingers gripped the headboard. He managed a ghost of a smile. "Do it."

With a clean towel over his chest, she sterilized the knife with alcohol, doused his chest and then cut exactly where Izzy told her. Trace's jaw worked and his arms twitched once, but he didn't make a sound.

Blood welled over the towel. Somehow she kept her hands steady.

After what seemed like an eternity, Gina lifted a small sliver of gray silicone from under the skin of his collarbone and set it on the nightstand. "Did you find it?" Izzy's voice sounded loud through the speaker she had activated on Trace's cell phone.

"Removed. It was just where you said."

"Good job. You did exactly what he needed, Gina. Now clean him up with alcohol and bandage his shoulder. Trace, can you hear me?"

"I'm here. Where the hell are you?" His voice was still harsh with strain.

"About an hour out."

Trace looked glad to hear it. "You think what I think?"

"Not much doubt." Izzy sounded grim. "He's flexing his muscles. He must have picked you up."

Who? Gina wondered. And what was the gray piece of metal she'd pulled from Trace's shoulder?

It was time they gave her some answers. She couldn't help if she was kept out of the loop like this.

She glanced at Trace. "I need to know what's going on. What did I just cut out of Trace and who is flexing his muscles?"

The man called Izzy cleared his throat. "What you cut out is classified, Ms. Ryan. And the man in question is even more classified. Trace will tell you what he can, but I can assure you now that it won't be much. You're going to have to trust us."

Before Gina could reply, the phone went dead.

Twenty minutes later Trace was a little pale, but on his feet, shoving one hand into his shirtsleeve. Gina fumed in silence, then pushed away his arm and pulled on the shirt for him. "You're an idiot," she snapped. "Both of you are. You should be in bed recovering. You should also be telling me exactly what is going on."

"Can't." His voice was steady.

The bleeding had stopped, Gina noted. He seemed to heal amazingly fast.

"What happened to you? What was that thing I removed?"

He didn't answer.

More secrets.

"Okay, I get it. Boys' toys and security stuff." She shrugged. "Something else I didn't tell you. I used to be Seattle PD, so I know how to keep my mouth shut."

He turned awkwardly, one eyebrow raised. "You were a *cop?*"

Gina shrugged. "Operative word, *was*. As they say, shit happens. And no, I don't want to talk about it."

"But we will talk about it," he said quietly. He grimaced a little as he slid a shoulder harness over his shirt and slipped a compact SIG-Sauer semiautomatic into place. "As soon as this is over. I get the feeling you didn't leave because you wanted to."

"Not going to talk about it." Her tone was firm.

Gina watched him slide extra magazines into his pocket. So things were getting serious.

An enemy was aboard the ship, and Trace was going after him. Why did this feel like a *High Noon* moment?

She squared her shoulders. If she had her way, she'd be beside him. She had top skills at the shooting range—a little rusty maybe, but she could provide covering fire, if necessary. "You have an extra gun?"

He hesitated, then pulled out a smaller semiautomatic with a two-inch barrel. "Para Ordnance Warthog. Light and very powerful. All yours."

Gina felt awkward holding the small handgun. It had been five years since she'd carried.

Five years since she'd been charged with mismanaging

department-confiscated property, thanks to her greedy ex-partner and one-time lover.

But some things you never forgot, and the grip returned, along with the stance and the calm focus that came with carrying a lethal weapon. She checked the chamber, tested the sights and then put the gun and three loaded magazines on the bed. "I think I'd better get dressed. If the shit hits the fan, I'd rather not be in a bathrobe."

Trace was going through equipment in his silver case. "Be careful. Things may not be...the way you think they are. I can't say more, but take nothing for granted." He turned, his expression grave. "If I'm at the door, I'll use this signal." He knocked twice fast, then four times slowly. "No matter what you hear or see, if the code's wrong, don't say a word and don't throw the lock. If I phone or we meet, I'll call you Princess. Remember that."

"I'll remember."

He pulled her against him, kissed her hard. His fingers gripped her waist.

Then he released her and stepped back, his expression cool and blank.

Thousand-yard stare again.

Once Gina had been damn good at delivering the same stare. She'd been sure that world was far behind her. The laugh was on her.

She tugged on her jeans, feeling unreal, as if she were walking through a role in a movie.

Except this was real. People's lives would depend on what she said and did.

She pulled on her white chef's jacket. "Any other sage advice before you go?"

"Yeah," Trace said. "Stay here and don't go out. I'll

contact you if I have anything to report. Remember the Para's gonna have one hell of a kick when you fire. Keep your grip tight and squeeze off the rounds."

"I remember." Gina slipped the small gun in the pocket of her chef's jacket. "Small barrels mean evil recoil, no way around it."

She picked up something red from the corner of his desk and studied it carefully. It was her piece of stray yarn from the knitting club. She stared at him in surprise. "You kept this?"

He shrugged and put the yarn in his pocket. "My good luck talisman. Laugh and you die."

Warmth filled her. He would protect her at all costs. She would do the same for him. "Later on...I'll knit you something for real."

"You want us to have a later on?"

Gina didn't hesitate. "You're not ditching me now when I'm just getting my first taste of wild, reckless sex. How about socks, Lieutenant O'Halloran? Maybe a matching pair of gloves?"

"Take your time. I'll be around to collect." He brushed back a strand of her hair and then pulled his jacket closed, hiding the gun beneath. "One other thing." He stood in the room's single light, his face hard. "This could be a bad night, but whatever happens, we're going to get through it and any other bad nights that come along. We've got a future ahead of us. It may not include a white picket fence, but it will be damned good. Some way I'll see to that."

It was a clear, unbreakable promise.

Gina liked the sound of that just fine.

But something told her they had a long, long way to go until morning.

THREE DECKS BELOW, Ford McKay walked down the corridor toward the infirmary, gripping his daughter's hand. Sunny had gotten sick again right before dinner. Her fever was up, too.

More flu. He was starting to think this whole cruise was jinxed.

The possibilities that Trace O'Halloran had outlined weren't helping his mood, either.

He glanced up as he passed the darkened security office. Inside a man was outlined in an interior office, talking on a phone.

"I'm sorry I'm sick, Daddy. I don't want to spoil the vacation."

"Hush, Sunshine. You're not spoiling anything." He made an effort to distract her, keeping the worry from his voice. "By the way, those were great photos you took today."

"Thanks, Daddy."

His voice tightened. "But I don't want you three running off again—not ever."

"Okay, Daddy." Sunny looked up at him, her brows drawn together. "Is something wrong?"

"Nothing I can't handle, Sunshine." Ford squeezed her hand as they reached the door of the infirmary. "Here we are. You'll feel brand-new in an hour, I promise."

Her fingers curled, linked with his, absolutely trusting as he pushed open the door and guided her inside.

SUNNY FELT FUNNY.

Ten minutes had passed. She was sitting in the waiting room, drinking a glass of apple juice and watching a lame cartoon show with talking giraffes. Usually she liked cartoons, but not tonight.

Her father was inside talking with the doctor, and she was pretty sure he was worried about something.

She hated to be sick.

It didn't happen often. Mostly it happened when she was thinking about stuff like going back to school and about whether Mei-ling would still be her friend when she got back.

Right now she was worried about what would happen to the white kitten and whether it would have a good home when she left. She hated the thought of leaving Trouble behind.

But she didn't tell her mom and dad that.

Then they'd worry, too, and this was their first real vacation in as long as Sunny could remember.

She wriggled in the leather chair, listening to her dad talk with the doctor, who had given her a pink pill to chew. It had tasted icky, but her stomach did feel better now.

She listened to the conversation through the open door and relaxed a little. The two adults didn't sound so worried now, and that made her feel better than the medicine had.

She bent down, digging in her backpack for her notebook.

When she looked up, she saw a door open down the hall. A tall man stood in the doorway, looking out. He had skin the color of burnt cinnamon and a little bit of gray in his hair. He stared down the hall, back and forth, for a long time.

Something moved near his feet, but he didn't notice. He checked his watch and then went back inside.

Sunny sat up. The thing on the ground near his feet was the white cat.

Her white cat.

She glanced frantically at the door of the exam room

where her daddy was talking to the doctor. She'd promised not to go off alone….

The cat turned, headed straight down the hall.

Her heart hammered. She didn't think or plan. If Trouble got loose again, someone might toss him overboard. Tears burned in her eyes and all her good intentions fled.

Sunny grabbed her backpack, opened the door and ran after the cat.

CHAPTER THIRTY-SEVEN

ENRIQUE CRUZ CROUCHED in the darkness, sweating.

His body was stiff, wedged into the small electrical room off the aft engineering area.

The appearance of the two women aboard the yacht had been arranged well in advance and had provided the perfect distraction, giving him time to wire in his remote network the night before. Cruz had made certain the crew in the nearby engineering room was otherwise occupied at the window before he went to work.

Cruz checked his watch, then slid his earphones back in place, scanning all ship communications in every department. Nothing new to note.

Riley's body had caused temporary panic, but the captain had wisely kept the news contained. Now Cruz had another set of wires to modify. After that, his key card would override all other access restrictions aboard the ship.

Once he was upstairs, he would deal with Tobias Hale. Izzy Teague's cooperation would have speeded up the process, but Cruz was prepared to handle any interference by Hale. The covert video feed Cruz had made over the past hours had revealed the location of the safe hidden behind the inside door, as well as Hale's access code. Cruz had actually passed himself off as Riley, one of the security staff, to gain entrance. Hale hadn't suspected he was seeing a perfect illusion created by classified chips and the focused energy of a superior mind.

Foxfire technology had its uses, Cruz thought coldly.

He spliced his last wire and then checked his watch.

Current mission complete.

Three minutes ahead of schedule.

CHAPTER THIRTY-EIGHT

TOBIAS WAS CHECKING a malfunctioning lightbulb in the hall outside his office when his cell phone chimed quietly. He glanced at the LED screen, walked back inside and closed the door.

Stay calm. Keep it professional.

"Hale here."

"Teague." His son's voice was cool and impersonal. "I just spoke to Trace. He's having some trouble."

"What kind of trouble?"

"Not at liberty to discuss it."

Tobias figured as much, but he'd still needed to ask. "How bad?"

"It's temporary. I'm just giving you a heads-up."

"Always good to know when you're headed into deep shit. Any other news I need to hear?"

Like *I miss you, Dad* or *Maybe we can get together and talk about why you left.*

But Tobias knew that wasn't going to happen. A reconciliation wasn't in the cards. His son considered him a stranger, and that knowledge broke Tobias's heart.

He sat down at his desk and tried to relax.

Tried not to care that his only son hated him.

"No, there's nothing more to add."

"Where are you now?" Tobias asked the question mostly to hear Izzy's voice.

"Less than an hour out. I'll contact you when my ETA is firm. Stay alert. Things are in motion."

Tobias clenched his fist on the desk. In an hour he would see his son. It was the last thing he should have focused on under the circumstances, but he was only a man.

Only a father separated too long from his only child.

"Roger. It would help if I had a few details, like what I'm up against."

Silence stretched out. Then Izzy's voice chilled even more. "What you're up against? Let me put it this way. Take the worst thing you've ever dealt with or imagined dealing with. Then double that. You just may be close. Our man on board will relay any other information as needed."

The line went dead.

Tobias stared at the phone. He knew that Izzy wouldn't exaggerate, and yet the conversation told him next to nothing. When he tried to put a face to the danger they were facing, all he could conjure up was shadows.

Finally he put down the phone, then turned out the lights in his front reception area. After rechecking the cameras and the lock on the outer door, he went back into his office. He opened the hidden safe, verified its contents were untouched, then secured the safe again.

All quiet.

He thought about the thick alpaca yarn stashed in a locked desk drawer, ready to make a vest with detailed cables. His fingers itched to pull out the project, but he resisted the urge. Work was work.

Meanwhile there was always official paperwork to tackle. If he worked 24/7 at nothing else, there would always be more to do. Somewhere the paperwork gremlins were laughing at him right now.

He put his feet up on the desk and pulled out a pile of recent personnel forms.

His cell phone chimed.

He glanced at the number and frowned. "Hello."

"Look, I'm sorry. I couldn't talk to you those other times. Now I'm—well, this is a private line."

Izzy.

Tobias's heart began to pound. He sat up slowly.

"I'm sorry, Dad. I shouldn't have said those things. After everything that has happened—" Izzy made a short, confused sound. "I want to understand. I really do. We need to talk as soon as this business is over."

Tobias felt his eyes blur. He'd waited so long and prayed so fiercely. Now he'd heard the words.

"Okay." Only a tremor betrayed his emotion. "You name the time and I'll be there. Obviously, it won't be right away."

"Things are happening fast. I can't fill you in over the phone, but I'm on deck. The chopper just put me down. Can you come meet me?"

Izzy was on deck.

Tobias shot to his feet. His fingers trembled as he shoved his key card in his pocket. "I'll be right there."

He strode through the room, a stupid grin on his face.

As his hand met the cold metal of the doorknob, he stopped.

Frozen.

Unable to move.

Too easy, Hale.

Too damned easy after all these years.

Slowly the joy and excitement left his face. Not like this.

It was exactly what he wanted to hear, which was why he couldn't believe it.

A long and often deadly career spent in dangerous places made him stand motionless, scrutinizing every detail of the conversation with Izzy. The words had been right and the voice pitch perfect.

But somehow Tobias didn't buy it.

He held his key card, frowning up at the cameras. What a fool he'd been to hope.

He fingered his receiver. Trace answered instantly.

"Teague's up on deck. He just called me on a new number. Apparently, the ETA was pushed up and he wants to talk with me, so I'm going up. You got all that? I know this changes things, so I wanted you fully informed. Izzy says you're hit pretty bad. Better stay in your cabin and take it easy for a few hours."

Like hell Trace would.

The thought made Tobias smile coldly. All warfare was based on deception.

This man Trace was after was smarter than Tobias dreamed possible. He had access to private details of his life and probably some kind of high-tech voice synthesizer. Tobias didn't reveal his suspicions to Trace, but the SEAL would get the meaning from the bungled details Tobias had dropped.

Trace would be the first to know when Izzy arrived— not Tobias. Trace would know Tobias had been given false information leading to what was almost certainly a trap.

If their unnamed enemy had access to Tobias's past, what else did he have access to? Could he have penetrated the security of this room, too? Hale looked around and saw that the drawer where the cat had been sleeping was empty. Hell. Tonight the stowaway was on his own.

Grimly, he unlocked a drawer in his desk and took out a Kevlar vest. Next came his old government-issue service gun. It was comforting to feel its well-oiled weight back in his hand after months of nonuse.

Time to start the party and head up to the chopper dock.

He squinted in the dim corridor, turning to lock his door.

A stun gun hit him from behind. The electrical burst drove him instantly to his knees. Tobias collapsed before he could warn Trace via the transmitter hidden in his shirt collar.

"I CAN'T HEAR YOU." Trace frowned, jiggling his small headphones. "Hale, are you there?" He had tried to contact Tobias twice, but all he heard was static.

He sprinted toward the nearest staircase, using his memory of the ship's layout to cut through the engineering department. As he raced up the stairs, a wave of cold energy hissed along the outside stairwell, circled back and drove into his head.

Cruz again.

The man was like a fungus you couldn't kill.

But with Trace's final chip removed, Cruz couldn't inflict any real damage.

As he raced toward Tobias's office, the lights flickered over his head, but not from loss of electricity or a power surge. It was as if the hall itself had flickered, going cold and sucking in all the light.

Only one person could create an energy effect like that.

Cruz was back. *Welcome to hell.*

THE NIGHT SECURITY FOREMAN strolled past the kitchen and nodded at the cook pulling pastries from the oven. He made a quick scan, noting that everything was normal inside, then continued down the corridor. When he looked to his left he saw a single light shining through the open door of the security office.

The officer frowned. Why was the door slightly ajar?

He slowed, checking for activity, one hand moving to his heavy flashlight. The long steel barrel was useful as a weapon in the event of an attack.

As he moved silently around the open door, he saw a man's leg sticking out beneath a table. Tobias Hale was stretched out inside the office, blood dotting one cheek. His key card was on the floor near his hand, and the door to his private office was open.

The inside alarm had never gone off.

CHAPTER THIRTY-NINE

THREE MINUTES ALONG the aft stairway, Trace felt a prickle of uneasiness at the back of his neck, and he sank back into the shadows. Not many of the crew were out and about at this hour of the morning. He passed two uniformed waiters carrying room-service orders, but no one else.

He descended two flights silently, alert to any activity nearby.

At the next floor he stopped. Something was tossed across the landing. At first Trace thought it was a rolled-up rug. When he came closer, he saw it was a man in a blue engineering staff uniform. The two bullet holes at the man's temple explained why he wasn't moving.

Trace didn't recognize the man. Judging from his skin temperature, he hadn't been dead for long. Quickly, Trace went through his pockets, but found nothing. He was preparing to call Izzy when he heard a low groan from the alcove at the next landing.

With his gun level he crept along the wall, keeping well back out of sight.

He heard another groan. When he reached the landing, he saw Blaine sprawled against the wall. A bruise covered her forehead, and blood pooled from a wound at her cheek. She blinked at him without any sign of recognition, and Trace realized she was slipping into unconsciousness.

"Blaine, can you hear me? Who did this to you?"

She blinked, her gaze focused over his shoulder. "Didn't know," she whispered, shuddering. "Not part of…plan."

Trace glanced around, looking for any cluc of how and when Blaine and the dead man had come here. Near the lower stairs, he saw a hint of red that might have been part of a bloody shoe print near an unmarked door that led to the crew dining room.

"Blaine?"

Trace heard the shocked whisper and spun around to find Gina one flight below him, her hands clenched on the stair rail. "What h-happened?"

"I told you not to leave, damn it. Why—"

She cut him off. "Ford McKay just called your room. His daughter is missing. She was sick and hc took her to the infirmary, but while he was talking to the doctor, she vanished. He's trying to find you and Tobias, but Tobias didn't answcr calls in the security office."

"I'll contact him," Trace said curtly. "Now go back to my cabin."

Gina didn't move. "I'm going to see Carly. If Ford wants my help, we can look for Sunny together. I know the ship better than he does."

"Like hell. You'll stay in my cabin. Let Ford go alone."

Trace covered Blaine with his jacket and took her pulse. Thready. The woman needed attention ASAP.

Now on top of everything they had a child missing. Another complication they didn't need.

Blaine shuddered and seemed to focus on Gina's face, reaching out one hand awkwardly as she gripped what appeared to be a crumpled silk scarf. "Didn't know," she repeated mechanically. "He lied. Just using me…."

Gina leaned down and straightened Trace's jacket around Blaine's shoulders. "Who lied?"

"No name." Blaine stared into space. "Has a scar." Blood trickled from her mouth.

"It's going to be okay, Blaine. We'll get someone to help you."

"Believe me." Blaine took a jerky breath. "Keep this." As her eyes closed, she shoved the silk scarf into Gina's hands.

"I'll go find the doctor."

Trace shook his head tensely. "You're going to McKay's cabin. I'll call the captain to send someone down here."

Gina stood up clumsily, unable to look away from Blaine's motionless body. "Carly is on E deck. Cabin 624." She took a deep breath. "The elevator's right over there."

"Take it."

As Trace checked the elevator, two tired-looking passengers emerged. They studied the hall, but Trace blocked their view of Blaine and the dead crew member. The last thing he needed was mayhem caused by a stampede of terrified passengers.

He opened his cell phone and cursed when Tobias still didn't answer his call.

GINA BLANKED OUT her confusion. She drove away the memory of the dead man, Blaine's white face and the thought of Sunny wandering the ship alone.

Hyperventilating wouldn't help anyone. When she looked down, she was surprised to find Blaine's silk scarf wadded up in her fingers. Without thinking, she shoved it into her pocket. The silk felt damp and slightly heavy, but she didn't pay much attention. Trace was already at the elevator door, motioning her to hurry.

THE WIND HAD PICKED UP, rattling the windows when Ford McKay yanked open the door of his room. Behind him Carly was reading to her two daughters, trying not to look frightened.

McKay nodded at Gina and motioned her into the small alcove off the bathroom. "I'm going after Sunny." He spoke in a cold whisper. "I need one of the security crew, too. Have you seen Trace?"

Trace strode inside and closed the door. "You'll get help," he said shortly. "Keep Gina here with Carly. Sorry I can't go with you myself. Keep your head down when you go out. Understand?"

A look passed between the men, and Ford nodded. "Any way I can contact you?"

"Too dangerous. Assume that all communications are monitored. I'll come back here once the situation is stable." He gestured to the door. "Don't let anyone in, and tell your wife the same. Make sure she understands this means no one. Not even me." Trace shrugged a Kevlar equipment bag in place over his chest. "*Especially* me. Nothing will be what you think it is."

Ford started to speak. Then he nodded.

"No one gets in. You've got my guarantee."

CLOUDS PILED UP along the Mexican coast, driven eastward by stiff winds off the Pacific. Stars shimmered and faded under the racing marine layer as the whine of the wind was drowned out by the thump of sleek, menacing engines.

A gray twin-engine Seahawk cut out of the darkness.

Plans had changed. As soon as the chopper hit the cruise ship's narrow emergency landing deck, eight men in black Kevlar poured onto the padded rubber. No words were spoken as they scattered.

In seconds the deck was clear.

Izzy Teague walked out of the darkness, talking on a cell phone. He hung up as Trace appeared. "Sitrep."

"Breach in the safe, contents missing. Tobias Hale was attacked. Two casualties, one fatal."

"Hale?" Izzy's head cut around sharply. "Dead?"

"Unconscious. Doc's looking at him now."

"So Cruz scored big." Izzy's voice held an icy calm. "Smart bastard. I gave as much incorrect information as I could when I talked to Hale via his ship phone. Cruz will think we're running short and late."

Trace looked up at the cloud-swept night sky. "Where are the dogs?"

"Second chopper, five minutes behind me." Izzy unzipped his black vest. "So where was Cruz headed? He has to suspect we'll lock the ship down tight."

"Hard to lock down a cruise ship," Trace said shortly. "One with over twenty-four hundred passengers and nine hundred crew."

Izzy pulled a laptop out of its case without breaking stride. "I want people watching all decks. We've set up radar and airborne surveillance of surrounding waters, but Cruz is smart enough to suspect that."

"So he'll hide somewhere else. A place where we wouldn't look."

Izzy pulled a headset in place. "We're going to take this place apart cabin by cabin until we find him."

Trace smiled coldly. "Sounds like my kind of job."

FORD MCKAY COLLARED the first security officer he met. "My daughter is missing. Get someone down here to help find her."

The officer frowned. "Sir, if you'll calm down, I'd be happy to—"

Ford leaned close, in the man's face. "Cut the therapy talk. Get a team down here ASAP."

The officer fingered his walkie-talkie, requesting backup. "How will I know her?" he called as Ford turned toward the elevator.

"Here." Ford dug in his pocket. "She's in six of those photographs. Purple shoes and purple backpack. You can't miss her."

For a moment his voice wavered.

Then his face went blank and he vanished into the elevator.

DOWN ON E DECK, Gina had been pacing Carly's cabin for almost fifteen minutes, unable to get the thought of Sunny out of her mind. Blaine's motionless body brought an equal dose of nightmares.

As she paced, her fingers slid restlessly into her pocket. She felt the outline of Blaine's scarf. Something was wrapped inside it, she realized.

Sitting down at the desk, she opened the scarf and stared at what looked like a plastic envelope covered with heavy-duty Cellophane.

Some kind of medicine? Was Blaine into drugs?

"Mommy, when is Sunny coming back from the doctor?" Across the room Olivia bit her lip, looking worried. "She should have been back hours ago."

"She's going to stay overnight so the doctor can check her tummy. Now close your eyes and try to sleep, honey."

Over her daughter's head, Carly met Gina's gaze. Something bleak filled Carly's eyes. Then she took a deep breath, gripped her two daughters' shoulders and began to read again, her voice calm and even.

Gina couldn't imagine how it felt to face the loss of a child. Her own worries seemed pale in comparison.

A throb began at her forehead. She winced, rubbing her neck, and realized she should have taken her pills an hour ago. Opening her shoulder bag, she dug into the inside zipper pocket where she had stashed her spare bottle.

The bottle was empty.

Anxiety hit her in an icy wave. She had to have her medicine. If the pain came full bore, she'd be completely useless. She couldn't let that happen.

She moved quietly to the bed. "Carly, I have to leave. Don't worry, I'll be back in three minutes."

"Ford said you needed to stay here." Carly shook her head firmly. "Something's wrong aboard the ship. You can't go."

Gina gave a quick smile as she tossed her bag over her shoulder. "I'll be fine. The head of security has taught me a few secret shortcuts."

"But Ford and Trace—"

"Shouldn't worry. Lock the door behind me."

Gina checked the view hole, then slipped outside. When she heard Carly slide the lock home, she sprinted toward a small laundry area at the stern. The small service elevator inside the laundry would get her downstairs and back in minutes.

"WHAT DID THEY GET?" Izzy stood in the middle of Tobias Hale's office and stared at the empty safe.

"Everything is gone." Tobias shifted on the couch, an ice bag at his head. His neck was covered with a white bandage, and he winced whenever he moved. "There was only one cardboard box in the safe. Whoever stunned and attacked me took it."

"You didn't see his face?"

"Too fast. He had a key card, because I heard it beep in the security slot right after I was hit. Somehow he knew my code to the safe, too." Tobias stared at the open safe. "I should have been faster, damn it."

Izzy didn't agree or disagree. "How did he get the key card?"

"Nearest I can piece together, the head of beverage services was involved. She might have gotten one from someone in the head office. We have reason to think she used a card to breach the kitchen and other areas of the ship." Tobias rubbed one shoulder carefully. "My junior security officer, John Riley, was found dead earlier tonight. I checked his cabin and turned up $15,000 in small bills, along with a plane ticket to Malaysia. He had to be involved. When I finished digging, I learned that he and Blaine had had a brief affair about three years back. I should have looked for that earlier," he said tightly.

Izzy met his gaze coolly. "It's usual to do thorough background checks on all security personnel."

Tobias flinched as if he'd been hit, although Izzy's tone was cool and impersonal.

Izzy looked away, studying the screen of his laptop, which was angled over his right arm. "I've almost got the signal. We can trace it."

Tobias's head swung up. "You had a homing device implanted in the package?"

"SOP." Izzy scrolled down the screen. "Bingo. He's in

engineering." He looked at Trace. "Port side. I've located the nearest stairwell."

Trace sprinted toward the door. "Use the codes we set up. He could be monitoring our comm."

Tobias looked up as Izzy moved past without a word.

When the door closed, a look of pain crossed the security officer's face. Grimacing, he pushed to his feet, swayed and then leaned against the wall, breathing hard.

He'd seen his son's computer diagram indicating the location of the stolen package. Tobias knew a faster way down to engineering than his son did. You didn't work security for nine years without stockpiling one or two useful secrets.

CHAPTER FORTY

WITH HER PILLS IN HAND, Gina slipped out of her room and checked the corridor. Buoyant with relief, she jogged back to the laundry service elevator. No passengers were in sight, which was unusual. At 3:00 a.m. there were usually a few stragglers returning from the casino, the theater or a late night with friends.

Any passenger questions Gina had were forgotten when she saw a small figure with a purple backpack walking past the crew lounge. Her heart pounding, Gina whispered a prayer that her two missions were about to be completed.

She ran down the hall past a service area where she and Andreas had occasionally prepared special events for the crew. Sunny was moving fast, holding something against her chest.

"Sunny, *wait*."

The little girl turned, and her pale face lit up. "Oh, I'm so glad it's you. I got lost when I went after Trouble and I couldn't find anyone to ask directions. Well, I could have, but I didn't want to speak to strangers, you know?"

Gina put an arm around Sunny's shoulders. "Everything will be fine, honey. We'll get you back upstairs to your mom and dad in a jiffy. But where did you find the cat?"

Sunny cuddled the squirming ball of fur proudly. "When

I was at the doctor's I saw him out in the hall. I couldn't let anything bad happen, so I followed him. But he was too fast, and then I got l-lost." Her voice shook. "I know Mom and Dad are going to be really, really mad at me. I did a bad thing when I left without telling my dad."

"Don't think about that now," Gina said gently. "We'll take that elevator upstairs and get you back."

But the little girl didn't move. She was smiling over Gina's shoulder. "Look, Mr. Trace, I found the cat. Now you can go with us. My parents will be glad you came, too." She bit her lip. "Maybe you could explain to them that I didn't mean to be bad."

Gina turned. Trace was coming down the staff stairway. "Are you finished?"

"Not quite. A few things to mop up down here." He checked his watch, straightening his black backpack.

Gina glanced over his shoulder. She hadn't seen him carrying the pack when he'd left. There was something different about his voice, too. It was lower and a little gruff.

She gripped Sunny's hand. Trace had given her clear instructions before he left that he would call her Princess as an identifying code.

The hairs prickled at the back of her neck as Trace came closer. The corridor seemed too small, too quiet.

"So...everything is okay?"

"Absolutely." He jogged past, one hand on the service pack. "Gotta go."

"Great. Princess and I will just head up to the kitchen."

He nodded without looking back, and Gina felt the cold air wrap around her, squeezing at her throat.

Nothing will be what you think it is. Trace had warned them not to trust anyone. What had happened?

She didn't plan to stay to find out. Calmly, she took Sunny's hand and walked toward the closest door of the staff lounge. "Let's get you some milk before we head upstairs, honey. You're probably thirsty."

Gina heard the sound of low laughter and glasses clinking beyond the open doorway.

Ten feet to go.

Suddenly she was hit by a dizzying sense of...*wrongness.*

Her pulse hammered as she fought to keep walking normally. Eight more feet.

Six.

Sunny's fingers trembled in hers. "I feel sick, Miss Gina."

"We'll get you something for your stomach, honey." Gina heard the sound of a chair sliding back. Her heart thudded....

A man's fingers gripped her shoulder, incredibly strong, covered in black leather. "You don't want to go in there after all," he whispered.

Gina froze. She couldn't fight the force of his voice as it wrapped around her.

"You want to come with me. Both of you. *Right now.*"

Somehow her feet turned without her control and she followed him, with Sunny's hand still in hers.

GINA LOOKED AROUND in a daze and saw metal walls covered in layers of white crystals. She was shivering with cold, and she couldn't seem to clear her head. Something warned her that she was in danger, but the uneasiness seemed to melt before she could figure out why.

Metal hissed and grated, and a tall man loomed out of the shadows. He crouched near a set of wires pulled from the wall. Sliding on a headset, he connected three of the wires to a small metal box.

Gina realized they were inside a freezer in a back storage room on the opposite corner from the kitchen. Heavy equipment lined the walls next to floor-to-ceiling boxes with canned goods.

No one would find them here until morning. Maybe not then.

A part of Gina's mind screamed for her to run, that this was a bad place, but she couldn't move. She stayed frozen, just the way he had told her.

Something wrong, her mind screamed.

Then that thought faded, just like the others.

Funny, at first she'd thought the man in the corridor was Trace. Now she saw that they looked nothing alike. This man was older, and his face had an unnatural pallor beneath his dark stubble. He moved quickly, crouched near the bottom of the wall as he shifted wires, then adjusted the headset. Gina guessed that he was listening to something aboard the ship via the computer network and telephone system.

Sunny yawned sleepily, leaning against her leg while the cat wriggled in her hands.

Go, Gina thought. *Have to go while he isn't looking.*

She touched the metal wall behind her and felt more ice. She tried to fight the mental fog that trapped her. The man looked sick, his face sweating as he pulled something from his field vest. The large bag was wrapped in the same kind of plastic that had covered Blaine's.

Gina felt the outline of Blaine's smaller package in her pocket.

Suddenly the man's eyes cut to hers. Gina had the sense that he was looking into her mind.

His eyes turned cold and assessing. He stood up and slowly walked toward her.

Beside her Sunny made a low, rumbling noise and leaned over to throw up. The man jumped back. He seemed uneasy as he gathered his equipment and took off his headset.

Weak and pale, Sunny leaned against Gina. "I don't feel so good," she whispered. "I want to go."

"I know, honey." Gina didn't want to draw the man's attention. She stared desperately at the outside door, but something still held her in place.

"He looks angry," Sunny whispered. "I don't like him."

Gina still couldn't remember how she'd gotten down to the backup kitchen storage area. Everything was fuzzy. "Don't worry. If we're quiet, he'll go away."

Sunny took a deep breath. "Can't we leave now?"

The man pulled tools and a lock out of his vest, and in that second Gina realized he meant to keep them here in the freezer. They were never going to leave.

But there were safety overrides on the equipment. Gina knew every one. She stepped backward, pulling Sunny with her. Even one small movement left her sweating, her energy drained.

Wrong. All wrong. It shouldn't be so hard.

The man zipped up his vest and turned. She felt the force of his gaze like a knife.

"I want to go," Sunny announced loudly, the cat clutched to her chest.

The man folded up a sheet of paper that appeared to be a floor plan of the engineering level. Then he glanced down toward the pocket where Gina was carrying the plastic package from Blaine. Something told her the package was very important.

"She gave you something, didn't she?"

Gina licked her dry lips and blocked the answer she felt

compelled to give. Grimly, she forced herself to recite food nutritional charts to keep her mind occupied.

"There should have been three bags. Where is the last one?" he said harshly.

Fruitcake, 659 milligrams of cholesterol.

Cheesecake, 2051.

"I don't know what you're talking about."

He backhanded her hard, and Gina tasted blood from a split lip, but she kept her face blank as she stared back at him.

Cop's stare. Yeah, she could do it, too.

"Who the hell are you?" he whispered. Then his brow rose. "You're sleeping with Trace. I'd offer my congratulations, but you aren't going to see him again."

"Let the girl go and I'll help you."

"All I need from you is the third bag. It's here somewhere, Gina. I know you have it." He jerked her leather purse off her shoulder and dumped the contents over the floor.

Her jacket would be next.

While he searched her purse, Gina pulled the small bag from her pocket and slid it into a corner of her mouth. She gagged a little at the heavy taste of alcohol when her mouth closed around the plastic. Liquid spilled onto her tongue and she felt her stomach churn, certain she would throw up.

Somehow she kept her face expressionless while he stared at her intently. Something oily crossed her skin.

Sifted through her mind.

Sorted through her thoughts.

She stared straight ahead. *Pecan pie, 556 milligrams of cholesterol.*

Her nausea made it hard to focus. "You'd better move away. Sunny and I are going to be sick."

He moved back uneasily, glancing at the wan girl still holding her white cat.

"You're afraid of that, aren't you? You're afraid of what illness we might give you."

He backhanded her again and Gina fell toward the cat, shoving him from Sunny's arms. "Run," she whispered. As the white cat shot across the floor, Sunny turned to follow.

The man in the black uniform blocked her way.

Too late.

"Inside." He pushed the girl toward the refrigerator. In the dim light, Gina felt a wave of icy air.

When the man reached for the door handle, Gina crouched and dug in her pocket. Sunny started to fight, swinging her fists wildly while Gina found her small handgun and leveled it at the center of the man's head.

"Back," she ordered. "Slowly. Hands up in full view."

He raised his hands, his face utterly calm. "Who the hell are you?" he repeated softly. "You act like a cop to me."

Gina ignored him, giving the girl a shove. "Run. Go now." Nausea roiled through her stomach as she kept the small package hidden in her cheek. Something bitter and soft slid onto her tongue and she resisted the urge to gag.

At the door, the little girl hesitated.

"*Go,* Sunny," Gina said again, keeping her gun level, moving to the door of the unit. Sunny still wasn't moving. Her eyes looked glazed.

The man's eyes were fixed on Gina's gun. She felt the oily thing move, attacking the edge of her consciousness, and she knew it was him, searching for weakness. Fighting nausea, she kept walking.

She was at the mouth of the refrigerator when she saw the white cat dart free into the shadows, but the man slammed her backward and sent her gun flying to the floor. He hit Gina hard and then shoved Sunny back into the unit.

Gina couldn't seem to move. Not even when he drove her down onto the floor next to Sunny.

Her vision blurred. She felt the force of the door being bolted shut. Shivering, she pulled Sunny against her chest. As icy waves of air crystallized in their breath, Gina felt the metal outline of Trace's chain burn at her neck.

IZZY CHECKED HIS LAPTOP. "Two floors to go," he said.

It wasn't going well. The dogs kept following fake trails that led to storage rooms or offices or garbage units. Cruz had always had the ability to project false sensory images, and it was clear that his skills were as strong as ever.

Maybe stronger.

Suddenly Duke, his Labrador retriever, froze, sniffing the air. Trace and Wolfe waited in silence while Izzy cradled his laptop, charting their progress through the ship and relaying the encrypted information silently to all the other Foxfire team members scattered on different decks.

The Lab moved forward slowly as a white cat shot out from behind a pillar. Trace caught the cat with one hand, frowning when he saw a bright plastic band tied around his neck. "Hell. This is Sunny McKay's camp band. She must have found the cat and then lost him again."

The other dogs ignored the cat and strained forward, turning toward the aft deck.

Trace gestured to Dakota Smith, who had joined them only moments earlier. "Backtrack and look for Sunny. Give King the cat's collar to scent, and get yourself back here once you've found the girl. Ford McKay is tossing every cabin looking for her."

The tall SEAL from Wyoming gave a little two-finger wave and took the black Lab's leash. The two vanished down the hall.

Trace hesitated. Ford had told Tobias that Gina had left his cabin, but still hadn't returned, and she should have been back by now.

He couldn't afford to think about how Cruz would react if he found Gina and decided she would be a useful bargaining chip. No emotions.

The mission came first.

He took a harsh breath. Where was an irritating ghost when you actually needed one? Why didn't Marshall do something useful like find Gina and keep her safe?

Are you listening to me here, Marshall?

Immediately he cut off the thought. He wasn't about to ask favors from a hallucination.

He looked at his pager. Still no word from Dakota.

No word from Tobias, either.

He seemed to catch the faint scent of lavender in the hallway, but when he turned around, it was gone.

CHAPTER FORTY-ONE

"HE'S NOT HERE," Izzy said tightly. "It's another false trail."

Trace watched Duke turn in a slow circle, looking confused. Cruz had thrown up half a dozen energy nets to confuse the dogs. As trained and experienced as they were, they were still no match for Cruz.

Trace's Lab waited restlessly, sniffing the air.

No sign of their target was indicated.

Dakota Smith, the other Foxfire operative, was still backtracking in search of Sunny while Trace and Wolfe stayed with Izzy. Tobias had indicated that he was going to check the breaches in the ship's phone system in an effort to trace Cruz's movements.

Izzy touched his headphones and stopped typing. He turned back to Trace and raised a warning finger. "Yeah, it's Teague. What do you want, Cruz?"

Izzy pointed to his computer, frowning.

Cruz. Calling via Izzy's laptop.

"Hale? Yeah, he's here. Except he's not my father." Izzy's voice was icy. "You're not getting off the ship, so what does it matter?"

All the time he spoke, Izzy was typing quickly.

"So you did your research. Am I supposed to be impressed? It's all old news. Besides, you've got your facts wrong." Izzy motioned to Trace and held up his laptop.

A flashing cursor moved along one of the ship schematics.

Trace gave a silent signal to Wolfe Houston, and the two
SEALs jogged along the corridor to the left, their dogs
close beside them.

IZZY STARED at his computer screen, fighting disbelief.

How was Cruz so damn well informed? No one should
have known his connection with Tobias Hale. Izzy had
worked hard to bury all those threads in the government
files.

Clever or not, this time Cruz was going down, no matter
what it cost.

"I've got Gina," Cruz said quietly. "Tell Trace she won't
be alive much longer."

Izzy followed Trace, keeping an eye on the cursor that
pinpointed the location of the call. "Why don't you find
him and tell him yourself? I gather you two have a lot to
discuss," Izzy said dryly.

"Like what? The good old days? Not since Lloyd
Ryker's been in charge of Foxfire." The rogue agent
laughed coldly. "I understand those tissue samples your
father was carrying could revolutionize our biotechnology.
Superior eyesight. Enhanced cell regeneration. Is there any
wonder I had to have them?"

"I don't know what you're talking about."

But Izzy did know, of course.

And inside he was churning. The tissues represented a
breakthrough in accelerated nerve growth. How had Cruz
managed to learn every detail of the newest Foxfire discovery? How many traitors were there inside the program?

"I was always the best. I deserve to have that new technology." Cruz's voice broke into static for a moment. When he came back on the line, he sounded out of breath.

"Out of shape, Enrique? Or maybe that sound is your lungs filling up with fluid. You're dying, and we both know it. It's a side effect of your last enhancements, but if you come in now, you'll be treated."

Cruz muttered a short, rough curse.

"Too bad for you. It won't be a pleasant way to go."

Izzy stared at the laptop screen and motioned Trace to halt. He pointed around the corridor to the left.

The red arrow was fifteen feet away.

He signaled the distance with hand gestures and watched the two SEALs move forward silently, flanking the double doors directly ahead.

Izzy waited, computer in hand. "Cruz, are you listening?"

"Who's the crazy one? *You* whistle off your own father. You're one sorry bastard, Teague. The old man had his reasons for leaving. Ask him what his reasons were— unless you're afraid of the truth."

More manipulation, Izzy thought angrily. With Cruz nothing was what it seemed.

He watched the SEALs hit the double doors. Their weapons faced a long wall of storage compartments. One door was open. A black radio transmitter hung from a cluster of wires that had been pulled from the wall.

Cruz was hacking into the ship's communications, just as Izzy had suspected. But the rogue SEAL was nowhere in sight.

Cruz's voice cut through the silence. "So you found one of my listening posts. Good but not good enough." His voice broke up in harsh coughing. "By the way, Gina doesn't have much longer to live, by my estimate. Tell Trace I said he'd better hurry."

The headphones went dead.

NO ONE WOULD CHECK this back storage room, she thought. No one would find them until it was too late.

She drove down her panic.

She had to stay calm and search the wall until she found the safety cable to unlock the unit. All the big coolers aboard ship had alarm buttons as a safety precaution. After long minutes of blind searching, she found the button.

Broken.

Someone—probably her captor—had disabled it. Now the wires hung loose and useless from the wall.

Think.

Try something else.

Shaking with cold, she dug in her pocket for her candy thermometer. As the frigid metal stuck to her numb fingers, she whimpered in pain. Icy metal pressed against Gina's back. Stiff with cold, she dug a piece of molding free with her candy thermometer while blood pooled over her palm, then froze along her nails.

Gina ignored the pain that welled through her cold fingers. As she tugged at the broken molding, the door's safety release cable dropped into her hand, hanging from the metal wall. She gave a vicious tug and felt the door vibrate.

But the metal didn't move.

Sunny had her arms around Gina's waist as the insidious edges of sleep began to close in.

Can't fall asleep. We'll never make it out....

Gina pulled the cable again, tearing skin from her palm and fingertips. As she struggled, the cold weight of Trace's chain broke free, dropping onto a small ledge in the metal wall. Shivering, Gina searched for the worn gold links, and for a second she caught the scent of lavender, probably a hallucination caused by trauma and cold.

As her fingers closed around the necklace, she felt the outline of an old piece of burlap, shoved into the side of the ledge. Wrapping the burlap around her fingers, she attacked the cable again.

The scent of lavender grew, spilling through the air around her.

This time the door creaked and moved slightly.

Dragging in an icy breath, she jerked the torn cable again, her fingers gripping hard through the burlap, her skin on fire.

Metal ground against metal; the door began to open.

A wave of warm air brushed Gina's face as she held Sunny tight and together the two stumbled forward out of the darkness, the faint cloud of lavender drifting around them.

"NOT THAT WAY. I know a shortcut." Tobias Hale gripped Izzy's arm, gesturing up the stairs.

Izzy stared at the security officer, who had appeared moments earlier from one of the passenger elevators. "We don't know where he's headed. What's the point?"

"If I were him, I'd try the lifeboats. He could detach one if he knew how to access the ship's electronics, and we know he's capable of that."

Izzy rubbed his neck, thinking it through. How did you put yourself into the mind of a madman?

"Here." Tobias pointed to the schematics on Izzy's laptop. "There's a service elevator behind this set of stairs. It will take us right up." He looked at Izzy, frowning. "This is personal for you, isn't it? What did he do to you?"

"Broke a few bones. Nearly killed me. Other than that, we're good friends."

"Never let it get personal. That's when you make mistakes."

"Tell me something I don't know, Hale."

Wolfe stood outside the elevator door. "It's worth a shot. Izzy, go with Hale. Trace and I will separate and sweep this deck. We'll regroup at the lifeboats."

WOLFE'S CHOCOLATE LAB stopped in the middle of the silent corridor outside the ship's gift shops. At that hour all the shops were closed, shadowed behind glass windows and locked doors.

Wolfe waited while his Lab sniffed the air intently.

Lights flickered in the corridor. The dog strained forward, then sank prone on the floor, facing a service storeroom.

Cruz.

Wolfe reached for his transmitter and then stopped. No noise. The last thing he wanted was to tip off Cruz that he'd been found.

Silently, the SEAL inched forward through the darkness. He crouched and inserted a slim piece of metal. In one swift movement he freed the lock and yanked open the door.

His flashlight beam picked up a camouflage vest hanging over a case of Jack Daniel's whiskey. Otherwise, the room was empty.

Wolfe said a short, silent curse.

Another dead end.

DAKOTA SMITH CHARGED into the engineering storage area and saw two bodies slumped on the floor. Two females. They looked dead.

Cruz was going to pay dearly for this, the SEAL thought.

Then the little girl shuddered and gave a hoarse cough. Still unsteady, she looked up at him. "You're here with Mr. Trace, aren't you?"

"That I am. You must be Sunny. Are you okay?"

"I'm fine. Gina is shivering, though. Could she have a jacket, please?"

"Sure thing." Dakota slid a silver field blanket out of his pack and spread it over Gina. "That should do the job."

He glanced around, his senses spread to scan all energy around the rows of kitchen equipment and ceiling-high boxes. There was no sign of Cruz, and no hint of his energy trail.

Dakota tapped a code on his walkie-talkie, notifying Izzy that he'd found Gina and the little girl.

One task complete.

Gina reached out for Sunny at the same second her eyes opened. They were a deep sea-blue, Dakota noticed. Even pale and groggy, she was a knockout. Figured that Trace had all the luck.

Plus, she could cook like gangbusters and handle a Para 9 mm. Nice skill set, the SEAL thought. "How do you feel, ma'am?"

"Like Montana just landed on my head." She rolled her neck, shivering a little. "Is Trace okay?"

"Just fine. He's a little busy right now." Dakota helped her to her feet. "How about we get you two up to the infirmary so the doc can look you over?"

"He was here." Gina's voice was shaky but precise. "He had a Kevlar backpack and he asked me about the things that Tobias was carrying. He stole the other bags, I think, but I have one."

Dakota's eyes narrowed. "One what?"

"A package of some sort. Tobias must have had them in safekeeping. I hid this one so he wouldn't find it after Blaine gave it to me. I think she was worried about that because she tried to warn me." Wincing, Gina pulled the small, gelatinous package from her mouth. "It tastes awful." She made a face. "It isn't—poison or anything, is it?"

"Not toxic at all, ma'am."

Dakota stared down at the wrapped tissue samples that represented Foxfire's next stage of development. The military and civilian applications of this top-secret discovery were mind-boggling. Of course Cruz had wanted to get his hands on these.

And this woman had managed to protect the only samples they had left following Cruz's theft.

"I hope it's okay. Not spoiled or anything."

Dakota looked down at the future of Foxfire cupped in his hand. "Ma'am, you don't know how okay it is."

TRACE TRIED NOT TO THINK about Cruz's threats. Was Gina safe?

His headset signaled three short bursts, static and then two more bursts, code to indicate that Gina and Ford's little girl were safe.

Trace let out a sharp breath. Another string of bursts indicated that Dakota was headed off to check the engineering area.

Trace leaned over Izzy's computer, charting Dakota's current location along with Cruz's most likely route of escape. On his surveillance tours of the ship, Trace had noticed a small row of lower balconies that hung out over the water, part of the staff recreation area.

The puzzle pieces snapped into place.

Cruz meant them to think he'd gone to the Promenade level lifeboats, but Trace sensed their target was four decks lower. A man could hide webbing and rope nearby, using the staff balconies for access to the water. The area was only two or three minutes via service elevator from the food storage area where Dakota had found Gina.

Trace tapped a swift code on his walkie-talkie to alert the others. Then he ran down the corridor, with Duke straining eagerly at his side.

DAKOTA TOUCHED his headset, assimilated the code and then scanned the staff room.

Gina and Sunny were sitting in armchairs, now wrapped in blankets and surrounded by crew members. Sunny was talking to her father via borrowed cell phone. They would be fine now.

According to Trace, Cruz was headed to a staff area one floor up.

The SEAL turned and sprinted for the aft elevator.

CLOUDS RACED before a thready moon that offered little illumination.

Hidden in the darkness beyond the first balcony, Trace watched shadows ripple over the hull of the ship.

Wind tore at his face as he tried to plot Cruz's next move.

Duke felt it first, his body going stiff. Then the dog dropped, head toward the next balcony aft. Object sighted.

There.

Movement rippled over the hull. A figure slid from shadow to shadow, rappelling down the side of the ship. With his night-vision glasses, Trace made out a new-generation oxygen rebreather and wet suit.

He aimed his rifle, but the ship's motion made a tight aim impossible, and he couldn't risk a shot that would alert Cruz to his presence.

Trace twisted the line ready at his feet, clipped in carabiners and went quietly over the rail, wind cutting his face. As he hung free he plotted a line that would keep him in the shadows, yet gradually bisect Cruz's descent.

No matter the cost, Cruz could not leave the ship alive.

The rope swung, shaking in the wind. Trace descended carefully, legs locked for stability around the line.

Suddenly the shadow to his side stopped moving.

Trace tensed as he was hit by waves of energy that slammed into his mind, shaking his concentration. He kept moving, despite a sickening sense of dizziness as Cruz's energy projection ranged off the charts.

Far below he saw a small fishing vessel bobbing on the dark water. The vessel had to be Cruz's arranged pickup.

Their lines were barely forty feet apart when Cruz turned. Two rounds exploded past Trace's head. The third tore into his shoulder, jerking his hand from his rope.

His fingers pulled free and he twisted wildly, banging the metal hull, then hooked his feet to restore his balance.

Cruz speed-roped down and kicked him in the face, but Trace feinted, blocked Cruz's feet and slashed upward at Cruz's rope.

As the two swung out over the water, a knife slashed through Trace's vest. He jerked Cruz's other foot, throwing him hard to the opposite side. His old team leader gave a skeletal grin and kicked Trace's shoulder, pain exploding like shrapnel in his recent wound.

But Trace kept one hand around Cruz's nylon vest. If the tissue samples were anywhere, they would be there.

From the corner of his eye he saw two figures roping down the hull. Trace recognized Wolfe and Dakota. A shot whined over his head and ricocheted off the hull.

Dakota turned. Aimed. Another shot screamed through the darkness.

On the hull Cruz jerked and groaned once. Then his grip loosened and he plunged toward the water. Only Trace's hold on the vest blocked his descent.

Trace twisted his arms, holding on despite the wrenching pain at his shoulder, feeling Cruz's dead weight.

It was over.

FIRST WOLFE AND THEN Dakota swung into place beside him, securing Cruz's inert body.

Subject immobilized. Classified materials restored. Ryker would be ecstatic.

Trace knew that he should have been relieved.

Instead, all he felt was exhaustion and anger at the memory of Cruz's betrayal.

THE TWIN-ENGINE CHOPPER banked in from Mazatlán. Nine men jumped aboard, carrying boxes of equipment and one motionless figure with a long scar above his eye. The dogs followed.

Trace was the last to go aboard. The ocean stretched black and restless beneath frothing clouds as he looked down at the cruise ship. His mind was already back at the Foxfire base in New Mexico.

But his heart was aboard the ship. Thanks to Dakota's report, he knew that Gina was fine. He had hoped to see her before the departure.

To touch her face one more time.

Not possible. The mission came first. It always would.

He swung around, looking east, where the first pink tendrils of dawn brushed the horizon beneath layered clouds. In that moment Trace made a silent promise to himself and to Gina.

He'd promised her a future.

Somehow he was going to keep that promise.

As the chopper surged from the landing pad, he thought he saw a dim image shimmer into view, slouched against one of the skids.

Good work, Lieutenant.

The phantom shape gave him a little two-finger salute and then vanished.

Trace rubbed his neck and sighed. As soon as they were back, he meant to do some digging into Marshall's death. He was also going straight to Ryker to cite precedents for bending the rules against personal attachments.

If Ryker didn't bend, was Trace prepared to leave the team?

The question weighed heavy as he thought of the men who had taught him and of the country he served. He thought of comrades fallen on dark nights in places with no names. Could he really walk away from that and stay sane?

He remembered Gina's face when she'd kissed him. Her smile when she'd manhandled the forklift truck. Her grace and laughter and sheer courage.

She'd given him her trust and her unqualified love. That kind of bravery made a man take stock of what he was missing.

Trace took a last look back at the brightly lit cruise ship. Yeah, he could walk away from Foxfire. Changing wouldn't be fast or easy, but he didn't want that future if Gina wasn't part of it.

Ryker was going to find that out first thing.

GINA AND TOBIAS WERE the first to reach the deck after the SEAL team pulled out. Tobias had given Gina the news in the infirmary, where she was being treated for hypothermia and dehydration. When she had insisted on at least a few details, Tobias had given her a statement of the success of the mission, though all names and departments involved were omitted. Now they stood on deck without a word, watching the chopper bank to the east against the pink light of dawn.

Tobias winced a little as his arm, freshly draped in a sling, brushed the rail.

"You okay?"

"Just a scratch," he said firmly.

"They had to leave already?"

"That's the job, Gina."

She took a deep breath. It was what she had expected, but expecting didn't make it hurt less. "He's good at his job, too. I just wish…"

She didn't finish. The list was too long. Besides, she'd never played *what if,* and she wouldn't start now.

"By the way, the doctor said to give this to you." Gina held out a white envelope. "He said one of the men left it for you."

Tobias studied the bold letters and slid the envelope carefully into his pocket.

"Is it important?"

He watched the helicopter bank to the east. "I think so. Damned important." He put an arm awkwardly around her shoulders. "You think you know how your life is going to turn out. You think you have every detail planned. Then fate comes along and kicks you hard in the butt." He looked at Gina. "Know what I mean?"

She knew exactly what he meant.

But there was a promise amid her pain. She wasn't giving up on her SEAL, not for a second. If he didn't look her up, she would track him down even if he was in a cave on the opposite side of the world.

They had a future to plan. Hopes and dreams to share. The thought was exhilarating, but terrifying, too.

As she faced the dawn, Gina swore that she wouldn't settle for anything less. Trace had taught her that.

She stood beside Tobias, watching the chopper race to the east. "Yeah, he's good at his job." She brushed a tear from her cheek. "And I had to make that crack about him lacking the skills to be a pastry chef."

"I think he forgave you," Tobias said wryly. "Don't worry, you'll find him again. I saw the way he looked at you. The man won't forget."

As the two stood on the deck, the sun broke free, bloodred above the horizon, and the helicopter faded to a vague dot in the distance.

CHAPTER FORTY-TWO

Foxfire training facility
Northern New Mexico
One month later

THE DOGS WERE on the move.

Trace O'Halloran lifted his binoculars, scanning the steep slope. Inside a dusty arroyo, Duke and two other service dogs nosed along the ground in search of a carefully hidden cache of weapons. The hunt was their third training exercise of the day, and the excited Labs showed no sign of flagging energy.

Trace crouched at the top of the slope, making notes as Duke jumped a row of boulders and skirted a fallen mesquite tree. A startled quail shot over their heads, and somewhere a spotted cactus wren shrieked a warning.

Duke sniffed at the air and went still.

As one, the dogs dropped to a prone position, their heads facing the buried metal box that held five shoulder-mounted Stinger missiles. They'd found their target in less than thirty seconds, Trace noted. Each time they searched, they had cut their target acquisition time by half.

Were these guys great, or what? His sister had done another fabulous job training these special dogs.

He noted final times and locations in his notebook and stood up. Ryker was going to be pleased with the dogs' progress, no mistake about it. In another six months they'd be ready for full field assignments.

Suddenly Duke's head cocked. Gunfire erupted from an outbuilding across the wash. Why was an idiot using live ammo near the testing area?

Trace grabbed his walkie-talkie and gave hell to the team doing maneuvers across the hill. When he turned back to the arroyo, his dogs were gone.

He skirted a cactus and ran down the slope, following the fresh prints in the sand. Behind a dead cottonwood tree, he found one of them sniffing in the sand.

Before Trace could give a signal to heel, Duke trotted up and dropped something at his feet. Trace realized it was a glove he'd dropped two days before during a night training session. The dogs had found it for him.

He was rewarding Duke with a thorough scratch behind the ears when another dog nosed in and dropped something pink on Trace's knee.

Satin and lace gleamed in the sunlight. Trace blinked down at the unfamiliar item while Duke shoved it closer, his tail wagging hard.

Trace realized the soft satin top belonged to Gina. He had found it in his cruise bag when he got back from the ship. It had to have dropped there by mistake after their night together aboard ship.

His rascals appeared to be matchmaking.

"I get the message. You want to see her, do you?" Duke squirmed closer and looked up intently. "Okay, I promise. It will be soon, if I have my way."

Wind shifted across the foothills while a hawk followed

the restless currents high overhead. Trace felt the cool silk slide through his fingers and wondered what Gina was doing at that moment.

Tension seemed to ripple over the wash. Trace had come to recognize the energy.

"Cooking." Light stirred above a gray boulder. Marshall's face glimmered in the shadows, barely visible. "Arguing with Tobias." Her eyes narrowed and she seemed to concentrate. "Thinking about you."

Trace folded the silk and lace and put it carefully in his pocket. He had only "seen" Marshall twice since leaving the ship. Each time she looked more indistinct.

He couldn't explain any of it, but he didn't need science or explanations. Now he accepted that she was real, if only for him.

Suddenly Duke turned, staring intently at the boulder where Marshall sat. The dog sniffed the air, then trotted across the wash.

"You're a beauty, aren't you?" Marshall leaned down, stroking the dog's head. "Smart, too."

Duke gave a little whine of contentment as Marshall's phantom fingers combed through his fur and smoothed his neck. The other dog curled up at Marshall's feet.

The dogs could see her, Trace realized. Why or how, he couldn't say. The reasons didn't bother him too much now. He accepted that he might never have the answers.

"They love you, you know. Especially Duke. Be sure to clean his left back paw because he picked up a cactus spine on that last search." Marshall smiled a little sadly. "I always wanted a dog. We moved so often that I never got one." Duke wriggled forward and sat in the space next to Marshall's leg. The dog whined softly, his head tilted up in the sunshine.

"It's done. You don't need me anymore so I came to say…goodbye." Her fingers stroked Duke's dark fur. "Don't worry about me. If you look, you'll find out what happened. But it isn't so important now. I'm moving on."

Duke made a little huff of contentment.

Trace didn't know what to say.

"You don't have to say anything. I'll miss you, Trace. But you have to know when to hold on and when to let go. For me it's time to let go."

I'm going to miss you, too.

Her face seemed to grow fainter. "There's one more thing. Protect what you've found. There's nothing more important anywhere."

Trace didn't need to ask what to protect. The feelings he'd felt since the day he'd seen Gina on a crowded San Francisco street had continued to grow, whether the two were together or not. And he'd find Gina as soon as Ryker lifted his ban on travel, following Trace's recent medical tests.

Sunlight shimmered over the slope.

Leaves stirred along the cottonwood tree, and when Trace blinked Marshall was gone. The air was warm and hazy, full of her presence as Duke sat up, whining slightly.

Trace didn't move. Without words he said the final goodbye he had somehow been unable to frame until this moment. He felt Duke's cold nose brush his hand as the three of them stared at the sunlight where Marshall no longer appeared.

She was gone for good. Trace couldn't explain how or why.

Suddenly Duke sat up, staring toward the top of the arroyo. His tail began to bang in the dust.

Boots crunched on sand and Izzy appeared, a black

backpack slung over one shoulder. "You three are a tough bunch to find. Hey, where's my greeting?"

Duke bounded up the slope and rolled over once, then shot into the air, front paws landing against Izzy's chest in a well-rehearsed routine.

"Yeah, that's better. How's O'Halloran treating you? Is he giving you those dog treats I left? Brushing you enough?"

"They're spoiled rotten, Teague. Stop busting my chops, will you?"

Trace hunkered down and watched Duke pirouette around Izzy, waiting for the piece of dried salmon that emerged from Izzy's high-tech backpack. "There goes my routine," Trace said dryly.

"Hell, you're way ahead of schedule and you know it. These two are doing things even Ryker didn't expect." Izzy looked across at Trace. "How about you?"

Trace's hand moved unconsciously to his collarbone. All his technology had been gradually reactivated over the past weeks, and the returning abilities had felt as natural as coming home. When Marshall had appeared, he'd sensed a powerful shift in the energy unlike anything else he'd felt before.

One more detail he wasn't fighting to analyze.

"Are the chips fully functional?"

"Better than before. It's already hard to be without them now."

"You won't be without them again, not if Ryker has his way. He has some new plans on the drawing board, but he'll tell you about that when he's ready." Izzy frowned, straightening his backpack. "I've got some information for you about Marshall. There was evidence of foul play that the local authorities missed in their initial crime-scene analysis. There were no clear marks indicating struggle near the edge of the river, but that changed when I tracked down a second set of crime-scene photographs that had been mislogged to another case."

"So it wasn't suicide." Trace took a deep breath. "I never believed it was. Marshall was too tough for that." His eyes hardened. "Any idea who did it?"

"There are several leads. Most likely it was a random, opportunistic attack. I'm following up, don't worry."

"I'm not worried. I don't think it matters to Marshall now." Trace stood up, brushing twigs and leaves from his knee. "Thanks for keeping an eye on the details."

"Not a problem. What's a techno-geek like me for, except to watch the data streams?" As Izzy scratched Duke's head, he glanced back over the hill. "Dakota said he's ready to take the dogs for their medical assessment as soon as you're done. He looked a little pale though."

"Too many green chile burritos last night, he said. The man has an appetite that doesn't stop."

Izzy rubbed his neck, frowning at the air above Duke's head.

"Something wrong?"

"Me? No." Izzy frowned at the backpack near his foot. "Hell, maybe there is. I had a call from Tobias Hale today. Ryker offered him a job here at the facility." Izzy spoke in tight, clipped tones. "He's starting as soon as the cruise line can find a replacement."

"That bothers you?"

Trace knew there was a rocky past between Izzy and Hale, but he'd never asked for details.

"It bothers the hell out of me," Izzy said curtly. "I'm going to have to see the man every day, eat meals with him, discuss data with him." He rubbed his jaw and glowered. "Treat him as an equal."

"He did a good job with Cruz. You know that."

"Maybe." Izzy shrugged. "We've got…issues, in case you didn't notice."

"You'll work it out," Trace said. "A really smart person told me that sometimes you have to hold on and sometimes you have to let things go."

Trace saw Duke paw at the small backpack he carried in training sessions. Trace realized that the dog had to have hidden Gina's silk top inside the pack that morning.

Schemer.

"By the way, Gina's leaving the ship next week. She's got a vision assessment in San Francisco."

Trace stifled a wave of anger. Ryker was reconsidering his personal policy for all Foxfire team members, but until he'd made a decision, Trace was under orders to have no contact with Gina.

For the moment, he was complying. But Izzy relayed small messages that neither man mentioned to Ryker.

Sunlight filled the arroyo, Duke panted happily and a quail chirped noisily from the shadows beneath the fallen cotton- wood tree while the desert drowsed in lazy contentment.

The snap of a twig made Duke's ears prick forward.

His tail wagged as Dakota Smith appeared at the top of the arroyo. "Sounded too quiet up here. Something wrong with the dogs?"

"No, everything's fine." Trace stretched a little, then looked closely at Dakota. "Maybe you should lay off the burritos, Ace. You look a little off."

Dakota made a dismissive sound. "Probably that new strain of flu Ryker told us about." The SEAL hunkered down and scratched Duke's head thoroughly. "By the way, Ryker's down in the Jeep and he's getting impatient." Dakota smiled as Duke bumped his hand, urgent for more scratching. "Come on, you two miscreants. Let's hit the trail."

The dogs shot off through the sunlight while Dakota followed, laughing.

This was what you had, Trace thought.

Now.

Not yesterday, not tomorrow. Just a long string of nows. If you were very good and very careful they made something unforgettable.

Marshall would have agreed with that.

The sun felt very warm on his back as he shouldered his pack and started up the slope with Izzy close behind.

"Did you hear about the test Ryker's got planned for the dogs tomorrow? He's got a new medical expert coming in to observe."

"The dogs will do fine." There was pride in Trace's voice. "Count on it."

Birdsong filled the air. Lavender swirled up, drifting through the wash behind the two men as sunlight shimmered.

Then all was quiet.

EPILOGUE

Las Vegas
Four months later

GINA KICKED off her shoes, dropped her purse and tossed her white chef's jacket onto the closest chair. She was tired and hungry, but she'd never felt better.

Her eyes ached a little. She sat down near the window and rubbed them gently.

The day she had dreaded had come. In the past month her peripheral vision had declined steadily. She couldn't drive now. Walking alone in a strange place required her full attention.

But in an unusual compensation, her nonperipheral vision was sharper than it had ever been. Though her new doctors couldn't explain it, she could see clearly in the dark.

She had been astonished when Trace's civilian boss, Lloyd Ryker, had come to see her aboard the cruise ship. During his visit he had directed her to a new doctor as a way to thank her for her assistance aboard the ship. Soon after that, she found out that Tobias Hale was leaving to work for Ryker as soon as his replacement could be found.

Her life had changed overnight.

None of it was expected.

None of it had been easy.

But Gina knew this was the place she was meant to be—at least for now. Part of her new job was organizing select cooking weekends at the best resorts in Las Vegas. In the process she discovered she had a flair for performance as well as teaching. And though she missed her friends aboard ship, she didn't miss the grueling, nonstop pace of production.

She didn't miss skirmishing with Blaine, either. Though her old nemesis had survived the attack on the ship, she faced long months of rehabilitation, most of it in prison, due to her involvement in the shipboard murders. Imogen was still facing questioning.

Not that her new job was laid-back. Today she'd finished an eight-hour workshop on advanced pastry techniques, and now she was exhausted.

Her stomach growled loudly.

She gave a silent prayer of thanks for room service.

Someone tapped at the door. "Room service, Ms. Ryan."

She stood up and straightened her blouse, then opened the door. A man in a white uniform backed toward her, pulling a cart loaded with dishes.

"Hold on. I didn't order steak." Gina sniffed the air. "I didn't order fettucini Alfredo, either."

The man sidestepped, then leaned around her to close the door.

Her heart began to pound.

She grabbed her knitting needles from the table near the door and backed up. It wasn't possible. The man from the ship had been arrested. Tobias had assured her of that after the SEAL team had left the ship.

She still had nightmares about being locked in the

freezer, and in every one she saw the cold, crazed eyes of her captor. Could he have escaped and come back for her?

She was groping for the phone on the bathroom wall, her knitting needles leveled as weapons, when the uniformed hotel attendant turned.

And his crooked smile sent her heart racing out of her chest.

"Trace," she whispered.

She couldn't breathe, couldn't keep the heat from swirling through her cheeks. She ran an anxious hand through her hair, certain she looked like a mess.

She had sworn to be fresh from an uninterrupted spa weekend, polished and gorgeous, when she saw him next. Instead she was shoeless, her hair wild after a long day in the kitchen. "What are you doing *here?*"

"Serving you steak, apparently. And there's a whole lot more on the agenda tonight, honey." He pulled off his room-service jacket. "Izzy told me where you were. If your class had gone on any longer, I was going to pull you out of there under pretense of an emergency in the hotel kitchen."

Gina just stared at him. "I don't understand."

He threw the bolt on the door and pulled her into his arms. His fingers moved gently, tracing every detail of her face. "You look tired. You did too much at your class today. When that jerk started arguing with you about the proper temperature for making ganache, you should have walked out—or decked him."

"You were *there?*"

"Most of the time. I sat in the last row. I wasn't going to say hello in front of thirty strangers." His hands tangled in her hair. "Room service to the rescue." He slanted her head slowly while his eyes filled with dark hunger.

The force of his look made Gina's mouth go dry.

She leaned against him and held on hard, afraid this was another of the many restless dreams she'd had over the past months.

"You're a damn good teacher." Trace reached around her and took a white linen napkin off the tray. Stepping back, he snapped it open crisply and guided her to a wing chair, spreading the napkin on her lap.

"But—"

"The teacher's gotta eat, kid, and I'm the man to see that she does. As usual, your nose was excellent. We've got lasagna, fettucini Alfredo and steak. I brought you chocolate espresso cheesecake for dessert. Figured I'd cover all the bases."

He pulled the clips from her hair and ran his hands through the warm strands. "God, I've missed you." He took a harsh breath. "I think that food may have to wait."

Gina saw the urgency in his eyes, felt the barely leashed hunger in his body. Not a dream, she thought.

He was here, absolutely real.

"Izzy told me you were in good shape." His voice was low, uncertain. "I hated to go without saying...without explaining."

She touched one finger to his lips. "Tobias told me all I needed to know. You had one more month, anyway."

"One month before what?"

Her chin rose defiantly. "Before I loaded my old Smith and Wesson, tracked you down, shoved you against the nearest wall and brought you to your knees."

His mouth curved in a sudden grin. "No shit. You were going to do that?"

For answer, she pulled off his belt and unbuttoned his shirt. With a few deft movements she sent his pants flying.

"Patience, focus and excellent reflexes," Trace muttered, kissing her fiercely as he carried her to the big, silk-covered bed. "I hope you haven't got anything planned for the next three days, because you aren't leaving this bed."

"I'm all yours," Gina whispered.

"Damned right you are." His eyes were hot and possessive as he stripped away her blouse and slacks, savoring the sight of her naked body. "You're still wearing my St. Christopher medal."

"I never take it off. I just wonder about that day aboard the ship." Gina frowned, sorting through the memories that were already blurred. "I dropped it somehow. If it hadn't fallen where and when it did…"

His fingers tightened. "Put it away. It's done, Gina."

She took a deep breath. "There was something that smelled like lavender. I think I must have been hallucinating by that point."

Trace's eyes narrowed. "You smelled lavender?"

"No question about it. It had to be from the stress, right?"

Trace was silent. Then he nodded slowly. "Maybe. Or maybe there are some things that we can't even imagine. I'm starting to believe that." He looked down and shook his head. "You're even more beautiful than I remembered. Hell, I didn't think that was possible."

Gina caught his palm and nibbled until he pulled her closer. "Not you. You're exactly the way I remembered."

"That bad?"

"I wouldn't change one detail." She hesitated. "But there's something I have to tell you. My eyesight…" She forced out the words. "I've lost most of my peripheral vision."

"Hell." Trace pressed a slow kiss against her hair. "That means you can't drive."

She looked up, nodding gravely. "No work over open flames, either. Does that…change anything?"

"Yeah, it definitely does." Trace looked thoughtful. "It means I'll have to find you a good chauffeur. Anything else I need to know?"

Gina felt something bubble up, hot and light in her chest. For days she had worried about how to break the news to him, and now it was done. But she wanted to be sure that he understood the full picture. "My peripheral vision may be gone forever, Trace. No one seems to know what to expect."

"In that case I need to find a *really* good driver for you. I'll put Izzy right on it."

Gina bit back a shaky laugh. "Can't you be serious about this?"

He looked at her intently and then shook his head. "Afraid not. You're alive. We're together. Nothing else matters."

Gina sighed as he kissed the curve of her neck. "Your friend Izzy says my night vision is abnormally strong. He said it may even become stronger."

Trace's hand stilled on her hair. "Night vision? That's interesting." Her breath caught as he bit the curve of her ear.

"Stop. I want to finish."

"Go ahead and talk, honey." Trace's voice was rough. "I'll try to listen."

"Izzy says it may have to do with that package I had in my mouth. He didn't explain too much, but he thought I should know that. By the way, your boss is very nice. He's come to see me several times, and he arranged for me to see a new eye specialist last week."

"Lloyd Ryker, nice?" Trace stared at her thoughtfully. "So he approves."

"Approves of what?"

Trace pushed her back onto the bed. "Everything, I'd say. Score one for the home team." He skimmed her waist and brushed her tight nipples slowly, fitting his hands to her breasts. "Enough about Ryker. We've got more important things to do. I only have four days of leave, and I plan to make every minute count."

"Hear, hear," Gina whispered.

He kissed her with slow, biting nips while he explored her wet heat.

She trembled, reckless with the memory of too many dreams. Ryker had mentioned he might have some work for her, something connected with the research institution where Tobias Hale had gone. He didn't give her details, but Gina gathered it involved top security clearances.

The work would give her more opportunity to see Trace, Ryker had explained. At the same time she could do a valuable service to her country by participating in further study of her changing vision.

But she'd think about all that tomorrow.

Tonight was for a man with shadows in his eyes. Tonight was for making him know they had an unshakable future.

"So what did you have in mind for your leave, Lieutenant? Sightseeing? Poker, maybe?"

"Something better." His fingers teased and inflamed as he brought her up and held her on the knife edge of pleasure. "Starting with this, I think."

He cupped her hips. Pressing her back onto the bed, he eased her legs apart. Then he savored her with his mouth.

Every slow, expert brush of his lips and tongue made Gina's breath catch. Her nerves seemed to stretch taut as his tongue met her trembling skin.

The room blurred. Reality faded.

Caught in a wave of need, she drove her body against his and dimly heard him mutter her name.

But she meant to draw out this pleasure for them both.

Her hands tangled in his hair as she wrapped one leg around him. "No poker? Can't you be more specific?"

Trace whispered a fierce, graphic phrase that lingered in the sexually charged air. Then he brushed her with his tongue and she came apart against him again.

His hands stroked her with a care that bordered on reverence.

"That's what I had in mind." In the quiet room Trace watched her face, caught by her honesty and her passion. This was as serious as it got, he realized. "A whole lot more after that. I'm going to be damned inventive about how many ways I can make you moan my name, honey."

She didn't see the small velvet box shoved inside his jacket pocket. He had hidden it there several hours before, feeling its weight in every movement he'd made.

Trace had agonized over the ring in two cities and five different shops. He'd wanted something different, something she would always remember. In the end he'd chosen a single diamond surrounded by dark tanzanite chips because they reminded him of her eyes when they made love.

He didn't realize that any stone would have been precious to her. That homes or cars or salaries didn't matter.

The future was what mattered, and that future was starting here and now.

Not yesterday, not tomorrow. Just a long string of nows.

If we are very good and very careful we'll make something unforgettable, Trace vowed.

He knew that Marshall would have agreed with that.

Then Gina circled his neck and pulled his body against hers, and Trace forgot about everything but how beautiful she was and how much he needed to feel her against him again.

The ring could wait.

The things he felt in his heart couldn't be put aside any longer. Meanwhile, the look in Gina's eyes was open, giving.

And just a little teasing.

"About your comment, that day we met. You mentioned chocolate and sex."

Trace felt her rising need, her lush heat. "I remember."

"You were definitely right." She fitted her body to his. "But don't tell anyone or I may be out of a job."

Author Note

I hope you enjoyed this wild sea voyage with Trace and Gina!

If you are curious about Ford and Carly, you'll find them in my earlier Navy SEAL book, *Going Overboard.* Suspense, deception and sizzling heat make their Caribbean cruise a voyage to remember.

Does Izzy seem familiar by now? The man first appeared in *The Perfect Gift,* my last paranormal romance set at hauntingly beautiful Draycott Abbey. From computers to medicine and espionage, Izzy has skills that would fill a SEAL training manual. But the man makes noncommitment an art form. Now that you've met his father and had a glimpse into his past, you can see why this tough guy wants nothing to do with commitment.

Did I say *nothing?*

Hint: the tougher they are, the harder they fall. Stay tuned.

Tobias Hale is another wonderful character who appeared with no notice while I was writing one day. As I recall, Izzy was being particularly troublesome and opaque. When I demanded to know why, Tobias simply appeared. Then I saw it all clearly.

I have a nagging suspicion we're going to see Tobias again, and Gina may be working closely with him. The mere thought of it gives Trace nightmares.

Time will tell.

Sometimes authors complain about research.

Not me.

I researched every kind of pastry technique while writing *CODE NAME: BIKINI*. Ditto for varietal chocolates. (Is writing a great job, or what?) If you'd like to see some of the desserts that Gina demonstrates in her new line of work, take a look at *The Secrets of Baking* by Sherry Yard (Boston: Houghton Mifflin, 2003). This meticulous book by the pastry chef at Spago will leave your mouth watering; better still, it will explain the science behind great pastry.

I highly recommend the caramel gelato with chocolate chunks and her Chinese almond cookies. (I'd substitute a portion of almond flour in the recipe, but that's another story. For more details, see my Web site.)

If my book made you think about Mexican food, be sure to read *Mexico One Plate at a Time* (New York: Scribners, 2000). The amazing Rick Bayless dishes up history, culture and nutrition on the same page. Great reading!

For a down-and-dirty food book, nothing cuts deeper than *A Cook's Tour,* by Anthony Bourdain (New York: Harper Perennial, 2002). The man can write! If you're not cringing, you'll be laughing hysterically. As I can guarantee from personal experience, if you have to ask what you're eating, you probably don't want to know.

Any knitters reading this? Yes, I mean you there with the secret yarn stash. You who can't help petting the merino and stroking the suri alpaca.

My secret is out! I learned to knit ages ago, dropped it after college and only returned to it by accident. But it's a new world, the yarns are amazing and I'm hooked all over again. I've even designed some special pieces to share. You can find the patterns at my Web site.

For more details, visit me online at *www.christinaskye.com.* I'm posting a special contest for readers of *CODE NAME: BIKINI* there, and you'll also find recipes, excerpts for all of my books, character diaries and knitting patterns to support some excellent charities. I will also be posting some new and exiting story content at my site, so be sure to drop by and say hello.

Meanwhile…

My next book.

You probably already guessed. Dakota is in my sights. The man is serious hero material, even if he doesn't realize that yet. One night his car breaks down and he's shot and…

Never mind. Just watch my Web site for all the details. And check out the exciting new contests you'll find there.

Here's to happy reading,

Christina